HAWKEYE

DANIEL STRYKER

J
JOVE BOOKS, NEW YORK

HAWKEYE

A Jove Book / published by arrangement with
the author

PRINTING HISTORY
Jove edition / February 1991

ISBN: 0-515-10509-0

Jove Books are published by The Berkley Publishing Group,
200 Madison Avenue, New York, New York 10016.
The name "JOVE" and the "J" logo
are trademarks belonging to Jove Publications, Inc.

PRINTED IN THE UNITED STATES OF AMERICA

10 9 8 7 6 5 4 3 2 1

ACKNOWLEDGMENTS

Major Richard Groller, USAR, acted as my primary consultant on Hawkeye. Especially in the task of developing a fictional, lucrative target, his expertise was invaluable. Thanks, Rich, for your help and support.

And thanks, also, to all the guys at Space Command who read the manuscript and made helpful suggestions. If not for you, USSPACECOM officers would be driving around in Wagoneers.

My appreciation, as well, to those who helped from the intelligence community, who loved the book and would have praised it publicly if they dared.

Any errors that remain, of course, are my own.

—D. Stryker

1

Day 1: Molniya Orbit

The American spy satellite *HE-12*, code-named *Hawkeye*, was over the U.S. Trust Territory of the Pacific Islands when it died.

Far below, on Kwajalein Atoll, the U.S. Space Command ground tracking station was preparing to take *Hawkeye*'s data dump when the satellite fell silent—before it could deliver all the intelligence it had gathered during its pass over the Middle East, half a world away. *HE-12* was a semisynchronous satellite in a Molniya orbit, 35,800 kilometers high at apogee: It routinely completed two eccentric east-to-west orbits per day, dwelling longest over the Middle East before it overflew American ground tracking stations to deliver its reconnaissance data from a mere 370 kilometers during perigee.

But there was nothing routine about this particular pass over the Pacific. *HE-12*'s stable, predictable, eccentric orbit brought it to within a kilometer of a satellite remnant traveling west to east in low earth orbit (LEO).

The spherical "remnant"—a shaped charge containing C-4 plastic explosive, an embedded nonmetallic timer, and 50,000 corundum pellets, each ten millimeters in diameter and weighing two-thirds of a gram—was coated with fluorocarbon resins, nearly invisible to the radar that ground stations employ to track space junk. A communications satellite, while breaking up two weeks before, had positioned the seventy-five-pound sphere in a decaying orbit painstakingly calculated to bring it within striking range of *Hawkeye* on June 1 at 1430 hours, GMT.

It had taken a great deal of number crunching to get the timing, the CEP (circular error probability), and the orbits precisely right. It had taken a great deal of money to conceive and execute the plan. The launch of a communications satellite with a lifespan of four months had to be proposed, approved, and contracted to Priane Space, a commercial space-launch provider. The host satellite had to be designed, built, and launched without error, without discovery of its hidden purpose, and without much fanfare.

This host satellite then had to be destroyed exactly and precisely on schedule. For this operation, as well as for future similar components of the plan, an entire covert ground station, capable of tracking and directing satellites, was constructed: the host's self-destruct commands, even encrypted, were too incriminating to risk letting a subcontractor transmit into orbit.

Once the host comsat had broken up—supposedly as a natural end to its short lifespan—the operation was subject to serendipity: money could be spent, experts could be hired, equipment could be built . . . but in the final moments, only luck would decide if every computation would be correct, and if every piece of equipment would perform flawlessly.

In their secret groundside tracking facility, the architects of the plan could only watch and wait. And then, when all the destroyed pieces of the host comsat fell out of orbit and burned in the atmosphere, there remained nothing to watch: the virtually invisible basketball-shaped charge, steered into orbit by the death throes of its host, would either serve its purpose, or not.

The sphere, with its Teflon-like shell, corundum pellets and plastic, gave minimal radar return. It was as invisible to its creators as to its target or to the groundside caretakers of America's satellites.

All anyone could do was watch the clock and wait. The spaceborne timer aboard the killer sphere, on a direct collision course with *HE-12*, was the final arbiter of success. Or of failure.

At 1430 hours GMT, the timer detonated. Due to a tiny error of computation, *HE-12* was twice as close to the remnant as had been expected.

HE-12's fragile solar wings were punctured, its lenses destroyed, its electronics rendered useless in an explosive shower of industrial rubies. Its onboard impact sensors registered the attack, but were unable to transmit that information to the ground station on Kwajalein.

The inoperable six-by-ten-foot hulk of *HE-12*, inclined at 63.4 degrees to the equator, continued in its Molniya orbit, thrown only infinitesimally off course.

Hawkeye was now little more than space debris. Its synthetic aperture radar (SAR) was blind; its two-meter black-and-white imaging capability useless. But, to the distress of its attackers, *Hawkeye*'s orbit was still reasonably stable. *HE-12* wouldn't break up and burn in the atmosphere, chunks tumbling groundward, for nearly a year.

It would continue on its rounds, turning a blind eye on Syria and Jordan, dwelling uselessly over the Middle East before it made its way, twice daily, back toward the West and the tracking stations waiting to download the data it was no longer capable of collecting.

2

Day 1: Kwajalein Atoll, Marshall Islands

"Goddamn," muttered Lieutenant Phil Young when the *HE-12* data dump quit just after it began. The comm jock had been watching the light flash on his modem and the CRT screen in front of him that said DOWNLOAD IN PROGRESS.

Then the modem light went off. His screen started flashing TRANSMISSION INTERRUPT.

"Why me, Lord?" the spectacled, baby-faced Army Space Command officer asked, staring at the machine in front of him.

No answer was forthcoming from Young's terminal. *HE-12* simply wasn't dumping. Or his own system was down. No, he had power.

Young's world telescoped into a tiny point containing only his terminal in its cubbyhole. That terminal was part of the space surveillance network, responsible for space object identification in the Army's ground-based sensoring role here at Kwajalein.

Young pushed back from his desk, looked up over it and called out to the watch officer. "Major, I've got a problem over here. Will you pull the *HE-12* data dump up on your console and see what you get?"

The operations officer on watch, Major Hall, came to the railing of the landing encircling the bay of terminals and leaned his paunch on it. "What's the problem, Young?"

"I'm not gettin' anything from *HE-12*, sir," Young called

back, conscious that around him, at a dozen other terminals, heads were turning his way.

Next to him, a female lieutenant named Porter craned her neck over the partition to look at his screen. Young's hands were beginning to sweat.

"Porter, take a look at *HE-12*'s coordinates," Hall called down to the pert, fine-boned redhead Young had been dating.

Allie Porter's SOI (space object identification) terminal was part of ALCOR (Advanced Research Projects Agency Lincoln C-band Observable Radar). ALCOR tracked objects in real time; its radar returned images of whatever was observable in orbit.

"It'll take a minute, Major Hall." Porter turned back to her terminal with a shake of her head at Phil Young and began pecking keys.

Belatedly, Young wondered if his operating system was down. He hit a function key and TRANSMISSION INTERRUPT disappeared; another, and his terminal was ready and waiting to receive anything further from *HE-12*.

So there was nothing wrong with his workstation. Therefore, something else was down. His mind shied away from the thought that *HE-12* itself was malfunctioning. His hand went blindly to the polystyrene coffee cup by his keyboard. Staring at his monitor, waiting for somebody to tell him something, he tilted back in his chair, took a sip, and closed his eyes. It was 0231 hours, local time. Young was going to open his eyes and everything would be normal. *HE-12* would be happily dumping its data. The lady soldier at the terminal next to his would smile an A-OK smile and they'd resume a low-voltage flirtation. The sudden silence in the bay would be broken by the normal banter of the night shift in the SOI facility, and his heart would stop pounding.

Young opened his eyes. His terminal stared back at him, still waiting, ready to receive *HE-12*'s data dump if it should start up again. Above his head, the watch officer, Hall, was bent to his own console.

Allie Porter stuck her head back over the partition and said, "Phil, I'm still looking, but so far everything seems nominal up there. The only anomaly I've had all night was a paint fleck or something, a little bitty radar debris image in that vicinity. Sorry." She smiled, concern making the skin around her eyes crinkle, and went back to her work.

Young swallowed a cold, foul mouthful of coffee, slid forward in his chair and put the cup aside in one abrupt movement that brought him up against his desk's bumper.

Everything Young could check was nominal, too, except that *HE-12* was giving him zilch for a data dump.

His heart thudded while he waited for news from Major Hall. The watch officer seemed to be taking forever. Finally, Hall came to the railing again and said, "I'm not getting anything either, Young." Then he turned his head: "Kimball, what's ALTAIR got on *HE-12?*"

It was one minute, twelve seconds since *HE-12* had stopped transmitting.

"Right with you, sir," called Kimball to the operations officer. The silence in the bay was so complete now that Young could hear the tap of Kimball's keyboard, a dozen terminals away. ALTAIR (Advanced Research Projects Agency Long-Range Tracking and Instrumentation Radar) was part of the U.S. Army Strategic Defense Command, with multiservice staffing here on Kwajalein, which meant that Navy and Air Force personnel were as likely to be staffing the sensor support facility as Army folks.

Kimball was Air Force. He stood up and Young could see him now: his balding forehead was creased with wrinkles as he directed his response to Major Hall, who was leaning on the rail, stiff-armed.

"ALTAIR's got a track, Major. *HE-12*'s still up there. Orbit's okay, maybe just a slight deviation . . . couple more minutes, I'll know for sure. Could be some meteorite nudged it. I'll send the data up to you when I'm certain. Maybe the glitch is groundside—some fifty-cent relay."

"Send me the ALTAIR track now, Kimball. I'm going to boot this up to CSOC. If there's an orbital deviation, maybe their telemetry controller'll want to nudge it back."

"Yes, sir," said Kimball, and disappeared from Young's view as he sat back down at his terminal.

Young looked again at his ready terminal, then up at Major Hall, who was spooked enough to want to contact CSOC. CSOC (Consolidated Space Operations Center) was headquartered at Falcon Air Force Base in Colorado Springs, which hosted the Air Force's 2nd Space Wing.

Hall caught Young's eye and said, "Any change, Young?"

Young shook his head: "Still nothing, sir." Hall was an average-looking guy, with a pleasant, unremarkable face. That face was white as the operations officer left the rail to return to his console.

At least the damned spacecraft was still up there. *HE-12* was behaving normally, according to ALTAIR ground track.

With a sinking feeling in his stomach, Young logged the anomalous transmission interrupt. When he'd finished, he had only his ready screen to look at. So he looked away, and saw Allie Porter watching him, a sympathetic expression on her face.

"Anything new?" he asked. Her ALCOR screen just showed radar returns—pretty pictures. Allie Porter probably didn't know any more than he did. But then, she was good; she was qualified on ALTAIR as well as ALCOR.

"It does look to be a little off track," she said with a weak smile of encouragement. "But just a little . . . not enough to indicate that it took a hit, at least not from what I can add to ALTAIR's data."

Then the watch officer called down for Allie Porter's take on *HE-12* and she got very busy.

That left Young alone with his ready terminal. *HE-12* still wasn't transmitting and neither ALCOR nor ALTAIR could confirm any reason why this should be the case.

3

Day 1: Peterson AFB, Colorado Springs, Colorado

When Major Chuck Conard of Army Space Command Intelligence walked into the USSPACECOM breakfast meeting in Building 1470's conference room, his mouth was dry and his pulse was pounding as if he were walking into an ambush. Maybe he was. Eleven superior officers, many of them from Air Force Space Command, were waiting for Conard to tell them what happened to *HE-12* and what they could do about it. And he wasn't sure. He was winging it.

The first thing they'd tried at CSOC when Kwajalein called was stabilizing the wobble in *HE-12*'s attitude. That was all it seemed to be—a wobble. But when the telemetry controller here tried to correct it, he'd gotten no response from *Hawkeye*. For all intents and purposes, *HE-12* was dead in space.

An opaque projector was throwing a bright square of light against the wall behind the table's head. A conventional briefing easel stood catty-corner to the commander-in-chief's chair at the head of the table. Over his head, on the commander's right, Conard could see the hastily prepared briefing material, a three-by-five-foot cardboard diagram slugged PROBLEM.

The bottom half of the card showed a portion of the curving Earth, from the Nubian Desert up to Syria's border with Turkey at the horizon. Superimposed over the Middle East were the Bright Star exercise parameters: the Egyptian staging area in detail, with mobile terminals and radar installations as well as tanks and planes labeled TACTICAL USER. Also represented were Libyan, Syrian, Jordanian and Israeli installations and defenses because, exercise or not, Bright Star was taking place in a real and potentially explosive warfare theater, where other nations fiercely protected their interests.

The top half of the card showed more aircraft at different altitudes and inclinations, and spacecraft as well: tactical and command theater mission satellites, relay crosslinks, and piggyback satellite relays were all depicted as if representatives of each category of spacecraft were dwelling over the exercise theater simultaneously. Among the drawings of satellite types were scattered a space shuttle, a NASP (National Aerospace Plane), a TR-1 high-altitude reconnaissance aircraft, two low-orbit photo-return satellites, and a fighter version of a TAV (trans-atmospheric vehicle), plus various missiles.

Over in the right-hand corner, from ground to space, were various configurations of "enemy" missiles, theater and strategic, and tactical varieties.

Up near the top of the chart, under the block-lettered PROBLEM, the *HE-12* in its Molniya orbit had been circled by hand with a wide, black marker. From it, black strokes extended through various other components meant to be simulated or postulated in the Bright Star exercise.

Conard's practiced eye took in the PROBLEM card at a glance, and he winced inwardly. It was a good thing that Bright Star was only an exercise. The black marks radiating from *HE-12* through various components of the Bright Star scenario left Space Command with pitifully few assets to bring to bear on any threat.

Space Command's role of "Space Force Enhancement" tactical support for ground forces during Bright Star was about to be radically reassessed. Every man in this room knew that his career might hang in the balance. CSOC had to come out of here today with a new support scenario that would demonstrate its value on Bright Star's electronic battlefield without *HE-12* as its linchpin.

You could cut the tension in here with a knife. As Conard slipped into his seat, Pollock, the Air Force's big, sandy-moustached deputy chief for special operations, and Manning, the Army's florid Strategic/Aerospace Defense planning chief, nodded to him. Everybody else was looking through the briefing material beside each plate.

Feeling somehow as if all eyes were on him even though he knew differently, Conard leafed through the briefing in its folder slugged with the U.S. Space Command logo: shield-chested eagle-and-stars over a globe circled by satellite tracks. Conard was a fast-tracker with God-given good looks and a bright smile, but at that moment he felt stupid, ugly, and awkward.

According to the briefing material, CSOC had already gone into computational mode: a chart showed what was available in the way of LANDSAT coverage, GPS (global positioning system) data, low-orbit photo-return satellites that covered any part of the exercise area and time frame, as well as a pitifully short and tentative list of satellites that might be maneuvered in to support Bright Star.

The briefing material also bluntly stated that *HE-12* had been expected to give a data dump at low earth orbit during perigee, but that Kwajalein didn't receive the data. It also surmised that ground tracking couldn't do anything about the problem. This was, Conard realized, a first draft of the report that must go back to Washington.

Conard didn't think the glum prospectus was exactly fair, although it was true enough. If he had six hours to work on it, maybe things would change. Just because he hadn't been able to get *HE-12* working didn't mean that he wouldn't. His eyes weren't reading the material any longer; he was mentally countering the tacit accusations.

Then he heard his name and looked up. USSPACECOM's commander-in-chief was talking to him: "Conard, why don't you open with a thumbnail of where you think we ought to go from here. Everybody's read in; there's no need for formalities when our response time's so short." The commander's jaw was thick and jowly. The Old Man's lips had brown spots on them.

Conard considered going to the briefing easel, but he hadn't been ordered to and, rebelliously, he sat where he was.

"Sir, I've been thinking about this all the way over, and I'd like to A, continue trying all means to get *HE-12* to respond to telemetry; B, bring the contractors in and see what they say, ASAP; C, consider buying ground tracks from SPOT, *System Probatoire d'Observation de la Terre*, right now, provisionally, so we don't have CENTCOM, Eighteen Corps, and every Delta commando out of Bragg laughing up their sleeves at us in Cairo; and D, get DIA to recall Dalton Ford's ass out of the Med, back here where I can kick it, if we can't jerk him in on our own. That is, sir, if everyone—if you're in agreement."

Conard sat back, dry-mouthed, hoping to hell that U.S. Space Command as a whole saw the priorities as he did: covering its collective ass was running neck and neck with getting overhead coverage for CENTCOM (U.S. Central Command) during Bright Star, so far as Conard was concerned.

The Old Man growled, "We'll tell CENTCOM, Eighteen Corps's three-star, and whoeverall from Special Forces—when this leaks, which it will—that we'll handle their needs, but their need-to-know isn't high enough for us to tell them how we'll handle them. Defense Intelligence Agency'll back me on that; this'll be in their laps by lunch." Against the wall was the Old Man's aide. He signaled for the aide to come to the head of the table.

When the kid reached him, the commander-in-chief whispered in his ear.

Pollock, beside Conard, leaned twenty degrees toward Conard and said, "Nice going, starting a turf battle. Anything that turns the heat down is fine with me."

So Conard had one supporter in the person of Pollock, the Air Force Special Ops chief.

Manning, on Conard's left said, "Yeah, black money got us into this, black ops ought to take the weight."

When you were talking "black"—special access—projects in Space Command, you were talking Dalton Ford, a "purple suit" who held down a DIA (Defense Intelligence Agency) slot and a Space Command slot simultaneously.

Now people began unbending at the table, picking up forks and starting to bitch and bounce the SPOT suggestion around with nervous laughs and wry comments.

For the next few hours at least, Chuck Conard's head was going to stay on his shoulders.

He watched the commander's aide slip out the door. The Old Man had already made his decision. The aide's quick leave-taking was proof of that. No matter whether all or only some of Conard's suggestions were implemented, Space Command was about to pass the buck to the Defense Intelligence Agency.

What Ford did with it wasn't Conard's problem. Conard's problem was still serious—finding a way to restart *HE-12* or make up for its lack during the upcoming Bright Star exercise—but no longer lethal.

The Old Man was confirming that, not in so many words, but in his demeanor, as he asked the table generally, "Let's see how much of Conard's proposal we can buy, gentlemen. Then I'll entertain any other bright ideas you've got. We have some time before we can get Ford back here with his whiz-kid black bag of tricks."

Suddenly, Conard realized that he was hungry. You had to feed a brain to use it. He reached for a sweet roll from the pile in a nearby basket and looked at the briefing chart again, with everything on it from the space shuttle to ballistic missiles. And for the first time his gut remembered that all this damage control was focused on an exercise, not a real war. He could feel that way, now, since he was back in good standing with the Space Command team, no longer fighting for his professional life.

Conard wouldn't have changed places right now with Dalton Ford for anything in the world, or orbiting it.

4

Day 2: Cairo, Egypt

Word didn't get to Dalton Ford until a little before dawn on July 7, although CSOC had been calling around trying to find him since about seven the previous evening, Cairo time.

It wasn't that CENTCOM (U.S. Central Command) in Cairo was inefficient; it was that Dalton Ford didn't want to be found. Cairo was an easy place not to be found, especially after hours, if you were staying with friends instead of the hotel where you were booked.

Ford was in Cairo to interface with CENTCOM during Bright Star. He had a piece of developmental hardware he wanted to try out that was meant for special applications—which meant he wanted to see how his friends in Special Forces liked it. The official description of the box said that it would facilitate "joint interoperability": allow the Army to use Navy (FleetSatCom) communications. Bright Star was the perfect environment for field-testing the (actually) black box.

The box was a prototype of a new Fleet Intelligence capability terminal upgrade. It was a downsized C^3I (command, control, communications and intelligence) terminal, hardened and (it was hoped) parachute-jump-capable. Because it was built with money from a black program, and there was only one copy, somebody like Ford had to go with the box and test it personally.

And he was having one hell of a good time in Cairo with his new toy, doing just that.

So when the knock came on his room's door just before dawn, Ford rolled off the girl and grabbed his gun from its holster slung over the bedpost, croaking, "Yeah, hold on," as he kicked free of the tangled sheets.

It was hot as the devil in Cairo, and Ford's host was old-school Egyptian: no air-conditioning, just ceiling fans that whispered in the shadowy dark above his head. The girl from last night was a local as well. She sat up without a word, clutching the white sheet to her throat, knees against her chest.

Staying in one of the pre-Mandate villas belonging to a honcho from Egyptian intelligence had its pros and its cons. If this was a local coup or inhouse squabble and Ford was caught in the middle of it, the cons were about to outweigh the pros.

What's-her-name from last night was either thinking the same, or was part of whatever was coming down: she didn't ask a single question or make another move as Ford scrambled to the hinge side of the door and flattened himself against the whitewashed wall.

Old habits died hard. Memories never did. You never took a single chance more than you had to, no matter how much you wished you had your pants on.

Again, the knock. This time, it was accompanied by an American-accented voice that said, "Sir? Sorry to wake you, but you've got a message that won't wait."

An American voice. The sweat dried on Dalton Ford's bare skin and he realized that he had the slide of his Beretta pressed against his forehead, and the pistol in condition zero—hammer down on a live round. You couldn't tell, out here in the Med, whether somebody on the other side of a door wouldn't decide to shoot through it.

He lowered the gun, flipped on the lightswitch with his left hand, and said, "Right with you." Then he squinted around for his pants.

The girl on the bed motioned questioningly to the adjoining tiled bathroom. She flashed him a quick smile when he nodded that it was okay.

As she fled in a flurry of bedclothes, Ford saw his chinos

underneath and grabbed for them. His pulse thundered in his ears as he bent over to dress. He'd really hammered himself last night.

But so had everybody else, and whoever was out there must have waked at least the houseboy to get this far . . . assuming *American* meant *friendly*.

He still had the gun in hand as he opened the door—first a crack, then all the way to admit the American soldier holding an envelope and spewing apologies.

"I'm supposed to wait for you, sir," said the blond Marine corporal who hadn't yet mastered the art of shaving.

It was 0413 hours local time and the envelope said "U.S. Central Command," even though the corporal was from the American embassy.

The pretty, blond kid was staring around the somewhat wrecked but still-elegant room Yousef had given Ford—staring as if the Marine had never before seen empty bottles, woman's underwear, or a half-dressed forty-year-old DIA officer with a hangover and a gun in hand.

"Fine with me if you wait," Ford told the kid. Ford's mouth was gluey, and the lights blazing down from the ceiling fan were making his eyes water. He stepped over his black aluminum attaché and sat on the bed with the envelope in his gun hand, fumbling with his other hand for his sunglasses and whatever was left in a tumbler by the bed. The drink was mostly melted ice, but it was wet.

When he read the message in the envelope, he said, "Shit. Assholes."

"Yes sir," said the kid from the embassy.

"Yes *sir*," Ford repeated snappishly, and then told himself to relax. Somebody at the embassy was thinking on the fly: once he'd read this, Dalton Ford had to get to a secure phone or report to CENTCOM HQ. There was a secure phone at the embassy. Hence the kid, who'd drive him there.

"Honey, I'll be back in a couple hours," he told the closed bathroom door, letting the kid know they weren't alone. Then he put on last night's shirt and socks, a pair of sneakers, shrugged into his shoulder holster and grabbed his windbreaker and the black hard case.

It was 0417 hours. "Let's go. Move, Corporal." Cold fury was chasing the effects of the night before from his body and mind.

The kid hustled, and they were downstairs and out in the courtyard where the embassy sedan was parked before the houseboy could come around asking questions.

Traffic in Cairo was less of a horror than it would be two hours later, when the sun was up. The kid could drive. Ford sat in the back, attaché case on his knees, and considered his reply.

Not enough damned information in the envelope to really scope the problem: CSOC wanted him back at Falcon. The message traffic on the "request" was listed, with times and offices queried.

If Ford had all the data there was in hand, his bosses at Space Command and DIA were only informing him of CSOC's request. That meant he had some leeway. The handscrawled postscript said, "Do some damn thing about this, Dalton, ASAP—J."

He was about to do just that. He left the car before it had come to a complete halt in the forecourt of the American embassy compound, waved to the Marine on duty, who knew him, and fished for his security badge as he climbed the steps.

By the time he'd clipped it to his jacket pocket, he was inside and on his way to the CIA station.

It was 0502 hours. The day shift was just coming to life. He could smell fresh American coffee, and it made his mouth water.

In the comm section, Jay Adamson was still at his desk in the little "clean" room used for sensitive communications, among banks of electronics. "It's about time. It's one thing for you to play hard to get with the military, but not with us . . . it's embarrassing." The sharp-nosed, thin man in a rumpled tropical shirt got up. "Guess I'll go get coffee." He patted the STU-3 (secure telephone unit) on his desk, which was downsized and not much different in appearance from a regular telephone. "Have fun."

"You bet," said Ford as Adamson closed the door on his way out.

It took a while to get the desk he wanted at Falcon. When he did reach the desk, Chuck Conard had gone for the day. So he had himself transferred to Pollock's secure phone and said, "Dalton Ford here. What's the bloody problem all you space jocks can't handle?"

"Where are you, Ford?"

"On a Company phone. You got me out of bed. Again: what's the problem?"

"Get back here and we'll tell you."

Ford took a deep breath, realized he still had his sunglasses on, took them off and folded their stems together. Then he closed his eyes to concentrate on the other man's voice. "Tell me and I'll troubleshoot it from here." Mustn't lose his temper.

A long, tremulous sigh came over the wire. Then: "*HE-12* cut out in mid data dump and is unresponsive to telemetry."

Dalton Ford opened his eyes but didn't see anything in the station's comm room. "Get a copy of what it did dump, however little that is, and send it to me care of CENTCOM." What the fuck? And what did they think he was going to do about it?

Ford's mind raced. He wasn't giving up his camping trip, complete with old friends, young girls, palm trees, and explosive ordnance, without a fight.

"The problem's bigger than that. We have to cover our part of Bright Star, Ford—you know that. We need you back here, in the trenches, in case this is more serious than it looks. Sabotage or something."

"'Trenches,'" Ford repeated. "'Sabotage'? You're not inferring some kind of aggression from a run-of-the-mill techno-screwup?"

"We've got to look at all the possibilities," came the voice from Colorado.

"You've got to cover your asses. Seems to me I'm going to do everybody more good over here interfacing with CENT-COM and finessing any failures than I will back there."

"That's not what CSOC wants."

CSOC wanted a scalp, preferably Dalton Ford's. "Look, get a copy of the fleet manifest and see when the next shuttle launch from Edwards is scheduled—or any military payload launch;

maybe we can beg a flyby or an EVA." Extravehicular activity:
Get somebody out there in a space suit to eyeball *HE-12*
or, if the payload bay was empty, bring it home. "We'll get a
look-see, maybe a hands-on if we're lucky. That's the only way
to settle the aggression question, and it's not quick. Probably
unnecessary, but we'll go through the motions. You want a
more likely culprit, you talk to the damned contractors, for
chrissakes. Meanwhile, I'll talk to people in the agencies and
see if we can pop up a cheap sat or divert some LEO-mission
sats that you can't access—in time for Bright Star." There were
plenty of choices, spy sats that didn't officially exist. "If I get
coverage, we'll route through NSA to you if we have to. That
take care of it?"

"No, it doesn't take care of anything. We've still got the
problem."

"You'd still have the problem if I were sitting on your desk
massaging your toes, friend." Ford was going to make all those
calls himself, but he was beginning to give up hopes of staying
out here in Egypt for the entire exercise. Any possibility, no
matter how remote, of a hostile source for *HE-12*'s troubles
brought the agencies in, and Dalton Ford on board inarguably.
Maybe he could hop a flight to the States, certify the problem
as in-house, implement some quick fix, and be back in time
for the real action.

The Libyans and Syrians and the rest of the Arab hard-liners
always got crazy during Bright Star, what with Eighteenth Airborne Corps on the ground and the Seventh Fleet offshore. Ford
really didn't want to miss all the fun.

"Look, Ford, I didn't cut your orders. Talk to your director
of operations. Far as I know, he's in agreement that you
should handle this the way CSOC wants. CSOC wants you
to troubleshoot this thing personally—be the investigator for
Kwajalein, look everything over on-site. You're the most
familiar with the system. You might see something somebody
else would miss."

That was the truth. "What's Conard doing? This should be
his problem back there. You need—we need—somebody on-
site here, especially if lots of mission specs are about to change
radically."

"Conard's . . . doing his job. Look, when am I supposed to say you'll be here?"

"You're not. Tell 'em what I suggested. I'll talk to my shop, to everybody inside the Beltway I can think of, and get back with you. If we can't make *HE-12* perform, we'll find another way."

"Yeah, we were thinking about SPOT—"

Caught off-guard, Ford let out an explosive snort. "Well," he said when he'd smothered it, "that's a novel approach. See, you guys don't need me."

"I can't comment on that. I'll tell them what you suggested, and that you haven't scheduled a flight."

That wasn't going to sound great. "Say I have an idea that I can't talk about, one that might solve the overhead problem. Say that if I can swing it, we won't need to worry about overhead reconnaissance for Bright Star. And say I said that if I can do it, I can do it from here."

"What's this, spook shit?"

"You got it, Pollock. Have a nice day—night, that is. . . ."

"Hold on, Ford. Don't hang up. How can we get to you?"

"Same as before. You want to cut the response time down, go through the Cairo station. I'll check in with you within twelve hours. Okay?"

"I guess, but we're in a world of hurt here."

"You'll survive it. I told you, I've got an idea. Bye."

Ford took the receiver away from his ear and felt for its cradle without opening his eyes. Then he pressed his palms against his closed lids.

From the way Pollock was talking, CSOC would blame *HE-12*'s troubles on Dalton Ford, Soviet dirty tricks, or sunspots if it would absolve them of responsibility. But nothing did that: you either got the job done, or you didn't. If you didn't, it was your fault.

And *HE-12* was one of the most competent pieces of spacecraft Ford had ever worked on. The chances of it going dead like that—unless it had been messed with—were pretty slim.

He leaned back in Adamson's chair, trying to figure what his next phone call should be. Conard was at the heart of this move to recall Ford. Conard was a slick yuppie bastard, but Conard could wait.

If CSOC had really implied to all and sundry that it suspected foul play from a hostile power, then the intelligence agencies were going to be running the hottest right now.

Ford reached for the phone to call somebody at DIA and his hand froze, not quite touching the receiver. A slow grin spread across his taut, dark-stubbled face. He wasn't a purple suit for nothing. He hadn't reached forty, while looking thirty, by being slow on the uptake.

He'd make every call and request and inquiry he'd told Pollock he would. He'd even make the ones he'd asked Pollock to make.

But if he was to start managing this crisis, he'd do it by seeing if his own shop liked the idea of mirroring—eavesdropping on—a Soviet overhead satellite to get Bright Star the data it needed. He liked the idea a lot.

With enough cooperation, he could provide Space Command with Soviet-gathered overhead of the Bright Star exercise area, and the Soviets would never know it was happening. Just steal the data right out of their system. He was liking it better and better. And, just in case *HE-12* was down because of Soviet mischief, and that fact later came to light, having stolen their overhead reconnaissance would prevent any knee-jerk demand for reprisal or open confrontation.

You had to understand your government. You had to recognize inertia when you saw it. You had to minimize the risk and maximize the fun at the same time.

Anyway, nobody'd ever tried stealing Soviet recon on such a massive scale before. If it could be done, even though the agencies couldn't admit that they'd done it or how they'd done it, it would be one hell of an intelligence coup for Dalton Ford.

5

Day 2: Baghdad, Iraq

On the third day of the Baghdad International Exhibition for Military Production, the principal responsible for crippling *Hawkeye* arrived with the rising sun at the pavilion where one of his coconspirators had a booth.

To gain entry at so early an hour, he had been provided with an exhibitor's badge. This he showed to a succession of Iraqi security guards, his smile steady, until he gained entrance to the exhibition's main concourse.

There he strolled down aisle after aisle, past exhibits from not only Arab nations, but from American, Brazilian, British, French, Italian, Portuguese, Spanish, Russian and even Israeli providers of defense equipment.

True to the Iraqi Ministry of Industry's boasts, "combat-tested equipment from the host country and many other countries" was on display here and elsewhere on the grounds. The biggest defense contractors had separate facilities, but here, in the great pavilion, where some booths were no bigger than a man's outstretched arms and others were larger than a studio apartment, the commercial scope of the defense industry was most apparent.

Here were the displays of the communications experts, the satellite and ground station purveyors, the masters of targeting and range-finding devices. Although many shelves and display stands were empty of equipment, art and photos on the booth walls showed soldiers in the field, using solar-powered listening stations and remote command trucks to guide men, planes, tanks and even remotely piloted vehicles (RPVs) in the conduct of war.

Elsewhere on the grounds, missiles, small and large arms, entire trainer aircraft, aircraft simulators, and fighter aircraft were on display, along with troop carriers and tanks bristling with armaments.

Those did not excite him the way the high-tech electronics in this pavilion did. On display here were the most sophisticated tracking and sensing systems available on the open market; here were uplinks and downlinks; here were the contractors who would make your tactical dreams come true if you could pay the price.

Much that was here, and much that was not, had gone into the covert ground station he'd designed, built, and finally used successfully against an unknowing America.

He had stayed behind at the ground station, while the other principals had come ahead to Baghdad, as agreed. Here they awaited him, waited to learn the outcome of Phase 1. He had remained in his camouflaged facility until Phase 1 was well over with, to make sure of his facts.

This was not the sort of result one reported, even encrypted, by telephone or telex or modem, by fax or mail, or by human courier. This was the sort of result one reported in person, face to face.

Considering the difficulty of the undertaking, the result, when it came, had been spectacular. Next time, they would do better. Perfection was an elusive goal. Success, in general terms, was theirs . . . so far. Their mission had proved to be worth all the risk—past, present, and future.

As he approached the booth he sought, he was nearly overwhelmed by the excitement he'd been suppressing because there remained so much yet to do. The plan in its entirety was dauntingly complex.

Yet he couldn't help feeling elated, walking among the contractors' booths at seven in the morning that seventh of July. Here and there, exhibitors were beginning to set up shop for the day, much like street vendors in a Moroccan bazaar. But unlike street vendors, these men were preparing handouts: giveaways of literature, flashy decals, posters, note cubes, coasters, pens and tote bags emblazoned with their company logo or a favored product.

In a more fundamental way as well, this souk was unlike any other in the Arab world: it convened for a few days and then moved on, hawking its wares in this nation or that, a marketplace of destruction that wandered around the globe. He had witnessed this same scene in Britain, in Germany, in France and in Australia while shopping for his ground station. It had come to feel like home to him. He was not unfamiliar with many of these men, and certainly not with their kind.

He felt a little thrill when he spied the man he was looking for, readying his booth for the day. His coconspirator was rustling around with a glass of tea in hand: sturdy, balding, looking for all the world like a human tank, despite his Huntsman silk-and-linen suit.

Given the venue, and the possible eavesdroppers from Portugal and Germany on either side, he greeted the heavy man in English: "Good day, old friend."

"Ah," said the other, coming forward, arms outstretched. "I was hoping to see you here." His eyes were sparkling crescent moons as his face folded them up in a wide smile.

The big man's embrace, enveloping him, smelled of Bijan. He endured a kiss on each cheek and gave back one in kind. The greeting, once Continental, was now merely common.

"How was your trip?" his associate asked.

"Successful."

"Ah. This is wonderful news. Come in, sit down. Have some tea. I'm having lunch with three friends of yours. Can you join us?"

"Thank you." All of this was as arranged.

In the booth was a thermos shaped like a teapot. While his host poured, the principal unable to contain himself, said, "I should get back by tonight. I merely wanted to drop by while I'm here and share my news."

"That good, eh?"

"Good enough." There would be time at lunch to explain that things had not gone perfectly. *HE-12* had not been knocked out of orbit sufficiently that it was even now falling from the sky, eradicating all evidence of an attack. Nor had it been blown to bits too small to analyze.

But the second operation would be smoother. Everything was already in place. The next target had been chosen long ago, before the host satellite had been successfully launched. All that remained was to confirm that everyone was still steadfast in resolve, ready to proceed.

During the Iran-Iraq conflict in the late eighties, the Americans had been able to use an older generation of Defense Support Program System (DSP) satellite, much less sensitive than *HE-12*, to observe 166 missile attacks between warring nations, and to observe aircraft flying on afterburner. The French routinely monitored the entire world with intrusive clarity. The Soviet Union had similar satellites, good enough to analyze oil fires; such satellites could not be blinded by ground-based lasers.

This ability of developed nations to monitor tactical missiles, aircraft, and ground-attack forces could not be tolerated at the moment.

This was why he was being paid such a goodly sum by the other principals to clear the skies during critical time windows over certain sensitive areas without any overt sign of aggression.

This was also why, as much as he would have enjoyed the three remaining days of the Baghdad show, he could not stay. He had agreed to come only because the heavy man worried that it might look odd if he did not.

Now that he was here, he was glad he'd agreed. This way, all of them would be seen here, among their fraternity. There was no alibi for such as they; but suspicion, when it fell, would not fall on them so quickly as it might if some or one had stayed away.

So they'd come here, where they could be seen where they would be expected to be. Baghdad presented an opportunity for all of them to meet publicly and unremarkably, so that he could deliver his report and discuss any last-minute concerns or instructions.

After briefing the principals on the exact degree of his success and the exact state of his preparation for his next strike, he was going back to his ground station, to baby his equipment, to take every precaution—to watch and to wait.

6

Day 2: Alexandria, Virginia

"You get it," Jenny Land's husband said when the phone rang in their darkened bedroom. Chandler Land was still in the adjoining bathroom, brushing his teeth.

Jenny groaned and glared at the little red light on the phone that pulsed with each ring. If Chan had been in bed, he would have taken the call. The phone was on his side.

And she couldn't just let it ring. It was the second line; that one didn't have an answering machine. It was for calls you had to take. Less than a quarter of their callers had that number.

"It's the B line," she warned Chan as she reached across the pillows for it. She could feel her gut tighten. It was past one in the morning, and no incoming call on that line at this hour could be good—or trivial.

She hoped to hell her mother wasn't in an ambulance right now, headed for the hospital again. Almost sure Mother was the problem, she said only, "Yes?" apprehension and resentment combining to make the single-syllable sound unpleasant to her own ears.

"Hey, Jen," came an intimately low male voice from what sounded like a long distance. "Did I wake you?"

"God, Dalton, it's past one here. I'm not your only phone call, am I? If you're looking for bail money, it's too close to the end of the month for us."

Dalton Ford always sounded like he was about to unbutton her blouse; Ford never gave his name if she took his call because she was supposed to know that voice even if, as now, she hadn't heard it in six months. Despite the fact that he'd never landed a paw on her, she gave a guilty start when Chan called from the bathroom, "It's Ford? At one in the morning?"

"I just said that, dear," she reminded her husband, slipping the mouthpiece down into the hollow of her neck. "Get on, if you want." Then she rearranged the handset and said into it, "Chan'll be right here."

"Damn, how long have we got?" came the low voice, this time laced with amusement because Ford loved to tease her.

"Not long enough. Is this call part of a billable hour?" She and Chan had done some consulting for Ford in the past. They were still on retainer to DIAC (Defense Intelligence Agency Center), she calculated quickly, although working mostly for other intelligence agencies and the occasional independent contractor.

"Only when Chan gets on, love: male chauvinism isn't dead in the land of the palm trees. How's America's sexiest national resource?" asked Dalton Ford.

Her husband opened the bathroom door and headed for the living room to pick up an extension.

Jenny rolled onto her back and put her free arm over her eyes to shield them from the bathroom light: "Not feeling very sexy at the moment."

"We can fix that."

"Not likely, Dalton. You sound pretty pleased with yourself."

"I'd be in paradise, but we're short on white women. You should come out here. It'd relax you. Promise."

"Here?" She wouldn't have asked unless he'd given her the opening. Consultants learned what not to ask.

"Cairo. And yeah, I'm havin' more fun than you are."

Chan had picked up by then: "Ford? This is a surprise. Did I hear Cairo? Sounds exotic."

So no one had warned Chan, either, that Dalton Ford might call. Jenny Land was now wide awake.

"Hot as hell," Ford said. "I've got a brainstorming problem."

"What are you working on these days?" Jenny interjected cautiously. The last she'd heard, Ford was at Space Command in Colorado.

"The question is," her husband said from the living room, "is it something we can handle?" Chan loved his spooks and their subtext.

Jenny said, "Dear, he wouldn't be calling if he thought we couldn't handle it. Dalton, I can't go to Cairo. My mother's sick again."

"Don't have to," said Ford from half a world away. "Somebody'll be around in the morning with the material. I'll be back there," Ford sighed deeply, "probably by tomorrow night. Want to have dinner?"

"Dinner's okay with us. But you don't sound happy about it," Chan observed.

"I just didn't want to come back right now. I'm hoping that you'll put everything aside for me and give me as much time as you can, so I can wrap this up and get back out here in, say, three days tops."

"It would be nice if you could give us a hint. As it is," Jenny said throatily, "I'm not going to sleep all night wondering."

"First tell me if you have the time."

"Chan?" she asked her husband. They had some work in progress: one project that was trouble ridden and stalled because of turf battles among other participants; another that was ahead of schedule; a third one, a spec project that was hers and didn't involve Chan, would probably sit on the shelf a while without harm, if necessary. Right now, with her mother's medical bills, they could use a quick and dirty money earner.

"Ah, Dalton, if this is top priority, we can move things around for you. But it's got to pay our freight."

"I promise, Chan, you won't regret it. Meet you both at the Pleasant Peasant in Mazza Gallery at . . . eight . . . tomorrow night."

"Fine," Jenny said.

"Jenny and I can't wait to see you, Dalton," added her husband.

"Fuckin'A," said Dalton Ford.

"What, if anything, does that mean, Dalton?" Jenny hated

gung ho. She forcibly reminded herself that Ford was a civilian suit. And he was being careful: he wasn't suggesting an agency hangout like the American Cafe.

"Means thank you, in this case."

"No sweat, Ford. We'll have all we need by then?" asked Chandler Land.

"Promise. Jen, I wouldn't want you not sleeping because of me: it's overhead. You're gonna love it. Make history, I bet."

"Uh-oh," Jenny Land groaned as her husband made enthusiastic noises.

When they'd hung up, she waited for Chan to come back into the bedroom, arm crooked over her eyes again. As she heard him moving, she said, "I really don't like this. Whenever we get involved with him—"

"It'll be all right," her husband said, clicking off the light switch.

He reached for her across the bed, but he wasn't serious about it. And she was unresponsive. The last thing she needed was Dalton Ford in her life right now, bringing one of his covert national emergencies with him.

7

Day 2: Cairo

Colonel Jesse Quantrell was having lunch in the Camel's Eye along with half of the cowboys in Cairo, when Ford brought his black box to Quantrell's booth and thumped it down on the table.

"I'm on a plane home in three hours. Hold onto this and don't break it before I get back." Ford shoved the heavy case toward Quantrell, enough to joggle one of the beer glasses on the table, which tipped toward the other two. The Soviet across from him caught it before it fell.

Jesse Quantrell had chosen the Camel's Eye, which competed with the in-house watering holes of the Western-style hotels close by, because it was dark and intimate. Quantrell thought Ford might not have noticed the nature of the two men sitting with him until Ford was too close to back off.

"Dalton Ford, do you know Klement Ignatov?" Quantrell said by way of introduction. "No matter what the scuttlebutt says, Iggy's just a Bulgarian cultural attaché. And in the corner's Gaspar Larka, who isn't Spetznaz any more than Iggy's from KGB's T-for-technology section."

Ford always managed to seem jump-ready to Quantrell. The tanned, unshaven DIA man didn't turn a shaggy hair as he digested the warning.

First Ford waved to Larka, the Spetznaz (Soviet Special Forces) colonel in civvies, whose huge shoulders jammed the

shadowy depths of the booth. Larka nodded his bullet head and
growled a sarcastically intimate Russian greeting: *"Privyet."*

"You bet," Ford replied and leaned over the beers to offer
his hand to Klement Ignatov, the pale, overfed Bulgarian KGB
agent: "Hiya, Ignatov. I'm one of Colonel Quantrell's technical
advisors."

Not a bad way to pull your foot out of your mouth, once
you'd stuck it in there in public, Quantrell thought with grudg-
ing admiration.

Ignatov's piggy eyes lit up as Ford's tanned hand disappeared
in his huge, white one. *"Que pasa?"* said Iggy, who'd been in
Central America and was proud of it and the ease with which
he charmed his targets of opportunity from all nations.

"Not a fuck of a lot." Ford stepped closer to the table,
nudging the case with his thigh.

Quantrell swept it up and put it between his booted feet,
where it wouldn't demand to become a topic of conversation.
"You might as well sit down and have a drink, Ford, now that
you're here. We're waiting for Seti, so we can have a foursome
for bridge." His dry delivery would not be lost on Ford. Yousef
Seti was an Egyptian intelligence officer. Quantrell knew Ford
was staying at Yousef's while he was in town.

Whatever the brass said back home, whatever the intelligence agencies would like to be the case, you knew the players if you'd been in the field long enough to be any good,
in Quantrell's line of work, which was very special forces.
Commando teams and special operations just didn't run like
spy nets.

Maybe you had connections into the intelligence shops, or
maybe you were run from the basement of your nation's capi-
tal, but basically you did missions on foreign ground. When
those missions were covert actions in Third World nations, or
counterterrorist square dances on the aprons of foreign powers'
airports, you ended up running into the other players. When
a man's face appears in your sight picture, you don't forget
him.

Quantrell slid inward, dragging the black box between his
legs, making room for Ford on the outside, opposite Iggy and
in front of Quantrell's Michelob.

Quantrell was here on behalf of the First Special Operations Command at Fort Bragg, paving the way for some Delta commandos of his who were long-haired and bearded and were going to run a war game of their own during Bright Star. He was also expecting some other hardballers, assigned to him from CIA's Special Activities Group (SAG).

All in all, it was looking like a real good time. And yeah, if Ford was going home early, you bet he could leave his black box with Quantrell and only bend the rules a little: it was Quantrell's boys who were really going to use the prototype. Ford had put it together with them in mind, after an all-nighter with Quantrell when the two men got talking about what you ought to be able to do with all this new and expensive technology in the field.

Watching Ford wiggle out of a potential security breach he'd just opened up was going to be worth the price of a Michelob, even in Cairo. Dalton Ford was ex-Special Forces. Now a civilian employee of DIA, he was currently holding down a slot in a joint military organization—Space Command. That made Ford a purple suit—a civilian joint intelligence agency employee currently holding down a slot in a joint military organization and reporting to a military officer. In this case, that officer was no less than the director of operations, U.S. Space Command: Rear Admiral Leo Beckwith, his badass self.

Civilian or not, DIA or not, Space Command or not, if you were once Special Forces, you never stopped looking out for Group, despite the fact that when a man put on a purple suit, he left his service prejudices behind.

This year's Bright Star was CENTCOM's biggest exercise ever, involving (among others) elements of the Seventh Fleet, Space Command, Air Force, even a Marine or two, as well as Eighteenth Airborne Corps units from Fort Bragg and the 101st Air Assault Division from Fort Campbell. Literally thousands of American servicemen were involved in Bright Star, many on Egyptian soil. But, no matter what the official description said, Dalton Ford had put this black box together specifically to fill the Bright Star requirements of Quantrell's multiservice special activities group.

It warmed your heart.

So when Ford tensed up beside him, Quantrell began paying close attention to what Ignatov was saying:

" . . . data retrieval is nil from *HE-12*, yet the message traffic to and about the satellite is considerable, so we've heard. Tell me what you've heard, Mr. Ford: Is the mighty United States' *Hawkeye* surveillance satellite really 'out of commission,' as you Americans say? And will you then maneuver in a Block 14 DSP satellite to observe Bright Star's simulated regional conflict, or does your Air Force Space Command keep the DSPs too busy where they are—in geosynchronous orbit over the Indian, Atlantic, and Pacific oceans? After all, watching Soviet missiles surely has a higher priority than watching an American exercise, even if your *Hawkeye* was as important to Bright Star as some are beginning to think it is. *Was*. Tsk." Ignatov shook his head sorrowfully.

"Iggy, I'm surprised at you, leaking Soviet intelligence to an American when we haven't agreed on a price yet," Ford scolded mildly. "Although I admit it's nice to know you're there if we need you. Even if it's all garbage, or a provocation, it's nice to know what the other guy's saying. Isn't that so, Larka—or can I call you Gaspar?"

Larka half-choked on his beer and growled, "Mr. Ford, call me what you will. But don't take my friend too seriously. He has a lamentably poor tolerance for Western liquor."

"Well, who doesn't?" Quantrell boomed expansively, hoping to lessen the tension. "Iggy, you ought to know better than to believe all of what you hear."

"Did you get this intelligence flash off Intersputnik?" Ford continued relentlessly, as if Quantrell hadn't given him a chance to quit while he was ahead. "Or off one of those nuclear-powered Cosmos 2100s that keep almost raining the Earth with radioactive debris because the automated boost systems are faulty? Or did you hear it from your astronauts on the *Mir* station? Because if you did, you know those poor bastards get punchy, you keep 'em up there so long, Iggy."

"*Mir* is the Soviets', not ours," said Ignatov heavily. "We Bulgarians just keep track of superpower stories, and repeat them if they are interesting."

Quantrell noticed that Ignatov, having bitten off more than

he could chew when he decided to bait Dalton Ford, was beginning to sweat.

And Ford was now having too much fun to quit. Or there was some truth to what Ignatov had said, and Ford was trying to shut the rumor down before it spread.

The DIA man leaned forward, arms splayed on the table. "C'mon now, Iggy. I bet your friend Larka here wouldn't like it if I started repeating stories about classified Soviet spacecraft. He might even report you for provoking an information leak." Ford was showing his teeth, but there was no humor in the smile.

Larka shifted enough that his lantern jaw caught the light. "You are belligerent, Mr. Ford. Why is this? We are all cooperating, these days. *Glasnost* means space is for everyone."

"It does?" Ford looked amazed. Then he snapped his fingers. "That's right. I forgot. Then if we ever do have any trouble with one of our remote-sensing spacecraft, I bet we could hire *Soyuzkarta* to give us topographics, cartographics, and photo-returns lots cheaper than we could, say, SPOT, given the relative value of the ruble and the French franc."

Quantrell touched Ford's thigh under the table.

Ford turned his way. "I gotta go, Quantrell. Have a good bridge game. Tell Seti I'll see him in three days, more or less." The tightly wound DIA man got up in one quick motion.

"Yeah," Quantrell said, aware now that he only had to babysit the box a while, not do the whole field test. "Bring me a carton of Salems, okay?"

"You bet," said Ford.

When Quantrell turned back to his companions, Larka was dressing down Ignatov in rapid-fire Russian.

"Hey, guys, Dalton's always been a little prick. Don't let that bother you. He's just self-conscious, being a civilian and all. What probably got him stoked was you calling him 'mister'—because that's all he is, these days. Just a hired hand."

Quantrell didn't care if the Soviet and the Bulgarian bought the line. He just needed to change the subject. There was lots he wanted to learn from these two—or trade for—before he got his boys on the ground.

You always had to be prepared for an emergency, watch out

for an accident before it happened. That was what pre-positioning was all about. You had to be willing to give a little, in order to get a little. And there was always a certain amount of unclassified information, which still was of value because being given it meant you didn't have to dig for it, only confirm it. Time was always money.

Sometimes, it was lives. Especially after seeing the way Ford behaved, Quantrell wanted to know if these two Soviet players had anything for him that might affect the survivability of Group on the ground.

Bright Star was just an exercise, but it was a big exercise, with real hardware in an explosive venue. People got killed in exercises all the time, even exercises in California.

And this exercise would be played out virtually in the laps of Libyans, Syrians, Iranians, and various other hard-liners, some of whom were trained terrorists with no love for Americans, who'd like nothing better than to see Bright Star turn into a casualty-ridden embarrassment.

Of course, that was one of the reasons you did Bright Star where and how you did it: you were projecting American power where that power most needed to be projected—right under the noses of a bunch of crazies who needed to be reminded just what they might be facing if Bright Star weren't only an exercise.

Sliding back into the space that Ford had vacated, Quantrell dragged the black box along the floor, careful to keep it between his legs. Sitting once again behind his Michelob, the Special Forces colonel wondered just what Dalton Ford had on his plate, to take him out of Cairo when he most wanted to be here.

Then Larka asked, "What is it Mr. Dalton Ford left with you, Quantrell? Anything interesting?" and Quantrell began seriously trying to change the subject.

While he did, he made a mental note to ask Ford, when next they met, if Ford thought the Soviets were up to something that Quantrell ought to know about, with the arrival of his special activities group imminent.

The trouble with spooks was that, all too often, they underestimated your need to know.

Just as Quantrell was thinking about spooks, Seti showed up and Quantrell had to slide himself and Ford's case once more into the booth's corner. The darkly handsome Egyptian was the ranking officer on this, his own turf, so the stakes ratcheted up a notch. So much so that Quantrell nearly forgot to tell Seti that Ford had said he'd be back in three days.

But not quite. Quantrell had the case between his legs to remind him that Ford was up to his neck in something serious enough to drag him back to the States on short notice.

8

Day 3: Plesetsk, USSR

It was cold as hell, pouring rain, before dawn. You couldn't see your hand in front of your face. McMurtry squatted in the Russian bushes, shivering but otherwise motionless, and cursed everybody back in Helsinki who'd had anything to do with shoving this mission up his ass on three hours' notice.

The list included everybody from the Tenth Special Forces Group colonel back home, to the damned pencil-necked intelligence officer from the Helsinki embassy who'd thought up this stunt, to the major who grinned when he tapped McMurtry on the shoulder, to the skipper of the Trident sub that snuck him through the Barents Sea, up the arm of the White Sea, to the Soviet coast.

This wasn't even close to diving for Soviet mines in Helsinki harbor, which was how come McMurtry had been in Finland in the first place. Dennis McMurtry knew the Group commander was doing this to him because that Marine guard he'd knocked up blew her head off the night before last.

Testing a system wasn't any damned reason to risk your ass behind enemy lines. The least his major could have done was not tell him why he was supposed to tote this handheld telemetry terminal into the USSR. He hadn't asked to know. He didn't need to know. A test. Knowing made him feel like this was some kind of punishment, and that made him feel both regretful and resentful when all he ought to be feeling was a determination to get the job done and get out of here with Dennis McMurtry's butt still intact.

But he couldn't concentrate worth a damn, now that he was at the specified grid coordinates. His positioning meter verified that he was where he was supposed to be, despite the lack of visibility.

He couldn't even see the lights or the fences or the big radar dishes or the gantries of the Soviet space facility, just a sort of vague lightness relieving the wet dark, as if there were a city behind a hill.

It better be the right bunch of lights. He had to be inside the footprint—in this case, the telemetry dump radius—of whatever satellite he'd trekked in here to steal data from. If he was out of range, and didn't get anything they wanted back home, then it was their fault, not his. He was right smack in the middle of his grid square.

He turned his meter off and put his positioning electronics away. No use pushing your luck. Never could tell what kind of alarm even a passive receiver might trip; everything depended on the enemy's capabilities.

Dennis McMurtry commonly depended only on his own capabilities. But that was what had gotten that cute—dead—Marine guard in such a state. Everybody knew that maybe you'd promise a girl everything, but there was no way you were going to deliver: Group came first. *Married* was for guys who did something else for a living. You'd think, in goddamn Finland, the dizzy twit would have just gotten an abortion. He'd have paid half.

Something moved in the foliage and McMurtry jerked his legs under him reflexively. Did they have sables this far west? Sables were mean as hell. Even a fox could chew you up pretty good, if it had a mind to, if you were near its den, or if it was rabid. Sables were worse.

Well, anything came at him, he'd have to chance shooting at it. He had a silencer, and subsonic rounds in his pistol. But he wasn't comfortable even having the pistol. He'd got out of his wet suit on the beach and was now in what was supposed to pass for local peasant clothes. The local peasants apparently didn't believe in raincoats. They sure as hell didn't carry expensive handguns, even Makarovs. Or multifunction wrist chronometers, let alone satellite downlinks.

Still, you had to trust your equipment. If he had to shoot a fox or a sable or even a bear, shoot he would. If he had to shoot an intruder-sniffing dog or a car full of Soviet guards, he'd do that too. If he couldn't see much of the Plesetsk installation, he had to trust that he was in the right place.

Sure he was. That glow out there was Plesetsk, some sort of Soviet Vandenberg that conducted military-related space launches. And he was right here, as close as he could get without "incurring an unacceptable risk" of running into mobile guard patrols, dogs and automated perimeter sensors.

He could testify that this spot was colder than a witch's tit, only a hundred klicks from the White Sea inlet where the Trident had surfaced to let him paddle to shore in an inflatable, where a Czech motorcycle was waiting with a full saddlebag of necessaries.

Plesetsk was 62 north, 43 east. If he missed his Trident pickup, McMurtry could still try making it back to Finland overland on the bike, about five hundred klicks from the shore where he'd stashed the inflatable gray Zodiac among some rocks. Sure thing.

He checked his watch. He was supposed to be out of here by dawn—had to be, to have any safety margin, to make his rendezvous with the Trident.

Any other time, he'd have gloried in all the fuss made over his mission: command didn't risk a nuclear-powered submarine on anything low-level.

But this was just a test, just a dry run to see if the black box he had in a waterproof pouch would do what it was supposed to do.

What McMurtry was supposed to do was get the box out, turn it on, run a self-test, and baby-sit it for an hour while it sucked up Soviet telemetry. If it got the data quicker, it would tell him "DOWNLOAD COMPLETE."

If it took longer than an hour, McMurtry was going to start getting a little nervous. And not just because he had to hike, then bike, through enemy territory to hitch a ride on a sub that wouldn't—couldn't—wait forever.

The black box in his hands had an "armed" switch that he was supposed to engage when he fired it up. That switch had to be retripped every sixty minutes from then on, without fail, or the box blew up.

This was a precaution meant to destroy the evidence if he were killed and the box was captured, but it made McMurtry antsy.

He checked his watch one more time, and set a one-hour stopwatch.

Then he turned on the box and put it through its self-test. The box thought it was working just fine.

His finger hesitated on the "armed" switch. Then he depressed the stud. What the hell. He checked his stopwatch function: It would beep once, three minutes before the box's auto-destruct sequence initiated.

That ought to give him enough warning.

If he wasn't discovered in the ensuing hour, all he had to do was listen for the beep and he and the box would make it through just fine. If he was discovered, or if he thought he couldn't make it to his rendezvous with the sub, or if he had trouble hiking his fallback escape route, he had the option of bursting the data out.

A burst transmission was real detectable, and bursts didn't always get received uninterrupted, so Helsinki didn't want him to burst-transmit the data unless he thought he was going to buy it—or the box was.

The box had an auto-burst that kicked in once the detonation sequence triggered.

So, McMurtry supposed, looking at the handheld's little plasma screen blinking READY, he could probably leave the damn thing in the mud under one of these bushes and get the hell out of here now, saving lots of wear and tear on his nerves.

Nobody was going to argue with him if he said he'd been chased by Rusk and left the box, armed to auto-destruct, hoping it would burst-transmit everything Helsinki wanted, the way it was built to do. At least, he didn't think anybody'd argue.

But he'd never hear the end of it—turning tail just wasn't his style. Even if Group never found out, McMurtry would know what he'd done. And, anyway, Helsinki wanted a human operator along just in case the satellite dump in question took longer than anticipated, or the intelligence time-framing was off by a few minutes and the download started later than intel expected.

Not for the first time, McMurtry wished he didn't know that this was just a test. A gust of wind blew up, howling, pelting him with gritty rain, and he consoled himself that it must be one crucial test, if they didn't want to burst the transmission.

They were probably going to courier this box out of Helsinki by diplomatic pouch once he brought it back.

Because he was going to bring it back. He cradled the box on his lap and bent his head, watching the plasma display, ignoring the water that streamed down his face and dripped from his nose and chin.

Watch the pretty pictures, kid. When DOWNLOAD IN PROGRESS replaced READY on the backlit little screen, he gave a start.

A second later, he thought he heard something.

Then he wasn't watching the screen anymore. He was watching the rainy dark. He checked his watch against the counter on the black box's plasma screen. He had better than fifty-nine minutes to go on his transmission hour, and forty-eight to go on his auto-destruct hour.

And he wasn't about to leave the area, now, with his download in progress, unless he was damned sure that he was in trouble.

He slid his Makarov out of the pocket of the peasant coat. The coat was heavy, coarse wool, half-soaked.

The gun's front sight fouled for an instant in the pocket's lining and scared the hell out of him.

When he had the pistol free, his heart was pounding so loud he wasn't sure what he was hearing. Funny how a little thing like having your weapon tangled in something will overload your nerves.

Holding his breath, McMurtry sat with the pistol on one knee and the box in his lap, utterly motionless, holding his breath, waiting for a branch to crackle under a boot or a paw, or a tire to slosh mud or throw gravel.

When he remembered to breathe again, his mind was working: nobody'd be out here without at least a flashlight—even McMurtry had one, though he wasn't about to use it.

Headlights were more likely. And you could see animals' eyes in the dark—they glowed.

If this had been a different kind of mission, he'd have had night-vision goggles. But night-vision goggles would look really odd on a Soviet peasant. McMurtry wished he wasn't so good at languages. He'd be packing for Cairo by now, if he weren't.

But he was an excellent Russian speaker. That facility might come in handy yet, if he fell afoul of the local militia.

Now that the scare an errant noise had given him was receding, he was feeling sleepy: adrenaline overload. He knew what it was, but there wasn't much he could do about it. If you got all pumped up and then all you could do was sit still, your body chemistry played tricks.

And the only thing moving out here was the counter on the black box's plasma screen. Everything else was just a blur of wind and rain and nothing in particular to focus on.

He realized he still had the Makarov in hand and stuffed it back into his pocket, tearing the lining as he did. He'd been watching that counter on the plasma screen so long that he'd lost touch with the numbers' significance. The procession of digits was hypnotic.

But he had to piss and his legs were numb, half-asleep from sitting cross-legged so long.

Dennis McMurtry carefully put the box down beside him and started unfolding his numbed legs. He had to use his hands on his left knee to help maneuver his left leg out from under him; its circulation was restored and pins and needles began.

He'd gotten up too fast once on that leg when it was asleep and it had gone right out from under him. He'd sprained his ankle in the process, and the snapping sound of the tendon slipping over bone face had told him he was lucky that it hadn't broken.

So he was very careful about rubbing the leg back to life and waiting until the worst of the pins and needles had passed before he tried to stand.

You could piss down your leg if you had to; he'd done it once when he was waiting to jump from a C-141. But he didn't want to be a peasant who pissed himself anymore than he wanted to be a peasant with a sprained ankle.

So he got up and walked a few paces away from the box before he pissed, to test his legs and walk them back to normal.

When his wristwatch beeped, he was just finishing one of the longest urinations he could remember.

"Shit." Stuffing himself into his pants, he nearly dove for the black box. He had three minutes.

But the box wasn't where he landed.

Okay, he had that flashlight in his belt.

He was just reaching for the flashlight when something growled at him. Maybe it had growled once before, when he dove into the mud like that; he couldn't remember.

But whatever it was had yellow, glowing eyes and it was probably as scared as he was.

He decided against the flashlight and reached for the Makarov in his pocket.

The growling got louder. He heard something move in the dark.

The pocket lining started to come out with the pistol. The front sight was really stuck in the little tear he'd made putting the pistol back in there.

Finally he ripped the pistol free, just as whatever it was rushed him in a scramble of mud and leaves.

"Shit!" He shot once blindly, and again when whatever it was sunk its teeth into his calf.

The second time, he knew right where to shoot.

Whatever had its teeth in his leg clamped down harder as it shuddered. He tried not to scream as it convulsed.

Instinct made him shake it loose, a demand that overwhelmed his mind's caution that he should get out the flashlight and look at the thing, or reach down and disengage its jaws with his hand.

He wasn't getting his shooting hand anywhere near those teeth.

Suddenly, he realized his leg was free. But by then, the box was burst-transmitting its data and the auto-destruct sequence was under way. He could hear a little whir that told him he was in trouble.

He knew that. His calf was all torn up and the pain was making him see red and white lights, like sheet lightning in the night.

He scrambled for the whirring sound, ignoring the pain in his leg, while he fumbled for his flashlight.

By the time he found the flashlight's rubber nipple and depressed it, his left hand, searching for the box in wide swings across the muddy ground, had found it.

He'd just picked it up and was feeling for the "armed" button he had to push to defeat the auto-destruct sequence when the box exploded in his hands, obliterating itself and the top half of Dennis McMurtry in a bright flash of plastic explosive.

The explosion brought guards from Plesetsk to investigate, but little could be made of the remains except that some peasant had gotten hold of a plastic explosive, which subsequent analysis would prove to be of Bulgarian manufacture.

Given the toothmarks in the peasant's calf and the signs of a wounded animal, perhaps a fox, or even a feral sable roaming far from home, the peasant was listed as a poacher on the Plesetsk perimeter guards' report. Why anyone would use plastic explosive for poaching was explained by the simple observation that peasants could be very stupid.

As for the sable and the Makarov, the first guard on the scene secreted the carcass and pocketed the weapon immediately. He forgot to mention either one to his colleagues or list them in his report. The pistol alone was worth good money on the black market.

9

Day 3: Bethesda, Maryland

When Jenny first saw Dalton Ford again, he looked like death warmed over, as her mother would have said. She and Chandler were already seated in the Pleasant Peasant's urbane dimness. As Ford followed the hostess to their table, Jenny kept trying to shake the impression that something serious was wrong with him.

But she just couldn't. And that apprehension made her elegant meal tasteless, her comments too sharp. If something was wrong with Dalton Ford, what business was it of hers? Why was she feeling sadly protective?

She didn't feel sadly protective of her mother, who was dying brain cell by brain cell—at least, she didn't feel protective of her any more.

Ford certainly seemed well enough, now. He was cheerful, fighting Chan for the last of the fried bread that was a Pleasant Peasant specialty. Under his loose windbreaker, what she guiltily thought might be the best shoulders in the District seemed too relaxed to support her initial impression that the world was resting on them.

She'd always liked Ford's looks—his fine-featured, dark head with its intelligent, guileless eyes and the unexpected touch of sensuality about his mouth; his graceful, lean body that nobody who made a living at a desk could match. But she also knew the type: Ford was an ex-Special Forces, government chauvinist who thought of women as recreational conquests.

The last thing Jenny wanted was to be conquered. The only way to deal with someone like Ford was by forcing him to treat you as one of the guys, because Jenny's marriage wasn't an impediment to Dalton Ford; it was a plus.

So why was she feeling so much sympathy for him tonight? Her eyes kept straying to his hands as he played with his dessert fork. Were they pale under his tan?

The material a courier had left with Chan didn't give her a clue. The job was intriguing, difficult, but hardly crucial: it involved an exercise, nothing more.

The restaurant served outlandish desserts; she had a fruit salad drenched in white chocolate sauce before her. Instead of tasting it, she sipped her espresso. Chan had already told Ford that the two of them thought the project, in general terms, might be doable.

Now the ball was in Ford's court, but he seemed hesitant to get down to specifics. He kept staring at Jenny's silk top. She tried to tell herself that he was waiting for her to demand an end to the macho small talk of Washington politics.

So, okay: "Dalton, let's get to your problem. I appreciate the dinner, but as far as I'm concerned, you've been on the clock with us since we walked in here." The restaurant had wide, striped chairs and wonderful, pale antique mirrors and breakfronts. The meal, with Ford's expansive choice of wines she hadn't drunk, was going to be as expensive as the folk sitting around them: political fund-raisers, congressional aides, image makers—the insiders who made Washington run. "You didn't fly over here just to see if you could make me gain half a pound."

"Okay, Jen." Ford leaned forward. So did Chan.

She didn't. Nobody else called her "Jen."

"Chan said you two think this project'll fly. I have to run options by Beckwith from Space Command and put together a threat-assessment briefing on possible Soviet involvement."

You almost had to read his lips, so quietly was Ford speaking. His intensity surprised her.

Then the words sank in: "Soviet . . . involvement?" She

stopped before Chan could elbow her. "You think that's what caused the . . . blind spot? That's why you want to do this?"

"You know, Jen, I didn't think so until just before I left Cairo. Then I ran into a Bulgarian who knew nearly as much about the . . . blind spot . . . as I do."

Chan put both forearms on the table, encircling the mound of whipped cream on his plate, and leaned forward another inch. "Ford, there are maybe two thousand Cosmos series spacecraft alone up there." He raised his eyes to the ceiling and returned them to Ford's face. "Some check out other people's hardware—whether it's on or off. You can get some good data when a spacecraft's running—what it's doing in general, how it's doing it in general. But to get more than that, to 'eavesdrop' the way you're suggesting, is going to take some committed technical means. And some serious decryption, once you've got the download. Monitoring spacecrafts' performance is a long way from acquiring the data they're collecting."

"You're telling me not to worry about foul play, before, during or after?"

"What Chan's saying," Jenny said, hoping she was correct, "is that it's unremarkable that they're keeping tabs on what's turned on and what's not. That's all."

"I'll keep that in mind," said Ford. He was looking hard into her eyes and it seemed that she could see his skull right through the skin. "Given that you don't think they're routinely doing what I'm proposing we do, how do you think we should go about it?"

Chandler Land actually looked over his shoulder before he spoke. "Carefully. Maybe we should go somewhere—"

But they were probably as safe here as anywhere except a clean room under the White House or at one of the agencies. Jenny suddenly wanted to cut through the bullshit:

"Dalton, if you need something right away for DIA to brief with, I can give you some easy options." You couldn't have this conversation without focusing it. "There's lots of ways."

"Shoot," said Dalton Ford, intensity and a trick of the light making his eyes glow like diodes.

"Okay." She saw Chan tuck in his chin. She also saw his profile: school tie, elegant, and disapproving. She'd better make sure her husband wasn't still angry when she was done speaking.

"Dalton, if you're satisfied with intermittent overhead, which was all you'd have been getting if nothing had gone wrong, then all you need to do is get in under the footprint. You might do it with a sub, but the sub would have to surface close to a Soviet receiving facility for an hour or so. You'll have the same time-related vulnerability with overflight. You could send up a TR-1 or a U-2 or even an SR-71 reconnaissance aircraft, but he'd need to circle on station a good long while. Then there's ground access. If you've got deep-cover agents near the appropriate facilities, then all you need is the opportunity to plant a receiver-transmitter near or in those facilities." She shrugged. "Those are the easy ways of mirroring."

"Yeah," Chan said. "Of course, you run the risk of getting caught at it."

Ford's face became absolutely emotionless. "I tried a test like that. Just got the results." His voice deepened, coming from somewhere below his breastbone. "The test worked well enough—we bursted out everything but maybe the last two minutes of encrypted download. But we lost somebody," he said thickly. "I hate like hell to lose people."

So that was it.

Chan proposed, "How about popping up a short-lived mission sat, maybe a fourteen-day job boosted into LEO by a Titan? Sync it to orbit right below the target—in the target's footprint—and use it to relay the data."

Ford's eyes lost their glassiness. He nodded once, and said, "Yeah, that's more like it. I've thought of some of this. But I've got to put a specific proposal together, and for that I need you guys—you're familiar with more spacecraft than most folks."

Dalton Ford wasn't fooling Jenny any longer. He was torn up by having run a spur-of-the-moment test and losing someone doing it.

Trying to cover her shock that the man was grieving, she said softly, "How about something that doesn't risk any lives, and can give you real-time data, or close to it?"

"We haven't got time to build something exotic from the ground up, Jen," Ford said, sitting back now, fingers interlaced behind his head. "We've got days—less than ten days."

"Come here," she said.

He sat forward again, leaning toward her until only the little candle on the table was between them. "Here I am," a glimmer of the old Ford told her.

"Your concerns are, first, doing the job; second, not getting caught doing the job; third, doing the job without casualties. What if I could give you real time, or close to it, overhead reconnaissance of your exercise's venue . . . in a virtually deniable fashion, without endangering reconnaissance aircraft or putting up a single new spacecraft or maneuvering any of our existing spacecraft out of their current positions? *And* without endangering any human operator on-site or in a sub or a plane or a rubber boat or under a haystack in Siberia."

"I'd settle for that," Ford said, "but the Easter Bunny's come and gone and I don't have it."

"If you'll put me—us," she amended, so excited now because she'd found an opening to float her plan that the words were rushing out, "in touch with the proper people and in a position to make use of the proper facilities, I think we can do that."

"Okay," Ford said. "I'll bite. How? Not specifically, just generally."

Jenny hadn't thought her chance would come so soon. She hadn't even talked this over with Chan. He was going to kill her when they got home. But it was too late to turn back now. "By 'spoofing': we preempt their telemetry. That is, we tell their satellite to dump on us, on our schedule. We're careful not to interrupt its current schedule. We could even dump to high-altitude reconnaissance aircraft—"

"Of course," her husband interrupted, seeing where she was going and not all that pleased, "we'd have to write the spoofing program and let your people execute it, unless there's some way, with a dual coding system, we could write the instructions into a computer and they'd be sent in the appropriate encryption for the satellite."

"Or," Jenny said breathlessly, "if you don't *have* the appropriate encoding for the satellite—which I doubt—we could try to help you break it." The gleeful taunt just slipped out. "Spoofing to relay sats is hard, but it'll give you close to real-time coverage. Spoofing to ground stations is safer, easier. It's up to you how much you want. It's riskier the more you do."

"Jesus Christ." Dalton Ford ran a hand over his mouth. "You're worth your fee, you know? Okay, let's get it straight: You're proposing to write instructions to the . . . target spacecraft, in essence to take it over intermittently, turning it on and then returning control of it in so timely a fashion that the proprietors never know it's been dumping to us—and to do that on a sufficiently regular basis that we'll have as good or better coverage than we would if we hadn't had our problem."

"Yep." Chan said with a sigh. "Good as your downlinks or relays will allow. Just keep in mind, 'never' is a long time."

Dalton was excited, Jenny knew. But even when he was excited, he wasn't going to say, *Use Soviet-encrypted telemetry commands to take over a Soviet satellite without interfering with its response to actual Soviet telemetry*.

But that was what she meant, and that was what Ford knew she meant.

The difficulty was largely domestic: NSA—which had the charter for breaking Soviet telemetry encryption—wasn't going to hand Chandler and Jenny Land such highly classified data, even though they were both CIA alumni. They'd probably have to work at NSA, if they were allowed to work on that part of the project at all.

"We've got to impress upon you, Dalton," Chan said, "that there are considerable performance-related risks. This is a very complicated problem. If you get greedy—try for too many dumps a day—then at least *what* has been done, if not by whom, will eventually be discovered."

Jenny thought Ford murmured, "I don't give a shit about that."

"What did you say, Dalton?" she asked.

"I can't wait to try it on the honchos," he answered. "We're going to do this in three days?"

"Once you give us the go-ahead to concentrate on Jenny's approach, we'll get started," Chan said.

God bless her husband. Sometimes she was afraid he'd hate

her, because she was a little quicker than he in certain situations. But he didn't.

"So, Dalton, are we going to try it?" Jenny pressed when Ford just looked at her pensively. "And if so, where? And when can we get the data we need?"

"Damned if I know," Ford said with a chuckle. "Now you're talking politics—sensitive toes, strings to pull. I've got to go to Kwajalein; then I'll be at Falcon. My flight leaves in three hours. You get started. Do whatever you can by yourselves. Call my old DIAC office if you get stuck and need help. The lady there's been told to expect to hear from you. If I don't get with you before I land at Falcon, I'll call you from there first thing."

Ford twisted in his seat and gestured for the waiter to bring the check.

"He likes it," her husband murmured, leaning toward her.

"I like it too," she replied under her breath. "I just hope we can do it. I wish Ford would sit still long enough for me to ask him more questions."

But Dalton Ford wasn't about to do that, and Jenny knew it. He was running from a ghost; trying to make everything work out right, so that whoever the ghost was could rest in peace.

10

Day 4: Kwajalein Atoll

Dalton Ford kept trying to sleep on the plane to Kwajalein, but his dreams were haunted by a faceless commando named McMurtry, some kid Ford had never met but managed to get killed anyway.

It always messed with Ford's mind to cross the international date line. He kept telling himself that was why, every time he dozed off in the Air Force jet, his dreams were full of the dead kid, who was being tortured by Gaspar Larka, the Spetznaz colonel from the Camel's Eye, while Ignatov—a fatter, pastier Iggy than Ford had encountered in real life—played interrogator.

The third time, he came up out of the dream like a trapped whale breaking the surface of icy water, gasping.

Okay, if he couldn't sleep, then he'd stay awake. He went over every bit of data from the Helsinki CIA station. They'd had an entire day to decide that McMurtry didn't make it, before writing the report that had caught up with Ford when he checked in with DIAC. Helsinki's presumption that McMurtry was dead was based on the burst-transmitted dump from the black box, which was interrupted near the end by the self-destruct commands of the ground terminal itself.

This, Helsinki station was sure, plus the fact that the Soviets weren't bitching that they'd caught an American spy red-handed, indicated that the Russians didn't have McMurtry alive, or a corpse they assumed was American—or the box.

The Trident sub had surfaced a second time at the pickup point—at great risk, Helsinki was at pains to point out—just in case the commando made it there late. McMurtry hadn't. He hadn't been sighted by any deep-cover agents on the overland route, either.

Anyway, in Ford's dreams, the kid was dead. Ergo, the kid was dead. You didn't do fieldwork for a living and not develop reliable instincts. If, for reasons of their own, the Soviets had decided that holding McMurtry incommunicado would be more fruitful than screaming to all and sundry that they had him, and in three months or so the United States had a screwup named McMurtry on the front page of newspapers worldwide, Ford would slap himself on the wrist for jumping to conclusions.

Right now, he had too much on his plate to let a single putative casualty obsess him like this. He had to analyze all the rest of his data before he conducted his Kwajalein investigation. And that data was prompting him to put his DIA persona out front.

If Ford found anything, the smallest hint at Kwajalein, which might corroborate Chuck Conard's suggestion that *HE-12* didn't go down because of defense contractor mismanagement or a Space Command fuck-up, then Dalton Ford's DIA hat was going to get him farther than his Space Command hat.

In that case, he'd be talking to all the agencies about more than access for an ex-CIA consulting team named Land.

When the plane landed and he stumbled down the ramp, blinking and reaching for his shades in the searing sun, it was midafternoon on Kwajalein.

A jeep was waiting for him. He took off his jacket as he headed for it across the baking tarmac, but he was already starting to sweat. This was his year for palm trees.

The nut brown MP driving the jeep was ultraefficient, taking him to the installation's commander. The base commander, freckled, balding and tense, was determined that—whatever was going on—Ford would receive every cooperation in proving that nobody on Kwajalein had put a foot wrong in the whole *HE-12* mess.

The commander had all the regular suspects waiting for Ford in an air-conditioned rec room. The poor suckers were all from Kwajalein's night shift and their eyes were bleary. Some were watching TV, two playing pool, and the rest were pretending to play poker.

What each one was doing was trying to stay awake: there were more coffee cups strewn around here than beer bottles, even though these people weren't due to go on duty until well after the sun had set.

Ford sympathized. He met with each one—from Major Hall, the unlucky operations officer on whose watch all hell had broken loose, to all the Army and Air Force radar operators who'd been at their terminals when *HE-12* quit in mid dump—in a little office off the rec room.

His desk in the borrowed office was stacked with their personnel records. Initially, he didn't even bother with those. When each person came in, carrying a duty log of that evening, he'd take the log and scan it, asking general questions if no specific ones came to mind.

When the comm jock named Phil Young came to sit in the folding chair in front of his desk, Ford saw how nervous the young lieutenant was and that woke him up—a little.

"So what do you think, Lieutenant?" Ford asked, playing for time as he scanned the log report and—this time—reached for Young's personnel file among those piled before him.

"Sir, I think . . . " Young took a deep breath. "Everybody performed creditably. I never had a minute when I thought somebody wasn't doing their job. All the radar operators, I mean—Allie and all."

"Allie?"

"The lieutenant on the ALCOR terminal next to mine—Allison Porter."

Bingo. But what had Ford found? "Do you think the lieutenant needs a character witness, Young?"

"Ah—no, sir. I'm just—she's my . . . we're good friends, is all. I'm not sayin' that the ALTAIR jock, Kimball—he's Air Force—wasn't on his shit, either. Major Hall will tell you, we've got a damn hot shift, sir. Nobody's skatin'." Young was freshly shaven; he had a brand-new haircut that looked positively painful where the skin around his ears and on his neck was mottled red and white.

"I'm not here looking to blame this on anybody, Lieutenant. I'm just here because somebody's got to go through the motions. And maybe I'll see something that'll give us a clue to what might have happened. In all the excitement, little things tend to get lost."

"Yes, sir, Mr. Ford," said Young, his guard even higher. He didn't believe a word Ford had said.

"Did somebody tell you guys that a civilian investigator was coming out here to take a scalp or kick any available ass— is that what's bothering you? You know, I just hate it when people are scared of me. I get to feeling like I'm not loved. Then I get suspicious because I start thinking nobody wants me around. Then I start wondering if people don't have good reason to worry. You get my drift, Lieutenant?"

"Yes sir," said Young miserably, managing to sit at parade rest.

Ford looked away from the nervous lieutenant, scanning the personnel file one more time. There was nothing in it to warrant the way Ford was treating the poor guy. But he was tired, and he didn't like the size of the pile of files in front of him. The base commander had decided to hide any possible impropriety under an avalanche of paper.

And Dalton Ford had no intention of staying on Kwajalein overnight. He was going to be on the Air Force jet that had brought him in here before it had to leave without him, flying back over the date line before he lost any more time on this wild goose chase.

He put down Young's personnel file and picked up the lieutenant's log. He had to blink to make the letters stop blurring. There wasn't a damn thing in it that was unusual, except maybe the discrepancy between the time of the log entry and the time cited as the subject of the log entry, when *Hawkeye* stopped dumping.

"What were you doing, Lieutenant, in the three minutes between the dump interrupt and when you logged it?"

"Waiting for confirmation, sir."

It was such a tiny interval, it wasn't even a screwup. But

the young lieutenant's lips were white as he'd answered.

"Okay, that's all, Young. You're out of here, squeaky clean. Go take a piss or have a beer or whatever. And don't think so harshly of us poor civilians—we've got a job to do, just like you do. Okay?"

Young shot out of his chair. "Okay, sir. Thank you, sir. I won't sir. Thanks again, sir." The short, staccato bursts of relief kept coming out of Young's mouth until he'd reached the door and charged through it.

There he fell silent, holding the door open for the next radar operator, who happened to be a woman.

She marched over to Ford's desk and handed him her log folder. But she didn't sit down then. She stood there.

Allison Porter was trim and slim and had a pixie haircut. Ford didn't blame Young for feeling protective.

"At ease, Lieutenant. Have a seat." Ford ducked his head toward her open folder on the desk, because somehow she made him want to smile, and this was serious business.

Then he heard, "Sir, I'd like to point out something. Maybe it isn't anything, but . . . "

"Well, go ahead, Porter."

She came around the desk, stood over his shoulder, and reached down to flip pages for him.

She smelled like lemon soap and her hand was steady as her scrubbed fingernail pointed to an entry. "There, sir. As I said, maybe it isn't anything, but it does make the anomaly category . . . at least it's not a catalogued piece of junk, and it's on the right track."

"Oh yeah," he said, leaning back to crane his neck so that he was looking up at her. "Thanks. You sit down, now, Porter."

He had something. He didn't know what, but something.

After he'd looked at Porter's log entry for a bit and compared it to Young's log, he asked her, "What do you think this 'fleck' indicates, Porter?"

She was sitting primly in the chair, her hands folded in her lap, back rod-straight. "A fleck. I'm not free to speculate. But it's a fleck that could well be construed to have been on a collision course with *HE-12*."

At least she wasn't afraid of him. "Okay, Porter, you're not free to speculate. That's why you didn't make any further mention of the fleck in view of the *HE-12* incident. I'm not asking you why you didn't report it. You did. I can see that. Any fool can see that. But what do you *think?*"

"I think my duty was to bring it to an investigator's attention—to yours, Mr. Ford—because there's an investigation under way, but that I don't have the rank or the right kind of equipment to do more than say I noticed and logged what seemed to be a radar return from a paint fleck or small piece of debris in the area and near the time that the investigation's concerned with, sir."

"That's okay, Porter. Thanks for coming forward with this. Who knows, I might have missed it. I'll be sure and note that you brought it to my attention."

"Thank you, sir."

"You can go now, Porter. Maybe you can calm down Lieutenant Young."

Porter flushed as she got up to leave. "I'll do my best, sir."

"And Porter," he said as she jerked open the door to step through it, "good work."

The smile that lit Allie Porter's face was as bright as the sun outside. "Thanks again, sir."

When Kimball came in next, Ford had a place to start. But he didn't find anything else. Nothing irregular. Nothing illuminating.

By the time he'd gotten through the rest of his interview, he knew what he was going to throw on Chuck Conard's desk at Space Command. Allie Porter's log was going to keep the boys at Colorado Springs busy for a while.

Which suited Dalton Ford. He wanted to take a copy of Porter's log to DIAC (Defense Intelligence Agency Center), personally, as soon as he could manage it. Then he wanted to go back to Cairo.

He wasn't tired any longer. But he was brusque with the base commander. He had some kind of evidence of something in the area of *HE-12* that shouldn't have been there. If that something turned out to be a hostile Soviet something, then there was real trouble ahead.

If it was just a paint fleck, then he could go back to Egypt the way he'd planned. One way or another, he was glad he had the Lands working on the spoofing project. If the Soviets had taken out *HE-12*, it'd serve them right if he used one of their satellites to make up for the loss.

The only way to get rid of some of those "ifs" was to hop back on the waiting Air Force jet and get the hell out of the Marshall Islands.

Damn, why couldn't he have found nothing out here? But Ford had found something, and now he had to follow where it led.

11

Day 5: Cairo West Air Base, Western Desert, Egypt

The runways of Cairo West were lit up like the light show at the Pyramids. The military gate was buzzing with activity just before sunset as Quantrell arrived in his VW van to pick up his Special Activities commandos. Bright Star wouldn't be officially up and running for two days yet, but Quantrell was—had been for three weeks.

This wasn't the first Bright Star exercise for CENTCOM, headquartered at Cairo West in old bomber hangars that had once housed Russian aircraft. Everybody else made do with tents. The communications and lower-echelon command elements had new, wooden-floored tents with air-conditioning. Near the flight line, the interoperating Egyptian airborne units had pitched orange tents with white linings that vented the heat. If you weren't from the host country, or high in the command chain, or from the "Eighteenth Imperial" Corps (the Eighteenth Airborne) who knew what favors to ask and borrowed Egyptian tents, you got your first taste of desert misery at Cairo West.

Some of these poor bastards, Quantrell knew, would never even find out that there was relief just twenty miles east, in Cairo proper. The American grunts who weren't down at the port of Alexandria off-loading equipment that could be shipped, rather than flown, were going to endure this exercise in "redesigned" basic desert bivouac tents—rank was jealous of its privileges in this venue, and a large proportion of the National Guard, MP, and Signals soldiers were first-timers.

And no manual or briefing could prepare you for the Western Desert. Your average twenty-mile-an-hour wind, complete with dust devils, drove the talcum-like dirt into every crevice of man and machine all day and all night. You sweated in the hundred-twenty-degree heat during the daytime and drank your thirteen quarts of water; you shivered once the sun set.

Quantrell's VW was attracting enough attention in this wholly military venue that he had to stop and show his authorization five times before he got through the maze of organized confusion to the tent he wanted. By then he was testy: the logistical problems of Bright Star were enormous because of its size, but they weren't his problems.

Quantrell's concern was to pick up his commandos without getting hung up here and get them back into Cairo, where the VW was appropriate to his mission parameters, before it was goddamn five A.M. and he ran into an Egyptian "thunderstorm": low foglike clouds overhead that impaired visibility when you were driving at the speed of Egyptian traffic—a hundred miles an hour—over roads treacherous with the slick dew that coated everything before dawn.

He had only two days to meld his Airborne and Agency boys into a working unit. And he'd had a cryptic communiqué from Ford, who ought to rot in hell, about finding Ford a Mossad agent who could get the Israelis to run some RPV (remotely piloted vehicle) missions without too many questions.

As if Quantrell had nothing better to do. Wrenching the VW through the chaos of trucks and troops, he wondered if Ford thought he was God or a rabbi or something. The Israelis only listened to God and their own; Ford should know that.

Out of the (gorgeous, purple and cobalt and rose) sunset came jet fighters, drowning out the lesser din as they approached. Quantrell looked up.

Over the heads of the American troops unloading C-5As, C141s, and C-130s on Cairo West's main runway, Egyptian Air Force pilots, who felt like they owned the flight line, buzzed the Third Army with MiG-21s and F-4s, fifty feet above the heads of American soldiers.

It could make you real nervous when those hot dogs buzzed you in the dusty twilight, but it was one way to remind the Americans that the Egyptians taking part in Bright Star had been trained to Soviet doctrine, and in many cases, were still wedded to it.

Quantrell knew all about the Egyptians' love for Soviet methods. They still classified *fucking maps*. They drew their damned mission graphics directly on their maps, even at brigade level. Like the Soviets, in the Egyptian Army, the battalion commander (supposedly an expert in every aspect of battalion operations) trained his officers, who then trained the soldiers. To accommodate convention, the Egyptian officers (who spoke varying degrees of English), rather than their troops, had to be trained by U.S. instructors. This meant that what the Egyptian grunts learned was their own officer's second-hand version of what the Americans were teaching.

If the American trainer was a woman, you had a real problem, because the Egyptian soldiers still thought it was demeaning to look a woman in the eye, let alone speak to one, regardless of rank. Women in uniform were camp followers, you bet.

During Bright Star's night assaults, a couple of lady Blackhawk pilots were going to teach the Egyptian Airborne a lesson or two that the Egyptian boys wouldn't soon forget: it was as inevitable as command and control problems with the satellite link to Somalia or the radiotelephone link to Jordan, or whatever screwup Ford was preparing for.

When he found the command tent he wanted and showed his Egyptian ID one more time, Quantrell consoled himself again, as he waited outside, that the Egyptian Army and Air Force components of Bright Star weren't his problem this year.

It was taking one hell of a long time for somebody to come out of that tent with a clipboard on which were the names of the men he was here to collect.

Quantrell got back in the VW and sat there with the door open and the radio tuned to a local station. After a while he turned the radio off to save the battery. He heard some snatches of conversation inside the tent that he hoped didn't have to do with his mission, but all he could see was a jumble of silhouettes—men and equipment—inside the lit tent.

Eventually, the second increment commander himself came out, a closer and larger silhouette, and Quantrell realized that night had fallen while he'd been waiting.

"Quantrell?" said the commander. "Don't get out. I don't have your men. Half of them flew by Company jet from Langley Field; I don't have to tell you which those are. The other half debarked at El Amirya . . . that's an Egyptian military post fifteen miles outside of Alexandria proper. And all of them are staying in the Hotel Venezia, about three miles from the port of Alexandria, down near the docks in a very indig—"

"I know where it is, Commander." If the man knew enough to talk to Quantrell as an equal and not require a salute, why the hell didn't he realize that Quantrell would know Alexandria? "What I don't know is how our signals got so mixed." Quantrell was holding onto his temper hard. He was a superstitious man, and he didn't like the way this mission was starting out. He didn't like it a bit.

"Well, you know the players, that ought to tell you something. It took me all this while to find out for you where the hell they were." The commander wasn't too pleased, either. "Want me to have some of my MPs deliver 'em to you? Just say where."

"You know, I think that's a great idea—for your boys as well as mine." Quantrell named an address in Cairo. "I'd like 'em before 0500, if that's doable."

The commander chuckled nastily. "It's my pleasure, Quantrell. Have a nice Bright Star." The commander turned and hurried back into his tent, rubbing his arms.

It was getting cold. And Quantrell now had a few hours to kill. Maybe, since he had nothing better to do, he'd rustle up that Mossad contact Ford wanted. Whether the Israelis would accommodate him, knowing as little as Quantrell did about why Ford wanted the favor, Quantrell couldn't say.

But it never hurt to ask.

Quantrell picked up his cellular phone and began punching presets as he headed the VW toward the Cairo West gate.

The phone was secure; a general back in the States had become an ex-general by leaving his keys in his car where his cellular STU (secure telephone unit) could be stolen, even though the phone was later recovered from a Washington pawn shop.

If you lost an STU-3 out here, you'd be in worse trouble than a body was likely to survive, what with all the hostile operatives around who'd love to get a chance to break the encryption.

But Quantrell had no intention of losing his phone, his special activities group (SAG), Ford's black case, or anything else during Bright Star. It was a matter of professional pride.

When somebody answered the phone, he asked a couple of questions and was told to meet an "attractive young woman with long black hair, wearing a red raincoat and carrying a purple purse, outside the Nile Hilton in two hours."

"Great," he said, and hung up.

Hot damn, cloak-and-dagger stuff.

But when he met Anu Soukry, Quantrell realized it was more than that: it was lust at first sight.

"*Amid* Quantrell?" she wanted to know, when he came stumbling toward her feeling huge and ungainly, a grizzly bear in rumpled khakis blinking rapidly under the Hilton's glittering lights.

"Just a poor *aqid*"—a colonel, not a brigadier general, as she'd called him. Her heart-shaped face tilted up to watch his face as he talked.

"*Aqid* Quantrell, then," she answered with a toss of her head that said it didn't matter if her information was wrong. "You may call me 'Meri,' if you'll take me inside and buy me a drink in the Taverna."

Quantrell had never seen a woman as beautiful, and he'd been knocking around the Near East, South Asia, and Central America for twenty years. She had cat-brown eyes, a delicately Mediterranean nose, and a refined but sensual mouth that was naturally pink against translucent skin free of makeup. Her long hair was blue-black and slightly wavy; it brushed her high rump, which shaped the red silk trenchcoat belted loosely at her waist. The whole package that was Anu Meri Soukry stood five and half feet tall in black riding boots and couldn't have weighed more than a hundred pounds, but she had the stopping power of an elephant gun.

Dumbstruck, thinking over and over again that *anu* meant *miss*, Jesse Quantrell had to forcibly remind himself that this exotic creature was his Mossad contact, an Israeli from the most dangerous and effective "action service" in the world. Caught in the kind of distended time that normally swept him up only during battle, he recalled all that he'd heard about Jewish girls, free from Original Sin or Muslim constraint, in bed.

Finally he realized she was staring through his eyes into his soul because he hadn't answered her, and managed, "Sure thing, Meri, a drink in the Taverna," pretending he wasn't transparently overwhelmed by her.

"Good." She stepped in front of him and stood on tiptoe, brushing each of his cheeks in turn with her lips as lightly as a butterfly. As she did, her breasts pressed against him and he burned.

He knew it was just tradecraft, that now they looked like a pair of lovers reconciled on the spot. But every step he took, with her hand through his arm, surprised him as she led him into the huge Hilton and deftly through its labyrinth of gift shops and barber shops, casino and restaurants, to the Taverna, a hangout of American and European expatriates and cruising gays that might have been in New York or London, except that the east bank of the Nile was outside.

There, at a quiet corner table, she sat opposite him and ordered a virgin colada, and when he'd asked for a beer, he realized he couldn't remember a thing she'd said, or he'd said, on the way in—just her soft, bantering tone.

He wanted to hear her say something else, and he didn't much care what it was. Quantrell couldn't remember the last time he'd felt like this; he could barely recall why he was here. It was enough to be here—with her, to ignore the envious glances of other, luckless men.

But she remembered why they were meeting: "So, our friend says you're a drinking companion of Sarwat Hatim's. We must first agree that he shall never know you are seeing me in my . . . official capacity." She leaned forward, breathing the words at him. "So we shall be lovers, yes? So far as he or any of your friends—any of them—know. Yes?"

"Yes," he said. "Lovers. Anytime. Tonight. Maybe I should get us a room." He grinned. "For our cover."

"I have one, here." Behind him was a mirror. By looking over his shoulder at it, he realized, she could watch the bar, most of the room, and the door. "But you haven't agreed to my conditions."

"Conditions?" He really had better pay attention. What had she said? "Oh yeah. No sweat. I'm not about to share you with anybody, Meri, if I can help it. And I don't gossip. Cuts down my survivability. As for Sarwat Hatim, I don't know anybody by that name."

"Sarwat Hatim? But of course you know him. My sources are never wrong. It cuts down our survivability. Perhaps you know him as Yousef Seti, but surely you've been in Egypt long enough to know what kind of name that is—a work name, a war name if you like, good for foreign contacts and so unlikely that no Egyptian would be born with it."

"Everybody knows Seti—Hatim—is Egyptian intelligence." Had he seen her before, if they knew Seti in common? No, he'd have remembered. "You don't have to warn me."

"I warn you that I know him, and many friends of his, but none of them know my . . . provenance. We have been here many years, Aqid Quantrell. My family is well entrenched in Cairene society. Our legend is valuable, so much so I am frankly surprised that I am here with you." She shrugged, "*Inshallah.*"

"I'm glad you're here with me, whether it's the will of God or just somebody keeping track of favors. And I promise, you're safe with me. In every way."

"This is always nice to hear." She smiled and the sun rose and set for Quantrell in the duration of it. "You know we wish always to be of service . . . " She trailed off.

The drinks came. She showed her key before he could find his wallet.

"I thought I was paying," he objected.

"You will, in time, Aqid."

"'Jesse,' please. And your sources were right enough—in Group, I'm something more than a colonel." He wanted to impress her.

"Ah yes." She sipped her fruit drink. "Your Group fights well, when it is allowed. But you don't fight continuously, as we do."

"Yeah, well, we don't have land borders with our enemies. Did your sources tell you what I'd like to arrange?"

"Ah, to the point, Jesse. . . . That's why I'm here. Are you sure you need this, want this help? There could be real-world repercussions from it, if anyone finds out we're helping you, now, with such a thing." Meri leaned even closer; her breasts cleared the edge of the tabletop.

"I love real-world repercussions," he said in his most jocularly dangerous voice.

"So, then, you want us to send our remote toys over a place and tell you what we see. What place? What shall we look for? And who gets the results? Do you need the pictures themselves, or only answers to questions?"

"Shouldn't we drink up and go to that room of yours?" He looked around with care. "This is getting to be a pretty specific conversation." And he really wanted to get her alone. He had a few hours before the MPs delivered his boys to his own hotel.

"Yes, we can do that." She signaled in the direction of the bar.

"Meri," he said. "*Meri*."

"Yes?"

"Doesn't that mean something in ancient Egyptian—*pretty*, or something?"

"*Love*," she said as the waiter approached. "It means *love*; or it can mean *lovely*. A whim, a little joke."

Quantrell didn't understand the joke, even when, in her Nileside suite, he began to wonder if she wasn't too accomplished a lover not to be professional, and whether some case officer had given her the name.

But he was getting his RPV overflights, just the way Ford wanted, without disclosing for whom or exactly why Ford wanted some extra aerial surveillance, so all this was in the line of duty.

Sometimes the line of duty was goddamn spectacular. He was going to have to thank Ford, when he saw him next, for putting him to all this trouble in his nation's behalf.

Meanwhile, there was nothing in the world that could take your mind off tomorrow like the thighs of a woman.

12

Day 5: Cheyenne Mountain Complex, Colorado

"Captain, I don't want to hear why you don't have what I need. I want you to call me back with the data, within the hour," Beckwith barked into the speakerphone on his desk. "I want a full analysis of this purported 'fleck' that treats it as a Soviet antisatellite weapon. I want a computer simulation showing me if some Soviet Cosmos satellite could have been responsible for placing that thing in *Hawkeye*'s path, and I don't give a fart whether a multiple launch from a single carrier rocket at a seventy-four-degree inclination seems unlikely to you to decay into a collision course with *HE-12*'s track. We're *looking* for the *un*likely: a secondary launch from orbit, perhaps. Let the computer do the thinking. If you can't make the numbers work with Plesetsk, try Tyuratam or Kapustin Yar as a putative Soviet launch site. If you need to bring in NSA's computer types, that's fine with me. But I want some tracks showing where this thing would have come from if it was an antisatellite weapon launched by the Soviet Union covertly. And I want them before I leave here today. Is that clear, Captain?" Beckwith paused for breath.

"Yes, sir," came a tiny, clipped voice out of the speakerphone. "Crystal clear, sir."

"Then hop to it, mister," Beckwith nearly snarled at the speakerphone, mopping his wide, tanned brow with his damp handkerchief as he stabbed a button to break the connection.

Beckwith despised the ass-covering mentality that made men afraid to try something just because the resulting data might not support the desired conclusion. That was why you tested hypotheses: to see whether you were right or wrong. Some of these desk jockeys who tweaked intelligence to make the customer happy ought to spend some time in the mid-Atlantic, as he had, trying to finesse their way around fifty-foot swells.

Rear Admiral Leo Beckwith was still a sailor at heart, even if his Space Command assignment meant that he was concerned with the sea of space surrounding the blue seas he loved so well—a starry sea he was too old, at fifty-one, ever to sail.

So far as Beckwith was concerned, sailing any sea was preferable to being landlocked here at Cheyenne Mountain.

Whenever he was inside the hundred-million-year-old mountain, wherever he was among the complex of fifteen steel buildings that housed the NORAD (North American Aerospace Defense Command) and USSPACECOM operations centers, he was acutely aware of all that granite over his head.

At the best of times, Beckwith could convince himself that the granite-shielded excavation was the equivalent of a giant submarine, and no more oppressive. Beckwith knew that in reality he was safer here than in any submarine. The capsulized amphitheater provided shelter from anything but a nuclear bull's-eye for the men and women, and equipment of its worldwide surveillance, warning and attack networks.

NORAD and USSPACECOM facilities here not only kept watch on anything air- or spaceborne that might threaten the United States and her allies, but also provided Space Command's commander in chief (CINCSPACE) and his battle staff with real-time overhead data from ground- and space-based sensors, as well as aircraft, which was automatically displayed on huge background maps of the United States and the world.

Cheyenne Mountain ran twenty-four hours a day, keeping eight hundred people busy during daylight and three hundred per shift on its two night shifts. Leo Beckwith was willing to bet that not a single one of them—from the elite guardsmen of the 1010th Special Security Squadron, to the 1010th Civil Engineers who maintained the prime power plant of six 1,750-kilowatt Delavel diesel generators—sweated the way he did every time he had to come over here in his capacity of director of operations, U.S Space Command.

Hell of a note, having rampant claustrophobic reactions to your command center when you were a USSPACECOM ops director. Beckwith always carried a half dozen fresh linen handkerchiefs with him to his Cheyenne Mountain office because he sweated bullets from the time his car nosed into the tunnel to the time he wheeled it out again into the fresh mountain air.

When he left tonight, he'd take the soiled handkerchiefs with him for his wife Carol to wash, as he always did, secreting them in his briefcase so no one would know. The last thing he needed was a fitness review sparked by counseling or therapy for what wasn't really a problem, unless he got trapped in here indefinitely by a nuclear conflict. And in that case, claustrophobia wasn't going to seem too serious or pressing a difficulty.

Beckwith was dealing with his claustrophobic demon the way he dealt with everything else: he toughed it out. His staff was accustomed to seeing him come in with sweat streaming down his face in rivulets; only once had a new girl asked him if it was raining outside. Nobody commented on the chill in his office—sixty-two degrees Fahrenheit, as low as his most temperature-sensitive computer would allow—except the occasional visitor, for whom he had prepared the response, "It keeps my blood thick."

When he said that, he always bared his teeth. Beckwith had carefully cultivated his ferocious reputation; it did him a world of good in the military pecking order.

But no amount of snarling or desk-pounding was helping to make the *HE-12* problem any less diffuse or more amenable to solution. Beckwith was nearly convinced that his Soviophobic staff—including Chuck Conard, boy astronaut—was wrong about *Hawkeye* being the victim of sabotage, that everybody from Dalton Ford to the DIAC boys who were backing Ford had a case of "Soviopia" (an eye ailment defined as seeing Russians wherever you looked) brought on by an acute attack of Cover-My-Ass Syndrome that had swept through his staff like the flu.

No one wanted Space Command to be embarrassed during Bright Star, least of all Leo Beckwith. But Beckwith was a sailor, and he knew the Seventh Fleet could take up most of the slack left by *HE-12*, at least where command, control, and communications were concerned.

Intelligence was another issue, but intelligence was always another issue.

And of course, interoperability or not, Space Command didn't want to go to the Navy for help in doing Space Command's job. Beckwith understood the situation with painful clarity.

If he'd had the foresight to speed up development on Ford's interoperable FleetSatCom laptop project, and had a couple of hundred, or even a dozen of Ford's black boxes on hand instead of one prototype, Beckwith could have used the downlink boxes to enlarge the Navy's piece of the Space Command pie and improve relations between Naval Space Command and the seagoing Navy. AFSPACECOM (Air Force Space Command), the "action service and lead agency" who got the lion's share of Space Command money, needed its wings clipped.

But Beckwith didn't have a dozen of Ford's boxes. What he had was a radar return from a putative paint fleck that might indicate foul play by the Soviets, and might not. And he had a contractor's rep waiting in his outer office with a smile and a couple of pounds of *mea non culpa* documentation.

At least lunch with the contractor would get Beckwith out of this grave of a complex. He could conduct the balance of the meeting back at Peterson, in his nice, airy above-ground office.

But he had one more call to make first, and he'd needed to ride herd on the computer workup on *HE-12*. So that left the phone call, and he was out of here.

Beckwith turned his chair to face the computer terminal behind him, punched up the fleet manifest for space shuttle launches and checked to see that the mission he had in mind hadn't been scrubbed.

It hadn't.

He swiveled back and punched presets on his phone. This time he picked up the handset. The number he'd chosen would ring on the desk of the man he wanted to talk to, bypassing chain of command and outer offices.

When Lundgren's voice answered, Beckwith said, "Terry, Leo Beckwith. What would it take to get my Army astronaut, Chuck Conard, on flight 55 of shuttle-C? It's a Department of Defense launch, I've already checked, and the inclination and altitude are right for my purposes."

"You want to tell me your purposes, Leo?"

"I need to send my boy out to eyeball *HE-12*, which is malfunctioning, and bring it home if the payload bay's as empty as it looks to me like it might be. That's a billion-dollar piece of worthless junk we've got up there currently. If we bring it home, maybe we can fix it. Everybody looks good; everybody wins."

"Everybody wins," said the military mission director at Vandenberg. "That'd be nice for a change. You're asking me to boot a mission specialist who's got a job to do, who's been prepped and passed a physical. I assume your Conard can handle all that?"

"He's done it before, Terry. I really need this one."

"You know who you want to bump, too, I bet."

"Somebody who doesn't have an intelligence specialty. This boy of mine knows just what to look for. I'll take care of my end if you'll handle the rest."

"You've got it, Leo. Sorry about your *Hawkeye* glitches. Anything else I can do, just let me know. I'll fax the initial paperwork to your Peterson office before lunch and you'll have the rest by ten tommorow morning."

"It's nice to talk to somebody who runs a tight ship," Beckwith said fondly.

"You trained me, Leo. My best to your wife."

"Thanks again, Terry," Beckwith said heartily and rang off.

Now all he had to do was tell Chuck Conard to stop bitching about who was going to do how well at what on the shuttle recon—Conard could do it himself.

After that, Beckwith could stop keeping his primary contractor's chief troubleshooter waiting, and use the fellow as his ticket out of Cheyenne Mountain for the day.

When, finally, the contractor was shown in, Beckwith noticed that the man was perspiring from the long, stressful wait.

He felt an instant rapport with the contractor and determined to make the man's trip here as painless as possible.

"Hungry?" he said expansively. "I know I am. Let's get out of here and have lunch. I can investigate you over a steak as easily as grill you down here." He beamed at the perspiring man, who was offering him a clammy hand to shake.

Beckwith almost forgot to get his damp hankies out of the drawer before he left with the contractor, whose relief was not only palpable, but audible. On the way out, Beckwith left an itinerary with his aide-de-camp, in case Ford called in or the *HE-12* simulations came through while he was out.

As an afterthought, and to demonstrate to the contractor that he was checking all possible error-chains, he told his aide to "have somebody get a list of all commercial launches in the relevant time frames. I know it'll be voluminous, but have Pollock run 'em all down for pertinence once we've got them."

It was important in your relationship with major contractors to make sure they understood that the government didn't consider contractors whipping boys or handy scapegoats. Especially in this case, Beckwith wanted to demonstrate that the government was going to great lengths in its investigation to determine exactly what had happened to *HE-12* and how it had happened.

Because if it *was* a contractor's screwup, Beckwith was going to hang those bastards out to dry, showing no mercy, taking no prisoners. And he'd enjoy every minute of it. Anything that took the heat off the Soviet Union was fine with him. Beckwith liked *glasnost*. His personal feeling was that the real battle, coming into the twenty-first century, was increasingly between the industrialized nations and the fundamentalist Third World.

Beckwith liked to think of modern geopolitics in terms of a decisive confrontation between civilization and barbarism. As a student of history, he was aware that, in all such previous confrontations, barbarism had prevailed.

He didn't want that to happen on his watch.

And he'd served in the Gulf, in the Mediterranean, in the

Indian Ocean, and in the Arabian Sea, so he knew the difference between armchair philosophizing and wisdom gleaned from experience.

As far as Leo Beckwith was concerned, the Third World War had been in progress for years. It was a war of low-intensity conflict that was more effective because the citizenry of industrialized nations didn't recognize it for what it was, and the warriors of the World War II generation didn't understand how to fight much weaker nations and not look like bullies in the eyes of the world press.

Beckwith didn't have the solution to that one, so he'd jumped at Space Command when it had been offered to him. He understood what the Europeans called the "Third Age" of space utilization as a race he was qualified to run, even if the Soviets were his main competitors.

Everything worth safeguarding that belonged to the industrialized nations was now in orbit, except the populations themselves. And everything in orbit was vulnerable—in need of his personal protection.

So Leo Beckwith was feeling positively cheery as he led his contractor's sacrificial lamb out of Cheyenne Mountain. He was serving his country the best way he knew how. He was working as hard as he could to avoid an unnecessary confrontation with the Soviets, and he was headed toward the light of day.

13

Day 6: National Security Agency, Fort Meade, Maryland

There were twenty ugly buildings at Fort Meade that belonged to the National Security Agency, plus acres of underground computers, and Jenny Land never wanted to see any of them again.

If it weren't for the fact that Dalton Ford had shepherded Jenny and her husband into NSA's Defense Special Missile and Astronautics Center (DEFSMAC), she'd be so afraid of never getting out (despite her clip-on plastic pass) that she wouldn't be able to work here.

DEFSMAC was hooked into Cheyenne Mountain, as well as having direct circuits to the National Military Command Center at the Pentagon, various war rooms, and even to the White House Situation Room. DEFSMAC was supposed to utilize the entire spectrum of threat-detection assets from the defense and intelligence communities, including CIA. Yet Jenny and Chan were being treated like unwelcome visitors from a rival camp.

The little white computer room that Ford, Chandler and she were using had no windows, a combination lock on the door, and enough active and passive surveillance systems to make the hair on Jenny's arms stand up, as if she were picking up a static charge from all the energy frequencies bathing her.

But static was the enemy in a place like this. The little white room had antistatic carpeting, antistatic floor mats over the carpeting, antistatic pads under the computers themselves, and cans of antistatic spray strategically placed where you could get to them without getting up from your ergonomic, wheeled chair at your workstation.

The only static in here came from people. And they'd had plenty of that. People from a black agency whose concern was reconnaissance and who didn't like outsiders, even CIA alumni, had come knocking on their door almost as soon as they'd gotten here and begun a heated discussion with Ford about bringing outsiders into the facility.

"Show your badges, kids," the unflappable Ford had suggested airily. "Come on, guys, go watch us do your jobs for you from a secure third location."

The reconnaissance specialists had glared at her as if they wished they could laser her into a pile of steaming meat on the spot. She'd fingered the badge clipped to her collar and stared at her terminal screen, wishing she hadn't let Ford talk her into coming along.

"It'll be fun," he'd said on the way in, with that almost-smile. "You'll like it. And I'll like knowing that my experts are uploading the program themselves. Less chance of error."

Chan had wanted to come. Chan loved the idea of going somewhere most people could never go. He'd even enjoyed the little turf battle that forced Dalton Ford to use his estimable clout.

Jenny was beginning to feel as if she'd stepped into a past she'd been grateful to outgrow. Ford had wanted to do this at DIAC, but the Defense Intelligence Agency couldn't get NSA to go along.

Even Ford couldn't say why. Once the Soviet satellite's encryption was determined by NSA cryppies (cryptographers), any competent programmer with the required clearance could have enabled the spoofing program that the Lands had written using sensitive compartmented information (SCI) chunks prepared by DIAC.

Both Jenny and Chandler Land had current SCI and top secret clearances, so it wasn't that they'd never get out of DEFSMAC alive—it just felt that way.

To the extent that it existed officially at all, the Defense Special Missile and Astronautics Center was supposedly a combination of NSA and DIA SIGINT (signal intelligence) capabilities that had a charter for quick action, including telemetry interception. Because it worked so closely with a black reconnaissance office, Jenny had been afraid to ask whether the data she was keying in would go real time from here to the chosen Soviet Cosmos 2100, or be relayed to another telemetry facility for rebroadcast.

She finished verifying her program and sat back, staring at the white glass wall beyond her CRT.

Looking over at Chan, she saw that he was nearly done as well. Not very exciting when you couldn't see the results, she thought.

Chan felt her attention on him. Lacing his fingers together, he stretched, stiff-armed. "Well, that's the whole ball of wax." He turned to Ford. "Dalton, all you've got to do is run it, now. We're done."

"And ready for that steak I promised you, as soon as somebody checks your work."

"We can't check it," Jenny reminded him stiffly, "except as a simulation—and we can't do that. Somebody else will have to run the simulation—somebody cleared for more compartments than we are."

"Come on, Jenny, don't get petulant." Ford walked over to her terminal and said, "What do I do to make it run?"

She typed a line, then rolled away from the keyboard. "Press enter, Mr. Ford. But nothing's going to—oh."

Ford had reached over and pressed the key.

Beyond her workstation, the white glass wall had come to life, showing satellite graphics with flashing letter-number groups beside the representation of the Cosmos spacecraft they were trying to spoof.

"Damn, that's nice," Chandler Land said admiringly, as a colored path of dashes ran up the graphic display and contacted the satellite simulation.

The winged Cosmos satellite changed color. The letter-number groups beside it ratcheted upward like a speed-maddened digital counter.

Then the Soviet satellite spewed a tight, yellow beam toward some off-screen receiving facility.

"She's dumping," said Ford excitedly; "right on command."

"In the simulation," Chan amended.

"Ah, right," Ford said in a way that made Jenny glance at him. There was an impish look on Ford's face.

Watching the screen as it shifted to a longer view of the Soviet satellite dumping to a high-flying graphic that represented a sophisticated reconnaissance aircraft, then to a lower-orbit relay satellite when the aircraft moved on, and finally to a simulated American "ground station" that looked as if it were on a ship, not on solid ground, Jenny realized that someone at another computer terminal somewhere in this facility was controlling the graphic display.

Then she noticed how excited Chan was. Her husband's open, boyish face was positively gleeful; he looked only a little older than he had on the day she'd met him.

Chan reached out and took her hand. "We did it." His eyes were sparkling.

"Yes, dear," she said. In three days, with lots of overtime and Herculean effort, they had done it. "Congratulations, team."

"Yep," Dalton echoed. "Come on, I'll buy you that lunch. Then I've got a plane to catch."

"You're on." Why did Dalton's revelation, that he was leaving, dull her pleasure at getting out of this creepy place, mission accomplished and a big check assured?

As they made their way through the building's nearly empty halls toward the exit, she chided herself for feeling less elated than she might. She was so preoccupied that when someone stuck his head out of an office, congratulating Ford, she didn't even worry that the man was going to say something had gone wrong.

Okay, she was disappointed that Ford was leaving, going back to his precious war game, no doubt.

When they all piled into Ford's Cherokee and headed out the gates of Fort Meade, toward civilian America once again, she wasn't even relieved.

Dalton was telling Chan, "You don't know how much you've contributed, Chandler, and you know I can't be specific. But you do know I'm counting on this spoofing project more than I like to count on any one asset. So I want to keep you two on the clock for the next few days. Ideally, I'd like you both to come out in the field with me."

"To Egypt?" She spoke up disparagingly from the back seat before Chan could jump at the chance. "I told you, Dalton, my mother's illness is keeping me close to home."

"You need to get away from your mother, Jen. You're living in a terrorist environment and it's wearing you down. What's she going to do, die while you're away?"

Chan said, "God, that would be a blessing."

"Chan!" Between themselves, they hoped for her mother's death, but outsiders couldn't understand what it was like to deal with grinding geriatric crises when the hulk you were trying to keep alive wasn't the person you loved anymore. "He didn't mean that, Dalton. I can't explain. I have to stay. Chan can go, if it's really necessary. But I don't see why—"

Dalton Ford wheeled the big car onto the Beltway. "Because we're trying something tricky, and I may need on-site tweaks, and you two are my consultants—my hired guns. Maybe we'll want to dump to the National Aerospace Plane, for all I know. Maybe we'll want to dump to a FleetSatCom laptop in Egypt, or to some of the Navy's goodies offshore."

"A dump's a dump, Dalton, you ought to know that," Chan said. Even though she could tell by his posture in the front seat, without seeing his face, that Chandler Land would love to go to Cairo as a guest of Dalton Ford and the U.S. government, Chan would never pretend he was needed when he wasn't. "I don't see what else we could do for you."

"I'm not sure there's anything you'll be able to do," Dalton admitted. "But I'll feel better with you two on board."

Jenny noticed that Ford wasn't speaking hypothetically, but as if they might agree to the trip. "Then give me a good reason," Jenny insisted, "why you think you need our sort of expertise, Dalton." She crossed her arms over her breasts, though he probably couldn't see that in the rearview mirror.

"I'm going to try for real time, or close to it—lots of dumps, to lots of different configurations: relay satellites if we can position them, maybe some aircraft, as I said—"

"I told you," Chandler Land frowned, "not to do this too much. If the Soviets find out, they won't be happy."

"They won't find out. We won't push too hard. That's why I want you two along. I've got some ground terminals you'll have to see to believe."

"No," Jenny said.

"We'll talk more about it over lunch," said Chandler, over-ruling her.

"Thanks," Ford said. "Remember, I lost a man doing that mirroring test. I don't want any more casualties as a result of action or inaction on this exercise."

Jenny Land looked at her sandaled feet. Surely Ford wasn't trying to suggest that the death resulting from *his* test, with his equipment and spook protocols, was in any way their fault.

But she knew she'd already lost the battle. Chandler Land was determined to go to Egypt, and that meant Jenny was going too. The long fight with the Grim Reaper over her mother's body had made her too frightened of losing a loved one to stay home and wonder if Chan's plane might crash, or something awful might happen out there among the palm trees. Losing what was left of her poor mother while she was gone could only be a blessing.

Losing her husband while she stayed home was an unacceptable risk. They'd already had all the right inoculations. And Jenny knew her own psyche. With Chan adamant about taking Ford up on his offer, and money to be made in the process, Jenny Land was going to Egypt.

14

Day 7: Jabal an-Nusayriyah, Syria

The ground station that Fouad Aflaq had built for his fellow principals lay north of Damascus, overlooking the Homs Gap, an ancient trade and invasion route along which the railroad and highway connecting Homs to the Lebanese port of Tripoli now ran.

High in the Jabal an-Nusayriyah range, Fouad could look out over the Homs Gap, on the fertile western slopes and the Mediterranean beyond, on Lebanon to the south.

It wasn't the view, or the height of the mountain range, or the dry winds, that had convinced the others that Jabal an-Nusayriyah in Syria was the best site. There were other mountain ranges in Syria that would have served. There had been talk of situating the covert ground station on Jabal ash-Shaykh (Mount Hermon), or beyond the Iraqi border, or even in the Yemens.

But Fouad Aflaq had prevailed in his choice over all objections. Tonight, as he sat on a rock in the wind overlooking the gap, he mentally thanked the railroad below. It was the railroad, more than any other single attribute, that had secured him this site. There was no safe place to do such a thing as they were doing, this everyone knew. There was no place where the superpowers and the European Space Agency and the Israelis might not find them out with their electronic snooping devices.

For a time, all the other principals had said, "Yes, we must do it, but not in my country." No one wanted to risk reprisals if they were found out. Yet Fouad had gotten his way, because of the railroad, because you do not ship complicated electronics unnoticed, because you were foolish to put such an installation where nothing at all similar existed.

The relatively dense population of Homs and Jabal an-Nusayriyah's western slopes offered a certain degree of camouflage. The trade route offered logistical advantages. And, of course, there was the view . . . not only for himself and his workers, but for the ground station itself. In the rocky terrain, radar dishes and telemetry equipment were nestled where they would not create an unacceptable profile. Syria had many defense installations. The ground station had been created to give the impression that this was merely one more.

And if reprisals came eventually, then the principals would deal with the consequences of that. They were not afraid of conflict. Conflict had provided the impetus for the secret ground station in the first place.

Fouad Aflaq stood up and took a final look at the panorama on the peak. Time to see the show.

He climbed with sure familiarity down from his perch, and descended first wooden and then concrete stairs until he came to the steel door of the bunkerlike structure buried in the side of the mountain. There he pressed the studs of the combination lock, and opened the door.

The lights inside were bright. Two guards had their rifles trained on him in the open doorway. Normal security.

"Masa' al-Khair, Jundi"—Good evening, soldier—he said to each in turn.

They each responded, *"Masa' an-nur, Mudir"*—Good evening, Director.

He passed on by, down the main corridor with its overhead lights. As a principal of the struggle, and creator of the ground station, he was hoping it would be a very good evening indeed.

When he'd met with the others in Baghdad, he'd found them steadfast. This was good. Also, he'd learned that the first blind spot in surveillance that he'd created by destroying *HE-12* had been put to good use.

While he had waited here, seeking signs of error or discovery or—worse—repercussions, the others had used the darkness that night to move some of the most crucial equipment to the chosen staging area. One could not tolerate night-imaging surveillance if one was moving missiles into position. Some troops, too, had deployed with their equipment—enough troops to make sure that the armaments were secreted undetectably before the next dangerous satellite came over the horizon at dawn.

Tonight, all was in readiness for the second phase. Men and equipment would move on his signal. To give that signal, he and his ground station must be sure of a flawless operation in orbit.

No one had ever hesitated to give him all the money he desired to make the plan a reality. Consequently, he had redundant terminals in a private office—a complete secondary system sufficient for any emergency. During the initial satellite launch from Priane's Guiana Space Center in French Guiana, he hadn't needed his backup system. During the first attack on the enemies in orbit, he'd waited in the ground station's main operations center with his crew.

But tonight, he wanted to be alone. Tonight, he was not as certain of success. The second spherical space mine launched from the host satellite had been in orbit by itself for seven days. In seven days, many things not immediately apparent can go wrong.

Although his ground station tracked the sphere around the clock, and all was nominal, there was always the hand of Fate to consider. Fouad Aflaq had learned, during his undergraduate studies at Caltech, the power of Murphy's Law.

Thus he went immediately to his private office and there he sat behind his black desk and watched his redundant display screens. There was nothing he could do if the second corundum sphere did not respond to its timer when it came within striking distance of the Soviet satellite. There was nothing he could do if the Soviet satellite was simply lucky and was not crippled or completely destroyed by the mine's pellets of industrial ruby.

If the sphere performed perfectly, the Soviet Cosmos 2100 that dwelled so long over the Middle East with its infrared eye would be totally destroyed, its pieces falling immediately out of orbit to a fiery death in the atmosphere. But this had not happened with the American satellite, although the sphere had performed its task well enough that success could be proclaimed.

But success was relative. With the Soviet Union, one didn't want to leave the slightest trace.

Watching his display screens carefully, Aflaq was acutely conscious of the countdown in the lower right-hand corner of his screen—now a matter of minutes, not hours.

Those minutes dragged interminably. A ground station such as this could not deliver the fanciest graphics, or the finest of images. But it could track with the best of them.

Aflaq, a principal, had made certain that this was so. He could watch the target satellite in real time if, as now, it was dwelling over his area. He concentrated on the radar return he was getting from the Soviet satellite that had troubled his dreams for the last few nights.

When his sphere exploded, that image should react to the event.

At the moment that his countdown indicator reached zero, and began counting positively, the Soviet satellite's track began to diverge from its course.

With a dry mouth, Aflaq sat forward, chin on his fists. Three minutes later, he was reasonably sure that he had succeeded.

He sat for twenty more minutes, watching the radar return and the other screens that showed him numbers which seemed to confirm success, before he got up to go to the main room of the facility, where his crew waited.

They would be slow to celebrate in the covert tracking station's operations center. They needed to be certain. Under Aflaq's direction, they would begin searching for Soviet reaction.

But within the hour, if no contrary indications appeared, a true celebration would get under way.

Then troops could begin to move under the cover of darkness. The plan was structured in such a way that men and machinery were ready to move on schedule, regardless of risk.

But eventual triumph lay in proceeding undiscovered, in the

enemy not being forewarned. And only here at the station was there any chance of achieving that, except by luck.

This time, Fouad had arranged with the other principals that one of them would receive a phone call from him, thanking the other man for a gift of Iranian pistachios. If all was well, he would tell the man that these white pistachios were as big as knuckles and as sweet as a woman.

If the success were only qualified, or uncertain, he would praise the pistachios less ardently.

One way or the other, he must go down to Homs to make the phone call, as soon as he was certain beyond doubt of his results.

As he strode into the main room of the facility, men cheered for him. He blushed. Every one was on his feet now. A smile shone from every face.

Then he knew that he could go down to Homs now, that he didn't have to wait any longer.

And in his heart, joy began to grow, while above his head, a mapping screen worthy of a superpower tracked the tumble from orbit of the Soviet Cosmos satellite his genius had destroyed.

15

"DIAC's in an uproar," Conard said miserably to Colonel Pollock from AFSPACECOM (Air Force Space Command). "Everybody's in an uproar. The Soviets are going to be ripshit. I bet Beckwith pulls my shuttle ticket. And it's all Ford's fault."

In the Officers' Open Mess at Peterson, Conard was having a coke while Pollock got beer froth on his moustache.

The Air Force's big deputy chief for special operations wiped the back of his hand across his sandy moustache and said, "How do you figure it was Ford's fault, Conard?" in an unfriendly fashion.

Conard blinked and took a closer look at the other man. Pollock had been one of Conard's strongest supporters throughout this whole mess. Pollock had fielded Ford's callback from Egypt and covered Conard's butt for him, making sure that Ford did indeed come back to the States.

Now Pollock was looking at Conard very coldly, waiting for an answer.

"Come on, man. Ford pulls some dumb stunt like spoofing a Soviet Cosmos 2100, and then—whammo—the damn thing falls out of the sky?"

"Don't they teach you Army brats anything about the survivability of jumping to conclusions? We don't even know if that Cosmos wasn't due to decay its orbit about now, Conard. And we don't know—officially—anything about what Ford's doing, or not doing. You get me?"

"Yeah, sure, but you can't be taking that bastard's part after the way he handled that Kwajalein investigation . . . "

"He found something, which ain't half bad. So he didn't bring it back to CSOC personally. He's busy and that's what telecommunications are for, buddy. Stop bitching and let's talk about what you might see and might not see on that shuttle flight of yours. We don't have but a couple hours to get you specced up to my standards."

"You think I'll still get to go, then?"

"Either you go or the Air Force is going to have to find another way to get that information."

"Meaning what?"

"Meaning we'll find a way, that's all."

"Fly one of your black toys up there? Nobody's gonna risk the space plane on something like this."

"That's why we're making sure you get the job done, Conard." Pollock tapped a briefing pack on the table, then reached beyond it to pick up a blue-and-silver matchbox with a space shuttle depicted on it. He lit a cigarette with a wooden match from the Officers' Open Mess matchbox and exhaled the smoke slowly through his nose. "Damn, I'd love to be sitting on the shoulder of the mission director at Plesetsk right now— or in Moscow when the fur starts to fly if that Cosmos wasn't decaying on schedule."

"You know it wasn't. The descent was too abrupt."

"Yeah, I know it wasn't." Pollock smirked. "I wonder if our guys are going to admit to their guys that something similar happened to us."

"I don't think *glasnost* reaches that far."

"Still, it'd be slick if we could pool Soviet and American resources—if there really is something happening, and we're not dealing with an unfortunate coincidence." Pollock looked at the tip of his cigarette. "Could still be just that—a statistical glitch that doesn't mean anything more than sinking thirty baskets in a row one day, and sinking none the next time you're on the court."

"How could our brass admit that we know what happened to their 2100 without—"

"And how could their brass admit it knows what happened to our *HE-12?* That's the billion-dollar question, Conard. So count your blessings: down here in the ranks we don't have to figure out answers to questions like those. We just fly 'em and fry 'em."

"Somebody's going to need those answers," Conard said, wondering if he dared put in a recommendation to offer to share intelligence on the *HE-12* failure with the Soviets if they'd share their Cosmos data. If he did, it might turn out to be a good career move. Of course, it might make him look dumb as a post, too.

Maybe, Conard decided, he'd better just fly his shuttle mission. He'd be two hundred miles above all this craziness, safe from any repercussions that might come his way because he'd been among the strongest advocates of the theory that the Soviets were behind the *Hawkeye* debacle.

Once Conard was out in space, he'd get a firsthand look at whatever had happened to at least one of the two satellites in question. Maybe what he found would settle all the arguments, although he didn't expect anything that unequivocal to turn up when he eyeballed *HE-12*.

You just didn't get that lucky in the space business.

16

Day 7: Dzerzhinsky Square, Moscow

This was a meeting one held in the old KGB building, not the new one. This was a meeting suited to the downstairs cafeteria with its green paint and its awful food, Aleksandr Shitov of the First Chief Directorate told himself morosely.

Here they sat in the cafeteria, all the once-mighty masters of the security directorates, and they munched their hard rolls and drank tea from glasses and listened while their progressive leader told them, once again, how things had changed.

Fiercely, Shitov bit into his stale roll, which only underscored the breadth of this change: Dzerzhinsky Square was now the recipient of stale crusts and scoldings. Security officers now slept the uncertain sleep once reserved for traitors and spies. And all because of this new leader who would make himself a dictator, if he could.

"And this, comrades," said the Executive President, rubbing his blemished forehead, "is one more example of why we cannot afford to jump to conclusions. A faulty piece of spaceborne equipment cannot be allowed to destroy all the progress we have made. We cannot assume, any longer, that everything which happens is the fault of the Americans. We cannot, any longer, blame everything—" the bug-eyed monster of their sleepless nights glared around at the gathered Chiefs tutorially "—on the Americans."

Shitov had been in Iran and France with the KGB Information Bureau, in Latin America, Argentina, and Cuba. He knew a dictator when he saw one.

And he knew that things would get worse in his beloved mother country before they got better. This made his tea hard to swallow, and the Executive President's personal oversight of this situation nearly unbearable.

"We will do as our scientific sections and the space experts from Plesetsk suggest," said the Executive President, "and open a dialogue with the Americans. We will not retaliate against them for something we are not sure that they did."

From Shitov's right, Nikolai Levonov asked to be recognized. He, like Shitov, had also received a "promotion" and been recalled to Moscow from Cuba, to take a desk job which included a KGB seat on the Commission of Space Exploration and Utilization.

A dozen heads turned to watch Levonov destroy his career.

Levonov was still handsome, though short by Shitov's standards, and frail. He had an intellectual's face with a full head of pale hair. His face was equally pale as he said, through bloodless lips, "Executive President, colleagues . . . how is it that we are not considering the possibility that the Americans did just what you caution us not to do: that they retaliated against us, destroying our satellite, because they assumed that it was we who silenced their *HE-12?*"

The downed Cosmos 2100 was only one of many, but the territory it watched was explosive. Everyone here was present because the technical experts from Plesetsk, Kapustin Yar, Tyuratam, the Space Research Institute, the State Committee on Science and Technology, and the Ministry of Defense had finished making their excuses and bucking the blame up the line. Now it was up to the security chiefs.

Face time was the term for briefing your higher-ups in a fashion that shifted the burden of error from yourself. Levonov, a good friend of Castro's, was a master of propaganda, but Shitov sensed that this time his hatred of the *Amerikanski*s and his horror of his new Moscow desk in the Technology Directorate had combined to make him overestimate his influence.

"What are you suggesting, Levonov?" said the Executive President, dropping his comradely smile and his egalitarian mask. When the Executive President was happy, he reminded one of a kindly uncle. When he was displeased, he became a drill sergeant. "That we move troops around, that we rattle cages, that we start a new era of confrontation when we are still in debt from the last?"

Debt. Debt was at the heart of everything, these days. Shitov sat back in his chair, so that he could cross his long legs.

Three men looked at him, so still was everyone in the cafeteria, which had been cleared of all service personnel and closed to the public for the occasion. Shitov kept his own gaze steadily on Levonov: *Old friend, this man and this issue are not worth professional suicide*, his eyes tried to say.

But Levonov had many years of risk under his belt and many guilts on his conscience, all sustained for the good of the State. Shitov's dear friend squared his shoulders and said without flinching:

"Executive President, I suggest just that. Let us move troops, to alert the Americans to our displeasure—move back into Eastern Europe, in strength. This is a perfect pretext. Turn our lasers on their jets—just enough to warm the pilots' pants—as we have in the past; or move ships and submarines, into the usual locations. But move we must, or else the Americans will feel they can destroy our space-based assets with impunity."

"Outmoded KGB thinking, Levonov," said the Executive President with a kindly weariness that had a hint of impatience in it. "If the Americans thought we damaged their equipment, you should have known it. And if they did, and you knew it, why have you not reported to me sooner?"

"I . . . " Levonov closed his eyes for an instant. His penetration agents should have apprised him of any American shift in intentions. He opened his eyes again. "Intent is the most difficult determination to make. I am not saying I know that the Americans blame us for their loss of *HE-12*. I am only saying they made inquiries. They instituted computer simulations. They examined the possibility that we might be at fault."

The Executive President half-rose from the table. "And what were the results of those inquiries?"

"Inconclusive. But suspicions could have motivated—"

"Shitov," snapped the Executive President. "What have you

to say? Do you think we should take the destruction of our Cosmos to mean that the Americans have used an SDI weapon against us? That we should signal a readiness to respond in kind?"

First Chief Directorate always ended up with the spoiled milk in its lap.

"First Chief Directorate bows to the specific knowledge of the Technology Directorate in this instance. We have looked at every report from our space weapons facilities, from the U.S. and Canada Institute. We have studied the text of every briefing. We have spoken with our space specialists at length. We see no clear pattern. But that does not mean that such a pattern of retaliation on the Americans' part does not exist." Shitov took a deep breath and uncrossed his legs. They were trembling.

In the Executive President's eyes, Shitov fancied he could see a reflection of Levonov's disappointed face.

But who knew what the Americans had in mind? The new Soviet regime was so accommodating to the West in its search for cheaper and more profitable coexistence, the Americans might believe that Russia had lost her will to survive.

Sometimes, Shitov thought this was the case.

"So, Shitov," said the Executive President, not satisfied with evasion, determined to make one friend betray the other completely and publicly, "you are saying you do not favor moving our troops and our submarines and shaking our fists, which are nearly empty, at the Americans?"

"I am saying only that if—as you yourself have suggested, *Glava*—any action by the Americans resulted from a misunderstanding of our intentions, and our actions, then reparations would be preferable to confrontation."

This was the particular sort of hogwash that the Executive President was demanding to hear.

"And does the First Chief Directorate have any reason to assume that the Americans made such a mistake?" asked the leader of the Soviet Union.

Shitov longed for the days of Brezhnev, since he was not truly old enough to long for the days of Stalin. "Through back channels, as you know," *if you've been reading your briefing memos, you fat, greasy farmer*, "the Undersecretariat has conducted a quiet exploration using the various secretaries of the various ambassadors in positions to make pertinent inquiries of their opposite numbers. We have said nothing. They have insinuated nothing except that they are as surprised and concerned as we ourselves."

"And do you recommend a strategem, Comrade Shitov?" The Executive President's voice cracked like a whip.

"We could send a secret memorandum by diplomatic pouch." Shitov shrugged, to show he was not personally committed to this plan. "In it, we could suggest that we would appreciate an opening of a dialogue on this situation. We do not have to say that we think they may have retaliated against us mistakenly, since they have not yet accused us. But either covertly or clandestinely, we must either discuss this matter or do something such as my colleague Levonov has suggested. Perhaps, to be safe, we should do both."

"To force them to do what?" said the man who ruled the USSR. "Move *their* troops around? Move *their* warships, *their* submarines, *their* satellites? Lase our fighters until our pilots sweat? Or simply to force them to ask the first difficult question?"

Then Shitov was sure that the Executive President knew exactly the answers he wanted to hear—probably had known them all the time. And he knew what he must say. This man hated the KGB more than any external power; he would use every opportunity to divest it of authority. Shitov must protect his own—and himself.

"If the Technology Section has no objection, we could surely draft a query which would not give away how much we know about the destruction of their *HE-12*, and then there would be no strategic impediment to asking a few simple questions. One can always move troops if one does not like the answers." There was, by the Executive President's design, no representative of the Ministry of Defense or the GRU here to whom Shitov could defer.

The Executive President sat back, beaming his television smile. "Good. Draft such a memo, to be addressed to the appropriate person. Speak to all your fellows here, and make sure it meets all security requirements. Have it on my desk in an hour. My protocol chief will look at it." Then the Executive President's face hardened. "Once I have a document that all you in this room have approved as secure and appropriate, then I can get on with the business of governance."

The Executive President rose to leave.

Levonov looked over at Shitov and shook his head sorrowfully. Levonov might have risked censure, but he wasn't stuck with the blame if this went wrong.

Since the draft memorandum would be Shitov's, whatever repercussions came of it would be Shitov's fault. If a confrontation developed, or should develop and did not—this, too, was Shitov's fault, from this moment onward.

Feeling the noose tighten around his neck, Shitov rose glumly to thank his tormentor, and to say he hoped he could live up to the Executive President's faith in him.

And since Russia's new and charismatic leader was clearly and openly out to discredit the KGB and all its senior officials, Shitov was going to need more than hope to see him through this day, and those to follow.

He was going to need a phenomenal amount of luck. If the First Chief Directorate was wrong in its assessment of American intentions, Shitov's head was going to roll before this was over.

Somehow, Aleksandr Shitov wasn't so worried about his friend Levonov any more. By the time he turned in a draft memorandum, he had to find someone in GRU to support a simultaneous move to a heightened state of readiness: only moving troops, nuclear submarines, or at least lasing American aircraft could save Shitov's neck, and KGB's, if he had just walked into the Executive President's trap unarmed.

17

Day 7: Cairo

Not only Jay Adamson, but Quantrell and three of his Special Forces kids, too, were on hand to greet Ford's plane when it touched down at Cairo West.

The look on Quantrell's face was so cautionary that Ford tried to slip away from the Lands, telling them, "Why don't you meet me at Mena House? I've got something to take care of—oh, hi, Jay."

Then he'd had to introduce Adamson, who was abroad in daylight and wearing a suit and tie, to the Lands: "American Cultural Attaché Jay Adamson. Chandler and Jennifer Land."

Behind their backs, the Special Forces boys picked up everyone's bags.

"Guess we're not going through customs, huh?" Ford tried his insouciant smile, which didn't seem to be working today. He should have known, when Adamson and Quantrell cut him off before even going through customs, that something was really wrong.

"Not today, Ford. This way, please." Then Jay led them through a door that said AUTHORIZED PERSONNEL ONLY and down a hallway, toward the blazing daylight and a waiting car.

"Look, Jay, we need entry stamps . . . " Ford was acutely aware that, without a properly stamped passport, he couldn't get back out of the country. Worse, none of his special cre-

94

dentials, from his Egyptian ID to his Get Out of Jail Free card, were going to be worth much in the light of illegal entry.

Adamson knew it too. Ford couldn't fathom what the trouble was. Something was seriously wrong. Wrong enough to necessitate Quantrell having to come along with a dour look, muscle on hand, and nothing to say.

Jay said, "We'll fix it when we need to. Let's not talk yet."

Terrific.

Ford kept looking over his shoulder to see that the Lands were still behind him. Every time he did, he saw the three long-haired commandos. And he saw Quantrell, grim as death, bringing up the rear.

If Quantrell had been walking backwards with an M16 cradled in his arms, he couldn't have looked any scarier.

The car was an armored Cherokee, sitting low on its axles. Adamson opened the rear door for Jenny Land with a flourish, She smiled brightly at him and got inside without hesitation, though when her glance met Ford's it was troubled and full of questions.

Chandler Land started to ask one, but she silenced him. You could forget that Jenny was a pro, sometimes. Ford thanked his lucky stars that she was smart enough to realize what was happening and composed enough to show no sign that she did.

Women like that always belonged to someone else.

In the front seat with Adamson, Ford all but expected Jay to hit a button and a glass partition to arise from the back of the front bench seat, isolating the two of them from the Lands and Quantrell in the rear seat. Behind, the three commandos piled their luggage into an identical yellow Cherokee.

Jay turned on the radio. It wasn't great noise masking, but it would have to do.

"What's the damned trouble?" Ford asked.

"Those are the people you used at Meade?"

DEFSMAC. The spoofing program. Oh, shit. "Yep. Good friends of mine. Is there some problem?"

"That depends on what you call a problem. Whatever you did seems to have destroyed a piece of Soviet hardware. Lots of people who love *glasnost* want to talk about that. Some with you. Some with them."

Adamson's eyes left the road in front of him. He had yet to pull away from the curb. "There's a lot of saber rattling going on. Some weird messages. How the hell did you get yourself in such a mess, Dalton? If they hang this on you, it's your ass."

"Have I still got a job?"

"So far."

"Physical liberty?"

Adamson raised one hand and rotated it twenty degrees from horizontal. "We need to get some good, or at least sustainable, answers. Until we do, you're not here. You're not anywhere. Neither are your friends."

"They're civil—"

"They're alumni. Don't give me any shit, Ford. Quantrell and I are trying to save your neck. The least you can do is help us."

Cosmos 2100. Christ. "It went down?"

"Blew up, is the term."

"Damn."

"You can say that again." Adamson hit his brakes twice to alert the follow car before he gunned his motor and bullied his way out into the airport traffic.

"Any good news?"

"Not that I can think of. Maybe some neutral news. Your Admiral Beckwith left a message for you with us. Don't let me forget to leave you alone in my office to pick it up."

"Thanks, Jay."

Adamson jerked the wheel to the right to avoid a suicidal taxi driver. An announcer replaced the music on the radio, and above his voice, Ford could hear Jenny Land asking Quantrell about Bright Star.

Jesse said, "Ma'am, Bright Star's an interoperating exercise between us and the locals, but its specifics are classified. Have you been to Cairo before?"

Ford kept telling himself that at least he was with friends. His body was reacting as if he'd been captured by enemies. If the spoofing project had brought down the Cosmos, and Jay's intimations of repercussions were true, then Ford was in about as much trouble as he could handle.

Maybe the ghost of McMurtry was still tagging along, trying to pay him back for a wasted life.

But even if the Cosmos had gone down, that was no reason for everybody to jump to conclusions.

Ford told Adamson so, after they got to the embassy and he was herded into Jay's bug-swept office where they could speak freely.

Jay gave him the silent treatment.

Ford tried to focus on Adamson's face, but he kept seeing Jenny's, as it had looked while she and her husband were being escorted down the hall by the three commandos dressed like tourists.

Still, he had to defend himself: "So it went down. So what? Stuff crashes and burns all the time. Satellites decay. How come everybody's so anxious to blame me—or anybody?"

"Because the Soviet Union is making inquiries as to whether we know anything about what happened to that 2100, so I gather. I know for sure that their military's on the move: our DefCon's gone up. Everybody's on security alert. Their fighter-bombers are shaving our coast on the way to Cuba over the Pole. They're lasing our fighters. A couple of subs surfaced just off Libya. A Soviet battle group is sailing our way out of the Indian Ocean . . . "

"I get the picture. What am I supposed to do about that? We didn't do anything to that satellite that could cause it to fall out of orbit, let alone blow up."

"Okay, we'll say that to our people. What else?"

"What else?" Ford realized he hadn't yet sat down. He was leaning against a filing cabinet. "You're asking my technical people some questions next door, or down the hall, right? You know they're ex-Agency, so I'm sure you'll be polite. But I need to go back to work. Especially if what you say is true."

"Why's that?" Jay wanted to know, pulling on his thin nose.

"Because maybe something's happening to these spacecraft that's *not* normal. Somebody ought to ask the Soviets what they think is going on."

"I'll pass along your message," said Adamson dryly.

"Come on, Jay. You're not going to make me sit here and play twenty questions."

"I can't make those kinds of decisions, Ford. You'll have to stay here, and your two friends too, until I get some response from the States."

"I've got to get back in the field. I'm already tracking the anomaly of—" was Adamson cleared for the *HE-12* compartment? "—the satellite we lost just recently. I want to know how similar the circumstance are."

"I don't know, Ford."

Not "Dalton." Not friendly, not now. "Let me see what Beckwith sent up for me. Maybe it'll shed some light on all this. And maybe you ought to get on the horn and tell your people that they have my assurances that nothing done at DEFSMAC could possibly have affected the functional life of that Soviet Cosmos."

"I'm sure everyone will be exceedingly relieved to hear that, Ford. Especially since, with the Soviet satellite completely destroyed, there's no proof one way or the other."

"So we just say we had nothing to do with it. They couldn't have caught our telemetry that fast. And if they did, it was in their own encryption." Ford shrugged. "Not only did we not do it, it can't possibly look like we *did* do it." Ford hoped to hell he and the Lands *hadn't* done it, somehow.

"As I said, I'll pass the word along."

"And get me off the hook, enough at least so that I can go back to work on what I was doing—with my consultants. It's not as if I'm here for a picnic."

"I'll see what I can do." Adamson got up, his face unreadable, as if to leave.

"Hey, Jay: I want that encrypted message you've got of Beckwith's—if I've still got the clearance to read it. And I want my passport stamped." He took a chance, fishing it from his pocket and throwing it on Jay's desk. "And my guests', as well."

The passport landed on Jay's desk. Adamson looked at Ford pensively.

"I assume you're telling me by this that it's all or nothing as far as you're concerned?"

Ford's was a black—official but not diplomatic corps—passport. "Yep. Either I'm trustworthy enough to go back to work, or you can ship me home to Leavenworth or wherever you want me. I can't work like this. And I don't want my heat falling on my guests."

"I'll do my best. Have fun with your Captain Midnight decoder program while I'm gone." Jay indicated a TEMPEST-secure computer behind the desk. "And don't leave, Dalton, even to take a whiz. Or your friends will have even more explaining to do."

Adamson left his office, closing the door behind him with a slam.

The Lands weren't really players. Ford hoped Jesse was handling their debrief, but knew it was unlikely. Jesse Quantrell didn't have the finesse. If the Lands' debriefer was somebody heavy-handed, then there was no telling how the couple might react.

Cairo station was big enough to get lost in. Permanently.

Ford told himself that things weren't done that way anymore, but the part of him that was being threatened didn't believe it.

Then he set about decoding Beckwith's message, first pulling up the computer fax program and punching in his access number so the computer would release the encrypted document from storage, then typing in his decryption algorithms, still without putting the document on the computer screen where its emanations might be vulnerable to electronic surveillance.

Finally, he printed the decoded document and sat back in Jay's chair to study it.

Leo Beckwith had run simulations that convinced the admiral that *HE-12* wasn't taken down by any Soviet killer-sat whose configuration the American intelligence community could model.

Beckwith's boys had simulated every recent Soviet launch from every launch site the Soviets had, and nothing from those launches could have emplaced a special device in orbit. The launch windows were all wrong.

But the fleck was still looking to Beckwith's people like a telltale.

Ford rubbed his jaw. *Come on, Beckwith, where're you going with this?*

Beckwith's final entry was unnecessarily cryptic, unless you knew the admiral the way Ford did. Beckwith had gotten hold of the entire Priane Space flight manifest from French Guiana, and from it culled a list of launches that might have components whose orbits "accidentally" decayed into interception with *HE-12*.

If there hadn't been a half dozen of them, Ford would have gone running out of there, despite Adamson's orders, hoping to find Jay.

But there were a half dozen, and only paranoia like Beckwith's could connect two- and three-month-old commercial launches with what had just happened.

The only trouble was, it made sense to Ford.

It just wasn't anything you could sell to a government—not his, or anybody else's. Not yet.

Ford sat back, staring at the decoded message. He couldn't even call Beckwith to talk about this until he got Jay Adamson calmed down.

And Jay might let him sit in here and stew for hours.

Dutifully, Ford got up and fed the decrypted document into the shredder by the fax machine.

Then he sat behind Jay's desk and said, "Get me Quantrell, Sally, if he's still in the building." Couldn't hurt to try.

Quantrell came on the line. "Ford, don't you know better?"

"I should, but I don't. How'd you do with those RPV over-flights I wanted?"

"I can't answer that question now, here. I may not be able to answer it at all, at least not for you, unless something down-right wonderful happens pretty soon or the hazard light comes off your dashboard."

"Don't worry, Quantrell, it will. And thanks for setting that up for me. When we get out of here, I'll need to talk to you about the specifics."

"I didn't say I did, did I, you crazy bastard?"

"Now, Jesse, I know you well enough to know when you've done a good job. I'll want that box you're holding for me when I leave here."

"You're awful sure of yourself. People have faced firing squads for less."

"Not when they haven't done anything wrong. At least, not in our civilized society. Take care of my friends, Jesse. The three of us are going to take you out on the town tonight, when all this is cleared up."

He hung up. Let them wonder why he was so calm. He wasn't. But he had to get through this witch-hunt, somehow.

He needed to talk with Leo Beckwith; he needed Beckwith's support on his side and working for him.

When Adamson finally came back, Ford was nearly asleep. Adrenaline does funny things. For a minute, he thought Adamson was McMurtry's ghost.

Then he sat up in Jay's chair and said, "You know, Jay, I'm an AmCit and I'm entitled to one phone call. I want to make it now."

"Okay," said Adamson. "Use my STU, if it's that kind of call." He threw Ford's passport on the desk.

Ford ignored it and picked up the receiver. Adamson left the room again.

Only then did he open the black book to see if his entry stamp was where it should be.

It was.

Dalton Ford carefully put the STU's receiver back in its cradle before he put his head between his knees, breathing deeply until the desire to retch subsided.

That was close. The stamped passport meant that, while he still might be under suspicion of having screwed up, he wasn't going to be prevented from doing his job—at least he had slack enough to clear his name and reputation.

And the Lands'. He shook his head. He still wasn't thinking clearly. Maybe it was only fair that he washed out on this one— he'd gotten an innocent kid killed in an unnecessary test. But he didn't want to take Jenny Land down with him, even if she had married a wimp with good shirts. The last thing he wanted was Chandler Land being able to blame anything on him.

He sat up straight, then leaned back in Jay's chair.

Dalton Ford had been a lucky camper all his life. A sour smile crept over his face. He'd call Beckwith in a minute, with some relatively good news, and share the bright side, now that he'd found it:

Since the Cosmos 2100 had gone down over the same place that *HE-12* had gone down, you could at least postulate that both satellites had been destroyed by the same external means.

If that was true, there hadn't been a damned thing wrong with Jenny's spoofing program—or with *HE-12*. Ford's spirits lifted somewhat. Maybe his baby wasn't flawed. Maybe Beckwith was on the right track. Maybe it really was foul play.

If the Soviets hadn't attacked *HE-12*, which was seeming more likely by the minute, then maybe somebody else had.

18

Day 8: Low Earth Orbit

About six hours into its flight, shuttle-C was over the central Pacific and Major Chuck Conard received permission from the Navy mission commander to leave his seat in the middeck.

That was the deal: hitch a ride, bump a physicist to do it, and you get the rumble seat. Conard had been riding the middeck since the flight began, segregated from the regular crew, which was deploying classified Department of Defense payloads.

Well, Conard's job was classified, too. Just because there'd been no time to brief Conard on the DOD missions in progress shouldn't have given the crew an excuse to treat him like a pariah.

He had work to do, just like they did, even if his name wasn't embroidered on some mission patch. Conard pushed off his couch and floated past a rack-mounted canister of biotoxin being grown in zero g.

Nobody on the flight deck was any better cleared for the *HE-12* data compartment than he was for their main mission— a communications satellite launch from shuttle-C's big cargo bay. But the crew had trained together for this, and Conard wasn't even a standard alternate on their roster.

The physicist-astronaut Conard had bumped wouldn't have fared much better, judging from the way Conard had been sandwiched back in the middeck among the five middeck payload experimental packages. One of those packages was a special 70-millimeter IMAX camera modified for SDI plume phenomenology and intelligence work, which was handy for Conard's purposes.

So, despite the virtual freeze-out coming from the four men on the flight deck, Conard had kept busy, reading the IMAX manual and programming IMAX to take pictures of *HE-12* as it came into range. All through the initial launch that placed shuttle-C in a 158- × -105-nautical mile orbit, and the subsequent maneuvering system burn, forty minutes into the flight, which raised the cargo shuttle to a 160-nautical-mile circular orbit, Conard had felt as if he was cramming for an exam. By the time he was asked to come forward, he was feeling like he'd passed that exam with flying colors: IMAX would eyeball *HE-12* for him.

Up front, Navy Captain Coates, the mission commander, was joking with the two Marine colonels and Air Force Colonel Byron, who was the mission pilot.

The fact that he could hear the chatter but wasn't included, that he could almost but not quite make out the words, and that everybody up front wanted it that way, reminded Conard that he was considered an interloper.

He might yet have to do an extra vehicular activity with one of these guys. There hadn't been time to fit this bay with a remote manipulator arm. No use worrying about what you didn't have. On an EVA, you wanted to worry about nothing but your objective. You sure as hell didn't want to wonder whether the people you were with liked you.

But then, Conard wasn't the most well-liked man in the Army; and up here, he was all the Army there was. Space was still too competitive, and Conard had never learned how to really be one of the guys.

He couldn't seem to let the truth slide for the sake of expediency, and he couldn't seem to drop instinctively into that pocket of good-fellowship that protected so many of his colleagues. Maybe his intelligence background was the problem: because he was never totally off-guard or because he was perceived as untrustworthy; or dangerously bright; or insufficiently gung ho.

Whatever the problem was, he couldn't solve it up here. But he couldn't shelve it, either. Space missions made you acutely aware that the equipment sustaining you was built by the lowest bidder.

Floating in zero g, the way Conard was now, made you even more clearly aware of how insignificant you were in the greater scheme of things. Looking out on the blue Earth always made Conard feel fiercely protective of it.

As Conard pulled himself forward, one of the Marines was coming back to middeck to make room for him on the four-place flight deck. Gibbons, the Marine colonel, said, "Anything you want me to do while you're forward?"

"Just watch my camera. You get anything interesting in the finder, let me know."

The two men both stopped themselves and hung, inches apart, clad in shorts and T-shirts, eye to eye.

"What are you looking for?" asked the Marine colonel who'd do the spacewalk, or EVA, with him if Conard had to go.

"Something indicative of whether it's worthwhile to bring *HE-12* home because it's got to be fixed on Earth, or whether it can stay here and somebody else can bring up whatever we need and do a quick fix on the spot." Conard couldn't be more specific, because he hadn't had orders to be.

Damn these closely held mission parameters: he couldn't risk saying the wrong thing to Gibbons. Now he thought he knew how the guys up front felt.

Colonel Gibbons nodded gravely. "You've got all your sequences computerized, right? I just look through the viewfinder and see if I see anything interesting?"

"That's right. If it's been centerpunched by a meteorite, then obviously we'll have to go get it."

"I can't wait," said the Marine, and winked at Conard as he pushed off, toward the middeck.

Maybe the rest of this mission wouldn't be as bad as the ride up here had been. Maybe Conard worried too much about what people thought. If you were back where you couldn't see what was happening, and flying a direct ascent trajectory at 104 percent throttle on three main engines, you had plenty of time to get paranoid.

And wearing the partial pressure suits for lift-off didn't make life any easier.

Neither did being an add-on.

The mission commander, Captain Coates, who sported a rusty moustache, looked over his shoulder at Conard as he pushed with his feet to maneuver toward Gibbons's empty seat. "Well, Major, it's time for your dog-and-pony show."

It didn't help being the lowest-ranking officer here, either. Conard settled into Gibbons's seat.

Colonel Byron said, "If we're going to maneuver for your quick flyby, Major, we've got thirteen minutes to dump our payload and start the burn."

Byron, the pilot, was asking if Conard had heard anything from Space Command on his middeck com patch, or seen anything with the IMAX that would make the rest of his mission unnecessary.

Coates watched him out of the corner of one eye, waiting for the answer. The Navy captain who was mission commander was rumored to be ultracapable, but Conard's extra mission was jeopardizing the rest of the flight's schedule.

Captain Coates didn't say a word about that, just waited for Conard to respond. Behind him, the other Marine was drinking juice through a straw and lying unsupported in midair, parallel to a computer bank.

At least shuttle-C had central processing units with more memory than personal computers. The first-generation shuttles had flown with less RAM than Conard had on his desktop at Falcon.

"I need the flyby. I'm still hoping for an EVA." It was Conard's gut that wanted the hands-on. Even if it turned out that *HE-12* could have been repaired in orbit, he wanted to bring it home, just to shut down unnecessary debate. If he was very lucky, the spacecraft would exhibit a good reason for him to do that . . .

"Okay, Major, then that's what we'll do," Coates said decisively. He turned to the Marine floating before the terminals. "Doug, you've got ten minutes, tops, to get that tilt table back in the bay and shut her up."

The crew had launched the satellite, Conard gathered from

Coates's comment: you used the tilt table to elevate a heavy payload to the appropriate inclination. Then springs pushed it out of the bay.

The cargo shuttle, shuttle-C, was built specifically for larger payloads. Conard wasn't going to have any trouble getting *HE-12* nestled safe and sound in there.

"I guess I'll go get ready for the EVA."

"Sit tight," said Byron, the pilot. "Until we've attained the orbit you need."

Conard did, in Gibbons's seat. He was committed now, despite whatever might be seen when they came up on *HE-12*.

His palms were beginning to sweat.

"And relax," Coates said, smiling under his moustache. "If we make your rendezvous, *then* you can worry. You want something to eat or drink, this is about your last chance."

You didn't want to get all suited up for an EVA, shrug into your manned maneuvering unit, get the joystick in your right hand, and then realize you had to go to the bathroom.

So Conard passed on the drink and waited, just watching and being glad that he wasn't stuck, alone, back on the middeck.

At six hours, fifteen minutes into the flight, the crew of shuttle-C performed a flawless thirty-one-feet-per-second orbital maneuvering system burn that placed shuttle-C in a 177-×-160-nautical-mile orbit that would bring it to within spitting distance of *HE-12*.

Conard went back to the middeck to prepare for the EVA with Gibbons.

As they were getting into their suits, Gibbons said, "What did you say you thought hit that thing?"

"I didn't say I thought anything hit it." Conard was doing his best to check every part of Gibbons's suit.

"Something hit it," said Gibbons positively. "And not a single something."

"What do you mean?" Conard froze, then forced himself to continue helping Gibbons.

"I was looking through the IMAX camera, like you said. Really nice system, that IMAX—"

"Come on, what did you see?" Conard couldn't access the

IMAX film and replay what was on it; the system was still operational.

"Couple o' holes."

"Holes? Punctures, you mean? What kind?"

"Holes," said Gibbons, and grunted as he settled the unwieldy helmet on his shoulders. "Roundish holes. More than one, unless it was a trick of the light."

"Holes. Where?" Holes? Did Gibbons mean that he'd seen punctures in general, or did he mean what he'd said? "What kind of holes?"

"Roundish holes in the solar wings, like bullet holes. Some more, I think. That thing have an impact sensor?"

"Yeah. But you didn't see what looked like ragged punctures? The sort shrapnel would make?"

Gibbons stuck his head as far forward as he could in his helmet, so that he looked like a turtle trying to come out of its shell. "Shrapnel? As in Soviet killer-sat that sidles up to one of ours and explodes, destroying its target with chaff and shrapnel? If that's what you're asking, Major, the answer's negative. I did not see anything that even vaguely resembled a Soviet strike on that satellite."

"You're too quick for your own good, Colonel Gibbons."

"You're taking me along on this EVA. Whether you take me into your confidence or not's up to you. Somebody's going to talk to me when we get groundside, if I just made a lucky guess—or if we see anything weird out there."

"Holes are weird enough, Colonel." The Marines didn't have a strong space or intelligence component, but they seemed to get everywhere they wanted to be.

Whether Gibbons wanted to be on this EVA or not wasn't pertinent: Conard couldn't do it alone; regulations prohibited it.

He was beginning to regret insisting on the EVA as they went through their final systems checks. In the shuttle bay, they helped each other into their manned maneuvering units, thruster harnesses controlled by joysticks. Then they were looking up into the heavens from the open cargo bay of shuttle-C, and the beauty and the quiet took his breath away.

Every time, you felt it. The whole universe was out there, all part of the process that had created you, every bit of it. . . . Maybe you weren't seeing the face of God, but you weren't seeing a whole lot less.

"Beautiful," he said to himself, and his helmet mike picked it up.

"You bet," Gibbons said proudly in response. "Any closer, and we'd have bumped her."

Byron had put them nearly under *HE-12*. She hovered at eleven o'clock, sunlight glinting off her wings.

"The wings are going to be a bit of a problem, if we can't depress them manually." If *HE-12*'s electronics were working, they could have done it electronically.

"Naa, if we're bringing it into the bay, and we can't get 'em down flush, we can still secure the package well enough."

Gibbons knew shuttle-C better than Conard did. The Marine was the flight engineer.

"Okay," Conard said. "Lead the way, whenever you're ready."

Protocol demanded that Gibbons lead. Once they'd done their final com check with the flight deck, Gibbons did just that.

Conard watched the other astronaut rise up out of the cargo bay, and then toggled his own joystick slightly, pushing off at the same time.

The feeling of exhilaration as his MMU thrusters propelled him toward the crippled satellite disappeared abruptly as Conard got close.

HE-12 was crippled, all right.

"Damn, look at that," Conard muttered, then remembered that the flight deck crew in shuttle-C could hear everything he said. Hell, there was no way to prevent them from looking out and seeing at least some of what he was seeing: holes, like big shotgun holes, in the satellite's wings. At least three of them, Four. Five.

Six.

His MMU brought him closer, and he shifted the joystick under his right hand to the left to jet around toward *HE-12*'s rear.

He could hear his own breathing, and Gibbons's. "Hey, Gibbons, let's start pushing her in."

"Seen enough, huh?"

Damned bureaucracy should have cleared everybody on board for this. Gibbons had seen enough, for sure, even if he hadn't seen what Conard was looking for, on *HE-12*'s off side.

HE-12's impact sensor was tripped. The multiple impacts had been hard enough and fast enough that there hadn't been time to transmit that data before the transmitting system itself went down.

Conard ran a hand over the impact sensor, almost in disbelief. He'd had this half-assed theory of Soviet mischief. He'd never in his wildest dreams thought he'd see anything like this.

"I'm ready, Conard. We gonna push it together, or what?"

Gibbons was beyond the satellite's wings, with one hand on *HE-12*'s forward end and another on the wing strut itself.

"Yeah, here I come." Again, Conard used his joysticks, which gave him good control over up and down, forward and back, left and right.

The wings were the most obvious telltales. There the punctures were almost perfectly round. And there were enough of them that no one would claim this mess was the result of some accidental collision with space junk.

Conard's chest felt tight. Gibbons was verbally coordinating their MMU movements in a careful, precise fashion.

Conard didn't mind taking Gibbons's orders. In fact, he was relieved that somebody was telling him what to do. The shock of seeing *HE-12* impacted this way still had him in its grip.

He followed Gibbons's instructions like an automaton. He wasn't even looking at the impacts any more. He was looking at the blue planet he could see beyond the space shuttle's bulk.

Why did it have to be something like this?

Chuck Conard was holding in his hands the first proof of aggression in space, a concerted attack on an American spacecraft.

You really didn't want to be the bearer of bad tidings, especially when you were basically an unlikable guy with minimal political skills who had got where he was because he was too good, and too bright, not to get somewhere.

But he couldn't figure out how this satellite he was holding (the way a kid might push a plastic submarine around a swimming pool) wasn't going to start more trouble than he could survive.

Or maybe more than anyone could survive.

Conard said, "Hey, Gibbons, we've got to get these wings collapsed. They're evidence."

"Yeah, I figured. Don't worry, we'll do it once we've got her inside the bay."

Now *HE-12* was a female. Gibbons, the Marine, probably understood what he was seeing as well as or better than Conard did. Space Command was a new service, dedicated to an evolving mission. Space Command wasn't the service in which you expected to be eyeballing impacts and guessing what kind of hostile fire made those impacts.

Gibbons had seen *HE-12* in the IMAX and realized then what Conard was only now figuring out: *HE-12* had been attacked.

And it hadn't been attacked by a Soviet killer-satellite. Soviet killer-sats threw shrapnel which would have torn entirely different kinds of holes in *HE-12*'s wings.

At least, *HE-12* hadn't been attacked by any kind of Soviet killer that Conard was aware of, or had even heard rumors of.

So what had hit the satellite? And more important, who? And, most important of all, why had they attacked *HE-12?*

Conard couldn't answer any of those questions. He could just try to shake off the numbness, try to tear his eyes away from cloud-swathed Earth. He had to pay attention.

He and Gibbons had to get *HE-12* into the cargo bay, secure it there (if possible with its wings flat to its fuselage), and bring it home.

Then somebody else would answer the hard questions.

But try as he might, Conard couldn't keep his eyes off the blue Earth. Space deployments were supposed to safeguard the Earth, not endanger it.

Every fiber of Chuck Conard's body was telling him that this was the most dangerous situation he'd ever been in. His mouth was dry and his eyeballs seemed to have a cool breeze blowing over them.

You didn't want to come home with something like this. You didn't want something like this to happen. He no longer cared that a Marine colonel was sticking his nose into sensitive, compartmented information.

He was glad the Marine was with him. He was glad somebody was with him when he'd found the shot-up satellite.

He just wished, as Gibbons kept talking and they maneuvered *HE-12* down into the cargo bay, that nobody'd found *HE-12*.

If the Soviets had a new space weapon that was stealthed and capable of this sort of destruction, and had used that weapon on *HE-12*, then there was going to be real trouble down on the blue planet now obscured by the walls of shuttle-C's cargo bay.

But that didn't make any sense. did it? The Soviets had just lost a satellite themselves, in mysterious circumstances. And if Ford's spoofing team hadn't been responsible for the Soviet Cosmos going down, then maybe it was something like this.

Whatever this was.

The Soviet Union was too smart to start something, weren't they?

The United States was too controlled to respond, weren't they?

All of a sudden, Conard wasn't sure of anything, not even if what he thought he knew about his own side's motives and performance was correct.

Then Gibbons's voice said jocularly in his helmet, "Got the sucker."

Conard looked down *HE-12*'s length, and saw Gibbons triumphantly holding up one of the satellite's punctured, solar wings.

As the cargo bay was closing over their heads, a shaft of light hit the wing, and it glittered in Gibbons's gloved hand.

19

Day 8: Cairo

When Sarwat Hatim, alias Yousef Seti, of Egyptian intelligence, threw a party at his neocolonial villa, every foreign national of any stature who was within fifty miles of Cairo invariably showed up. Tonight, the pretext for the party was to celebrate today's official commencement of Bright Star. Looking around her at the glitterati wandering the white rooms and lit grounds of the villa, Meri Soukry couldn't find a single guest for whom Bright Star was anything more than a pretext.

Yousef Seti's villa was one of those sprawling affairs that was a confection of Parisian nineteenth-century architecture filtered through Islamic conventions. From its veranda, she could see through the wide-open French doors into the reception area and beyond, to the front foyer. Every new arrival seemed to have a brittle smile and a stiff walk. When people laughed, she thought she heard a hysterical tinge to the men's chuckles and women's giggles.

An American couple drifted by—a man who was handsome enough to be Vice President and a woman in a practical cocktail dress chosen because it packed well, not because it looked well.

With the couple was a small, dark Egyptian matron, who was asking the American woman, "But what does it mean, that this American 'DefCon' is at 'three'? What was it before?"

The American woman looked at her husband, who said, "DefCon: defensive condition. Three is a higher readiness state than usual. As for what it means . . . probably nothing."

His wife snapped, "Nothing? Four's duck and cover . . ."

The matron, an Egyptian antiquities dealer, tittered. "Mr. Land, don't tease an old woman. With so many American forces here, surely we . . ."

The threesome drifted off. Meri Soukry left the veranda and headed for the group gathering around the buffet. There was no air out here anyway. So those were the Lands; they didn't look much like their dossier photos.

Time to go to work. If the Lands had arrived, then Dalton Ford was here somewhere, as well. The exchange she'd overheard was typical tonight: with the joint exercise under way and the DefCon suddenly raised, everyone was nervous. Egypt could not help but be drawn into whatever might happen, if the staging area for American force projection chanced to be Cairo West.

Her light, white silk shift was clinging to her, despite the rapid cooling now that the sun had set. She simply wasn't one of those people who didn't sweat when she was working.

And tonight, here where everyone who was anyone was also working, it was important that she did not look more rumpled or ruffled than was appropriate to her cover. Sarwat Hatim was one of her most lucrative contacts, because she was useful, because he thought she was beautiful, and because she was a woman. Hatim was an old-school Egyptian. He couldn't take her seriously enough to be worried by the occasional rumors that she was someone's agent.

In Cairo, everyone was someone's agent, and Hatim thought of her as his. She went right up to him, cutting through the drinkers of Moët and the nibblers of Soviet beluga, and insinuated herself under his arm.

Hatim had the face of a B-movie star, with smoldering eyes and a full head of graying hair that set off chiseled features. If his lips weren't that awful purple of the Nile people, his gums brown, and his heritage more Iraqi that Egyptian, even Soukry might have found his tall, princely bearing irresistible.

As it was, she frequently resisted Hatim. They had a business arrangement. She acted as an escort for some of his more exotic guests, who needed an entrée into Cairene society, and he did her favors where visas and customs regulations were concerned. To Hatim, Soukry was a genteel smuggler of antiquities whom he had by the short hairs.

Hatim was Meri Soukry's hole card in Cairo. Only a sexist pig of Hatim's extremity would be so blind and so accommodating.

"Aren't you going to introduce me, Yousef?" she prodded when Hatim—Yousef Seti to all his guests—trailed his hand down to her rump without pausing in his conversation with two men she wasn't supposed to know.

"Of course, my dear. Anu Meri Soukry, this is Aqid Gaspar Larka, a Soviet guest, and Klement Ignatov, from the Bulgarian . . . trade delegation, isn't it?"

The plump Bulgarian reached out to kiss her hand, muttering a response as he did so.

She knew who both these men were. Larka, the soldier with the brush cut, was the lesser danger, despite appearances. The Spetznaz colonel couldn't flush a toilet in Cairo without Ignatov's permission.

"Anu Soukry's in trade as well, Klement, so you'll perhaps discover common interests."

She had more common interests with the Spetznaz officer, but now was not the time: she already had an agenda for this evening.

Larka, acknowledging her quizzical look with his own quick and detailed inventory of her body, offered, "Did you hear the one about the two Bulgarian border guards, Anu Soukry?"

"No, tell me. And call me Meri. Everyone does."

Ignatov moued in exaggerated anticipation of a joke at his expense. "Gaspar, must you—?"

"Come on, then, Larka," said Hatim, always happy to sow discord, "tell us the story."

"Two Bulgarian border guards," Larka said relishingly, steadfastly watching her face, "are on patrol. One says to the other, 'Comrade, what do you think of the new regime?' The second replies, 'I think exactly the same as you, Comrade.'

The first points his rifle at the second, 'Then, Comrade, it is my duty to arrest you in the name of the State.' " Larka finished triumphantly and waited for someone to laugh.

Heartbeats of silence passed before Soukry managed to giggle, while Ignatov apologized sorrowfully, "Soviet humor is an acquired taste."

Then, finally, Hatim, whose gaze had wandered during the joke telling, guffawed uproariously.

While he was doing so, Soukry had a chance to look over her shoulder to see what could have distracted the Egyptian Intelligence officer.

And there, barely ten feet away, stood not only Dalton Ford, but Jay Adamson, Cairo chief of station, the Land woman without her husband, and a Frenchman with a waxed moustache, Marc Brisson, legal advisor to the European Space Agency's African office.

"Excuse me," said Meri Soukry brightly, "but I see an old friend. Actually, Seti introduced us. He's a terrible horse-breeder." With an insouciant smile at the shocked Soviets, she left their group for Ford's.

Let her intention be clear. Let the scandal-mongering begin. Conscious of her body language and the often-unwelcome effect her feral beauty had on rooms full of men, she swept past three Arabs in *ghutra*s and placed herself squarely before Ford.

On tiptoe, she kissed him. All conversation in the group stopped.

For an instant he was stiff with surprise. Then her welcoming press woke his groin, his lips parted, and he returned her embrace.

She leaned back against his hands, locked at her spine. "Dalton, it's been too long."

"Way too long," he said with a quick smile and narrowed eyes. It was possible that he only vaguely remembered her, considering his condition when last they met, how quickly he'd left when summoned by a Marine from his embassy.

"This time," she said as she stepped back and he let her go, "I hope we don't have to borrow a room from Seti."

Then he was sure how he knew her. And he made up his mind on the spot, as she'd hoped. "Don't go away. Introduce yourself while I get you a drink."

A nice cover for the fact that he didn't remember her name. At the time, she'd been concerned that he remember as little as possible.

Adamson was talking quietly with Marc Brisson, the Frenchman, saying, ". . . SPOT can do the job for us. Quite a feather in your caps."

The three Arabs, whom she'd jostled, were right behind them. One was a skeletal, horse-faced Syrian, here as a rug merchant; another was one of Seti's men; the third was an Iraqi from their Defense Ministry.

Meri Soukry ignored them, though they were obviously eavesdropping. Everyone here was eavesdropping, and the American woman was looking steadily at her, waiting for the promised introduction with knives in her eyes.

"Jenny," Adamson said, "I think you're the only one here who doesn't know Meri Soukry. Meri's old Cairene society, so if you play your cards right, she'll take you where the average tourist never manages to go. Jenny is here with her husband, who's doing some technical consulting on Bright Star."

"*I'm* doing some technical consulting on Bright Star," corrected the fair American woman.

One forgot how prickly the Americans were. But surely no more so than her own people. Meri smiled and said, "These men will never admit you're doing anything but decorating their parties. Jay, do you know those three behind you?"

Adamson might or might not respond. But at least he turned and looked to see. Then he turned back and said, "Sorry, I can't introduce you."

But by then the Land woman was nearly smiling. "I'm learning. Women's liberation hasn't penetrated the mysterious Middle East. Yet." She crossed her arms and craned her neck to look over the crowd. "Where has Dalton gotten to?"

"Did I hear something about SPOT?" Soukry asked.

Jenny Land said, "Oh, we've bought some time on it for the duration of Bright Star—you do know what SPOT is?"

"I read the paper." This American woman was impossible. And unaware of what was politically embarrassing and what was not. Or uncaring. Also, territorial where Ford was concerned, which was strange. She'd brought her husband. "How embarrassing for you all," Meri said, probing.

Adamson had to respond. "Not at all. It's no secret. Just more international cooperation at work. Right, Marc?"

The Frenchman said, nodding, "Interoperability is the key to all our futures."

"Now here is a man accustomed to thirty-second sound bites," Meri said teasingly, and Brisson blushed.

So the Americans weren't trying to hide the fact that they were utilizing SPOT's remote sensing. She must get Ford alone.

And she must change the subject. The Arabs behind need not be the recipients of an intelligence windfall, even if the intelligence wasn't classified.

Keeping her eyes on the Syrian behind Adamson's shoulder, she said, "Where's Dalton, do you think?"

"There he is. No wonder," Jenny Land said.

She followed Land's gaze and saw Dalton, still by the bar, with two champagne glasses in his hands. Jesse Quantrell was with him.

For a moment, Meri panicked. She'd thought that since today was the first calendar day of Bright Star, Quantrell would have been out on exercise, or too tired, or at least too busy for this.

But there he was.

"I must go and claim my drink," she said absently.

All the way to the two men she weighed the situation: Quantrell had promised to keep her cover secret; she'd bedded him for an extra measure of certainty. This was going to be awkward, to say the least.

She walked up to the two and kissed Ford first, to let Quantrell know what was happening. Then she reached up to the Special Forces colonel and the big bear of a man leaned down to embrace her.

"Follow my lead," she breathed in his ear, though she had no idea how she was going to handle this.

"Anu Soukry, I see you've met Dalton—"

"I have for him what you requested," she said softly, as she put the glass to her lips.

The two men's eyes met. Then Ford's eyebrow raised. "Want to go somewhere quiet?"

"In a minute," she said. At least she now had control of the situation. The moment was passed when she wanted to use Quantrell as a cutout to deal with Ford. A pity. She truly liked the big man. She needed him to understand that. "I can't go off with both of you. It would start rumors." She dipped the tip of her tongue into the champagne and licked her lips with it, as if deciding how to handle things. "Jesse, is everything all right? Tonight I have heard about SPOT, and of course there is the DefCon."

"Fuck the DefCon." Quantrell managed to keep his rumbly voice low. "And you'll be hearing more about SPOT. It's open source." He rubbed his neck, looking at her.

Quantrell was obviously tired. He was freshly showered and shaven, and his eyes were bloodshot; the look in them was very guarded.

"But you're all right?"

"Yeah. All right." Increasingly, as he realized the delicacy of their situation, Quantrell was showing signs of discomfort.

"Good. Then I will take Ford tip my hotel. If you need us, you know where to find us."

"Some days, even a snail like you gets lucky," Quantrell told Ford, and then looked over Ford's head, trying to find some place to disappear to, someone whom he could say he must see.

"Jenny and Chan are over there," Ford told him. "After the airport, you three should mend some fence."

The big man said, "Okay," doubtfully. The he brightened. "Damn, there's Iggy and Larka. See you later, Ford."

When he'd gone, Meri said, "Shall we? I hate good-byes."

"Fine with me." Ford was right behind her as she climbed the steps, got her coat, and led him outside, where Hatim's houseboy waved at her and ran to get her car.

"Nice night," Ford said.

"It may yet be. Did you truly not remember me?"

"I . . . was pretty ripped. Of course I remember you. I just didn't remember how beautiful you were. Seti's a terrific host. But I didn't expect to see you, I mean—"

"You mean you thought I was a tart? A hooker, as you say? No, I am not that."

"At this point, that's clear enough. You could have knocked Quantrell over with that purse of yours."

"You would prefer to deal with us through him?"

"Ah—us. I still haven't absorbed all this. No, I wouldn't prefer anything to going to your hotel. It *is* going to be a nice night." He tentatively brushed her hip with his arm.

She shifted away. Her car's headlights lit, down the drive, and started bobbling toward them. "If we live through it, what with your country's heightened DefCon."

"DefCon's just automatic in this kind of situation, you know that. Don't let the loose talk fool you." He looked out of the corner of his eye at her. "Seti doesn't know about you, right? He would have warned me, at least . . . "

"Don't be so sure. Seti thinks I will tell him things. Help him with people. Sometimes I do. He is an Egyptian male. No woman is more than a chattel. No woman has a working brain."

"Christ."

"He'll think nothing of us going off together."

"I just don't want to make any mistakes."

The houseboy brought the car to a halt in front of them in a shower of summer dust and little stones.

"Then get in the car, please." She slid into the driver's seat, pulling out as soon as he'd shut his door.

"I ought to be pissed, you know. What were you trying to get out of me, the last time?"

"Trying? You're so sure I didn't get what I wanted? Now you want something from me."

"That's for sure."

She went slowly through the villa's gates and turned into traffic, still heavy in the early evening. "We have the photos you wanted; infrared and high resolution. The borders of Israel and Egypt, we were told. We weren't told what to look for."

"I don't know what I'm looking for. Something odd, somewhere in the area where we had no coverage for a time."

"What SPOT now covers?"

"Whoa, lady, Isn't this all kind of casual? How do I know that you're—"

"I was Quantrell's contact. I have your material. We will wait until you decide you need more from us." She shrugged. Then couldn't resist: "What is odd, that we know about, is not happening in the south. It is happening in the north."

His head came up and he stared at her. She had him. She passed a car, eliciting honks and a flat-palmed curse.

Then Ford said, "If we were to talk about the time frame we're concerned about—"

"The ground tracks you are concerned about."

"The ground tracks we didn't get, yes. And a subsequent set of tracks. If we were to talk about the missing routine surveillance, could you people fill in the blanks?"

It was such an audacious request that she chuckled honestly. "I doubt it. Everything? Tell us what you need, and we'll help. A remotely piloted vehicle has limitations: around fifty-kilometer range from its command car, if it's mobile. More, if it's dispatched from a stationary command center. But you are interested in more than border surveillance, which is all RPVs are good for."

Ford slid down in his seat. "This is going to be a long night. Maybe I ought to see what you got for me."

"I got you what I was told you wanted. You did not give Quantrell much specific guidance, or if you did, we did not have it from him."

She turned on the radio; they drove a while without talking.

When they neared the hotel, he turned it off. "You're sure about this? I could just wait in the car, you could bring it down, and we could go back to the party. There's lots of stuff popping over there."

"Such as?"

"Look." He sat sideways. "You people know the Soviets lost a satellite. You know we lost one. You know the DefCon's up. You saw Adamson in there, and Ignatov. Tonight, Adamson's

conveying backchannel condolences from our CINCSPACE—
commander in chief for space—to their equivalent about their
loss. And he's hoping to get some sort of pulse on whether
they've calmed down enough to want to compare notes."

"This is your job, the Soviets?"

"Honey, right now, *you're* my job. But staying alive in a
habitable landscape is everybody's job."

"Adamson should watch his back. The Arabs were all over
him while he was talking to that Frenchman."

"This is an Arab country."

"A Syrian and an Iraqi . . . I would rather deal with an
Iranian than an Iraqi any day. At least you can talk to the
Iranians. The Iraqis are purely mad."

"We've had a lot of trouble talking to the Iranians, you may
remember," said Ford dryly.

She pulled up in front of the Nile Hilton. "The Arabs are
very tense, with Bright Star officially begun."

"They aren't the only ones. I thought you lived in Cairo,
permanently?"

"I do. My family keeps a permanent suite here, for when
one of us must stay in the city proper. The traffic, you
know . . ."

"Yeah, I know. Well, ma'am—"

"Meri. Someone will take the car."

She got out and left it, keys inside, knowing that he would
follow.

In her rooms, she immediately pulled out the RPV photos
and dropped the folder in his lap. "As requested."

He looked through it while she got him a drink from the bar.
He took it without comment, leafing through what had come
from Israel.

"I should have asked for more," he said.

"You can do that."

He tasted his drink. "Scotch?"

"It's wrong? It's what you drank at Seti's when . . ."

She stood up, to take it. He took her by the wrist. "It's fine.
I'd like to ask for more. What do I do, fill out a form?"

She let him pull her down onto the couch. "We need better
guidance, to be helpful."

"I've got to think about how helpful I can afford to let you be."

She knew where this was going. So did he. But it must go her way. "Our concerns, right now, are in the north. Yours are in the south."

"I don't know where mine are." His pulse was beating visibly in the hollow of his throat. "How about I give you some time frames and you people tell me if, during those time frames, you saw anything unusual or worrisome, anywhere you're surveilling."

She pulled back. "They won't give you that much. It's too revealing of our capabilities."

"We have an intelligence-sharing agreement, have had since '58."

"Through much better monitored channels."

"You mean we can't trust each other well enough?"

"Give me your time frames, and I'll see what I can do." She needed to get the Americans interested in the north. It must be on their own initiative. Otherwise, with such sketchy data as Mossad now possessed, they would seem to be baiting the Americans, leading the investigation, if there was to be one.

"Great," Dalton Ford said. "Now let's work on getting to trust each other better."

Trust was out of the question. But when his fingers slid from her throat to her lips, she took one between her teeth and sucked on it for a moment before she let go. Intimacy was another matter.

20

Day 9: Space Weapons Center Research Facility, Kirtland, New Mexico

Leo Beckwith had the local CIA man in a borrowed office, and a fractured ruby pellet on the desk before him. Chuck Conard had found the ruby fragment rattling around in *HE-12*'s fuselage once the shuttle had touched down at Edwards and he could perform a thorough examination. For the first time in Beckwith's memory, he was cold, down here in Albuquerque. There was gooseflesh on his arms. He got heavily to his feet and went to turn up the thermostat.

"Admiral," said the pock-faced Agency officer attached to Space Command, "I'd like to send this over to the Air Force Intelligence labs for identification. Industrial corundum—if that's what this is—can only come from so many suppliers. Maybe we can find out who sold lots of this, in pellet form, to somebody recently."

"Fine. You do that." Having adjusted the thermostat to seventy degrees, Beckwith lumbered back to his chair. "We can use all the help we can get."

"Can you tell us anything else, sir?"

"*HE-12*'s available for hands-on, if you boys want to get in line," Beckwith growled. He hated the implication that he might have missed something or, worse, be withholding something. "I'm going out now to look at a data-gathering option. Want to come, son?"

"Nesbitt, sir. Al Nesbitt. And yes, I'd like to come."

124

So off they went, without Beckwith having used even one hankie this morning, to see Pollock's demonstration, which had had to be held at Kirtland for mysterious reasons.

The office where Beckwith and the CIA man had been asked to meet Pollock looked like it had been in a localized earthquake. The sandy-haired Air Force Space Command colonel wasn't there. The kid at the desk said, "Sirs, Colonel Pollock asks that you meet him on the test flight line."

Then Beckwith knew what Pollock had in mind. But the CIA liaison didn't, so Leo Beckwith went out of his way not to tell Nesbitt anything that would spoil Pollock's surprise.

Instead, when they got back into the Cherokee to drive over to the flight line, they talked about other avenues of inquiry into the satellite kills.

"Ford says he's getting some results working with the Israelis out there, and he's going to stick with it," Beckwith told Nesbitt, "unless anyone's got objections at your Israeli desk or wherever. After all, since this is happening right around Bright Star, it's shortsighted not to look closer at the Arabs, even the moderates."

"As long as it's unofficial and you don't step on any toes," Nesbitt said, putting on aviator glasses as he talked, "it's fine with us. We've got an alumnus out there and we're keeping tabs through him—a guy named Chandler Land. If Ford's got questions for us, he should route them through Land. Right now, all I need is an idea of how close you're thinking you need to look at Arab moderates—after all, the Israeli desk needs to keep the peace."

"Nothing significant." Beckwith wheeled the car around a tight curve and stopped at the guardpost, where he was waved through almost immediately.

"Nothing significant such as what?"

"Nothing significant enough to upset your moderate Arabs, unless they're involved. We're popping up a tac sat: very low orbit, short lifespan, at a hundred ninety miles. We had it sitting around. We're making sure to tell the Soviets before we launch it. And I've arranged with Eighteen Corps to do some nap-of-the-earth missions. We'd like you people to consider maneuvering one of your photo-return satellites in where we need it, and let us have the data for a couple days."

"I think we can do that, no problem," said Nesbitt. "Are you prepared to exonerate the Soviets out of hand as perpetrators of the *HE-12* kill, then?"

"For the record?" Beckwith was no fool. "Absolutely not. That's what you and the Air Force technical people are going to be working on—identifying the provenance of the pellets."

Ford's last call had convinced Beckwith to go back farther with his Priane Space commercial-launch search, but Pollock hadn't given him the results of it yet. Right now, the Kwajalein fleck data and the Priane Space data were too thinly connected to discuss with CIA, even with this local liaison officer. Nesbitt's proprietary reaction to Beckwith's mention of the moderate Arabs was proof of that.

The CIA man said, "We'll find your pellet manufacturer for you, I guarantee it. It just may take a while. Is there anything else we can do for you?"

Maybe this was Leo Beckwith's lucky day. "I'd like State to broach pooling our *HE-12* data and the Soviet's Cosmos data. If the problem's not the Soviets, and we can figure out what's wrong together, it'll be a *glasnost*ian triumph everybody can be proud of."

"And if it *is* the Soviets who took down our sat, and then lost their sat as an accidental result, they won't pool data and we'll look at them harder. Not bad. I think I can sell that to Langley, sir, easier than I can sell the Israeli interface by an unqualified operative."

Oh boy. "Ford's out there on the line, doing his best. As you say, he's unofficial. So is your man, Land, whom nobody even bothered to tell me about, until now. . . . "

"That's because he wasn't doing anything significant or within your need-to-know. Land was there when the shit hit the fan, he's got unique qualifications, and he's still among our consultants."

"Right." Beckwith knew all about Agency consultants. "Well," he said as he pulled the Cherokee out onto what looked like an empty apron and put it in park, "here we are."

"I don't see anything."

"Watch the sky, Mr. Nesbitt."

Beckwith got out his binoculars and handed them to Nesbitt, content to watch without magnification. If Pollock didn't kill himself, this was about to be one hell of a show.

The black dot of the hypersonic x plane didn't appear for nearly five minutes, and then it came down out of the sky like a swooping hawk.

Beckwith's heart pumped so much blood into his head that his ears rang with stress tones. The most dangerous times in the life of any aircraft were the moments of takeoff and landing. That went triple for x craft: experimental, prototype aircraft with x designators such as the X-29A, the X-30, and the X-31A. Pollock was a crazy bastard, and if he was checkriding this particular x plane for the reasons that Beckwith suspected, CIA might as well hear it from the horse's mouth.

The black dot was growing so fast now that Beckwith hoped to hell it wasn't crashing. The glide characteristics of the aero-space planes were different from anything else in the air.

The hypersonic plane came over the runway once in a low dive and a scream of scramjet engines, then went around for a second pass. Right over Beckwith's Cherokee, Pollock wiggled his wings in salute.

The bastard really was pushing it. Until the time-honored wiggle, Beckwith had been sure that Pollock was in trouble, and was plain overshooting to come back for another try.

What did Pollock think this was, the Paris Air Show?

The black-painted, ultrasweptwing space plane looked more like a missile with fins than a spacegoing aircraft. She could switch from air-breather to rocketship when she got out of atmosphere. She'd been designed to reach Mach 20, tested at Mach 8. She didn't officially exist. Even her x designator was so classified that, when the CIA man breathed, "What in the hell was that?" Beckwith just said:

"Space plane."

Nesbitt would recognized the areospace plane when Pollock parked her. Pollock must have left early this morning to have brought her over from Vandenberg so soon.

In spite of himself, Beckwith was impressed. But he was also concerned by what Pollock wanted to do with the trans-atmospheric testbed. There might not be any reason to risk the space plane for a reconnaissance mission like this.

If she crashed anywhere on Earth, the security breach, and technology loss, would be crushing. The prototype had been built out of the black segment of the Air Force budget, with intelligence-community money, in a manner safe from Congressional oversight. Nobody wanted to do any explaining: not Lockheed's Skunk Works, where she'd been built; not Space Command, where she was being evaluated; not the agencies, where her specifications had been determined far in advance of the announcement of the X-30 National Aerospace Plane, or NASP, program.

X-NASP was what everybody around the project had dubbed the officially nonexistent bird. It was a measure of how closely this one project had been controlled that Nesbitt hadn't realized what he was looking at immediately.

When Pollock came around for his second approach, Nesbitt said, "You people are crazy if you think we're going to risk something like this on a little dustup like—"

"Losing satellites isn't a little dustup. You think about whether you want to be on the recommending team, Nesbitt. I haven't made up my mind yet, either. If we've got a problem that's going to continue, there are billions at stake. Not to mention national pride and crippled defense communications."

"Yeah, I know." Nesbitt tossed the binoculars on the seat between them and leaned his head back. "Nobody's going to like this back East. There's no proof yet to connect *HE-12* to the Cosmos, let alone to anything having to do with Bright Star."

"Except that the ground tracks of *HE-12* were specifically targeted on the Middle East, and the particular Cosmos 2100 the Soviets lost had an identical area of concentration."

"I know, I know." Nesbitt pulled off his sunglasses and rubbed his eyes in irritation. "I'm not saying you're wrong, Admiral. I'm just saying that using an expensive, classified asset is always hard to sell."

"You let me sell it, son. You just sit back and let yourself be convinced that Pollock's capable of bringing home whatever kind of bacon it is we need, using that bird."

Just then, far down the runway, the black, pneumatic-arrowhead shape of the x plane touched down, its nosewheel riding up for another second while Beckwith held his breath.

Pollock was an old man, as pilots went. But when you were talking about doing what Pollock wanted to do, you had to be able to do it yourself. Pollock, the Air Force deputy chief for special operations at Space Command, was probably the only pilot who could get cleared to fly the X-NASP to the Middle East.

The plane raced up to them in a cloud of smoke from her tires and dust from the runway. They'd have to do something about those tires.

"Let's go," Beckwith said, and got out of the car. Nesbitt followed.

The x plane was fully stopped, now, her automatic ladder deploying. Moments later, Pollock started climbing down.

As he went to meet the pilot, Beckwith was still wrestling with his own doubts. If he let Pollock take the X-NASP, and something went wrong, it wasn't just Pollock's life and Beckwith's career that were down the tubes. In this climate of research-and-development penny-pinching, a public failure could kill the whole project.

When the orange-suited Pollock took off his helmet, oxygen mask, and held out a hand, Beckwith said, "Pollock, you know Mr. Nesbitt. How was she?"

"Hi, Al. Leo, she's ready, if you are."

That was the question, all right. Circumstances had to warrant the risk of the space plane. And they simply didn't. Not quite yet.

Beckwith looked at Al Nesbitt, who was already practicing the opening line he'd use to tell his grandchildren about the day he saw the future.

21

Day 10: Moscow

Shitov was sitting in his Zil while his aide dashed into the bakery, when someone knocked on the car's window and tried the doorlatch.

Shitov's heart stuttered. All he could see was a raincoat and a hand, but the hand didn't have a gun in it. If it had, bullets would already be shattering the glass on the way to his skull; only the Executive President had an armored car in Moscow, these days. So it wasn't an assassination attempt.

Then, was it a crackdown on government corruption—again? Everyone in KGB Moscow used their clout to cut through meat and bread lines. Shitov had been using this particular bakery for so long that his raisin pumpernickel was routinely saved for him; it never saw the front of the shop.

The knock came again. Shitov rolled down his window and peered up and out: "So? What is it?"

"Will you get into the Executive President's car, please?" said the weasel-faced functionary who stood there with a sour look on his face, and indicated the car behind.

If the Executive President would travel by motorcade, with a decent motorcycle escort, embarrassing moments like this wouldn't happen.

Shitov got out of his own car heavily. How was he to know that the Executive President would sneak up behind him?

Still, he should have noticed the limo. But he was distracted with his personal problems. Levonov was boycotting Shitov because of the meeting in the KGB cafeteria, and Levonov's wife was treating Shitov's wife as a traitor, which meant that Shitov was getting no sleep and no sex either. . . .

Nothing for it but to get inside when he rapped oh, so delicately on the limousine's window and the door opened.

"Yes, *Vhozd?*"—*Great Leader*. Shitov slammed the door shut, hating himself for his servile tongue almost as much as the piggish little man who was determined to make the USSR's elite as poor as its peasants.

"Aleksandr, I would like an update on the investigation into the loss of our Cosmos satellite." The Executive President always made sure you knew exactly what he was talking about, as if you were a child or an imbecile.

Report? He'd not been told to have a report ready, or even that the call for one was imminent. This was a trap, an attempt to catch him with his dick out. But there was always something one could say. *Think!* What had come across his desk?

"Sir, so far our investigation into American complicity" (this sounded like a pig-raiser at a Central Committee meeting) "our investigation has uncovered the fact that the Americans have had to hire the French remote-sensing satellite, SPOT, to serve their overhead reconnaissance needs during their Bright Star exercise." Did the Executive President remember Bright Star? "This is proving very embarrassing to them. My people in Cairo tell me that an as-yet-unidentified Mossad agent is close to the American contingent there, perhaps working closely with them."

Shitov paused for breath. Ahead, his aide had come out of the bakery with the bread. Please, just get in the car. Don't flaunt the baked goods. . . . Too late. The Executive President's aide and Shitov's man were talking. Then both looked at the limo in which Shitov sat. Then, as Shitov watched, horrified, his man offered the Executive President's man a roll, and both stood munching, right in front of the bread line, leaning against the fender of Shitov's car. . . .

"And so," the Executive President prompted when Shitov said nothing more, "what does this lead you to believe?"

"Believe, sir? It leads me to think that we must keep an eye on the Americans, especially on those in their Space Command, such as the ones my Cairo field men have cultivated."

"And that is all?"

"All? I see no further—"

"I should tell you, Shitov, that their commander in chief for space has sent his condolences over the loss of our Cosmos, and wonders if the circumstances of their loss and ours are similar. Are they?"

Shitov was floored. Someone should have told him that the Americans had sent condolences. It was Levonov, paying him back for what Shitov had done in the meeting, who'd found a way to keep that information from him. If he hadn't already been sitting, he would have sat heavily. As for similarities in the two disasters, how did Shitov know? How could anyone know? Even if the Americans told you something, you couldn't believe what they told you: their CIA was running their country.

Shitov peered through the car's gloom at the dough-boy face of his country's most senior official. "I . . . I am not sure. We have not yet retrieved any wreckage from our satellite, which burned, for the most part, in the atmosphere. The Americans, I'm sure the Technology Directorate has informed you, sent a shuttle up to collect their satellite—intact—and bring it home for study." *Take that, Levonov!* "Apart from the fact that they have something to study and we don't, how could the satellite disasters have been similar, since ours was destroyed but theirs—they claim—was merely incapacitated?" He leaned forward, energized with relief at having found a way to respond. "It is entirely possible that nothing was ever wrong with their satellite, that the whole furor over the transmission failures of their *HE-12* was an elaborate ruse to allow them to test a new SDI weapon on our satellite and then avoid blame because it seems that one of theirs, too, was destroyed."

"You believe this, Colonel Shitov?" The Executive President's voice was very soft.

"Executive President," Shitov said carefully, sitting back, "I do not believe anything. I am an officer who is trained to believe only the evidence of his senses. I have no such evidence, as yet. If it would be forthcoming, then I will believe it. I only say it might be premature to trust the Americans in this matter."

"Then get such evidence, Shitov. And get it quickly. Have your agents in Cairo tell the Americans in their Space Command there—very cautiously, so that we can disclaim it as unauthorized later if we must—that we will give them whatever help we can in finding the trouble at the root of this matter. And have your agents give such assistance as is not damaging to our own security. But keep very close tabs on what is said and what is done, Shitov—very close."

"Very close," Shitov promised numbly, and nearly stumbled out of the car when the Executive President told him he could leave.

It must have been the bread, Shitov decided, which made the Executive President angry enough to give Shitov such an impossible and suicidal task. Flaunting the pumpernickel rolls in front of the people the way his man had, leaning indolently on the car and chewing his cud like a cow.

As soon as he found a punishment post severe enough, Shitov was going to reassign the man now driving him back to the office. Then he was going to call his wife and forbid her, under any circumstances, even to speak to Levonova.

He would find someone with whom he could swap ballet seats—someone whose seats did not adjoin the Levonovs. Levonov must have no excuse to say that Shitov or his wife had said this or said that. The battle lines were now drawn.

22

Day 10: Cairo West Air Base

In the air-conditioned, wooden-floored tent that housed US-SPACECOM at the airport command center, Jenny Land watched her husband studying the first SPOT transmissions to come down.

Before her, on a rickety folding table, were RPV and nap-of-the-earth reconnaissance photos. She couldn't do anything with this stuff, wasn't expected to, really. But she'd refused to stay in the hotel.

"Chan, switch with me."

"What? Oh yeah, okay." Chan was in his most abstracted mode. What he thought to find that could have been missed by everyone else, she couldn't fathom.

The ARCENT—Army/Central Command—facility even had a telecommunications system, used mainly for trouble-shooting and briefings, that provided videoconferencing. So pictures of what they were looking at were being looked at everywhere in the United States where relevant expertise existed.

As her husband passed her in the narrow confines of the tent, she stopped him with a hand on his arm. "I want to go home. If you had any sense, Chan, so would you. We're useless here. I don't see why Dalton insisted that we come. My mother—"

"Jenny, you know we can't go home." Chan's boyish face seemed comical when he looked grave. After so many years, she still loved his eyes. "Langley's counting on us."

"Oh, it's the honor of being drafted at the last minute back into service? You like the feel of your harness?" Someone from Langley had called, and then someone else, while they'd been detained in the embassy and—*wham!*—they'd been agents on the spot, serving the dear old national interest in a covert capacity. Jenny Land had never been a field operative in her life.

"I . . . think this is serious, and we're here, and we've got the right qualifications—"

"And we've got a better parking spot for our clearances, yes dear. You know what happened the last time a bunch of ex-pros started working with the military on a sensitive intelligence—"

"Ssh! A tent's no place to—"

"—mission that couldn't be subjected to congressional oversight!" she finished, uncaring of who might overhear them.

"Jenny, if you want to throw a tantrum don't do it here."

They'd known each other too long for that not to hurt. She crossed her arms.

"I know you're still upset about what happened at the airport, but Quantrell apologized. You just won't let it go."

"It's not Quantrell who should apologize. It's Adamson and—"

"Knock-knock?" boomed a voice from outside the tent. They'd been alone in here because what they were looking at was highly sensitive, Ford wasn't around, and the other Space Command people who could have handled this data were in the next tent, facilitating "comms."

Facilitating comms was a large part of Space Command's job on Bright Star: getting people in touch and keeping them in touch with the command, control, communications and intelligence that they needed.

"Knock-knock," came the voice again. The Lands eyed one another. Then Jenny unfolded her arms, kissed her husband, and began stuffing the data into blue-bordered folders while Chan went to see who it was.

"Colonel Quantrell, we were just talking about you," Chan said.

"Don't worry about that. You can't hear a thing outside these air-conditioned mothers. Recirculating systems make too much noise. Great impromptu security. Can I come in?"

Chan looked at her over his shoulder. This had become, somehow, against Jenny's better judgment, a CIA field station full of commandeered material. Now—or any time on a minute's notice—it had to turn back into a Space Command comm tent. She put the last folder in her briefcase, and locked the briefcase.

She wanted to get out of this nightmare more and more urgently. She'd been wrong to come. She didn't belong out here. Neither did Chan.

As her husband stepped out of the way to let Quantrell enter, she saw someone who did belong out here. Jesse Quantrell was so big he seemed to take up the entire tent.

The friendly-hound expression on his wide, craggy face seemed ludicrous, once you'd seen Quantrell in action, and Jenny had. She remembered the way his commandos had treated her. No American should ever be treated like that. Chan was right, she was still furious at Quantrell for not somehow refusing to let his "boys" (ever-so-politely) treat her like traitorous garbage.

Chan gave her a warning glance: *Say something, for God's sake! At least, be polite.*

She didn't want to be polite. She occasionally would admit that her standards were too high, that she bore grudges and turned them into crusades to teach lessons to those who offended her. She couldn't help it. But her husband's desperate look made her know, at least intellectually, that this time she'd better try to control the tendency.

"Hello, Colonel Quantrell," she managed icily.

"Come on, Jenny, all's forgiven, remember?" Quantrell came toward her, both hands out and open to take hers. "Call me Jesse, please, then I'll believe what you said at the party."

What had she said? Oh, that she'd let him off this time, but not to cross her again. Well, she could live with that.

She let him take both her hands in his but then shook free immediately. "Forgiven," she said faintly. "Now, if you could do something about the heat. . . . "

"Actually, I stopped by to see if you two wanted a ride into town. Nobody works, this time of day. Siesta or a long, cool lunch in your hotel, on me. . . . "

"I can't," Chan said; "but Jenny just said she wanted to go back. Why don't you go with him, honey, and I'll find a way later?" Her husband went over and leaned against the briefcase. "I'll bring this stuff with me when I come."

Fine. Let him be this way. She'd offered to kiss and make up, but Chan wasn't satisfied. She knew what he was doing. If she went into town with Quantrell, she'd have to come to terms with the man, or the ride would be unbearable. Sometimes she hated how well Chan knew her.

"Fine. Let's go, Colonel. I hope your car's air-conditioned."

"Bring a sweater," Quantrell advised with a grin.

When she stepped out of the tent, the blazing midday sun struck her with its heat. She put on sunglasses, which cut the glare, but nothing could make the air breathable. It was as if she were standing behind a laundromat, breathing the air coming out of the vent.

She followed the big colonel through the maze of tents until he pulled open the door of a VW minivan for her.

Inside, the plastic seats burned her though her cotton slacks.

"Just a minute, and it will be cool," Quantrell promised as he got in the other side, started the motor, and put the air-conditioner on high. "Leave your window open until the hot air's out," he told her.

So she sat there, feeling the moisture evaporate from her body nearly as soon as it soaked her, and desperately wishing for something to drink, while Quantrell drove them through the checkpoints and turned toward Cairo.

"Okay, you can close your window now. There's a jug of water under your seat. Drink as much as you can."

She didn't need to be told. She drank thirstily, and felt every crevice inside her where the water went. Then she handed the jug to Quantrell and leaned forward, directly into the vents on the dash blowing cold air, holding her hair up from her neck.

She should have stayed home. She'd been talked into this only because of her mother. They needed the money, God knew, but it wasn't just the financial drain of expenses that insurance didn't cover. It was that she wasn't treating her mother as well as she'd have treated a dog or a cat: You wouldn't let an animal live on in misery, long after it forgot its name or why it was living. She couldn't go to see her mother anymore; she couldn't handle the horror and the fear that something like that might someday happen to her. . . . So she'd run away at the first opportunity. Because it had been so long since she'd dared feel anything very strongly, she hadn't heeded her own instinct not to come.

And Chan was happy. So maybe it would be all right, somehow. Chan and she both needed something to occupy their minds besides finding ways to pay for someone else's living death.

Maybe this would turn out to be important, the break they needed, something they'd be proud to have done. But it certainly hadn't felt that way when they'd been all but arrested at the airport. And then there'd been that awful party, where Ford had made a spectacle of himself with some local vixen. "What did you say?"

Quantrell had been trying to get her attention: "I was making small talk," said the big Special Forces colonel. "Nothing earthshaking. Look, I really meant what I said: I want us to be friends. Dalton thinks the world of you two."

"We think the world of him too," she said, and was sorry when it sounded cynical. Outside, the baking, blighted landscape swept by; Quantrell, like everyone else, drove crazily here.

"I could take you to someplace real for lunch—not one of these tourist joints. Show you some real Cairo, indig style. Would that make us even on points?"

Points. "Oh, that's all right. I just want to take a shower." She shouldn't have said that, not to a soldier. She tried again, "I mean, I'll eat in my room."

"No problem. How's the work going? You people going to have Dalton looking as good as he wants to?"

She had no intention of talking to him about anything professional. She said, "I don't suppose Dalton will ever 'look as good as he wants to,' do you?"

A honk sounded. Then another. Then a horn blared continuously.

Quantrell spun the wheel in his hand, swearing like a dockworker. Jenny grabbed the doorhandle and closed her eyes. She heard her own voice demanding. "What is it? What is it?" as she felt the minivan lurch and veer sharply, as if it had gone off the road. Horns were still blaring. One of them, from its volume, was theirs.

When she opened her eyes, they were on the sandy shoulder, and another car was skewed sideways in front of them, so close their blunt nose was nearly in contact with the other car's passenger door.

Quantrell said grimly, "Wait here."

He got out and stalked toward the other car. The other driver was out of his car, as well.

Jenny, shaking all over, got out, too.

Quantrell heard her door open and looked over his shoulder: "I said, stay in the car."

She'd lost her sunglasses somewhere. It was so bright she could barely see the other men, two of them, who'd come from the other car.

Then one of them came over to her.

"Come with me, madam?" said a big man in a plaid shirt. His voice was accented, but at least it was English.

"I'm not going—"

"Jenny," Quantrell's voice called, "It's okay."

The man walked her over to Quantrell, who had his hands on his hips and was talking to someone who was about his height, with pale, crewcut hair.

"Jenny, I guess you remember Gaspar Larka, from the party." Quantrell was biting off his words. He looked as if he were about to explode in violence at any instant.

She thought, *This isn't just a traffic accident.* She took her cue from Quantrell: "Hello, Mr. Larka."

"Jenny Land," Larka said with a nod. "We are sorry about the . . . accident. If there's anything we can do to make your stay in Cairo more pleasant, you'll let us know."

"I—certainly will." *What the hell was this?* "But we're not hurt. At least, I'm not hurt. I don't think we need to report this—"

Everyone looked at her.

"Exactly," Larka said. "Good. Quantrell, again, I give apologies for the abruptness. You will pass on the message to your people: whatever we can do, unofficially. This is clear. And to you, Mrs. Land?"

"I don't know who you think I—"

"Jenny, say yes." Quantrell told her as if he were ordering a dog to heel.

"Yes," she said.

"Good. Then, if there is no damage to your vehicle, we will see you later."

Quantrell began, "Larka—"

"At the Camel's Eye, we will drink a toast to stupid orders, okay?" Larka said, and turned his back on Quantrell to go back to his car.

Then the man beside her returned to his car and Quantrell spun her by the elbow, nearly pushing her toward the minivan. Larka started his car and backed it off the shoulder onto the road in a cloud of dust that choked her and made her eyes tear.

She had to fumble for the doorhandle when they reached the minivan. Quantrell put his hands on her waist to help her up into her seat.

"I can do it."

Wordlessly, the big man went around to his side.

When they were both in their seats, Quantrell started backing the van onto the road, his face grim. The tires spun. He rocked the vehicle carefully, door open, head out, watching the tires.

When the minivan started rolling backwards, he slammed the door shut. "You ought to tell people if you're going to be the target of Soviet messengers," he said. "I'd have had my goddamned gun on me." He reached down and checked something under his seat.

"I'm not a—"

"Right. But don't forget to tell your husband that the Soviets are offering unofficial aid where your satellite's concerned."

"*My* satellite? That message was for Dalton," she flared. "You heard that Larka person. Where *is* Dalton, anyway?"

"I don't know." Quantrell let the wheel spin through his fingers and accelerated the minivan into traffic. "I thought you might know. I haven't seen him since the party." Quantrell was very angry, or very worried.

Jenny said, "Maybe I ought to go back and wait for my husband."

"That's a good thought." Quantrell indicated the car phone. "Call and make sure Chan knows you're coming back. I don't think I want to be responsible for you all by myself."

She wasn't sure if Quantrell's remark was meant to be funny. He bared his teeth, but the expression wasn't anything like a friendly smile.

23

Day 11: Southern Israel

It was after midnight, and Dalton Ford was in an Israeli facility with Meri Soukry. The damned helicopter that had come to get them had underflown radar, had run without lights, and bristled with countermeasures the Israelis weren't about to let him see. He'd been brought here blindfolded, after a discussion with Meri held at full shout in the chopper's wash.

It was bad enough finding out the woman was a Mossad agent, but this was getting nasty. There was something very disorienting about being led, blind and helpless, off the chopper, along what felt like dirt, then down a flight of stairs and through endless corridors. He knew he wasn't a prisoner. Meri had explained the conditions for this trip to him and he'd agreed. But the reality could shake you.

Here he was, in a room somewhere within the Israeli border, having a chat with people whom the Egyptians still considered their deadliest enemy, peace agreement or not. If it got back to anybody in Cairo that he'd even been spirited over the border, his butt was going to get kicked, hard. He might even be booted out of the country, especially with half the people he knew still suspecting him of committing some techno-blunder that might yet result in World War III. Did Meri care?

No, she did this all the time. No one ever found out, she'd said with that amazing smile. It was hard on your ego when a woman ran rings around you, Ford was finding out. Christ, he'd slept with her before he knew who and what she was. He ought to be able to handle her better, now, not worse.

But now Ford was faced with Mossad officers trying to find out how much he knew about Bright Star, *HE-12*, the Cosmos 2100, the DefCon bump and American-Soviet relations in general, while pretending to be interested in giving him more RPV recon data.

How'd he gotten himself into this?

There were three Mossad men in the room, clustered behind an old wooden desk opposite Ford's chair, plus a major from AMAN (Agaf Modiin), Israeli Defense Forces' Military Information Bureau, leaning against a wall papered with maps. And Meri Soukry, of course, lounging against a bank of chipped filing cabinets, who was holding her own, if this was an exercise to see who could get the most out of him while giving the least.

The RPV reconnaissance photos on the desk in front of him were exactly the sort of thing he'd initially asked for—more of what Meri'd given him in her hotel room. And of no more use.

Everybody in here knew it as well as he did.

But they were waiting for him to start the bidding.

"This isn't doing me much good," Ford said to the AMAN major. "I'm looking for something suspicious, something your people would have flagged anyway. You're giving me everything but."

"Everything is suspicious to us. You asked for specific locations," said the major, who ought to be on an Israeli recruiting poster: one of those Slavic or Soviet Jews who didn't look anything like the stereotype. "If you are looking for classified intelligence, then you'll have to be more forthcoming about what sort of problem you are expecting to have. We are always finding something sufficiently remarkable about movements of men and machines beyond our borders to classify them. If you want PLO troop movements, then—"

From behind the desk, a Mossad officer held up a hand and the AMAN major stopped speaking in midsentence. The Mossad representative was the only one besides Ford in the room who had a chair to sit in. He'd shown Ford some

pretty impressive credentials, and he looked exactly like the
stereotype: his name was Gazit and he wasn't more than five
foot five, with cocker spaniel eyes and rubbery lips in an
olive face.

"Let us stop fencing, eh? We, none of us, have much time
left, Mr. Ford." As he spoke, the lips quirked as if in amusement, but the eyes were sorrowful and guarded: "Mr. Ford,
what we have that might fit your description—oddities—are
data relating to the north of Israel, not the south. We don't
know if you'll be interested in such matters. While we," he
shrugged philosophically, "are always interested in anything
that might affect the security of Israel as a whole."

"And, of course, there's the west," said Meri, shifting
against the filing cabinet, one hip cocked. "The west is interesting this season."

"The west is always interesting to Americans," one of Gazit's
two underlings added. Neither had been introduced to him, and
neither wore uniforms. One wore a T-shirt that said Coca-Cola
in Arabic; the other, a denim jacket.

"This American's only interested in certain areas to the north
and west of Israel during certain very specific time frames,"
Ford declared. It was difficult to ask for what he wanted without confirming for the Israelis much of what they probably
already knew but couldn't verify about American overhead
capabilities.

Everyone, including Meri Soukry, stared at Ford.

Ford actually squirmed in his seat. He wanted their help.
Hell, he needed their help. But if he wasn't careful, he was
so far out on a limb here that the Israelis could control him
for the rest of his life by simply threatening to saw it off. He
wasn't in a position to decide what kind of information could be
swapped, and they ought to know it. Probably did know it.

He looked at Meri in near desperation. She'd set this up.
She set him up. A few hours ago, she'd been soft and warm
and hungry under him. He couldn't make it jibe in his head. He
kept thinking about famous cases of American spies caught in
sex traps, who ended up giving away the store and telling themselves it was for the benefit of all the nations involved. . . .

"Go on, Mr. Ford," said Gazit.

He almost asked to call his embassy. It was a gut reaction; he wanted Adamson's okay. Wanted *somebody's* okay, because, on reflection, Adamson wasn't the right guy.

He could call Leo. Beckwith would back him, even if he overstepped a little. . . . *Hi, Admiral. It's Ford, and I'm in Israel. The Mossad guys I'm with want me to tell them exactly what I need, and so does their girl superagent, and I'd really like to do that sir, but do you think I'd be endangering our security if I were to ask for everything covered by the HE-12 ground tracks? How about if I draw a little circle on one of their maps, just what we lost coverage on, and what we still can't cover, and . . .*

No way. He simply couldn't do it. Not even if he'd thought he was in love—which he didn't—or that doing it would give him exactly what he needed. Maybe he didn't know what he needed.

"Look, eleven days ago, we had a transmission interrupt in your area." That was as far as Ford was willing to go. Now, be careful. "Anything 'suspicious' by your standards that occurred—any damn where in the whole of MESA . . . Middle East–South Asia—that you people have flagged will be of interest to me."

"Now, Mr. Ford, we can begin to help you," said Gazit warmly. He looked like a crocodile climbing onto one of those Nile mudbanks with a fish in his mouth as he leaned forward, his eyes heavy lidded. "Is there a . . . secondary time frame of interest?"

So they knew all about the Soviet Cosmos, or at least they knew enough to infer the rest. "Yeah, I'd like to correlate it with any similar oddity that might have occurred when the Soviets lost that satellite of theirs, what—four, five days ago. Twenty-four hours after the events ought to be the time limit."

The AMAN major scratched his head and squinted at Ford. "So the north is okay for your purposes?"

"I'd like to see what you've got."

As if Ford had said the magic word, both the Mossad men behind Gazit leaned down, conferred with their boss, and left the room.

Meri had to get out of their way. She came to stand beside
him and touched his shoulder for a moment. Then squeezed
it. Then let go.

Dalton Ford couldn't have said at that moment, whether, if
he had the chance, he'd fuck her or kill her. But at least *she*
seemed to think things were going well.

Gazit was saying, "You're a smart man, Mr. Ford. We have
a few minutes before my people come back with a file or two
for you to look at. What do you think the Soviets have to
gain by rattling their sabers at the same time they're sniffling
around, hoping to get out of you people all the data on your—
lamented—satellite loss?"

"I . . . damned if I know." Phew, if he ever got out of this
alive, Ford was going to buy a fishing rod, a cabin in Montana,
and live off the land. He'd pension out. He wouldn't even have
a phone, let alone a computer or a downlink.

"Dalton," Meri Soukry said, settling herself on the corner
of Gazit's desk as if he were her uncle or some such, "we
want to help, this I've told you. Surely you know something
which can help us. What you're about to see is very disturbing to us. The Palestinians have a great deal of money right
now, and many friends. They are massing and they are moving—"

"Enough," said Gazit, and Meri stopped. She shrugged;
Gazit shrugged.

It was so similar a gesture that Ford began to seriously consider the possibility that the two were related. But what difference did it make? He had to get through this without doing
the wrong thing or saying anything he shouldn't. Even if she
was the daughter of the head of Mossad, she was still a woman
he'd slept with, drunk and sober, and a woman he'd trusted to
blindfold him and bring him here.

If he didn't trust her as much now as before, then he was
saying he didn't trust his own judgment. Damn, he was beginning to wish he'd never come. "Palestinians? The last thing
I'm worried about is Palestinians."

"PLO." Gazit spat the initials.

"Well, that's different," Ford said as if he believed it. "But
you've got to remember, sir, that I'm involved in a high-tech

sort of job, and that low-tech enemies aren't my . . . specialty. I can't foresee any scenario in which Palestinians would figure—"

"See?" Soukry swiveled on the desk. "His is Space Command, as I said. A communications jock. A software merchant. He doesn't understand that the PLO are a widespread group of thugs, in many nations, employing the men and methods of many nations. . . . You have to be one of us to know that."

Gazit looked up at her and shook his head, slowly. "Meri, Meri, this is no reason to become upset. Your feelings for your friend blind you. He will see what we have. It will be useful, or it will not. We ourselves don't know quite what the data we have collected signify. But some of it is not, as you Americans say, 'low-tech.' Not at all."

Ford said miserably, "Sir, I wasn't implying that you're running a low-tech operation. I just want you to realize that I can't do much but pass along information, at best. And the information I need is highly specialized."

"Like who might have benefited from nearly total lack of surveillance at specific times. Yes, you have made yourself clear, Mr. Ford. We understand your needs. I wish you understood ours as well." The big, brown eyes of Gazit seemed to bore into his soul.

Ford couldn't think of a damned thing to say. He was going to get Jesse to take him on one of his SAG's training jumps. He needed to come to grips with real enemies, like air streams and gravity.

To break an uncomfortable silence, Meri Soukry said, "So, Arik, tell our friend, while we're waiting, to beware of Yousef Seti. It will have more weight, coming from you."

"Seti?" Gazit frowned.

"Sarwat Hatim. Seti's his work name," Meri clarified.

"That snake?" Gazit's tongue flicked out, as if to get the taste of an enemy from the air. "Hatim is a player of the old school: If he were trustworthy, we would not need to be so close to him."

So where did that leave Ford? "I understand. Thanks for the warning. Look, I've got to be back before dawn. Maybe we could see what's holding them up out there?"

"I'll go," Meri said and she left Ford alone with the old man.

"An amazing woman, yes?" said Gazit when the door closed behind her.

"I'll give you that, yeah."

"Are you angry that you were tricked? This is not Cincinnati, my friend from the Space Command. This is not the Boy Scouts. We had to vet you."

"I'm not complaining."

"Ah, you think her methods are unacceptable? Men have different strengths." Again, the shrug. "She could not very well accomplish male bonding at a massage parlor, or challenge you to a wrestling match. Don't judge us, Mr. Ford, by—"

The door opened. Meri stopped on the threshold. Behind her were the two Mossad men. She said, looking first at Ford and then at Gazit, "SPOT's down."

"*What?*" Ford said, coming out of his chair. "Jesus. I've got to get back."

Gazit was calmer. "Sit down, Mr. Ford. We have your data for you. Meri will get you back, with a fine cover story we shall concoct to cover your absence. Now, you'll appreciate what it is to have a woman for a contact."

Ford's mind was reeling. Meri came over and crouched by his chair. Behind her, the Mossad men hurried with their folders to the desk.

"What do you think?" she breathed. Her eyes were too bright.

"Damned if I know."

Then something occurred to Ford: "Sir," he said to Gazit. "Would you agree that this is a time to put your people on special alert? I could get on the phone and get the exact tracks SPOT was covering for us." Excitedly, he detailed what he wanted the Israelis to do.

24

Day 11: Homs Gap, Syria

Fouad Aflaq was jubilant. Now he had truly done it. He had destroyed the most valuable spaceborne asset of his personal enemy, the repellent French homosexuals. Success after success after success.

Outside the ground station, he stared up at the sky, shivering with triumph. Who would have thought that he could have come so far, so far? *Allahu Akbar*. They sky was cloudy, another gift from Allah the Merciful. All the better for the troops moving about this evening.

The troops would scurry among the shadows and the hills, and do their jobs, as he had done his job.

When they were finished with their work, everyone would celebrate. The whole world would be a better place.

Tomorrow, Aflaq himself would celebrate. Tomorrow, he would be basking in the sun and eating in fine restaurants on Cyprus. Tonight, he must only prepare the station to function without him. Then he could leave for his rendezvous on Cyprus with his compatriots, where the planning for the last phase of this great undertaking would be finalized.

Tomorrow—yes, basking in the sun and eating stuffed grape leaves and washing them down with the praise of his fellows. Soon enough, the entire Arab world would know his name and revere him as a liberator.

For a while longer, he must keep his profile low.

Aflaq raised his hands once, to the heavens which now were the province of God once again, and not the spying eyes of his enemies. Someday, all such eyes would be blind. Today, only the most crucial ones must be plucked from the skies.

One of the finest and most appropriate details of this battle against the infidels was that, if you really thought about it, you were stoning them, blinding their eyes, plucking those eyes out.

He went inside, to put a trusted junior in charge of the nominal tracking functions of the ground station and to order the place spiffed up for the upcoming visit by his peers, who would come back here with him from Cyprus.

Theirs was a visit which would mean triumph was at hand at last.

25

Day 12: Kirtland AFB, New Mexico

"You're sure you want to do this, Leo?" Pollock asked before he fastened his oxygen mask.

"Sure as I've ever been about anything, Pollock. If you can't take me for a ride in this thing and convince me that it—and you—are mission-capable, then neither of you are going anywhere near the Middle East."

"Yessir, sir," said Pollock, and put his nose in his oxygen mask. At least his expression wouldn't be readable from now on, or any time during the ensuing flight.

Admiral Beckwith looked somehow ludicrous, sitting there beside him in a flight helmet and pressure suit. Maybe distress orange wasn't the admiral's color. Or maybe, Pollock thought, it was just that Leo looked his age today.

Pollock had to stifle the impulse to reach over and check the other man's equipment. This was almost as bad as having the Old Man—CINCSPACE—in the cockpit with him. Maybe Pollock should count his blessings that it wasn't CINCSPACE he was joyriding.

If Pollock was an old man, Beckwith was positively geriatric. The admiral really had no business in the cockpit of the X-NASP, but you couldn't tell the brass anything. As long as Beckwith didn't demand to fly X-NASP, Pollock had to go along, because Beckwith wasn't really pushing the envelope of privilege.

Pollock started his final checks, talking to Kirtland Control and wondering if this sudden need of Beckwith's to ride in the space plane had anything to do with SPOT going down like that.

Perhaps Beckwith was serious about letting Pollock take X-NASP to the Middle East. Pollock hoped so. All this money and all this capability wasn't going to do anybody any good sitting on the ground in a guarded hangar.

One of the 9th Strategic Air Wing's TR-1 tactical reconnaissance aircraft had been dispatched to Cairo West from RAF Alconbury; but the TR-1 was slow, and it took nearly five hours to complete its circuit on station at ninety thousand feet, covering six hundred nautical miles in surveillance mode. The advanced tactical fighters on carriers deployed in the Bright Star area had the opposite problem: they were too fast to do detailed surveillance, even if they had their gun replaced by a GPS navigation satellite receiver. And, worse, because they flew low, they were provocative. Nobody wanted a shoot-down. The Saudis had added their E-3A AWACS to the data-collection system, but the AWACS had nine monitoring stations each: too many privy parties for security, especially when those parties were Arabs, moderate or not. And the dome-carrying planes were such lucrative targets, and so recognizable, that CENTCOM was as hesitant to use the Saudi aircraft as the Saudis were to become deeply involved in whatever this was at so early a date.

So that left Space Command holding the proverbial bag: if you didn't want to use low-flying aircraft, and you didn't want to use slow-moving aircraft, and you didn't want to use much in the way of local talent, that left you pitifully few options.

You had tac sats, relay sats, photo-reconnaissance sats and downlinks. And you had the hot stuff. Most of the hot stuff was evaluated at Falcon's National Test Facility, the core of the National Test Bed of SDI. When you had something too superhot to test at Falcon, you pretended it was a "simulation and computer evaluation," and tested it from Kirtland's black facility. Of all the hot stuff, the X-NASP was the hottest.

Leo Beckwith was about to find that out.

When Kirtland tower cleared him for takeoff, Pollock asked

Beckwith one more time: "You're sure about this, sir?"

"Fly the plane, Colonel."

"Yes, sir."

Pollock let the g force of takeoff do the rest of his talking for him. X-NASP made you reassess yourself, the universe, and what human bodies could tolerate in the way of stresses, every time you flew her.

Not just Pollock, but every other X-NASP pilot he'd talked to as well, nearly lost it on takeoff: you saw little dancing lights; the edges of your vision got blurry, then dark, then darker. Your chest hurt and you didn't even think about turning your head; you thought about breathing.

That was why X-NASP had an Associate electronic copilot, an artificial-intelligence, computer-managed "expert system" which was supposed to bail you out if you passed out, execute voice commands if need be, and generally make sure that the plane made it home even if you didn't.

There were still glitches in the voice-command stuff: your voice did funny things when you were stressed enough, and high-g takeoff stress wasn't something your body reacted to exactly the same way each time.

So Pollock liked to fly the plane as much as he could, and not just sit there like a passenger trusting the technology to fly it for him. You learned to function in various states of altered consciousness, if you flew high-powered aircraft for a living. If you flew testbeds, the way Pollock had for nearly five years, you learned to do what you needed to do when you could barely remember your name.

But you never learned to do it and keep up your patter with a passenger. You talked to the plane, you talked for the cockpit recorder, you talked to ground control . . . you didn't worry too much about what you said.

So Pollock forgot all about Beckwith, and Bright Star, and SPOT, until he started leveling off high above the cloud layer. "Stratospheric conditions optimal for lidar test," he told those recording below and the box recording onboard, and started the procedure that would make his lidar work.

"Lidar?" somebody croaked from beside him.

Then, finally, Pollock remembered Beckwith. "Lidar on,"

Pollock confirmed. Lidar worked like radar, but used light instead of radio waves. "Right there at four o'cock, sir, is the display."

Beckwith grunted as he moved his head to look.

It really hurt your neck, coming up through that much atmosphere that fast. Pollock sympathized.

"See the heat shield, Leo?"

There was still some glow on X-NASP's nose.

But Beckwith wasn't looking at either the lidar screen or the space plane's nose. He was looking out and down, at the Earth.

Shit. Pollock had forgotten: Beckwith had never flown in a hypersonic of any kind, had probably never been higher than about sixty thousand feet. They were at nearly twice that altitude. You could really see the Earth's curvature.

Suddenly he thought he understood why Beckwith had been so eager to hitch a ride: the admiral had been working his heart out on these space-related projects for a long, long time, and he'd never gotten up here before.

Hell, here was where it all made sense. You had to be up here to really understand what you were fighting for. You had to see it with your own eyes. And X-NASP was the only way someone like Beckwith would ever see it: too old for the shuttle, he could have cut his own ticket only during some sort of emergency like this, where everyone was too busy to ask any questions, where whatever had to be done got done, and nobody cared about much but end results.

Finally, Pollock wasn't worried about what Beckwith had in mind; or resentful that some old guy with clout was abusing the privilege of rank: the admiral had a right to be up here, if anybody did.

"Sir, did you want to talk to me about anything?" Pollock asked. He could hear Beckwith's heavy breathing in his comm system; he hoped the admiral wasn't going to punk out on him.

That was all he'd need. If Beckwith died of a heart attack or something up here, then what?

But Beckwith said, "Yeah, I sure do, son. I want to know whether you really consider yourself deployable on this Bright Star thing."

"Deployable? You bet. Or do you mean, do I really consider the space plane deployable? Because I sure do—we ought to use her for something, sir. She's not meant to sit in a hangar until she's obsolete enough for a public rollout."

Beckwith coughed, or snorted. Then he coughed again. "Okay, you've convinced me." His voice was very soft. "Or looking out there's convinced me. Did you go back that extra month, checking the commercial launch manifests the way I asked you?"

Surprised, Pollock said, "Yeah, but you might want to remember we're recording, both down on the ground and in-cockpit."

"Right; I understand. You'll give me what you got when we get back on the ground."

There'd be plenty of time, on the ground, to explain to Beckwith that once Pollock had gone back the additional month, through all logged commercial launches, he'd found a Priane Space customer who was on CIA's list of companies who'd bought corundum from a particular West German supplier. Although Pollock hadn't been inclined to give CIA's Al Nesbitt the fruits of his labor, he'd be glad to give Beckwith the name of a telecommunications company with offices in Syria and Iraq, as well as Egypt and Libya. Then all Space Command had to do was get some Cray time to crunch enough numbers to prove that a putative telecommunications satellite, launched commercially, could have laid the sort of low-tech space mines Leo Beckwith was postulating, so that CIA would have a model to work with in their investigation.

Right now, Pollock had more important things to attend to. Beckwith's breathing really was labored.

"Can I check your oxygen mix, Admiral?"

Pollock started playing flight attendant, as best he could, telling the Associate package in his helmet, "Take over. Maintain present speed and heading."

It was time he started letting the Associate tend to X-NASP. He needed to test seriously that part of the system one more time: if he was taking X-NASP on a mission, he might need the Associate's capabilities.

26

Day 12: Cairo

Jesse Quantrell was slipping through the predawn murk, and betting himself an *ahweh*—a Turkish coffee—at Fash Awi's that it was going to rain on his urban war game before morning.

Rain or not, Quantrell was hoping to sneak up on one of his commandos, thereby taking the man out of play, before the team found its target, an apartment above Madame Senouhi's on Opera Square.

The twelve-man team, made up of six Deltas and six Special Activities Group professionals, were doing pretty well. They'd already homed in, using two Special Forces pistol-grip location finders, on the transmitter Quantrell had hidden over the Leather Shop directly behind Fash Awi's long, narrow coffee shop, to the left of El Hussein Mosque on the square.

Now, if they could just avoid Quantrell, whose job was to pick them off before they got to Madame Senouhi's antiquities shop, they had plenty of time to go clean: find the apartment, sneak in surreptitiously, get the bag of coffee beans with three raw eggs inside, and carry it back to the waiting minivan without waking the neighborhood or alerting the local police. Or breaking an egg.

The three raw eggs were Quantrell's little surprise: if they broke an egg—which they probably would, because a sack of coffee wasn't a wounded American hostage, even though the note pinned to the bag said that the bag was just that—Quantrell was going to give them hell. One broken egg, so far as he was concerned, was aggravated wound trauma; two meant that the hostage represented by the bag had gone into a coma because of the team's rough handling; three meant that the hostage's neck was broken and the would-be rescuers had killed him while getting him to the minivan.

Since the team didn't know about the eggs, the chances of them treating the hostage-bag gently enough not to break even one were slim. But that was why you did urban games: to make it tough, not to make it fair. Quantrell had never been on an urban assignment, whether it was rescue or a payback, where the intelligence he'd had to work with had been anything like current.

So he always tried to make his exercises realistic. Which was why he was doing his damndest to capture at least one of his people before they got to the coffee sack representing the hostage. You always seemed to find, doing the real thing, that somebody got fouled up. One time, there'd been somebody waiting with a truck for them who'd been backing up, ripped the door off of another truck, and ended up at the local police station. Another time, in another place, somebody'd flat forgotten to take his travel papers; one time, a nervous buck sergeant had blown the entire Plan A of a covert operation because he was so jumpy that he hauled out his gun and waved it at a traffic cop who'd only wanted to give him a speeding ticket.

There are only so many things a Get Out of Jail Free card can do for you, and there was nothing one could do for you if the person you showed it to wouldn't honor it. Quantrell had seen things come apart because of the unforeseen too many times not to give his people the experience.

So he was sneaking up on his choice of targets, the "low-intensity conflict" man who'd done most of his training in the Pentagon basement, when somebody's hand came down on his shoulder.

Spun him around. Spat Arabic when he kicked at the shadow and went for the .357 Desert Eagle under his windbreaker. Yelled, "Freeze, Colonel!" in English. Shined a flashlight in his eyes.

Jesse Quantrell froze. If the hand holding that flashlight belonged to Mackenzie, the only one of the A team who spoke good Arabic, Quantrell was going to bust Captain Mackenzie's chops for this. If it was anyone else but their operations officer, he was going to do a hell of a lot worse . . .

"Mackenzie?"

"Colonel Quantrell, please come with us quietly."

Definitely not one of his people. The flashlight was still shining in his eyes. Professionals.

"Who's 'us'?" Give yourself a minute. They hadn't disarmed him yet.

Then a hand reached out, past the flashlight, and did just that. Somebody clucked in disapproval.

The first voice ordered, "Search him," in Arabic.

So he saw a face, finally—an indigenous face, attached to a slight body in plain clothes.

"Who are you?" Quantrell demanded; his voice was a croak because now his mouth was dry.

The flashlight's beam wavered. The man searching him stood up empty-handed, then held out ID: Egyptian intelligence.

What the fuck?

"Come quietly, please, Colonel."

"Okay. As soon as you give me my gun back." He was permitted for the Desert Eagle; he had all the right Egyptian ID. "I'm a friend of Yousef Seti's. Whatever this is, he's not going to like it if I tell him you guys stepped over the line." Maybe Quantrell should have said *friend of Sarwat Hatim's*. But no, he'd never heard anyone call Seti that but Meri Soukry, and now wasn't the time to see if she was right about Seti. Right now, Seti's was the heaviest name he could drop.

A huddle ensued; voices buzzed.

"Your gun? Perhaps later," said the first voice he'd heard. The flashlight bobbled as if the man were uncertain. "Orders. Please come now."

Quantrell sighed and shook his head pityingly at the flashlight. "You poor bastards are getting yourselves into some serious trouble, interfering with an interoperating American officer in performance of his Bright Star duties. But yeah, let's go get this straightened out."

In these Third World countries, whenever something like this happened, Quantrell always felt like Gulliver among the Lilliputians. The six men surrounding him were all so much shorter and lighter than he was, he probably could have knocked some heads together, thrown one fellow at those remaining upright, and gotten himself out of this without more than a moderate scuffle.

But then he'd have big problems. And he'd have lost the Desert Eagle, which had come through without serial numbers and of which he was inordinately fond.

So he went with the little guys to their black Peugeot, and when he got in the nonregulation car, he started wondering if this might have anything to do with the French, because the car was French. The French were all upset about SPOT, and there still were plenty of Frog heavies playing Egyptian politics.

SPOT was only the latest in a long string of screwups that might be at the heart of this. Another one, Quantrell thought morosely as he was joined in the car's back seat by two Egyptians in polyester suits, was Meri Soukry.

Meri Soukry was one screwup that Quantrell was finding hard to forgive, or forget. The way she'd gone flouncing off with Ford like that had really hurt. Even though Jesse's mind understood that Ford was probably just as much a part of her job as he'd been, it hurt.

Jesse Quantrell had never in his life been with a woman remotely like Anu Meri Soukry. He'd been having fantasies of being with her a whole lot more. He'd written up the contact, like he was supposed to whenever he interacted with a member of a foreign intelligence service, but he'd left out the best part because he'd been hoping there'd be more best parts.

So maybe, he told himself, this wasn't a roust at all, just Soukry using her friends in Egyptian intelligence to bring him to a rendezvous. . . . Jesus, he did have it bad for that woman.

Well, it didn't look they were going anywhere but the main headquarters of Egyptian intelligence; he could see that much out the window. So it was probably just a screwup, some kind of problem he could solve when somebody told him what the hell was going on.

These guys couldn't, or wouldn't if they could. He knew better than to ask. He sat quietly, all pumped up with no way to vent, and catalogued the scenarios running in his head. Mackenzie's A team was going to go clean, or nearly clean, depending on whether any of the eggs broke.

He ought to try to think about whatever this was in the same light.

But it felt wrong. It felt real, and everything on this Cairo trip was supposed to be make-believe: exercises and games. You could break your leg out here, or your back if you were in a wreck or your chute streamed, or get yourself shot if you were extremely stupid—but those were just normal risks. You could do that at any American base.

This felt real. His gut knew real when it felt it; everything was looking different, because Quantrell's gut was absolutely convinced that he was in trouble.

The air itself looked different: clearer, deeper; he had more depth of field and he could see bits of dirt and specks of dust in the car's running lights. His body was in its customary fight-or-flight mode: he didn't have an ache or a pain, anywhere on his person; a remarkable state accessible to him only in combat-readiness, these days.

When the car stopped before the headquarters of Egyptian intelligence, as he'd thought it would, and the little guys herded him inside and deposited him in an empty interrogation room without a word, he was ready, he thought, for whatever the hell this was.

And then he had to sit there, in a wooden chair, looking at an empty wooden desk, bolted to the floor, whose drawers were locked shut. Sometime during the wait it struck him that maybe the DefCon had bumped to four. If so, and Egypt didn't want any American presence or any part in an American-Soviet conflict, that could explain this. Maybe. Sort of.

Jesus, he didn't want to play nuclear war. It wasn't any fun. There was no skill in it, and nobody could win. Jesse Quantrell was categorically against no-win situations.

When finally the door opened and a fat Egyptian in shirt-sleeves waddled in with a file under his arm, Quantrell shot out of his seat.

"Sit down, Colonel. We're sorry for the abruptness of all this. But, you understand, we have questions." The fat guy had a moon face and bad teeth. He sat down behind the wooden desk.

It didn't sound like a nuclear alert was under way and the Egyptians were booting the Americans out of the country. "You've got my gun, for which I have a valid permit. I'm a friend of Yousef Seti's. Does that name ring a bell?"

The fat guy actually winced: "Please do not jump to conclusions, Colonel. You will not need to talk to Mr. Seti. We can handle this among ourselves."

Great: "I'm going to want to talk to someone, before I talk any more to you. Like the American embassy." He began to give Adamson's phone number.

The Egyptian held up his hand, and a huge pinky ring caught the light.

"Do you know, Colonel Quantrell, the whereabouts of a Mr. Dalton Ford, one of your fellow Americans?"

"Fucking Ford!" So it was Ford that this was about. That meant it was Ford who'd spoiled his team's urban training session. And it was Ford who'd ruined Quantrell's warm, fuzzy fantasies about Meri Soukry. "Hell, I haven't seen Ford since . . . Seti's party."

"Then perhaps it would be of interest to you to know that your friend Ford has been in Israel."

"So? What do I care where Ford is?" This was not sounding good.

"You know, I'm sure, that we watch all travelers who are coming from Israel, or going to Israel, from our territory. But you may not have known that your friend, Dalton Ford, has gone out of this country into Israel illegally, with the help of those pigs from the Mossad, and that we have it on good authority that Ford was in Israel with his Mossad contacts as recently as yesterday."

"Why are you telling me this?" He barely got out the words. If Meri was with Ford, then Ford had blown her cover, from the sound of it. If that was the case and she came back into this country, she could be executed by the Egyptians.

If that happened, Jesse Quantrell was going to shoot Ford himself. It was only fair.

". . . also ought to know," said the Egyptian intelligence officer, "because you are such a good friend to Egypt and because Yousef Seti desires that you know it, that we are nearly sure that Ford's compatriots, the Lands, are CIA spies, loosed clandestinely upon our country using Bright Star as a cover. So you can see, Colonel, that the situation is very sensitive."

Sensitive enough that Seti wouldn't come himself? Quantrell still didn't quite get it. "What does all this have to do with me?"

"We wish to find your friend, Dalton Ford."

"I can't help you. I don't know where he is."

"Then perhaps some of your fellow soldiers, those you were stalking tonight, whom we have also apprehended and detained, will be able to tell us."

"Shit, you didn't arrest my—" He stopped himself.

"Bright Star, Colonel Quantrell, is an interoperating exercise of military nature. It is not, officially, an exercise that extends into Cairo itself. Yes, indeed, we arrested your Captain Mackenzie and his cohorts. We're not sure whether we will charge them with breaking and entering, or simply turn them over to your military police."

"*Get me Seti!*" Quantrell came out of his chair again. The next thing he knew, he was in the Egyptian's face, with only the desk between them to remind Quantrell that if he touched this fat, greasy bastard, he might have real problems.

He started strangling the lip of the desk instead. "Get Seti now, or get me my embassy. Whatever you think you've trumped up, it's not going to hold water, Mr. Noname."

"Sit down, Colonel Quantrell," said the fat man, who'd finally realized that Quantrell was close enough, and mad enough, that calling for help couldn't get him out of danger quickly enough.

"I want. My. People"—Did the Egyptian have all twelve? Better not risk it—"out of jail, and in here, and telling me they're all right. And I want my goddamn weapon back. Then I'll skip official apologies through channels. Otherwise, buddy, you'd better be ready to kill me on the spot to avoid repercussions, because I'm going to make the rest of your career—however short it is—a living hell."

Quantrell ought to have known that something was seriously wrong as soon as the fat guy walked in without identifying himself. But you miss little things like that when you've been sitting around in an empty room for a while. Damn, he should have been ready for this.

But he hadn't been. And now he had to wing it.

The Egyptian scrambled out of range. The chair he'd been sitting in scraped across the floor as he made for the door, folder clutched tight. He stormed out and slammed the door shut behind him.

Quantrell didn't even try it when it closed to see if it was locked.

He paced around and snarled at the walls until Mackenzie and the other eleven members of his crestfallen A team showed up.

"Wait over there." Quantrell pointed behind the desk. "Don't talk. We'll be out of this in a minute."

Then the weapons arrived, and apologies by somebody thin and harried looking, who carried them in so gingerly you'd have thought that the guns would go bang on their own.

"Mackenzie, make sure your electronics are all here too."

The lank, ash blond Delta captain got up and started apportioning the gear before the thin Egyptian had left the room.

"Hey, you," Quantrell said to the Egyptian. "Where's your fat friend? Where's Seti? Where's my damned phone call?"

"I know nothing about anything, sir. I was told to give you your equipment and allow you to leave." He rolled his eyes heavenward. "*Inshallah.*"

"Yeah, *Inshallah* I don't find out who that fat bastard is."

But nobody would tell Quantrell that. And nobody would give him a phone to call Seti.

When he got the team out of there, Quantrell was calm enough to realize he ought to be glad he'd gotten the .357 back. A permit to carry was one thing; a piece with no serial numbers was another. He was lucky nobody'd looked closely.

You just walked down the headquarters steps and off into the 0500 mist, making sure you had all your people right there with you.

When they'd turned two corners and Quantrell was sure nobody was following them, he said, "Mackenzie, listen up: the next part of this urban exercise involves apprehending three Americans. We'll apologize to them when it's over. It's more realistic that way, and they're friends of mine."

Quantrell wasn't really sure he had the balls to give those orders until they came out of his mouth. "When we get back to Cairo West, I'll get you dossier photos on the AmCits: Dalton Ford and a couple named Land."

Maybe Quantrell would never see the fat little Egyptian again, to get revenge. But revenge was a big word. And Quantrell was seriously pissed.

The SPOT thing was all over the papers, Ignatov hadn't been seen in the Camel's Eye or anywhere since Seti's party; Larka had dropped out of sight after the incident with Jenny Land on the road. And Ford decides to go to Israel, leaving the goddamn Lands, husband and wife spook team, on their own.

No other single man could manage to cause so much trouble and then be out of harm's way when the shit hit the fan. This time, Ford was going to take his own heat. And so were Chandler Land and his tight-assed wife.

Quantrell could forgive many things, but not this. His relations with the Egyptians were at an all-time ebb because of Dalton Ford.

If he could have found Ford that night, or the Lands, he'd have cheerfully wrung any of their necks.

But he and his team could turn up neither hide nor hair of those three, no matter how hard they looked.

27

Day 12: Kwajalein Atoll

Lieutenants Phil Young and Allie Porter met on the steps of the SOI (space object identification) facility as they were both coming off duty.

The sun was going to come up in a few minutes. The sky over Kwajalein was velvet black and royal purple with rents of gold and red between the clouds.

"That was one fine night's work," Young said as Allie came down the last step.

"I guess," she agreed with a tired smile.

Young fell in beside her. The anomaly that she'd found when *Hawkeye* went down was known far and wide as the Porter Fleck. It made him proud.

He reached for her hand and tugged on her arm, guiding her toward the beach instead of toward quarters.

Tonight the two of them had been part of a massive effort to make up for the SPOT loss, at least so far as Bright Star was concerned. In concert with CSOC in Colorado, Maui, and the Ascension Island tracking and telemetry stations, they'd gotten the newly launched Space Command tac sat into a make-shift circuit that included a Tracking and Data Relay Satellite (TDRS), elements of the Global Positioning System (GPS) satellite constellation, and a repositioned Block 17 satellite formerly targeted on the Persian Gulf.

"I guess those downlink jocks at Bright Star'll have just what they need, now that we have some working sensors," Young said lamely. Work wasn't what he wanted to talk about—not tonight. But how did you get started?

"I guess. You did a great job, Phil." The sunrise was beginning to saturate the darkness with color; he could almost make out the tones of her skin; her cheek was washed in lavender as they walked toward the beach.

They had to pass between two old wooden structures that were now used for storage. In the middle of the alleyway, where it was still totally dark, Young screwed up his courage:

"Hey, Allie, what do you think: are we going to have a war?"

"God, I hope not. All this . . . we're almost out of the woods. Almost to where we can keep from blowing ourselves up."

He couldn't see her face, but he felt her lean closer. He put his arms out and she was there. He could feel her heart pounding against him as he held her.

"I know," he said. "It seems so stupid, sometimes. All this technology, all this ability, and we still can't seem to get it right."

"We can; I know we can. A little longer, that's all we need. Then we'll have enough of a tech base to make mutually enforced peacekeeping a reality . . . if we've got a little longer."

Her hair smelled like lemon soap against his nose. He closed his eyes. "It'll be okay," he told her, though he wasn't sure he believed it. "This is some kind of aberration, sure. But it's not the superpowers, it's something else. Some glitch. Some uncatalogued junk up there—"

"If it's not us and the Russians, then what is it? Some kind of orbital terrorism? Who's doing it, and why?" She shivered against him. "God, why can't people grow up?"

"I don't know," he said, and meant it. Then, finally: "Allie, will you marry me? Now? Right now? As soon as we can find somebody?"

Young felt a shiver run over her. Then she was perfectly still in his arms. "Because of the satellites?" she said at last. Her voice seemed tiny, like a child's voice.

He knew what she was asking. "Naw, well, sort of . . .

because I'm scared, a little, and that's made me realize I don't have forever. But I've been trying . . . I needed something to give me the courage to ask you. I kept . . . well, will you?"

"I . . ."

She pulled back against his arms. He let her go.

"Come out in the light and ask me," he heard her voice say.

He still had a hold on her wrist.

They walked out from between the buildings and into the sunrise. By now, it was like fire on the horizon, and the blue of the high sky made you want to cry.

All those colors spilled over her face. and her eyes were huge as he put both hands on her shoulders, held her at arm's length, and said solemnly, "Lieutenant Allison Porter, will you marry me?"

She blinked twice at him. Then her wicked grin began to spread across her face. "Lieutenant Phillip Young, I'd be delighted to marry you. I've been hoping to move to better quarters."

He burst out laughing and tried to grab her. She evaded him and ran toward the beach. He gave chase. There was no reason that they couldn't be married by the weekend, even if the DefCon stayed high. Or went higher.

Phil Young couldn't fix everything wrong up in orbit, but he could fix what was wrong with his own life.

Maybe it took a little jolt, once in while, to show you what mattered. Right now, coming out into the sunrise after sweating all night at his terminal, praying to the laws of nature that his equipment would work and everybody else's equipment would work, a girl and a sunrise—his girl, his sunrise—were just what he needed.

It was about time he snagged Allie Porter, before somebody else did. There wasn't a better radar operator in Space Command than the woman who'd just agreed to become his wife.

After a night of saving the world, he had a right to do something about his own future. Now if only satellites would stop dropping like flies, maybe he'd have a future.

Whatever was going on up there, whatever the Porter fleck really meant, at least now the brass trying to evaluate it would have decent data.

That was all that he and Allie, and everybody like them, could do to help: get the data up where wiser heads could evaluate it.

Chasing Allie down toward the beach in sunrise, Young simply couldn't believe that somewhere, somehow, with all this high technology and all the brainpower that the U.S. defense establishment could bring to bear, they couldn't get America through this crisis so that Mr. and Mrs. Young could raise some little Youngs.

After all, keeping space safe for satellites was what their jobs at Space Command were all about.

28

Day 12: The Syrian-Lebanese Border

An Israeli pilot was flying Meri Soukry over the Bekáa in a
Soviet MiG painted with Syrian markings and desert camouflage.

"I don't see anything," she said. Her voice sounded funny
in the helmet and oxygen mask.

The pilot said, "Hold on," and then her entire world tilted
forty degress to the right.

Her stomach came up in her throat and she nearly blacked
out.

"See? There. Three o'clock."

She tried to see what the pilot thought he was showing her,
but she could barely breathe. She shouldn't have insisted on
this overflight. But if she was going to pass such a message
to Dalton Ford, she wanted to make sure that the message was
based on truth, and not paranoia.

Photos and computer-generated reconnaissance could be
cooked. Elements in Mossad were not above tweaking their
data to get the Americans' attention. And when it was a
matter of troops and weapons in Lebanon, one had to be very
careful. Many Israelis in the business still blamed American
interference for the failure of the Israeli invasion of Lebanon
in the early eighties.

If Mossad was imagining or concocting the troop movements
it found so unusual, if the pilots were hallucinating what seemed

to them to be truck-mounted missile batteries of the sort that
could reach Israel, then Meri wanted to find out before it was
too late.

The fighter jet was diving—or crashing.

She wasn't sure which until the pilot, breathing heavily,
said, "See? There, under that netting."

If they were more than a hundred feet above the ground,
Meri would eat her passport.

She tried her best to see what the pilot wanted to show her.
Then she did see it: shapes nothing at all like bushes, but nestled in the foothills where bushes might be.

"Yes, I see—"

The rest of her words died in her throat as the pilot screamed
into what seemed like a forty-five-degree turn and headed for
the open sea. Either he was content that she'd had her in-person
glimpse, or he'd seen danger.

Whatever it had been, when the fog cleared from her vision,
they were over open water.

Once again, it struck her how small the area was they were
all trying so hard to protect. Or to destroy, if you were the
camouflaged troops.

She'd known she wouldn't see the troops move now, in broad
daylight, since they'd been doing so under cover of darkness,
and were well dug in to their positions. She'd been briefed by
Gazit's pet AMAN major, the pretty one who kept eyeing her,
the one who'd been at Ford's interview.

The MiG leveled off, and Meri looked out and down, on
the sparkling ocean where, for thousands of years, ships had
plied the coast, bearing pottery and oil and bolts of cloth from
ancient Kush all the way to Tyre and beyond.

This land had been contested so mightily, for so long, at
such great cost, that on her bad days she thought that it would
never stop, that the land itself had been cursed by the gods of
antiquity who once ruled over vanished city-states.

Once again, the city-states contested here. The troops whose
camouflaged bivouac she'd seen had mobile missile batteries
as well as conventional heavy artillery, according to AMAN.
According to Gazit, they were PFLP General Command commandos, augmented with the inevitable Libyans and—not so

inevitable—Iraqi units and weapons.

These regular troops from Iraq, Gazit was sure, signaled a different, more dangerous threat than any Israel had faced before. If Mossad was correct, and this mixed force signaled an escalation of the hard-line threat, then it was crucial that the Americans be informed and brought on board, so that Israel could secure American concurrence before it acted.

Otherwise, it would be like Beirut all over again. And the Israeli government, shaky at best, could not afford that. Not now.

But neither could one afford to be massacred.

So, as she listened to the pilot telling first the American Seventh Fleet and then Israeli ground controllers that he was not what he looked like—a Syrian MiG—but a logged reconnaissance flight, Meri prepared to face Gazit.

Yes, she would tell him she was satisfied. Yes, she would pass on the information to the Americans exactly as Gazit wished. Yes, she would do her best to convince at least Dalton Ford sufficiently that, when the Arab moderates started making excuses and spinning likely stories to explain away Israel's photographic evidence, those stories would not be believed.

If only Mossad could find a way to link the Americans' concerns more closely to Israel's, Meri would be more confident of Gazit's plan to assure American support for a preemptive strike.

But the only thing the Americans cared about was SPOT, right now. And no one in Mossad, no matter how hard they'd all tried, had been able to link Israel's troubles on the ground to the satellites winking out overhead like blown-out candles. Only the circumstances, so far, pointed to any connection between the heavens and the earth in this matter.

As her pilot changed course to give the exercising U.S. warships a wide berth, Meri could only hope that those circumstances—coupled with the fact that, in the first few hours of darkness after SPOT went blind, there was definitely troop movement along the ground tracks Dalton Ford had asked Mossad to watch—would be enough to convince the American agent of the connection.

Then it was up to Ford to convince his government. Meri

had enough trouble dealing with her own. At least she'd gotten Ford the information he wanted, and she'd have all the surveillance data to go with it: infrared and light-intensified photos, medium-range RPV sensor reconnaissance, all that Mossad had collected. Getting permission to give Ford such raw and sensitive intelligence had been a feat in itself.

But she had done it. Now it was his turn to do the impossible: make the Americans pay attention to something out here besides Bright Star.

For there to be even a chance of Ford doing such a thing, Meri Soukry had to survive a jet landing by a hot-dog pilot, report to her superiors, and sneak back into Egypt by nightfall to find Dalton and give him the information he'd requested, before he himself made his report.

29

"The Seventh Fleet offshore can't confirm your Israeli sighting, and none of my sensor data is showing anything, either," Chandler Land told Jay Adamson irritably. "Where'd you get this crap, anyhow?"

"Oh, around and about," said the CIA station chief, who looked even hotter and stickier than Land felt in the supposedly air-conditioned comm tent.

"Come on, Jay, don't pull this 'we don't reveal our sources' stuff with me. How am I supposed to evaluate this data? Any of these pictures could be faked, or years old—from the Israeli invasion of Lebanon, for all I can tell."

Behind Land, the Space Command ops officer for low-intensity conflict was oblivious, his ears in headphones. Even the youngster had made a sour face when he'd looked at the data that Adamson had brought in for Land's assessment.

"If that's your last word, Chandler," said Adamson mildly, "I'll have to video these back to Langley . . ."

"Where the experts can pore over them? You do that. I'm just out here to facilitate comms, not to make judgments on photo opportunities. You'd need a 'crate-ologist' to make anything of those pictures, and cratology may be a science, but it's inexact at best."

"I'm not asking you to tell my fortune, Chandler. I'm just asking you if, given that these pictures say what my contact

173

says they do, you think that there's any significance to these movements having occurred within six hours of SPOT—"

"If you guys are seriously looking for an excuse to take out Arabsat because you want a target for retaliation, I'm not going to be the fellow who gives it to you." Chandler Land stood up as straight as he could, then moved three steps to the left, closer to the apex of the tent so that he could stand tall and stretch. God, his back hurt.

"I'm not going to comment on any rumors, Chandler. You know I can't. But you've been around long enough to know that people are getting very upset about these overhead losses. The French ambassador chewed my ear off about us withholding pertinent information. Brisson's about to have kittens; he'd nearly talked the Egyptians into a lucrative, long-term contract to buy SPOT agricultural remote-sensing data. The Saudis are huddling with their Arab League buddies and won't talk to us about anything they may know. What can you expect?"

"My wife was right, I'm beginning to think: we never should have come here."

The young operations officer—the man who'd have been in the hot seat if Land didn't happen to be in Cairo—had told Chandler about the Arabsat rumor, which meant everybody was talking about it. Arabsat was a comsat, not a spysat, and one of the proudest possessions of the Arab moderates. Only an idiot would spread rumors threatening retaliation against a peaceful-applications satellite.

But Chandler Land's father had been fond of reminding him that there were more horses' asses in the world than there were horses.

"We're glad you're here, Chandler. Don't think your work is unappreciated." Jay Adamson had a thin neck and a long skull and a high forehead, which made him seem almost tritely suited to his job as resident egghead. Right now, his job was to get Land to say something positive about this pile of Israeli photographs, and he wasn't doing it.

Where was Jenny when you needed her? She'd have told Adamson where to get off, in no uncertain terms. Chandler always had trouble telling people things they didn't want to hear.

"Look, Jay, I understand what you want, but I can't help

you right now. Maybe when Jenny shows up—I need at least one more opinion. Or Ford. Where's Dalton, anyhow?"

"I haven't seen Ford today," said Adamson, crossing thin, hairy arms. "I need an opinion on that data, so that I can send in a preliminary report." He actually tapped his foot once on the wooden floor of the tent.

"Fine. My preliminary opinion is that the data's too inconclusive at this time to support any assumptions or aggressive recommendations. Is that bureaucratic enough for you?"

Adamson frowned. "My contact's not going to like that."

"So? The Arabs won't like it either if you—"

The S-3 ops officer took off his headset. "Sir, I'm done, if you want to leave. Oh, I didn't mean to—"

"No, that's fine; you weren't interrupting." Chandler Land stood up. "I'm going back to the hotel. If my wife should wander by and you don't need her desperately, tell her I'd like to meet her for lunch." He got up and handed Adamson the photo-reconnaissance folder. "Better luck next time."

Adamson stood in his path so long before he stepped aside that Chandler considered what would happen if Adamson simply didn't move out of the way.

"I'll walk with you," Adamson said, and did.

Out in the open, Cairo West inundated them with the suffocating combination of hot wind, dust, and diesel and gasoline fumes that had become its hallmark. Breathing unfiltered Cairo West air could give Land a headache in a matter of minutes, so he hurried toward his rental car.

Adamson's was parked beside it, motor running: "Get in for a minute, Chandler." The other man's sudden grip on his elbow was unwelcome.

Inside the consular car sat Meri Soukry, the Arab woman that Jenny had taken such a dislike to at Seti's party.

"Hello, Anu Soukry," said Land as he got in the back seat. From the front, Adamson handed him the handset of his secure carphone and said, "Call your wife. See if she'll meet us all for lunch."

Us? Come to think of it, Adamson had handed the photos to Soukry when he'd slid behind the wheel. Well, it figured. Everybody here was a player.

As he dialed the number, he said to the woman, "Have you seen Dalton, Anu Soukry? If we could turn him up, then Jay would get off my neck about all this."

"I haven't," said the Egyptian woman in a low voice. "I was hoping you might know where he is."

"Nope."

The desk clerk at Mena House answered and Land gave his room number. The room phone rang eight times before the clerk came back on the line to tell him that no one was in the room.

Land handed the phone back to Adamson: "She's not there. Probably out shopping. She wasn't scheduled out here until evening." Land started to get out of the car. "If I find her, or Ford, I'll be sure to let you know, Jay. Unless I should let Anu Soukry know directly?" He wanted to make sure that they knew he understood what he was seeing. He didn't like the way Adamson treated him, as if he weren't really part of the team, just a dilettante.

"Calling the embassy will be fine," Jay told him.

By the time Land was in his own car, theirs had left. He had to run the air conditioner with the windows open; the cardboard he habitually placed behind his windshield was pitifully inadequate to these conditions. By the time he'd made it to the first checkpoint, he was soaked with sweat and the air conditioner was blowing as hard as it could, doing its best to make sure that his every muscle would be stiff by the time he got to his hotel.

But he didn't get to his hotel. Traffic was light, and he was driving along fuming, fiddling with the radio trying to get some American rock and roll, when a minivan pulled up beside him and honked.

Quantrell waved from the driver's seat.

He waved back.

Quantrell motioned him to pull off onto the shoulder, and started to do just that.

Land followed suit. "What's up, Colonel?" he said, rolling his window down regretfully: all his nice, cool air was going to be sucked out into the blanching heat.

Quantrell called, "I need to talk to you."

By then, two of Quantrell's commandos, whom Chandler Land remembered very well from the airport, were at the doors of Land's car. One reached in the driver's side window and pulled up the lock button.

"I don't need any help," he protested as the commando on his side pulled open his car's door.

The other one was already rifling his glove compartment.

"What's going on, Quantrell? What's the—"

The closest commando said, "Don't argue. Don't say anything. Get in the van." He felt a flat hand on his back.

The next thing he knew, he was being shoved—*shoved*—into the minivan and hands grabbed him.

For a moment, in the dark of the van, everything looked green and grainy. Then he couldn't see anything at all: a blindfold was over his eyes and his hands, jerked behind his back, were being bound with something like a plastic tie.

He would have yelled his head off by then, but there was a hand over his mouth, which was followed by a piece of tape. The tape hurt his lips and pulled on his beard hairs. Somebody shoved him down into what he assumed was the van's corner, saying, "Sit still. Don't make a fuss."

He could feel another person's body on his left. On his right was the side of the van.

What was happening? Had the whole world gone crazy? The commandos were obviously following orders—Colonel Quantrell's orders. Quantrell was on their side. Land's side. Wasn't he?

30

Day 13: Langley, Virginia

Rear Admiral Leo Beckwith was a fish out of water at CIA headquarters, and he knew it. Beckwith still considered himself a man of action; and action didn't include sitting around making macho noises at a bunch of over-age cowboys making macho noises back at him over their unpronounceable salad greens in the executive dining room.

If Beckwith had to eat one more haute cuisine "power breakfast" or "working dinner" he was going to die of a cholesterol overdose on the spot. Didn't these old fools realize that they were killing themselves with all this fancy food?

More to the point, was *he* as old as all these other old fools? As paunchy? He surely wasn't as pasty. Carol would kill him when he got home if he'd gained as much weight in thirty-six hours as he suspected he had.

As if reading his mind, Nesbitt, under whose auspices Beckwith was getting the red-carpet treatment from CIA, leaned over and proposed, "How about a game of racquetball after lunch, Leo? I've got to get some exercise or I'm going to go to sleep."

"You're on, Al," Beckwith said, and went back to pushing food around his plate until someone asked him something pertinent.

There were nine of them in the executive dining room this time. At the head of the table was the deputy director of

CIA, a man who'd come out of the Intelligence Directorate after running the Bureau of Intelligence and Research at State and, before that, collecting a purple heart during a stint in the 101st Airborne. His boss, the director, hadn't shown himself the entire time that Beckwith had been in town. Rumor had it that the man never attended these meetings and always left the building by three in the afternoon.

The deputy caught Beckwith watching him and said, "I think we're getting somewhere with this, Admiral."

The deputy was around Beckwith's age, but never called him by his first name. Titles were everything in Washington, these days.

"Where are we getting, sir? Given the readiness level, I've spent about as much time as I can out of my operations center." Even Cheyenne Mountain was beginning to look good, after a night in a Tyson's Corner motel.

"After correlating your data with the Air Force labs', and ours," said the deputy, laying his fork carefully beside the knife on his plate, "we think that the Syrian-Iraqi telecommunications company in question is run by the same people who're involved in building a chemical munitions plant in Libya along with officials of the Egyptian government." Eyeing Beckwith significantly, the deputy sat back.

Somebody picked up a water goblet and the clink of it against a plate was startlingly loud.

"So where does that put us?" Beckwith was damned if he saw what was so significant.

The deputy had white wings of hair above his ears; he ran his forefingers along them, as if sweeping them back. "I'm sure you realize we can't risk moving with evidence as circumstantial as what you've brought us."

Moving? Moving where? Moving against a target? Leo Beckwith wasn't going to need a racquetball game to get his heart pumping. He tried to judge how serious the deputy director was by the man's expression. He couldn't. The deputy had one hell of a poker face.

When Beckwith just stared at him, the deputy said, "The situation's especially delicate because it's not clear that the corundum came from any specific country: the purveyor sold that batch widely over the Middle East. Nearly all the Arab countries who have uses for industrial ruby customarily deal with the same supplier." The deputy, picking up his fork once more, sat back and toyed with his food.

Nesbitt, beside Beckwith, slid down slightly in his seat and looked at Leo.

So he had to say something. "All of which means, I presume, that I can go back to directing the operations of Space Command and leave this delicate matter in the capable hands of your staff. I wasn't expecting to come out of here with a quick fix. I'm just here to make sure that Space Command's point of view is represented, not to urge any specific type of action."

"But, Admiral, we need to do just that—decide on a course of action. The President wants to do something. He and your CINCSPACE and my director went fox hunting two days ago. Then all three of them had dinner with the boiling mad French ambassador. It seems that if *we* don't do something, the French will."

Beckwith wished he'd stayed in Colorado. "Do something? What sort of something?" He really didn't want to hear the answer to that question. Whenever he came back East, he felt like Alice at the tea party.

"We'd like you to work up a scenario with the Strategic Defense Initiative organization for using Brilliant Pebbles to take down Arabsat—nonattributably, of course."

"Of course," Beckwith repeated numbly. Brilliant Pebbles was an as-yet-incomplete constellation of SDI satellites that used kinetic energy in a hit-to-kill configuration. Brilliant Pebbles' space-based interceptors were about one foot in diameter and three feet tall, housed in pairs in small orbital platforms covered with solar cells to provide housekeeping power. Each "pebble" had a wide-field-of-view telescope and a multispectral sensor, multipurpose antenna to communicate with other platforms or the ground, and two sets of thrusters and propellant tanks. The Brilliant Pebbles sensors gave electronic, real-time image processing, utilizing an optical system so sensitive that, from an altitude of one thousand kilometers, its "electronic telescope" could resolve individual autos parked in front of buildings while imaging a land area the size of Virginia.

Brilliant Pebbles, when complete, would consist of a hundred thousand mini-interceptors. As yet, only a fraction of those were in orbit. But that didn't mean you couldn't use one, or ten, or a hundred. But it was one thing to have an SDI weapon up there, for emergencies. It was another to use it in a knee-jerk reaction to take out a hapless communications satellite incapable of behavior more threatening than degrading the transmission quality of your phone call to Riyadh.

Beckwith cleared his throat. Everybody at the table was still watching him. Everybody except Al Nesbitt, CIA's representative at Space Command. Nesbitt was playing with the hem of the yellow tablecloth. The kid could have warned him. . . .

"Of course," Beckwith repeated his first comment, "you'd want to proceed nonattributably. And of course I understand that the President is under some considerable pressure to act. But you don't use an SDI weapon 'just to see what would happen.' This isn't a fox hunt, gentlemen."

"We must placate the French," said the deputy director, all pretense of deference gone now. "And we must flush this bogey—we need proof of who's taking these satellites out. The cost per space-based asset is simply too high to tolerate another incident."

To the deputy's right was a honcho from the Science and Technology Directorate, who handed the deputy a note. The deputy frowned and read it. Then he looked up at Beckwith and said, "In this climate of satellite losses, no one is going to be able to trace the pebble to us, unless we're suicidally sloppy."

Beckwith was in danger of losing his temper. "I understand the pressure you're all under. I'm feeling the pinch myself. And I understand that when the commander in chief gives an order, we're all bound to carry out that order. But there might be another way to satisfy the French, without putting the President in such a difficult position." CINCSPACE was either chewing the rug, or champing at the bit: if this was the Old Man's idea, it was one of his worst. Brilliant Pebbles wasn't the way to go, unless you wanted public debate. "I, for one, can't sanction using a U.S. space weapon to destroy a nonaggressive, commercial satellite arguably performing a public service in its region, no matter how covertly you think you can do it. Everything blows eventually. This will, too." Didn't they ever learn?

"What's your counterproposal, then?" asked the deputy director, who looked from his Science and Technology man on his right, to his deputy director of operations, a hatchet-faced man who, until this moment, had shown little interest in the proceedings, but now was sitting forward.

Finally Beckwith understood why Nesbitt had cajoled him into coming back East. The kid was still playing with the table-cloth, his fingers nervous where no one could see.

"My proposal," Beckwith said, "is that we use the X-NASP to gather more data. We've got all the optics you could wish for on board: a new, Brilliant Pebbles–type camera combining spherical focal planes, fiber optics, and multiple charge-coupled devices. We can generate between one and ten billion resolvable spots, using pop-eye lenses, to achieve a constant angular resolution over a sixty-degree field of view while eliminating all angle-dependent aberrations. We can record meteor or satellite tracks, multiple targets across a large region of sky. If there's anything up there that shouldn't be up there, we can find it with X-NASP. And we can give you ground reconnaissance like you've never dreamed. If your people want to work with us—share your suspicions of where you think your ground proof might be—we can give you high-quality imaging of any-place on Earth. If you've got a fox out there, let's use X-NASP to find his burrow, before we start something we can't stop."

Beckwith sat back. No one said anything at first. Then the deputy started murmuring to the DDS&T man, and his DDO joined in.

Al Nesbitt stopped playing with the tablecloth and sat up straight. Beckwith could see the grin trying to break out on that pockmarked face.

The deputy said, "Okay, Admiral. You've convinced us—finally. I still don't like taking the chance of losing that space plane, but we're agreed that it's no more risky than the Brilliant Pebbles option, now that the pebbles are on the table. Go fly your recon mission."

"I will," said Beckwith, and clapped Nesbitt on the knee.

"But for heaven's sake, don't lose that space plane in the Med," the deputy warned him in a voice so thick that Beckwith again stared at the deputy.

"I won't," Leo Beckwith promised. "You can count on it," he added, knowing he'd just put his professional life on the line.

He hoped Pollock was up to it. Hell, he hoped X-NASP was up to it. If the pilot and the plane failed, then Brilliant Pebbles was the next weapon the administration would grab.

And Beckwith was too old a war horse not to know what would happen once SDI weapons came onto the playing field. You'd think that CINCSPACE and the President would have had more sense. But then, Beckwith didn't have the French breathing down his neck.

If he had, he'd have told the French to use their own goddamn assets, instead of maneuvering the United States into a position where America took all the risk.

But Beckwith was no stranger to risk. And neither was Pollock. Pollock had been dying for an excuse to put X-NASP through her paces. Beckwith just hoped he didn't die doing it.

One ride in X-NASP had convinced Leo Beckwith that she was a young man's aircraft. Beckwith could still remember the fist that had closed around his heart when that beast leaped into the air.

Maybe Leo should use a different pilot. Pollock was no kid. But then, there wasn't a kid in the whole of the armed services whom Leo Beckwith would be willing to trust with the fate of the world.

31

Day 13: Western Desert, Egypt

When Quantrell had ordered his special activities team to put
together a low-signature base camp in the desert, he'd never
expected to be using it for anything halfway real.

Certainly he'd never expected to be using it for anything
like this—interrogating high-powered American nationals in a
tent on a cold desert night.

At least it wasn't so windy here, in the lee of a sandstone
ridge in the handy depression that Mackenzie had found.
Mackenzie was turning out to be an all right officer. Quantrell
would take a seasoned captain over a fast-track lieutenant for
this sort of mission, any day.

But what sort of mission was this turning into? He stubbed
out his Salem and looked up at the stars. Even with the wind
blowing dust, the stars burned fiercer in the desert than anywhere Quantrell had ever been. He liked this venue: he even
liked the heat, most times.

But tonight, the cold bit and the heat of the day seemed to
have lodged under his skin, as if he had a fever.

"Sir? I don't mean to disturb you . . . "

"You never disturb me, Mackenzie. What's up?" The lank,
square-shouldered captain put both hands in his hip pockets.
"Should we feed and water the prisoners, sir?"

"Naa, not yet. We've got to keep this realistic. I'll take some
water in with me when I go back to continue the interrogation."

"Yes, sir," Mackenzie said without inflection. Mackenzie wasn't pushing him about the rationale for taking American captives as part of the A team's war game—yet. And Mackenzie wouldn't push, unless Quantrell did something very stupid. The captain knew damn well that if it weren't for Quantrell, Mackenzie would be spending every night in the desert, in worse tents, trying to teach pidgin Egyptian and read Russian maps and keep the sand out of his pits.

No, Mackenzie wouldn't push. He was from the Special Forces side, not the CIA side, of the mixed team. But some of the others, by now, must be asking questions. Hell, now that Quantrell had Ford and the Lands where he wanted them and his temper had cooled, Quantrell was asking himself some of those same questions.

Questions like: Are you making this personal? What do you think you're doing, asshole? How do you expect to survive this, professionally, once you turn these people loose?

Because he had to turn them loose, eventually. The kind of foul play he suspected wasn't the kind that was illegal by American law, or even frowned upon in the field if you were playing by American rules.

But Quantrell had been out here in the Med too long not to know that you played by survival's rules, and that anything that cut down your survivability was against those rules.

Mackenzie was still there, standing a little behind him. "Not a bad place to camp," Quantrell told him.

"Thank you, sir. Good cover; a decent view. Sandstone formations like this fuck with overhead sensors, so we're pretty safe from discovery by any kind of electronic means."

The captain was uncomfortable with this part of his mission and hoping against hope that Quantrell would tell him something that made sense.

"Why don't you come on in with me, Mackenzie? Just tell the rest where you're going, so we don't have a head count unexpectedly."

"Yes, sir," said Mackenzie, trying not to sound doubtful.

To the left of the desert-capable, indigenously produced tent was an A-shaped affair whose two solid walls were soft solar collectors. Inside it, the special activities team had set up their electronics and were testing different signature-readers fed from a collapsible dish antenna no bigger than Quantrell's hand.

Evidently, from the talk Quantrell had overheard, the biggest problem they'd had in locating and estimating the size and position of the "enemy" (everybody else whose gear had readable emissions), was in finding a good position for the antenna.

Of course, the solar station wasn't meant to shelter six people, which was why they'd brought the second tent. Even with three men walking the perimeter and two watching the prisoners—one inside, one outside—it was tight in the solar-powered tent.

Nobody was complaining. This was a good bunch of men. At this point, they weren't "boys" to Quantrell any longer.

But then, at this point, he wasn't playing a game any longer.

"Let's go, Mackenzie."

Once the two of them ducked into the tent and relieved the inside guard, who left, Mackenzie hunkered down just within the tent flap, waiting and watching.

Quantrell hoped the captain had as much sand in his craw as Quantrell was giving him credit for.

He put down his canteen where the prisoners could see it. Then he sat down cross-legged behind the canteen, where they could see him. Then he lit another cigarette, exhaled, and took a swig of water. All the time he watched three pairs of eyes follow his every move from above adhesive-tape gags.

"Mackenzie, you want to fix it so Mr. Ford can say a few words?"

Mackenzie got up, walked over to Ford, who was sitting with his bound feet in front and his bound hands in back, and went down on one knee. Then he looked over his shoulder at Quantrell.

Quantrell nodded. Mackenzie, with a shake of his head, ripped the adhesive tape off Ford's mouth in one quick motion.

The sound of the tape ripping away made Quantrell's own mouth tingle in sympathy.

Ford didn't start ranting. This was round two of the interrogations. Round one had consisted of Quantrell telling three bound people what questions he wanted answers to, but never removing their gags while he told them.

You couldn't interrogate purported friendlies and fellow citizens the way you could downright enemy shooters. But all three of these people were endangering Quantrell's performance of his duties, and, for all he knew, his life.

"Okay, Dalton, talk to me," Quantrell said as Mackenzie got out of the way, scuttling half-crouched back to the tent flap. "Where've you been, these last couple days?"

"I can't tell you that, Jesse. I wish you'd calm the hell down and think about what you're doing here."

"I'm calm, Dalton. I even remember you're a friend of mine. I was trying to remember it while officials of the Egyptian government were asking me—not real nicely—where the hell you were. And I didn't know what you'd have wanted me to tell them, Dalton."

There was a white, ragged line of adhesive gum where the tape had been over Ford's mouth. The skin within that oblong was a blotchy white-and-red, against which his stubble showed starkly. "Jesus, Jesse, I'm sorry. I really am. But you've got to believe me, I didn't know anything like that would happen. I'm in up to my neck on this one." His eyes slid sideways, toward the Lands. "I can't talk to you about what I've been doing."

"Because your two buddies are spooks and you didn't bother to tell me that, either? The worst kind of spooks—the kind the local government gets real upset about. Yeah, I know. I was told, in no uncertain terms. Dalton, we used to be friends." That was before Meri Soukry. "What happened, man? Where the fuck were you and how come you got so sloppy I'm taking your flak?"

"I don't know what happened with the Egyptians, Jesse. Maybe you want to untie me, and we'll go off and talk about it. But whatever it is, you can bet it's not because of these two." Again, he turned his head to look at the Lands. "The two of them together don't know enough about Egypt to order dinner in a restaurant."

"Put the tape back on him, Mackenzie."

Quantrell had trouble resisting the urge to turn to see if Mackenzie would do as Quantrell told him.

He shouldn't have worried.

And Ford, to give him credit, didn't try anything with Mackenzie, or even argue. He just looked at Quantrell as if Quantrell were making some terrible mistake.

Which he probably was. "Now the girl," Quantrell told Mackenzie.

This time Mackenzie shot him an anguished look before he obeyed.

Quantrell braced himself. Jenny Land had a big mouth. She was some sort of whiz kid, and she'd gotten used to being treated special because she was smart. He expected a lot of smart comments to come out of that mouth.

But the big mouth was pinched shut and red from the tape. The woman stared knives at him, and that was about all. Unless you counted the entreating look she gave Mackenzie.

Maybe this hadn't been such a good idea after all. "Do you want to talk to me, lady? About how come you and your husband are on every Egyptian shit list in town because they like their Agency spooks to be formally introduced? You saw all those boys out there? All of us just spent a while in an Egyptian facility being asked questions about you and your hubby that we didn't know how to answer because we didn't know squat. Now maybe that's Dalton's fault, but Dalton and I go back a long way. You give me a good reason to treat you with as much courtesy as I'm treating him." He reached out and took another drink from the canteen.

The only real-world pressure he'd applied was withholding water from the captives. It had been long enough, now, that such pressure wasn't insignificant.

The woman licked her lips. "You call this courtesy?"

Same woman, all right.

"Yep. I could have slit your throats and left you for the carrion eaters out here. There's still jackals, you know. And of course, there's vultures. And more exotic fauna. We don't need the kind of trouble you represent. Do we?"

"Listen, you—Colonel. I'm here at Dalton's request, as a civilian consultant. Ask him. That's all I am—"

Her husband groaned behind his gag, rolled his eyes heavenward, and stamped his bound feet in front of him.

Interesting. Wrong Land, obviously. "Mackenzie. Let's try
Door Number Three."

Mackenzie, this time, breathed, "I hope you're sure about
this, sir," as he passed by Quantrell to take the tape off Chandler Land's mouth.

"Leave the woman the way she is." Neither Quantrell nor
Mackenzie, under Quantrell's direction, had done anything so
irremediable—yet—that he couldn't talk his way out of it if he
needed to.

"Okay, Mr. Land. You had something you wanted to add?"

Bingo: "You idiot. Of course we're working for the Agency. How else could we being doing comms for Space Command
and interfacing with Ford at the same time? Do we look like
tourists to you? I have twenty years in the business, soldier,
and in those twenty years I've never seen or heard of behavior
as unbecoming an officer as yours."

"No shit?" said Quantrell, in a mildly surprised voice. "Oh,
right, you said 'Agency.' Look, Land, whatever you're doing
that's got the Egyptians so upset, maybe you'd better quit doing
it. Okay? And use your 'Agency' connections to get me off
the Egyptian shit list. I have to live and work here, friend.
And, while you're showing me how grateful you're going to be
because I let you out of here alive—even though, of course, this
is only part of my men's training that you and your wife volunteered to help with—I want you to promise to stay out of trouble, and out of anything that will make the Egyptians nervous,
until you go home to Georgetown or wherever you're from.
Which ought to be pretty damn soon, for all our sakes."

"Fine. I accept all your conditions, in front of your witness,
here." Chandler Land gestured with his chin toward Mackenzie.
"We'll make arrangements to leave as soon as we possibly can.
I'll talk to Jay Adamson myself about making sure that your
reputation has not been damaged by contact with us, nor your
standing among the local . . . professionals. And I'll forget all
about what happened here. Just *turn me loose*."

"Mackenzie. Untie him and help him outside. Walk him
around until his legs work. Then give him just a little water."
It wasn't anything that Chandler Land had said that convinced
Quantrell. Nobody that stupid and that arrogant could be a

danger to anyone but himself, let alone enough of a field presence to worry the Egyptians.

So that stunt at Egyptian intelligence wasn't really about the Lands at all. Or else the Egyptians had been misinformed.

Jenny Land was glaring at him, but she didn't say a word until Mackenzie had half-carried her husband out.

"And now I suppose you're satisfied, Colonel? Why couldn't you have asked us these insipid questions without all this manhandling, this—this idiotic game?"

"Yes, ma'am. War games. That's what we're doing here."

The flap opened; cold air hit the back of Quantrell's neck. He looked around: Mackenzie was ducking back in under the tent flap: "He'll be okay. He's real relieved. Marconi's helping him get his feet under him. They're talking about the war games." Mackenzie hunkered down and crossed his arms over his chest.

"You," Jenny Land said. "Captain Mackenzie, isn't it? Did you sanction this?"

"I'm following orders, ma'am."

"And so are you—right, Mrs. Land?" Quantrell reminded her. If she threatened his people, that changed everything.

Ford knew that. He swung his legs over and knocked the soles of his shoes against her knees.

"Let Dalton go. This is outrageous. You can't let Chan go and keep both of us—"

"Do it," Quantrell told Mackenzie. Quantrell worried, now that he'd gotten to this point, about just what he was going to do if the woman wouldn't be reasonable.

"Mrs. Land, you're a security risk, threatening the very survival of my soldiers in a venue where the DefCon is too high to consider the sort of thing that happened to me tonight as inconsequential. I want you to tell me if there's any reason that the Egyptians should be considering you a threat to their security."

"Certainly not. I—"

From beyond Mackenzie, who was stooped over, freeing him, Dalton Ford said, "Jen, Quantrell's done you a huge favor, even if you don't like the way he's done it. So you just calm down."

Mackenzie finished untying Ford and stepped away from him. Ford was rubbing his wrists. "For all we know, the Egyptian faction who was lying in wait for Quantrell might have been after you, too. Maybe following you. So if they saw Jesse's people pick you up, that's good. It'll confuse them. But we've got to figure out why they hauled Jesse's team in, and how to get you two out of harm's way."

"Send us home, Dalton. I keep telling you, you don't need us here."

"Yeah, well, that was true until your husband volunteered to make himself useful." Ford grunted as he leaned over to massage his ankles and calves. "Jesse, there's no problem about this. Not from Jen, either. You have my word."

"Gee, that's big of you, Dalton."

"Shit, Jesse, you've got my black box, don't you? I can't afford not to be nice to you."

"Do I?"

"Yeah, it's in your hotel room. Put it there when I left with Meri."

So Ford, finally, answered Quantrell's question: He *had* been in Israel—with Meri Soukry.

Quantrell was sorry he'd untied him.

But Ford was grateful enough for the warning, and worried enough about the situation as Quantrell had described it, that he was thanking Mackenzie and letting the captain help him up:

"Can I buy your team a drink? We put them through a lot today, Captain. And I should get to know them."

"Only if we drop the Lands at their hotel first," decreed Quantrell at the same time that Jenny Land asked huffily, "A drink? You want to have a *drink* with these thugs, Dalton, you do it without me. Or Chan."

"Fine," said Ford smoothly. "It's decided—if Jesse will let his people break camp?"

"Sure. They're done for the time being. I'll have Mackenzie drive you all to town and I'll be along when we're secure here."

"Fine. Great." Ford grinned. "Camel's Eye in, say," Ford looked at his watch, "three hours. And, Quantrell, bring my box."

"The hell I will. You stop by my room later to get it. I'm not finished with you."

That was the truth. When Quantrell and the nine men he had with him got to the Camel's Eye and found Mackenzie, at a booth with the two Deltas he'd taken along to ride shotgun, Ford was nowhere in sight.

Quantrell began to get angry all over again. "Where the fuck is Dalton—"

Mackenzie thumbed over his shoulder, toward the men's room. "With two big Sovs. Cozy."

Okay. Relieved that Ford hadn't run out on him, Quantrell sat down at Mackenzie's booth. "Where're they sitting?"

Mackenzie showed him a booth in the corner.

"Everything go okay, delivering the noncombatants, Captain?"

"Yessir." Mackenzie ducked his head slightly, turning his beer bottle in his hands.

"Something you want to say, Captain?"

"That woman's mightily pissed, sir. Still."

"She'll calm down. Hubby's with the program, right?"

"Hubby's on the payroll, from what I saw. Sir."

"Tell me later, Mackenzie." Probably just Mackenzie's native ability to put two and two together, thought Quantrell dismissively as he went to greet Larka and Ignatov, who were filing out of the men's room after Ford.

"Iggy! Larka, you old shit!" As scatological Russian pleasantries were exchanged, Larka grabbed him in a bear hug and whispered, "It is good you do not hold a grudge, my friend. Friends are where we find them these days, eh?"

"That's what I always say," Ford said, herding everybody to the back table. "Iggy wants to pledge allegiance, Quantrell—everything short of an honors defection."

Ignatov blushed so that his fat and pasty face looked positively sunburned. "This is not the truth. I thought Americans valued the truth. Did you not hear this fairy tale, Larka?"

Larka squeezed in beside Ignatov. Quantrell waited. He didn't like to be on the inside in a booth. Ever since the incident with Larka on the road, he'd been wearing the Desert

Eagle under his arm. He wanted to be able to get to it if he needed it.

Larka said, "This I have heard also, that the Americans like to think they tell the truth. But they also like to think they know the truth. If they will tell it, we will all like to hear it. But promises, among Americans, fall like apple blossoms in summer."

Once Ford had slid all the way in, there was room for Quantrell to sit. He put both arms on the table. "What's up, fellas? Iggy, where you been?"

Ignatov rolled button eyes, then squeezed them shut theatrically. "I have been," he pounded his chest with a flat, fat hand, "all the way home."

"To Moscow?" Ford teased.

"To my house, in Bulgaria. Where my babushka, poor soul, is ailing."

"Yeah, we know, Iggy," Ford said. "Now tell Quantrell what your babushka wants you to tell the U.S. government. It'll clarify some recent events for him. And you know how hard it is on all of us when Quantrell, here, gets unclear about who's who and what's what."

Larka snorted, making an ostentatious show of pouring his beer into his glass.

"Come here, friend Quantrell." Ignatov's sausagelike finger beckoned. "Closer. Good."

Quantrell could smell garlic and onions. "My government," Ignatov whispered, while Larka, no longer fussing with his beer, kept an obvious watch for eavesdroppers.

"My government," Ignatov said again, "is very . . . disturbed over the destructions of these satellites. Soon you will all have to be buying from us the remote sensing time. And we do not want this. It is bad for relations between our countries that parity, even in space-based sensoring roles—not be maintained. So we are offering, oh so quietly, very unofficially, through the persons of Larka and myself—"

"Christ, Iggy, just tell him before we all grow old and gray," Ford groaned.

"—we are offering, to you and our friend Ford alone, whatever help our government can provide, through our persons, in finding the reason for these terrible destructions of expensive satellites—and stopping them. Do you understand what it is I am saying?"

"I think I just heard something about 'nonattributable cooperation,' didn't I? Or did I not hear it?" Quantrell replied.

"You did not hear it," Larka growled and leaned forward on both elbows. "But you can count upon it, and us, where these matters are concerned. And we would like it if your government could know, without knowing, you see, that this the case."

"Gotcha. Well, knowing without knowing is more Dalton's style than mine, but I'll be glad to have Spetznaz assistance, anytime, anyplace, and you can tell your government, Iggy, that I hope Larka and I will have a happy life once we're married."

Iggy guffawed and clapped Quantrell on the arm. "Very good, yes. It is like this. We're all marrying each other, in secret. Don't you think, Ford?"

"I gotta get out for a minute—"

Quantrell was wondering if the enforced fluid deprivation, followed by what was looking like a considerable amount of beer, had done something to Ford's kidneys.

But then—getting up from the booth so that Ford could slide out—Quantrell looked around.

And there was Meri Soukry, walking up to the bar, her purse bouncing against her hip as it swung.

"We, too, must leave," said Larka, pushing Ignatov, then elbowing him so that the heavy man grunted as he struggled out of the booth.

"Why must we . . . ?" Then Ignatov saw the woman at the bar. "Oh, it is late, I forgot." He showed square teeth. "So, my dearest—" he patted Quantrell on the cheek "—you will think of some ways in which we can be busy helping you, yes? I must report that I am doing my best here—"

"—to dear old babushka. Yeah. I'll get with you. In fact, I'll come with you, if it's okay with Larka. We can find another bar."

And they did, leaving Ford and Meri Soukry in total control of the Camel's Eye, once Quantrell had told Mackenzie to give everybody twenty-four hours off.

Mackenzie's people had earned it. And it was going to take that long to make sure that there were no repercussions coming Quantrell's way—or theirs—from the Lands.

You couldn't count on Dalton any more. He didn't even care about his favorite black box, now that Meri Soukry had arrived on the scene.

And, despite himself, Quantrell couldn't blame Ford. He couldn't blame him one bit.

32

Day 14: Cheyenne Mountain Complex

Back in his office at the Cheyenne Mountain Complex, Leo Beckwith mopped his face with a clean, lightly starched, white linen handkerchief.

Then he hunched down before the teleconferencing terminal connecting him in a two-way visual circuit with Bright Star's CENTCOM headquarters' hangar 3, at Cairo West.

No sooner had Beckwith arrived back here from Langley than he'd been told that CINCSPACE had balked at Beckwith's plan: to hold off the Brilliant Pebbles attack on Arabsat, Beckwith must convince the Old Man to let him deploy the space plane.

To convince CINCSPACE, when the alternative was testing Brilliant Pebbles in the field, Beckwith was looking for ammo wherever he could find it.

When you were hunting for informational dynamite these days, on this subject, one of the most obvious places to look was into the eyes of Dalton Ford.

Somebody other than Ford came into view on the telconferencing terminal's screen. Beckwith said querulously, "Who're you, mister? This is Admiral Leo Beckwith at Space Command Ops Center, holding for Dalton Ford on a Priority One."

The snowy face before him was handsome and startled. "Admiral? I'm Chandler Land, sir, a Bright Star consultant—"

"I don't care if you're—" Then the name rang a bell for Beckwith. "Oh, the spoofer. Look here, where's Ford?" This Land was the last person Beckwith wanted to talk to; he'd talked to enough CIA people in the preceding three days to last him the rest of his life. And he was going to need to talk to more of them. But not field people. People with clout.

"I'll get him sir. He's right over—"

The face disappeared from the screen, which then showed a middling to poorly resolved view of the hangar HQ: desks and terminals and people moving around with headsets and file folders.

Then that scene was replaced by a waist, wearing a crocodile belt threaded through faded blue jeans.

Beckwith had a close-up view of a madras shirt. The person sat down and his face came into view.

"Hello, sir? Ford here. What can I do for you this evening?" Ford leaned into the camera and peered at Beckwith.

Signal processing for teleconferencing ought to be better than this by now, even from a portable field station. Beckwith made a note to chew somebody out about it.

"It's still morning here, Ford. Can you talk with me freely?"

"Just a sec, sir."

Ford got up, showing belt again, then butt, and closed a partition. The teleconferencing satellite link had a standard NSA encryption chip, but any secure unit was only as secure as your immediate environs.

"Go ahead, sir." Ford's face pushed forward, into the monitor until it took up most of the screen.

"I've got a problem with a deployment I want to make. If you have any data that could help me argue that whatever's going on out there at Bright Star is in some way connected to the . . . overhead . . . troubles that . . . we and certain other nations have been having"—you could never be too careful—"then I'd like to have that information. Now. In as much detail and with as much corroboration as you can give me."

"Ah, sir . . . Admiral." Ford's eyes narrowed and Beckwith was sure he could see Ford's pupils contract, despite the intermittent snow on the monitor. "I can make that argument," Ford said carefully, "only on circumstantial and unverifiable data. But that doesn't mean it's not good data."

"I'm listening." Beckwith bounced an eraser-tipped pencil on his desk.

"I've got good RPV overflight pictures—not fly-by-wire; pictures from somebody's intermediate-range RPVs, the sort that has a sensor-processor bay up front, navigation bay in front of the jet engine, and a recovery chute in the rear."

"I know the type and manufacturer you mean," Beckwith nodded. "Go on." So Ford had gotten his Israeli reconnaissance. Those RPVs could identify targets with pinpoint accuracy.

"Okay, good. These RPV overflight sightings have been confirmed by a . . . manned reconnaissance flight over an area that now looks to have an inordinate amount of activity—both human and electronic—which could indicate a problem spot. Only I can't get anybody here to support my analysis on the basis of the RPV data alone, and I can't show the other data: it's word of mouth from a trusted source."

From this, Beckwith confirmed what he'd been told by Nesbitt: Ford was in up to his ears with the Mossad.

"Well, Mr. Ford, write it up and fax it to me encrypted. I need something that will blow the legs out from under a counterproposal, and I need it now."

"Sir, this data's going to be suspect because of its source."

"What, exactly, do you mean by that?"

Ford leaned so close that it seemed his nose would touch the inside of Beckwith's VDT. "Sir, the venue's a little off the beaten track and everybody knows how my contacts hate the possible perpetrators in question. The links aren't strong enough to hang your hat on."

"I want it anyway, Mr. Ford. Right now. Let me see the RPV stuff, and I'll run a copy."

"Right away."

By the time Ford's head reappeared, Beckwith was ready to record on his unit's built-in VCR. Ford showed him one photo after another, giving an audio briefing with each and reaching in with a pencil at times to circle or point to various spots on the reconnaissance photos.

When he was done showing the photo-reconnaissance, Beckwith took Ford's commentary on the verbal information passed to him by a "pilot and highly qualified observer who overflew the area in question." He ended his briefing by saying, "If the electronic emissions I've been made aware of are really out there, there's some sort of high-tech facility where no previous Syrian installation is on record as being emplaced. So I'd heartily recommend a further study of these grid coordinates, before any more far-reaching response is contemplated."

Beckwith held his hand up and ran a finger across his throat to indicate that Ford had said enough. Ford looked blandly at the screen until Beckwith shut off the VCR.

"Nice work, Mr. Ford."

"I wish I had more for you, sir."

"I imagine you will, Mr. Ford. Call me when you can add anything."

"Yes, sir, Admiral."

Beckwith was about to sign off when Ford said, "Sir?"

"Yes, Mr. Ford?"

"I'm going up there to take a look, with some friends of mine, as soon as I can arrange it."

"No you're not—at least, not until I've won my battle over here and you've got the right sort of intelligence to work with."

Ford looked distressed. "But somebody's got to—"

"Mr. Ford, you still do work for me, remember?"

"Yes, sir. We'll wait until you're ready, sir."

"Thank you, Mr. Ford. The last thing I need is an accident that will draw the wrong sort of attention to the area in question prematurely. I need everybody looking in some other direction. Is that clear?"

"Clear, sir. I've got some feelers out to sources in the Soviet apparatus. If I come up with anything else—"

"Anything I don't have in twenty minutes won't solve my immediate problem, Mr. Ford. I'm taking your data to lunch with CINCSPACE." He shook his head ruefully. "Wish me luck—the Old Man wants a fish fry and I'm hoping for a chef's salad."

"I understand, sir. Good luck."

"Good-bye, Mr. Ford. Good luck to you, too."

Beckwith shut off the telecom link, ran the VCR tape, edited it down to show only Ford's RPV and verbal briefing, then stuffed the tape in his briefcase, along with two fresh hankies.

The one he'd been holding in his lap was sopping wet.

When he got to Peterson for his lunch with the Old Man, CINCSPACE looked at him with pursed lips, fingered the tape, and said, "Whatever this is, Leo, you know I've got to talk it over with CIA first."

"Fred," said Beckwith to the nation's commander in chief for space, Frederik Whelan, "it's sufficiently enticing that I'm going to have to insist that you at least delay the pebbles option until I've flown my overhead mission."

The little man looked up at him, from behind a desk on which was a picture of him and the President in riding togs. "Leo, let's just not get our bowels in an uproar, shall we? If the only way we can have a pleasant lunch is to get this matter settled first, then here's what we do." CINCSPACE rubbed gnarly hands together. "You prepare the space plane for imminent deployment. I'll view this later, and send a copy back East. If they don't balk, you're clear for takeoff. Does that satisfy your requirements?"

"It certainly does, Fred. Thank you. I can't tell you how relieved I am." And he was. All Beckwith really wanted was to be sure that X-NASP, and Pollock, got a chance to render the Brilliant Pebbles option obsolete before it was brought on line.

He had a distinct feeling that once the Joint Chiefs had seen X-NASP's reconnaissance, they weren't going to want to use Brilliant Pebbles. It was only a feeling, until he'd talked to Ford.

Now, that feeling had achieved the status of a premonition. Ford was onto something. And whatever it was, it was on the ground, not in Molniya orbit, geosynchronous orbit, low earth orbit, or any other orbit.

Whatever it was that had Ford so cranked up was out there, somewhere, in the mountainous deserts of Syria.

And X-NASP, with Pollock at her controls, was going to find it, and reveal it, before it was too late.

33

Day 14: Cyprus

Fouad Aflaq was having the time of his life, celebrating with his cohorts. They'd danced all night with women that Gerhardt, the German, had provided. They'd stayed in the seaside villa belonging to Rifaat, the Syrian. They'd listened to the toasts of their Egyptian colleague and drunk expensive champagne—though it was a sin—in his honor.

Those who were less fat and less Westernized than the Egyptian, those among them who had the most to lose, had gotten the drunkest. Aflaq had toasted Iraq and all the glory that would be hers.

Now, in the morning, his eyes ached and his brain sloshed in his skull every time he stood up. If he turned his head too fast, the whole room spun.

For this, the German prescribed tomato juice with a raw egg in it, but Aflaq was not in the mood for raw eggs.

Aflaq was in the mood for leaving. He stomped out onto the sun-splashed mosaic tiles of the patio and said, pulling his terry robe around him, "Gerhardt, Rifaat . . . " Starting with those two, he called all four of their names. "Sebek. Mohammad. We must go. There is no time to delay. Get ready, get packed! We will miss our flight!"

"What flight?" wheezed the pale German, brushing his hair from his forehead. "I've gotten us a seaplane, a charter to the mainland. Then we'll all disperse and come into Damascus on different flights from there. No use being incautious."

"You go by your seaplane. I'm taking the flight I booked," Aflaq said. "And I'm unwilling to wait any longer to depart."

Mohammad, the Libyan, said to the Egyptian who, for the purposes of this enterprise, was calling himself "Sebek": "Listen to him. He is a mother hen. He is a camel who spits when the master appears. He is—"

"Probably right, you know," said the German. "Anything can happen out here." He peered around, at the glorious sea so darkly blue and so calm today. "Maybe our enemies are even now climbing up from the sea to assassinate us." He raised his hands and wiggled his fingers. "After all, we are not a small threat to them, anymore."

"I had a dream," said Rifaat glumly, sticking his tongue into the tomato juice and retracting it, so that a drool of egg followed and lodged on his goatee. "I dreamed we all died in a terrible slaughter, in fire and smoke, in a great, horrible moment of—"

"It was the grape leaves last night," said Aflaq impatiently. "Too spicy. Spices give unpleasant dreams. Now, who is coming with me, and who is going to waste time as only a Westerner can contrive to do?"

There was going to be an argument. The argument would be deemed a "discussion." In the end, a compromise would be reached.

Such had been the methodology by which they had arrived at every decision consequential to the completion of this project: all of them would argue about things they barely understood, make portentous political pronouncements about their friends and their enemies and the state of world affairs. And then, when that was over, they would turn to Aflaq to make the practical decisions.

To do what Aflaq had done, one must be a practical man.

But, to be fair, to do what Rifaat had done, one must be related to a national potentate. And to do what Mohammad had done, one must have a hand in the till of a revolutionary state. And to do what Gerhardt had done, one must have been born with a German's ruthless skill and generations of mercantile connections. Of course, to do what Sebek, the Egyptian who never used his name, had done, one must be a camel trader descended from a long line of camel traders.

Although, without Aflaq, all their skills would have been worthless in this endeavor. He was about to remind them of that, because it pleased him to flaunt the new importance of technical competency.

Some day soon, all the old, entrenched power brokers would be replaced by men who understood the new world of technology, the world that so terrified some of his Muslim contemporaries, but was as familiar and welcoming to Aflaq as the family cat.

"Gentlemen, I say to you now: if you will be in the tracking and telemetry station, which I have built for you, by tomorrow evening, then you will be able to watch history take a new course. If you dawdle, that is upon any of your heads, not mine. All things will now proceed according to their timetable. The final preparations for our assault on the occupied city are beginning. Be there to bear witness, or not. There is still the one more technological feat to perform; there are still the chemical weapons to move. In the end, if you are not at the station, nothing will be lost to our endeavor—only to yourselves."

And Aflaq spun on his heel and stomped back into the house, stripping off his robe as he went.

Until now, he had been a mere hireling, even though the plan, in many of its facets, was as much his as it was any of theirs.

But now, the wheel was in motion. The time had passed to turn back, to lose heart. No longer did he feel it necessary to coddle these spoiled children of the oil empires. A new empire was about to arise in the Near East, one that was clean and strong and in harmony with the Will of God.

And he would be its Imam, for among all his brethren, he would be the one who delivered to his people an old prize and a perennial goal: the shrine of their struggles, for a thousand years—Jerusalem.

34

Day 15: Moscow

Aleksandr Shitov was clearing off his desk. Tonight, he and Shitova would go to the ballet, sitting in their new seats, across the theater from the Levonovs. Shitov was already so tense, contemplating the evening to come, that his shoulders were knotted and a headache was forming where his neck met his skull.

But he must go bravely to the ballet, show himself publicly, so it was clear to all that he remained unintimidated by Levonov's strategy to save Levonov's own career by destroying Shitov's over this Cosmos 2100 affair.

Shitov must not, under any circumstances, appear cowed. He must not behave like a man in disrepute, or a man thinking he might fall into disfavor with the Executive President. He must act like a man in the right, if he were to survive the coming purge.

Purge was a horrible word. His father had lived through Stalin's purges, and his uncles still spoke of those days. Whenever they did, they licked their lips and their eyes looked nowhere.

So Shitov would stride into the theater, well dressed and smiling, with his wife sporting her new sable stole, no matter how warm the evening was.

None of this had been inevitable, not until Levonov behaved like a craven fool. The Americans were responding with conciliatory noises, as Shitov had predicted. There'd been no need for open debate in front of the Executive President. There'd been no need, in fact, for any sort of discussion whatsoever.

They all could have nodded their heads and given the requisite opinions and gone back to their desks, and nothing would have changed.

But things had changed. Then there had been the incident in front of the bakery. Shitov could still see that imbecilic assistant of his, chewing on his raisin roll in front of the peasants—in front of the Executive President himself.

Since that moment, life had become a sea of treacheries for Shitov. Nothing he was learning from his people in the field was helping, either, because none of it was the sort of thing that the Executive President wanted to hear.

Shitov glanced at his Swiss watch, a memento of happier days in the Cuba Department, and sat down heavily before his cleared desk, propping his jowls on his hands. He must get home to shower and shave.

Where *was* that idiot Bulgarian with his report? The time difference between Cairo and Moscow was only one measly hour. You would think that even a Bulgarian could manage to compute the difference and report at the correct Moscow hour.

Shitov thought to himself that, in the future, he would ask for his report using Cairo time, and then he would not find himself sitting around in an empty office waiting for a man to call him who could not compute a time difference.

Shitov's stomach rumbled. He must get home. Shitova would become angry if he was too late, and then, no matter how he tried to smooth things over, the impression he was hoping to make at the ballet tonight would become an impossibility: if Shitova was angry, everybody knew it. She could exude a black cloud of wrath which would settle over the entire theater and make everyone miserable, and all that unhappiness would be credited, in whispers over glasses of tea, to Shitov's troubles in the First Chief Directorate.

Glumly, Shitov reached for his bulky secure phone. He would call Cairo himself. The *residentura* would send someone to find the Bulgarian for him, drag the dog in by the collar, and keep him there until Shitov could find a more convenient time to take his report. After the ballet, perhaps . . .

As he touched the phone's handset, it rang.

He jerked his hand away in surprise, then snatched the instrument from its cradle. "*Privyet*," he nearly snarled. If this was not the Bulgarian, it could wait. If it was, then . . .

Excuses and honorifics poured in a jumble from the earpiece, filling his ear and bringing his headache to fruition.

"Stop babbling, Ignatov. You're late. I have another appointment. Report and be done with it!"

"Yes, *Glava*," mourned Ignatov, "I am trying. Please, understand that I am having troubles here. The Americans are using the auspices of the despicable Israelis, and not our auspices, though we have offered and even been told that our offer is accepted." A deep sigh whooshed across the line. "So the Americans, sad to say, are not taking us into their confidence."

"Ignatov, this is not what I wish to hear." Shitov's headache crawled up his scalp and embraced his entire skull, then reached for his face. His cheeks began to hurt.

"I am sorry, but you know the Israelis. Ask anyone out here: ask the Egyptians. They will corroborate the Israeli influence on the Americans—especially the American Defense Intelligence Agency liaison who is their Space Command man, Dalton Ford, on whom you have my written report."

"Tell me something I can use, Ignatov, or . . ." Shitov rubbed the bridge of his nose. There was no point in threatening the Bulgarian field agent. The man was already too worried. Worried men, Shitov well knew, did not think clearly.

"*Glava*, Colonel Larka and I are working as closely as possible with the American Special Forces colonel. This man says that some strange movements have been seen above the Bekáa, and this is diverting American attention. Is this helpful?"

Shitov's headache began, ever so slightly, to recede. "It may be. You may tell the Special Forces American, off the record, that we Soviets have heard from Azerbaijan, both as a result of overflight and observation posts, of similar strange movements. Perhaps, using this tidbit, you can trade for information about the satellites—especially about this SPOT matter. Find out if it is true that the Americans were using SPOT time just when it went down. And find out," Shitov kept his voice neutral, "anything you can about this Brilliant Pebbles project of theirs. We have intercepted message traffic that discusses this Brilliant Pebbles—and Arabsat. If it is something they will be doing, and we do not hear about it from them first, we will be very unhappy. If it will be a real problem, then there is no telling what the Soviet military reaction will be."

"Yes, I understand, *Glava*."

"Do you?" Did Ignatov understand that this Brilliant Pebbles operation, if it was what Shitov feared, would earn Shitov a bullet in the back of the head? His wife would find him, behind the local militia station, dead and cold.

"I do, *Glava* Shitov. We will find a way to have intimate cooperation with the Americans. Larka and I are sure of the Special Forces fighter. It is only the one Space Command officer, the DIA man, who is in bed with the Israelis. And we will find a way to stop that."

"Or use it, Ignatov. Take desperate measures. Do whatever you must to get me good information on the American posture, before we all lose everything because of the damned Israelis."

The Bulgarian would understand that. Shitov didn't wait for Ignatov's response. He slammed down the phone. Obviously the man had nothing more for him but excuses. Bulgarians were always full of excuses. It came from being servile by nature, the product of a satellite nation full of men frightened by their new found freedom. You could only trust a Bulgarian to do one thing: save his ass.

And since Shitov was concerned with saving Shitov's ass, it had not been difficult to make Ignatov understand that, in this matter, Ignatov's career was on the line.

Why not? Everyone else's was. Shitov was only mildly regretful that he'd freed the Bulgarian to use "desperate measures." You could never tell, with a Bulgarian, what such instruction might lead to in the way of mayhem. They were a people devoted to violence.

So, if Ignatov called back and said that he'd murdered everyone, out of hand, who might be considered a threat or a stumbling block, then Shitov must be ready to take responsibility for Ignatov's overreaction.

Perhaps he should have been more careful in instructing the Bulgarian. But now it was too late to do anything about it. Shitov must leave at once, or face the wrath of Shitova, which was worse than the wrath of an entire company of Bulgarian secret service officers.

And why, really, was he worried about the Bulgarian? Shitov asked himself as he sealed the old Mosler safe in his office with hot wax before he left. What could Ignatov do to make matters worse? Kill a few Israelis? Interrogate some local players with less than consummate gentleness? Cause diplomatic remonstrances?

Shitov stopped thinking about Ignatov as soon as he'd shut his office door behind him. Ahead lay the Levonovs, and dangers much more immediate, such as putting on the proper appearance at the ballet. At least, having taken an eleventh hour report from his field person, if the Executive President showed up unannounced and demanded a briefing during intermission, Shitov would not be caught with nothing to say.

Not this time. He almost hoped it would happen, just so that he could see the disappointment on Levonov's face.

35

Day 15: Western Desert, Egypt

Ford had been putting his black FleetSatCom downlink box through its paces with Quantrell's team out in the Western Desert when a Marine pulled up in a jeep, telling him that Adamson wanted to see him immediately.

It was nearly dark. The most crucial test of the downlink's capability could be made in the next few hours, while the box was subjected first to a rapid drop in temperature, then to sustained cold on the heels of extreme heat.

Ford almost told the jeep's driver that Adamson could come out here to see him.

But since it was Jesse's team, and Ford was trying to mend fences, he left the box with Mackenzie and Marconi, both of whom knew what to do with it and were capable of writing a decent report.

You had to trust somebody, these days, and Ford was feeling as if he were running short on allies. Quantrell was still so torqued about Meri that he'd dragged the Russians pointedly out of the Camel's Eye when she'd showed up there the other night. Now Ford's only shot was to spend some time training with Quantrell's special activities team, trying to show Jesse that there were no hard feelings and get acquainted with the men.

If things went the way Ford hoped, he'd need the trust and respect of every one of Quantrell's commandos to pull off the mission he had in mind—if Beckwith would let him mount it.

If Beckwith said yes, Ford still had to be able to convince Quantrell it was a good idea. And even after that, the mixed A team, or some members of it, would have to volunteer. They were here for training. Ford, an outsider, had no right to ask them to risk their lives on an off-the-record reconnaissance mission that had a possibility of escalating into a payback. If Quantrell still harbored any resentment, Ford had to straighten things out before it spread to the colonel's men.

So Dalton was running around in the desert with them mainly to prove that *he* had no hard feelings toward them about being snatched off a Cairo street, blindfolded, gagged, and then interrogated at length. Doing that was going to take more than a couple of beers at the Camel's Eye with Mackenzie and his comm jock, Marconi. Both of them were very reserved when Ford entrusted his precious box to them, pointing to the waiting embassy Marine in the jeep:

"Got to go. Take care of my pride and joy, Marconi. And see if you can get a dump on this freq from these coordinates." Ford wrote the data on a piece of paper and handed it to Mackenzie. "Then destroy the paper."

"You want a dump from this low-orbit satellite while you're gone?" Mackenzie asked, squinting at Ford.

Mackenzie was really asking if a Special Forces captain ought to be taking a data-dump from one of CIA's highly classified, officially nonexistent surveillance platforms, the sort of satellite that usually relayed data to the States and seldom was accessed by field personnel. The CIA satellite made precise measurements of phased-array and space-tracking radars by recording their microwave emissions. This CIA satellite's primary target was a series of ABM installations in the Soviet Union, but Ford had arranged to "borrow" it as it flew by.

Mackenzie put both hands in his hip pockets and cocked his head at Ford, waiting patiently for clarification.

"You bet," Ford said.

"You're sure you want us to do that, without you here?" Marconi was shorter than Ford, dark-tanned, and very, very cautious.

"Just say hi to it; let it say hi to you. If it's got anything, you won't be able to read it anyhow. It'll store it for decryption by someone using my password. You'll see the file builder tell you when it's done."

Marconi nodded, his tongue playing with the inside of his cheek. "I'd rather try the tac sat."

"Do that too. In fact, see if you can get any baseball scores from the guys on the *New Jersey*." The FleetSatCom part of Ford's handheld prototype "intelligence capability terminal upgrade" could handle voice communications as well as data. "See you," Ford said.

And off he went, with the taciturn Marine, who might well have been the one sent to get him two weeks ago, when he'd first slept with Meri Soukry but hadn't known who—or what—she was.

That still rankled.

Hard feelings seemed to be spreading like a plague in Cairo. Ford still hadn't been able to figure out what Jay Adamson might want, when the Marine driver dropped him off at the Nile Hilton. Night had fallen while they were fighting Cairo traffic, and Ford was glad to get out of the open jeep into someplace warm.

Adamson was waiting for him in the Pizzeria, a trendy lunch spot for upper-class Cairenes that wasn't too crowded for a quiet talk at this time of evening.

"You're not actually going to have the pizza?" Ford said as he sat down opposite Adamson, whose eyes resembled the red-and-white checkered tablecloth.

"Pizza's not bad, really. But I think I'm drinking my dinner tonight. Or your blood, asshole. I couldn't see you in the station."

It was serious, then. If you couldn't talk about something in Jay's beloved clean room, it was something he really didn't want on record anywhere as having been discussed at all. He didn't even want a record that they'd been together, discussing anything.

"So what's up?" Ford said, opening the menu to show Adamson he wasn't afraid of Jay, or anything Jay might have to say.

"What's up," Adamson said, leaning halfway across the table, "is that I just had a visit from Ignatov and Larka—you do know who they are, I hope?"

"Shouldn't we be talking about this in a moving car or out on the ocean, or on bikes or walking through the Medina?" Ford was going to kill Larka, Ignatov, and then Quantrell, in that order, if this was some sort of revenge.

"Answer my question, Dalton. You're not denying that you know those two?"

"Stuff it, Jay. You know damned well I know them: you saw us together at Seti's party. Last I saw of Ignatov and Larka, as a matter of fact," Ford told Adamson flatly, "they were leaving the Camel's Eye arm in arm with Jesse Quantrell, looking for another bar—night before last." He looked up innocently. "You want to drop the other shoe now, Jay?"

"During this visit from Ignatov and Larka, they mentioned," Adamson lowered his voice, so that Ford found himself leaning in to catch his words, "Brilliant Pebbles and the Saudi's pet Arabsat in the same breath. Nearly accused the U.S. of planning to destroy Arabsat because we out here in Cairo, having become pawns of the Israelis, are sending bad information back to our decision makers. Would you know anything about this mess? It seems they think you do—"

"They're fishing, for Christ's sake." He absolutely was going to kill Quantrell, at least. All this because of the Egyptians roughing him up? "I hope you didn't react."

"I'm reacting now," said Adamson through bloodless lips. And he smiled pleasantly, tapping the menu under Ford's hand on the table, to show that he was in complete control of himself and the appearance they were making. "Have the pepperoni," he suggested. "And answer my question, before I start asking other people, people you might not want wondering about you right now."

"Look, Jay, I don't know how the Soviets got what they have, but I do know that the Egyptians—some fat guy—picked up Quantrell the other night and he's still mad about it. Did you know that?"

"Yes, I did. The Egyptians were concerned about Meri Soukry, so I hear."

"They were concerned about Chandler and Jenny Land, the way I heard it. Jen's not a problem, but maybe you should take a closer look at Chan. I can't imagine where else Pebbles information might have leaked from. SDI constellations aren't something that Quantrell or his people would have known anything about." It wasn't fair, siccing Adamson on Land, but Land was handy and Ford needed to deflect inquiries from Meri Soukry.

But it didn't work: "Are you in too deep with the Soukry woman, Dalton? If you are, tell me. We'll pull you out."

"I don't want out. I'm just getting up and running. I want to follow up what I've got. I talked to Admiral Beckwith about it, and I've got a provisional okay." That wasn't really true, but Beckwith was the right name to beat Jay over the head with. "So ease up, all right? This is a very complicated situation. And Meri's not the problem."

"Prove it to me."

"I don't have to prove it to you."

"This current batch of security breaches alone is worth my job, Dalton, and you know it."

"The Soviets probably got all that from message traffic, Jay. Maybe they're reading *Defense Electronics* in their Washington embassy while they're listening to National Public Radio. Don't worry so much. And no matter what you do, don't react until we know who's who, here."

"That's what I'm worried about, Dalton." Adamson's shoulders seemed to slump; his neck came forward a little; his face took on a sour expression which, in Ford's estimation, was a lot less threatening than Jay's former lack of expression. "If you're being manipulated by Mossad, Dalton, into something we can't see yet—into anything—I'm going to personally see that it's the last time. Because if you are, and it goes bad, it's going to be *my* fault." Adamson poked himself hard in the chest with a finger.

"Jay, I promise, if I think there's anything too deep for me to handle, I'll come straight to you with it. She's doing a great job for us, Jay. That's all I can tell you."

"Dalton—"

The waiter showed up, and Jay had to order.

Saved by the bell. The breathing space gave Ford a chance to remember that he couldn't afford any more hard feelings. One person you needed on your side in Cairo was Jay Adamson.

Ford ordered his pizza. When the waiter had left, he said, "Jay, if all these things *are* connected, that woman's the best chance we've got of sorting out this mess without a major, overt international flap. Please take my word for it."

"I guess I'll have to, Dalton. For now. But you've got to promise to keep me better informed. I don't want any more surprises such as Ignatov and Larka gave me today."

"There won't be, Jay. I promise," Ford said, knowing there was no way he could keep a promise like that, and that Jay must know it as well as he did.

For now, all anybody could do was try to keep a lid on things and remember who their friends were.

36

Leo Beckwith was with Pollock and Conard on the flight line when his secure carphone rang, beeping his car's horn automatically.

"Be right back, boys," Beckwith said, and hustled away from the two men standing before the X-NASP, waiting for him.

Beckwith looked back once as he reached in to answer the cellular STU. The X-NASP, crouched on the most restricted of Space Com's aprons, really did look like something from the future. His future. America's future. At the last minute, the Skunk Works boys wanted to shield X-NASP's windscreens with ceramic plates, which meant that there'd be no purely visual sighting possible for the pilot and copilot on this flight.

Personally, Beckwith suspected the X-NASP contractor of having cold feet, and trying to see if they could abort the flight with such a scary, last-minute change that Colonel Pollock would chicken out. But they didn't know Donald J. Pollock. And Beckwith wasn't sure he was going to accept the contractor's recommendation at the last minute. X-NASP's clear windshields had held up well enough in all previous tests. He wasn't convinced that the rigors of a long-duration flight would tax the windscreens sufficiently to warrant a replacement, or a reschedule.

"Hello, Admiral Beckwith here." When he picked up the handset, his car horn stopped honking.

215

"Sir, it's Dalton Ford."

"What now, Mr. Ford? I'm busy out here."

"I just need to confirm something on Bright Star, sir."

Bright Star was seeming less and less of a priority to Beckwith. "Don't you people talk to one another over there? You've got your Bright Star remote sensing: that tac sat we put up for your use is relaying by TDRS all the GPS data you'll need." With the GPS, the global positioning system, feeding through the tac sat by way of the TDRS, the Tracking and Data Relay Satellite, all the positioning data—and anything else that Space Command wanted to relay through piggy-back transponders on the GPS components—was accessible to Bright Star's mobile ground stations, electronic battlefield commanders, and so on. He barely remembered to tell Ford about the CIA satellite: "And the Company sensoring platform you wanted is available, intermittently, as well. Go check your electronic mail, Mr. Ford, before you bother me again."

Ford's voice, bounced by three comm satellites to reach Beckwith, was wispy and thin: "Yes, sir. I'll do that. But I need permission for that interoperating sortie to the north of where we are—the one I told you about."

This wasn't about the exercise at all, Beckwith realized. "Fine, you've got your permission, Mr. Ford." Beckwith was more concerned with getting the space plane off the ground without having to put blinders on her. "And I may have some considerable reconnaissance for you, later on. As I said, watch your mailbox."

Beckwith was about to hang up.

Ford sensed it, and said, "Another minute, sir, and I'll let you go. Do you still want data contraindicating Brilliant Pebbles utilization, even if it's Soviet data?"

"Ford, it's too late for petty intrigues. I need better data than the rumor mill can supply, but I'll take it from the Devil himself if it serves my purpose. You do still remember what that purpose is?"

"Yes, sir."

"Well, have you got anything that will fill the bill?" Anything he could stuff down CINCSPACE's throat to stop Brilliant Pebbles, Leo Beckwith meant.

"No, I'm afraid not, sir," Ford sighed. "Not yet. But after this sortie, I will."

"Fine, then call be back then. Good *day,* Mr. Ford. I've got my own mission to deploy, and you're holding up that deployment."

" 'Bye, sir," said Ford, and hung up.

Beckwith fitted the secure handset in its cradle and walked back to the space plane, shaking his head. Damned field people. Beckwith had to make a decision on the retrofit of the space plane. And he had to make it going by his gut. Otherwise, there'd be a string of holdups and hesitations that might mean he'd never get X-NASP off the ground in time.

And if he did get her up, with clear windows and no retrofit, he'd be solely responsible for what happened next.

He could feel every jar as his heels hit the hot apron while he walked back to his two men, who were standing around looking at X-NASP as if she could make her own decisions.

When he reached Pollock, he made his: "Well, Pollock, here's where the rubber meets the road: It's your call. You want to fly her with sensor guidance only, we'll wait. You want to be able to look out the windows, that's up to you."

Conard, who'd be the copilot if the mission flew, stared at Beckwith as if the admiral had lost his mind.

Then he said, "Admiral, those new helmet-integrated visual approach and landing systems aren't fully tested. It would be crazy to trade one kind of risk for another. We're already dealing with as much helmet-mounted display data as a human brain is capable of processing."

It might have been the flush that accompanied Beckwith's rising blood pressure that caused Conard to fall silent. Or maybe the annoying young man had simply said all he had to say.

Pollock had a half-amused expression on his face. He inclined his head toward Conard. "I think that says it all, Leo. If you'll back us, we ought to get into the air before somebody stops this flight altogether."

"And you'll be comfortable with the windshields the way they are, no matter the contractor's hesitation?"

"I'm ready, Leo. I'd like to do this by myself, but since you've insisted on a copilot, we'd better be sure Chuck's in agreement: we fly her as she stands, right, Major Conard? You got a problem with that, say so now."

"No problem, Colonel Pollock. If the Air Force is satisfied that X-NASP is aerospaceworthy without opaque cockpit windows, then the Army's satisfied, too."

Beckwith wondered, not for the first time, what made Conard such an infuriating little prick.

"Then let's do it, gentlemen," Beckwith said.

Conard looked away from X-NASP, behind which was a cloudless blue sky, and stared at Beckwith again. "Now?"

"That's what we've been talking about, sonny," Pollock said with a shake of his head. "What's the matter, you didn't pack your teddy bear?"

"All right, gentlemen. That's enough. If we're going to make our original departure window, we don't have much time to spare. I'll give you a lift back." Beckwith motioned Conard to precede them.

As they walked, a little behind Conard, back to the car, Pollock said to Beckwith, "I don't think I need him, Leo. I really don't."

"I was up in that thing, Don. I want somebody else with you. It's a long sit on station I'm asking for. I wouldn't want to lose you and X-NASP because you dozed off at the wrong time."

"Leo, are you telling me I'm too old for—"

"I'm telling you you're still not old enough to disobey my orders, Colonel. And I sympathize: I wouldn't want to be cooped up in a cockpit with Conard for twelve hours, myself. But, especially if we're ignoring the contractor's recommendations, we've got to go with a full complement."

"If anything goes wrong, Leo, it's not going to matter that I had a copilot. X-NASP can nearly do this mission by herself, with the Associate system and the amount of artificial intelligence she's got."

"We've been through all this. Let's not let the kid think we're holding out on him."

Beckwith knew men. That was the one, final, make-or-break skill you had to possess to rise as high as the admiral had in the armed services. Conard was exactly the right irritant around which Pollock was going to build a perfect pearl of a mission.

Competition should always be a factor, when the stakes were this high, he told himself.

The two men started to pull together as soon as Beckwith had them both in the car. By the time they'd suited up, had their preflight briefing, and driven back to the flight line, the sun was setting. Colorado sunsets were occasionally magnificent enough to take Beckwith's breath away.

A Colorado sunset with X-NASP leaping into it on gouts of flame, her scramjets screaming and her nacelles gleaming, made Beckwith want to laugh or cry, he wasn't sure which.

At moments like this, he sometimes wished that Carol could be with him, and the dear ones of the pilots, as well.

But that wasn't the way it worked, when you were flying black test-beds.

There was nobody out here but Beckwith. Not even a driver. And Peterson Control was on skeleton staffing for the event. That was why they'd chosen the dinner hour.

Beckwith watched until X-NASP was just a silver contrail in the glowing cobalt of the upper atmosphere.

Then he got into his car to drive over to Cheyenne Mountain. From his operations center, he could keep in contact with X-NASP for nearly the entire duration of her flight. It was going to be rough, spending all night in his accursed, underground office. Maybe he could cure himself of his claustrophobia by simply outlasting it.

For the first time ever, he was eager to go down into the heart of the mountain. He wanted to hear Pollock's voice, telling him that everything was A-OK.

He wanted to know he'd made the right decision, by going now, without opaque shielding. And he wanted to be there, in case anything went wrong.

He looked up once more as he started his car's engine, before he closed the door and drove off. But he couldn't see X-NASP. All he could see was the darkening sky and a twinkle near the moon that he hoped to hell was the evening star shining, and not X-NASP burning in the upper atmosphere because he'd been wrong, and she'd come apart up there.

He called Peterson tower as he drove, and got a patch so that he could listen to the controller and the hypersonic space plane through his hands-free speaker.

All the way to the Cheyenne Mountain Complex, he listened as he drove and night fell. By the time he got there, he was getting one hell of a heartburn. But X-NASP was safe above the clouds, on her way to the Middle East.

37

Day 16: Cairo

"Where the *fuck* do you get off, Land, putting a security block on my mailbox?" Dalton Ford grabbed Chandler Land by the left shoulder and twisted his right hand up behind him as the other man was turning around to lock his car.

"*Hey! Fuck you, Ford!*"

Dawn would break soon; behind the hangar, where the staff parked, the lot was nearly deserted: change of shift wasn't for an hour yet. Ford slammed Land first up against the side of his car, and then, face first, into the wall of CENTCOM hangar 3, too angry to speak.

"What's going on here? Ford, have you lost your—"

Ford banged Land's head against the corrugated metal of the hangar wall.

Mackenzie and his companion, a GS-13 named Kellogg whom Ford had specifically asked for as a CIA witness, each stepped back a pace, further into the shadows.

It was zero five-thirty hours, and a thin mist was falling. Ford was prayerfully glad he'd had the presence of mind to ask Mackenzie to come along, and bring his CIA commando with him. Otherwise, the way Ford was feeling, he'd have been tempted to kill Jenny Land's husband there and then, drive him out into the desert, and leave him for the elements to dispose of. Even now, the temptation was nearly irresistable.

"You're asking me what this is all about, *Land?* It's about

you fucking with my electronic mail, is what. Admiral Beckwith wanted to know how come I wasn't checking my mailbox,
and when I did, I found out I couldn't get at my own—" *bang!*
the side of Chandler Land's face hit the metal as Ford pulled
him back suddenly and shoved him against it, hard "—fucking—" *bang!* "—files!" *Bang!*

Ford heard Kellogg, Mackenzie's covert action specialist,
mutter something to the captain, but Mackenzie didn't tell Ford
to stop.

Which was good. Ford wasn't sure he could stop. Not yet.
Not unless somebody made him. Which was why he'd brought
Quantrell's people—in case he couldn't tell when to stop on
his own, this time. "Answer me, asshole!" *Bang!* "You make
me lose my fucking temper, and we're both going to be sorry!" *Bang!*

Land gasped, "Ford, cut it out! I'm the goddamned CIA liaison for your mission, remember? Anything going Stateside's
supposed to go through me!"

Bang! Kellogg said something else to Mackenzie, sotto voce.
This time, Mackenzie answered Kellogg, nearly inaudibly:
"Let's wait and see."

Bang! "That's not good enough, Land. That doesn't give you
the right to get between me and information from my mission
commander!"

"The hell it doesn't, Dalton. Stop hurting me, and listen.
You've been seen with Israeli and Russian nationals. Your
behavior's been queried by Egyptian intelligence. It's not that
you've lost your clearance—you've still got that. You just don't
have access right now."

"Wrong. I've got access, and you're going to go there with
me and take that block off my file and stand there while I read
it. Then you're going on a little trip."

"Trip?"

Bang! "That's right. Your choice: Either you go with one of
these nice gentlemen, over to the *New Jersey* where you can't
cause any more trouble, and sit this out at Fleet Intel, nice and
safe in the FleetSatCom installation on board; or you're going
home: in a box or in a seat, your choice. That's after you take
that fucking security block off my mailbox."

"No way, Ford. I don't work for you. I've got orders to—"

"You wouldn't even be out here, Land, if it weren't for me. Whose orders are we talking about, anyway? In my command structure, you don't just block a guy's access unilaterally. There're procedures to go through." *Bang!* "And you don't leave somebody twisting in the breeze—not out in the field, not in any command structure. Now, who gave you those orders?"

Ford was sure it must be Adamson, piqued over turf infringement, Meri Soukry, and the ruffling of Egyptian feathers. Why couldn't people be satisfied to get the job done, instead of spending half their time trying to make sure the other guy couldn't do his?

"I . . . it's nobody's idea, Ford. That is, you're not cleared for CIA compartments. The information your Admiral Beckwith sent is part of an ongoing CIA investigation—"

Bang!

"Mr. Ford?" said Kellogg softly. "There's somebody coming." Kellogg was a mild-mannered, dark-skinned kid who was fresh from the Farm and cool as could be.

Ford, still holding Land against the wall, looked over his shoulder. The sky was lightening, beyond the building's shadow. Two men, chatting, carrying briefcases, were coming toward the parking lot.

"Land, we're going in there. You're going to clear the block on my file. I'm going to read it. Then you're going with Mr. Kellogg, here, one of your fraternity brothers, over to the Fleet by chopper. Okay with you?" He had to stop. Not just because of the men coming. The more Ford heard, the less he liked. If he found out that Land, on his own authority, had blocked Ford's electronic mail, he might actually do the consultant some permanent harm, the way he was feeling.

When you had a temper like Ford's, you did everything you possibly could not to lose it. So it was a battle against himself that Ford was fighting. He'd never been gladder for backup: Mackenzie and Kellogg were Ford's hedge against his own emotional inflation.

"Okay, Ford. Just let me go."

"Mackenzie, if you please? Mr. Kellogg . . ."

The other two men stepped in close. Ford, with a shove that bounced Land's cheek against the hangar one more time, stepped back, poised and ready to defend himself if Land jumped him.

But Ford shouldn't have worried. Chandler Land had tears in his eyes as he rubbed his cheek. His puffy lips turned down as he said, "You're going to be sorry for this. When I tell Jenny what you've done."

Ford stuffed his hands in his pockets, where he could keep tabs on them. Mackenzie and the covert-action specialist crowded close to Land on either side.

"Jenny ought to find herself a man," Ford said. "Maybe if you tell her what happened here, she will." He was probably going to tell her himself, before Land did.

But when Mackenzie, Kellogg, Land and Ford piled into the electronic mail cubicle, and Land called up Ford's mailbox, Dalton Ford forgot all about Jenny Land.

The terminal showed three dated communiqués from Admiral Beckwith. Ford had to ask Mackenzie and Kellogg to turn their backs while he read them.

Chandler Land was right about one thing: the Porter Fleck had turned into a CIA-run investigation.

Ford sat back for a moment, once he'd read the first and second documents. Vindication was sweet: when *HE-12* was retrieved, there'd been a piece of corundum pellet caught in her fuselage. Her impact sensors had tripped, and the holes in her solar wings were nothing like the rents that Soviet shrapnel would have torn. The corundum manufacturer commonly sold his product widely throughout the Middle East. Now Ford understood why Brilliant Pebbles and Arabsat were being talked about in the same breath. And he thought he understood why Adamson had gotten so torqued, and the Egyptians as well, over Ford and Quantrell openly consorting with Russians and Israelis. Well, with Israelis, anyway.

And he understood why Larka had gone to the Lands first with his offer of Soviet help. Quantrell hadn't been so far off the mark, taking Ford and the Lands out into the desert. Ford should have known better than to distrust the colonel's instinct.

"I owe Colonel Quantrell an apology," he remarked to

Jesse's two commandos, who were stolidly looking in the other direction, Chandler Land between them.

"Yes sir, he'll be glad to hear that, sir," said Mackenzie softly.

Then Ford scrolled down to the next transmission from Beckwith. At first, he didn't realize what he was reading.

The significance of what he'd already read was just beginning to filter through his hyped-up nerves to his brain. Anger always made him dense; it was one of the reasons he tried not to get angry.

But: *HE-12* wasn't flawed! There'd been nothing wrong with his baby, nothing at all. The *Hawkeye* program was totally vindicated: the satellite wasn't hardened to withstand a kinetic attack of the magnitude that Beckwith described.

Ford began to feel better; he could hold up his head again in techno-spookish company. Then he focused on Beckwith's last communiqué.

The deployment Leo had been talking about was X-NASP. That was enough to make Ford blink. X-NASP was, probably by now, up there looking for bogeys. CIA's investigation had resulted in the name of a Middle Eastern telecommunications company, and X-NASP was hoping to find either some targeting intelligence or some physical evidence linking the company to the *HE-12*, Cosmos 2100, and SPOT attacks.

Leo also suggested strongly that Ford delay his sortie until X-NASP came back with her data. But he wasn't ordering it.

Ford wiped the files and sat back. He laced his hands behind his head and said, without looking around, "I bet you read all this—broke my code to do it, right, Land?" How else could Land have known what was in the message traffic?

"I'm not saying anything more to you, Ford. You shouldn't be reading those files."

"What files? There aren't any files. But if I find out that the locals—Jay Adamson, any of his Egyptian buddies—know what those files said, Land, there's no place on Earth you can run where you'll be safe from me."

Mackenzie said, "Sir, are you done? Can I talk to you?"

"Turn around, Mackenzie." Ford returned the electronic mail program to its main menu with a tap of his finger.

"If we're going to take him, we should take him. It's getting kind of crowded in here."

"Kellogg, do you think you can take your blood brother out to the *New Jersey* without getting browbeaten into doing something different from exactly what we decided to do?"

Kellogg had startling blue eyes under coal black hair. The eyes narrowed. "I'm ready to walk him right into the arms of Fleet Intel, sir. He can't give me orders."

Neither could Ford, but Mackenzie was another story.

"Mackenzie," Ford said, getting up, "I'd like you to come with me, back to take a look at what my black box got. That okay with you—Kellogg escorts Land; you come with me?"

Chandler Land watched unspeaking, his whole right cheek puffy and turning yellow.

"Sure is, sir." Mackenzie reached into his pocket and gave Kellogg the keys. "Don't wreck my car, speed demon, no matter how immune you are to traffic violations."

"Ford," Land said, "when Langley hears about this—"

"They won't hear anything from me about you unilaterally interfering with the flow of intelligence from one Space Command officer to another," Ford said in a voice far too deadly to match the pleasant expression on his face. "Kellogg, you sure you don't need us?"

"Trust me." Kellogg grinned. Then: "Let's go, Mr. Land."

Ford, motioning to Mackenzie, followed. Outside, they watched Kellogg and Land until the two men were in Mackenzie's Chevy and Kellogg drove away.

The sun was up, so hot and bright that Ford had to shield his eyes with his hand. "This'll take a couple minutes; then we'll need a car." He started walking toward the Space Command comm tent, far down the flight line.

"I'll get a jeep from Eighteenth Corps and catch up," said Mackenzie, and jogged away.

Ford wasn't halfway there when Mackenzie came back with the jeep. The lank captain winked at him. "Hop in, sir."

When he had, Mackenzie said, accelerating, "How bad is it, Mr. Ford?"

"Captain Mackenzie, we're in damage control." He shrugged. "That asshole. Five will get you ten he's been feeding all my data to Jay Adamson, and Jay's been judiciously trading it off to the Egyptians and the Soviets for whatever he thinks he wants."

"Shit."

"You said it, Mackenzie."

HE-12 was vindicated! Now maybe they'd stop thinking he'd taken down Cosmos. Ford was getting happier by the minute, so happy he wasn't really expecting anything he learned from the data dump to be a problem. Still, he needed to see if his black box had captured any information that Leo Beckwith could use, now that he knew exactly what the admiral was doing.

Inside the comm tent, the black box was locked up tight, right where Ford had left it. He and Mackenzie chased out the Army Space Command comm operator on duty, and started to look over what Mackenzie and Marconi had downloaded out in the desert.

"That's the tac sat," Mackenzie said over his shoulder. "It's probably got some good—oh."

Ford scrolled right past the tac sat reconnaissance, saying, "That tac sat's only got another three days, tops, useful life. Don't get too dependent on it."

When he got to the covert satellite's data, he sucked in his breath and said, "Mackenzie, does that look to you like what I think it is?"

"A space-tracking radar signature," Mackenzie said uncertainly. "But where . . . ?"

Ford keyed a command. The coordinates appeared in the black box's display lid. "Mother of god," Mackenzie said.

"Yep," Ford agreed. "Of course, what you're seeing is just part of my Bright Star test program."

"Ah, sir, isn't that where we're—"

"It's real near the sortie coordinates, yeah. I gotta send this back to Leo—Admiral Beckwith in Colorado. Maybe it's not too late to have his . . . deployment . . . take a look at these grid coordinates for us, before we drop in unannounced."

"I heard that," said Mackenzie with a strange, wispy edge to his voice.

Ford looked up at the Special Forces captain. "Still time

to un-volunteer, Mackenzie. For you and any or all of your people. I can go up there by my lonesome, or with some help from indigenous friends. You're not required to risk—"

"I really want to do this, sir—Mr. Ford. I'd just like you to tell me, if you can without breaking your security, if this is as serious as I'm beginning to think it could be."

"Looks like it. USSPACECOM at Cheyenne Mountain'll give us all the help they can, but somebody's got to go out there and take a look—get physical evidence, or at least a sighting."

Or destroy a site. Ford reached for the modem connection on the black box. Once he'd sent this to Leo, he'd know more. Then all he had to do was wait around to see if the X-NASP found anything he ought to know before he went up-country.

Especially knowing what he did now, Ford hated to delay the mission. As he completed the transmission, he could feel Mackenzie watching him.

He shut the box's lid. "That's it, for now. I'm taking this with me. Come on, Captain, I'll buy you a cup of coffee. Then we'd better find your colonel. You need to report on what we did and I need to apologize for not trusting his judgment."

Scary as things looked, Ford was feeling better than he had since *Hawkeye* had gone down. *HE-12* was off the hook. So was he. The Porter Fleck had led to something worthwhile. Some commando he'd never met named Dennis McMurtry hadn't died for nothing. And, especially in the wake of everything that had happened to Ford in Egypt, he couldn't wait to put a face on this enemy.

When the enemy had a face, you could confront him. If that face wasn't an American face, or an Israeli face, or a Soviet face, so much the better.

"Ready, Mackenzie?" Once he found Quantrell, Ford had to get to Meri Soukry, and Larka and Ignatov, to let everybody know they were on indefinite standby. Then there'd be time to have a little talk with Jay Adamson. Or not. Maybe the best revenge would be to let Adamson twist in the breeze a while, the way he'd let Ford twist, with no idea what the hell was going on.

Somebody had to tell Jenny Land that her husband had been

transferred over to the *New Jersey*, where Fleet Intel could keep an eye on him.

It wasn't going to go down well. But it had to be done, and Ford knew damned well that he'd better do it himself. Otherwise, he could find himself up on charges.

Chandler Land had plenty of grounds for an investigation. Ford was counting on there not being one. Land wasn't fool enough to drag them all through the mud. But even if there was an investigation, all Ford had to do was evade any MPs for a few hours, and he'd still be able to mount his mission first.

From what he'd seen in his mailbox, nothing mattered very much, compared to that.

38

Day 16: Jabal an-Nusayriyah, Syria

In the secret ground station's large tracking and telemetry bay, the perpetrators were all gathered, making fools of themselves before invited guests.

Aflaq had never dreamed they would be so foolish, his comrades, as to invite their backers to the facility. But it was always a mistake to underestimate the vanity of men.

To Aflaq, it was one thing to have his four cohorts present—this he could deal with, had been prepared for—it was quite another to throw a party as if this were a horse auction or a reception at an arms exposition.

This was neither of those. As women—some unveiled!—and men in fine clothes drifted in and among the terminals of Aflaq's white-coated technicians, he continued wringing his hands. He had warned them.

He had especially warned Mohammad, saying that he would not put on a show for ignorant politicians and soldiers. Consequently, he had just finished instructing his men to show no sign of their upcoming, final scheduled strike against an enemy satellite. They would not admit that they were preparing to commit aggression against a superpower—not before so many witnesses.

So now there would be only the most general capability display, until the guests left.

Then, if the four men he'd invited here apologized oh so very

230

profoundly, Aflaq would consider resuming his countdown.

Gerhardt, the German, came up to him, a glass of champagne in hand, as Aflaq stood on the raised gallery and watched morons move among his precious tracking stations. "Good show, Aflaq," said Gerhardt.

"If they touch anything, those idiots," Aflaq hissed, "all is lost. Over. Done. And without this final strike, there is still an eye above which can see the chemical—"

"Don't worry. Nothing is *kaputt!* Cars are already warming up to drive them down to Homs, where they can take the train, in a private car we arranged. You worry too much, Aflaq! We will have them out of your hair, no harm done, in an hour or two, at the most."

"An hour or two?" Aflaq's spirits sank. "How can you behave so foolishly? Don't you realize that things must be done at certain times?"

He broke off. There was no use. He turned his back on Gerhardt, striding around the gallery until he came to stairs, which he descended.

At their foot was Sebek, the fat Egyptian who must have arranged this awful show. "Sebek, get these people out of here."

"Aflaq," Sebek said, twisting his garish pinky ring, "we must see *some*thing. Show us something. A wonder of your technology. Then I can tell them the show is over and they will leave."

"Show you something?" Aflaq considered showing Sebek his open palm, a curse not to be denied throughout the Near East.

But he did not. He was above all that. He strode to the closest terminal and said to the white-coated technician, "Up. Up, I say."

And he sat down at the workstation, gazing blankly for a moment at his options.

Then he enabled the great main tracking screen to display real time, expecting only the standard display to appear. It was too early, by forty minutes, for the CIA photo-return satellite to come by on its trip Poleward. But a picture of Arabsat might do the trick. . . .

As he aimed his most powerful space-tracking radar, so that he could show Arabsat in all its glory, his monitor showed him something else.

An anomaly.

Forgetful of his guests, he punched up a standard grid that displayed all the satellite tracks that the station customarily monitored. This was shown on the great screen above the guests' heads and everyone murmured appreciatively.

Aflaq ignored their praise. What was this thing? It was moving very fast, very high. And then it seemed not to move, but to circle. As he watched, the track did things no satellite track should be able to do. Then it shot off his tracking screen and was gone.

His radar image was completely normal. He rubbed his eyes. Perhaps it was a meteorite, a piece of junk in some highly eccentric orbit that decided to fall out of the sky just as he watched. He told himself that it must be something like that, because no satellite could perform such astrobatics, and no plane could fly that high.

A horrible fear overtook him that something was wrong with his equipment: that there'd been nothing there at all; that what he had seen was a gremlin, a glitch, a ghost in his system.

If so, all his labors had gone for nothing: he would not be able to execute the final component of his plan.

But, praise be to Allah, with all the visitors here and this horrid party disturbing his timetable, he could blame any and all subsequent failures on the intruders.

He could say someone had spilled food or drink on his equipment, if he must. He could say, too, that his timetable had been irremediably disturbed.

What he couldn't say—what he most wanted to say—was that everyone must leave immediately, so that he could run systems checks. One of his operators leaned over his shoulder and asked if everything was all right.

The man had seen what Aflaq had seen. "*Bismallah,*" he told him, and got out of his seat at the workstation.

As an afterthought, he returned the display on the giant screen to the one that had evoked such awe from the guests.

Perhaps the fact that they were all idiots would work in his favor.

If he had a problem, he intended to make sure that no one knew that he did. No one at all.

And, because of that, he decided against attempting to hurry the guests from his station. It might not be necessary. He had one space mine left—his finest. Let the CIA photo-return satellite make its pass untracked, and let the night be spent without any more unpleasantness. In the morning, once the ground station was fully checked out, Aflaq would consider resuming the countdown for his single remaining mine.

Soon enough, when the guests were gone and the countdown tonight could not proceed as scheduled, and must wait a few hours extra, his Syrian, Iraqi, and Egyptian friends, as well as Gerhardt, would remember who was the man making all this possible.

Without Fouad Aflaq, even at this late stage, discovery was twice as likely, and the moment of attack twice as likely never to come.

Aflaq, squaring his shoulders, went to mingle with his guests. The sooner he met them all and satisfied them all, the sooner they would get out of his ground station, so that he could begin checking his equipment for signs of malfunction.

Signs which, if Allah willed, he would never see again. Too much depended on the ground tracking station to lose it now, because of technical problems. If the station broke down, it was arguable that the entire attack would lose momentum, that the push to Jerusalem might not happen at all. Or, happening, degenerate into a rout, a debacle, a disgrace upon all their heads.

With these unhappy thoughts in his mind, Aflaq tried to greet his guests as befit the Imam of technology he'd styled himself to be.

39

"What in hell was that?" Conard breathed into his oxygen mask.

Beside him, from the pilot's seat, Pollock said, "Looks like . . . telemetry, of some kind." He tweaked a readout on X-NASP's panel. "I don't know how much longer I want to maintain this—"

"Not just telemetry," gasped Conard excitedly. "Ground-based, space-tracking radar. Right where Beckwith wanted us to look. We'd better call that in."

"Fine. You do that, Conard." Pollock toggled a display up onto his helmet's visor, where he could read it without looking down. He wished nobody'd worried about the cockpit windows, because now he was worried about them.

But all the temperature sensors he could monitor were reading well within normal limits.

He sat back, trying to concentrate on the data he was reading off his visor. The heads-up display presented the information he wanted to his dominant eye only, superimposing the entire information grid over his field of view whenever he turned his head.

Theoretically, the display shouldn't obscure his vision. But he was asking it to do more than he was supposed to: he was trying to monitor what the reconnaissance pods were giving him, as well as what he needed to fly X-NASP to her next

234

station, where he'd coast her at higher altitude, slowly, saving fuel while she behaved like a satellite and he took ground tracks.

But he couldn't handle it all right now, not while listening with one ear to Conard, who was reporting verbally to Space Command and asking if CSOC wanted X-NASP to relay the Syrian data back right now.

Pollock hit his declutter mode and half of the reconnaissance-monitoring data disappeared from his visor. He'd preset it that way, so that he could take a break. His head was still swimming. He hit his second declutter mode and reduced his display to just what he needed to fly X-NASP.

Conard was saying, "Yeah, coming at you . . . three . . . two . . . one . . . transmission in progress."

Pollock was still not feeling right. He shut off the visor-display entirely and irritably retracted the visor on his helmet.

Then he saw the little fingers of ice crawling around the edges of his forward windscreen. "Oh, shit."

"What?" Conard's insect-eyed head turned to him.

"We've got some kind of cockpit heater problem." Pollock hoped that was all it was. He started flipping through his temperature and life-support screens, looking for a readout that matched his visual perception.

When he didn't find anything, he scratched with one gloved finger at the inside of the glass. He could write his name there, by scratching away the thin film of ice crystals.

"We're going back in. Tell 'em we're not in any serious trouble, but we'd like to cut it short."

Don Pollock hoped to hell the admiral had what he needed. Those windows were already beginning to spook him. X-NASP had punch-out—ejection—capability, but Pollock didn't want to be the first man to try ejecting from low earth orbit. He also didn't want to have to land anywhere but an appropriate facility in the continental United States.

Conard got on the horn to CSOC and Falcon cleared them to come back home: "You sure we have to do this, Colonel Pollock? Cutting the mission short like this?"

"No, I'm not sure. I'm cautious. Look, Major—Chuck. You're still one of the first guys to fly around the world in an operational aerospace plane. If this mission is ever declassed, you can tell your grandkids about it."

"Yeah, but there's no indication that this kind of icing isn't well within X-NASP's tolerances."

"Well, it isn't within mine." Don Pollock really did not like having his judgment questioned by a copilot, no matter how smart that copilot was. "Look, Conard: you do the mission, you go home. You don't take it personally. Okay?"

"I understand, Colonel."

"Then get back to watching the recon." Let the kid spend all that brainpower monitoring the reconnaissance scans from X-NASP's multisensoring arrays. "I'm just flying, from now on. You have a problem with your equipment, you tell me about it. Because I want to stay as close to X-NASP as I can. I don't care any more if she takes data or not. I just want her to get home safe and sound with us inside."

He shut off his comlink to Conard, flipped to his AI, and started talking to his Associate computer copilotry system, reading in new course data as he pulled the information on board from TDRS, which was relaying it from Falcon, half a world away.

If Conard wanted him, Conard could break into his computer voice-command circuit, either by voice or by tapping him on the shoulder.

Meanwhile, the ice was getting thicker and all Pollock wanted was to get a nice, smooth descent curve, into and through the stratosphere, warming up the windows as gently and as smoothly as possible, so they didn't crack from the sudden temperature change, or pop right off and hit him in the face as he brought X-NASP down through the atmosphere.

The Associate computer was very reassuring. But then, it wasn't flesh and blood. It didn't care if it died and, in so doing, spread pieces of classified hypersonic airplane all over the Eastern hemisphere.

40

At first Jenny had been angry, when Dalton Ford came round to her room at Mena House to tell her what had happened, and where Chan was—and why.

Then she'd been resentful that it had taken Ford so long to find her and tell her.

And then, somehow, she'd realized it wasn't Ford so much as Chan whose behavior she resented. She was always cleaning up Chan's messes. This mess was going to take a long time and some pretty thorough scrubbing to put to rights.

She wasn't sure why she let Ford take her to dinner: her schedule was so potty, with her working days and Chan nights, that she never seemed to be eating or sleeping at the right times.

Throughout dinner, Ford kept looking at her with those earnest eyes of his and smiling that ingenuous smile. By the time they'd eaten, she wasn't even resentful that he'd waited until she'd worked her entire shift to tell her where they'd taken her husband—under guard.

When he brought her back to Mena House, she was telling herself she wanted Dalton to leave. It was nearly midnight, and she was calm enough now to realize she had to make some sort of plan.

"What about Chan's shift, Dalton?" she said, sitting at the little round table in her Moorish room that overlooked the golf course.

237

"Don't bother. We've got Army SpaceCom personnel for that. I just want to make sure you're all right."

"Does that mean you don't need me—you never needed me—us?"

"Jen," Ford walked over to the table and took her hand in his. "Don't be so sensitive. If I'm not letting this get to me, then you ought to let it roll off your back, too. We're grown-ups."

"You mean, I ought to be used to this by now?" She bit her lip.

She'd always known that some day she'd be alone in a room with Dalton Ford and he'd have her hand in his. But she just wasn't the sort of person to betray the trust of her marriage. And, no matter what sort of man Chan had grown into, they'd married for the long haul. Unless she was going to leave Chandler, she'd never hop into bed with another man.

"Dalton, you and I . . . aren't the same sort of people." She tugged on her hand.

Ford, never one to push things, let hers go regretfully and took a seat on the other side of the table, looking at her soulfully.

Why did men do these things? Why couldn't friendship be enough? If she'd been a man, sex would never have entered even peripherally into their relationship, business or personal. Why did it always become a subtext when the chips went down between male and female coworkers?

And why did Dalton always pop up in her dreams as the most likely candidate, whenever she dreamed of running away from her life—Chan, her mother, the crushing drudgery of doing all her work and most of Chan's, too?

"Come on, Jen, loosen up."

"Dalton, nothing's going to happen."

"I wasn't asking."

He'd known exactly what she meant.

"See?" she said accusatively.

"You ought to get rid of him, Jen."

"Don't call me that. Call me Jenny, like everyone else does. I can't 'get rid' of Chan. What would he do without me?"

"He'd find somebody else, somebody like you, to clean up after him. Don't worry—"

She didn't want to have this discussion. She was beginning to perspire. "If you're content to let the matter lie, I'll convince Chan he should, too. Beyond that, all I can do to make amends is be as helpful as I can during the rest of Bright Star, no extra charge." She tried a rueful grin. None of this would have happened if her mother wasn't this horribly expensive hunk of semilucid protoplasm at which she was supposed to throw thousands of dollars per month.

"That's good enough. I told you, I wasn't asking. But I'm your friend. I can't lie to you. This guy's your biggest problem. He's holding you back."

"Dalton, what's the use of all of this when, even if we win— we lose? If we struggle on and survive, evading violent death and early death, then we've got—what—mental incapacity, incontinence, brain damage and lingering death to look forward to?" She put her palms against her temples, pressing hard to ease the pressure. "At least Chan is young, healthy, and not trying to get himself killed on a regular basis." One had to be a masochist to get involved with these cowboys, no matter how attractive they were. She'd seen too many of them come and go. She'd been to too many funerals of people her own age. "A casket full of debris is a poor substitute for a living being."

"I see Chan's been talking to you about my message traffic, too."

"I'm not brain-dead, yet, Dalton. Once I saw Larka on the road that day, I knew something was up. And then, of course, there was your friend Quantrell's stunt. . . . " She brought down her hands and folded them, because she was still angry about that.

Ford got up, came around the table behind her chair, and put his hands on the back of her neck, simply kneading the tight muscles there.

She was wearing a sleeveless sundress. Something in her became oddly still at the touch of his hands on her bare skin. Suddenly she was frightened, clumsy, tired and short of breath, all at once.

"Dalton—"

"We've got to put these glitches behind us—"

The phone rang, as if she'd planned it to save herself.

Automatically, she looked at her watch. It was just after midnight.

"Probably Chan," she told Ford, getting out of the chair so fast it bumped him as she went to get the phone. "It's about time he called."

But it wasn't Chan.

"Mr. Seti? No, you didn't wake me. Why, yes, Dalton is here, by chance."

She palmed the mouthpiece: "Yousef Seti," she whispered. "He wants me—and you—to come over to his place, now." She held out the handset to Ford. "You talk to him. It's so late . . ."

Ford, in two quick strides, was at her side to take the phone. At that moment, she'd never been gladder that Dalton Ford was in her life.

"Yeah, Seti. It's Ford, here. What's this about?"

Ford listened, saying, "Uh-huh," occasionally. Then he shook his head at her, raised an eyebrow comically as if in exasperation, and told the phone: "We'll be right over. No, we can find our own way."

Then he cradled the handset. "Powwow. Let's go, white woman."

"Why me? I'm not—do you think it's because of Chan?"

"Come on. I saw your face when the phone rang. You'd rather face wild dogs than be cooped up alone with me."

"Unfair, Dalton."

"Life isn't fair, Jen. No, it's not Chan, I don't think: he's invited too. We'll explain about that, when we get there. Let me handle that part."

"I shouldn't—"

"I thought you were going to cover for your husband to pay me back for all the trouble—"

"Yes, I am. I'll be right with you. Let me get a sweater."

If it was a matter of professional pride, then so be it. She had as much professional pride, and more basic ability, than ninety percent of the men out here. She'd been wishing he'd treat her like a male colleague, and now he was doing it.

So why was Dalton making her angry all over again?

They took his car, some sort of English Rover, and in it, as they jounced toward Seti's, he said, "If this gets too deep for you, remember to throw me the ball."

"Why do you think it might?" In the strobing of lights as they passed oncoming cars, Ford looked tense and grim. And beautiful.

But she'd had her chance, and she'd blown it. She just wasn't capable of personal treachery. "It's a character flaw," she murmured.

"Excuse me?" he asked.

"I'm worrying about what Seti has on his mind. Who else did you say—"

"I didn't. I really needed at least one Land to come: Larka and Ignatov are already there. You know the Soviets' view of you two: heavy Company players. So for tonight, you are one. Jay Adamson'll be there too, but don't worry about him. He'll follow whatever looks like the line of least resistance." Ford's voice was openly bitter.

"You think Jay and my husband conspired against you, don't you? Even after I've told you that's not so."

"Everybody knows my business, and in my line of work, that can get me killed."

"Surely not at Seti's."

"No, surely not at Seti's."

She could feel his distress. The only thing she could think of to do was reach out to touch him. He took her hand and brought it to his lips, never taking his eyes off the road.

"I'm sorry. I get snappish when I don't know what I'm walking into. Reach into the glove compartment and hand me the pistol there." He let go of her hand.

Wonderful. *Pistol.* She found the Beretta, its leather wrapped around it, and handed Ford the spidery little shoulder rig after she'd untangled it.

You didn't live this life and not learn about weapons. And you didn't associate with these men without learning when to keep your mouth shut.

They drove in silence the rest of the way to Seti's, once she'd helped Dalton shrug into the shoulder holster.

When they turned in the drive, he reached in back for his jacket. "You ready?" he said.

"Why not?" She was going to be as good as her word. It was a matter of professionalism. She tried not to think that Chan's career might hang in the balance: Dalton would never go back on his promise not to make waves, no matter how this turned out.

But she must be very careful.

Ford left the keys in the Rover for the houseboy who'd park it, and helped her into her sweater as they mounted the steps.

Seti's home was the sort of place Jenny had always dreamed she'd have: high ceilings, French crystal chandeliers, fine nineteenth-century paintings in huge gold leaf frames. And the rugs were such that one almost hated to walk on them.

But a home like this in Cairo wasn't the same thing as a home like this in the Washington area. Still, it made her wish she'd fulfilled more of her early expectations, walking through three palatial rooms to get to the group gathered in a small sitting room.

As Ford had predicted, Larka, the man who'd stopped her and Quantrell on the road, was there. And Ignatov, whom she'd met at Seti's party, as sturdy as a Russian bear, stood between open French doors. Jay Adamson, in a Hawaiian shirt, was leaning on the mantelpiece, spidery and very pale tonight under his tan.

Adamson said, "Good to see you, all. Thanks for being prompt. Where's Chan, parking the car?"

Jenny spoke up, too quickly: "Out doing some FleetSatCom work offshore."

Ignatov turned away from the night: "Ah, Mrs. Land. See, we said we would be helping you. My partner, Larka, is always as good as his word. My government, too, is always as good as its word."

Where was Seti?

Ford, too, was looking around.

Adamson said, "Seti'll be right along. Before he joins us, let me just say that I'm not about to commit to intelligence sharing for interoperability on this sort of scale—not when we're talking about something far removed from an exercise."

"What sort of scale, Jay?" Ford said.

Simultaneously, from behind Jenny, Seti's voice asked: "And why not, Amid Adamson?"

Well, Jenny supposed, if you wanted to stretch a point, a CIA resident was the equivalent of a brigadier general: *amid*.

Adamson, instead of answering Seti, just sipped at a snifter in his hand.

Everyone looked at Seti, who always reminded Jenny of a famous actor whose name she kept forgetting. Seti's handsome face took on a scolding expression: "Jay, the moderate Arabs, my friends from the League and from the Gulf Cooperation Council, must have a hand in it—"

"It?" Ford interjected sharply.

"*It*, Mr. Ford: Whatever is done about this . . . increasingly likely link between our area and your, ah, overhead problems. It—the adventure my sources tell me you Russians and Americans are planning—must *not* involve the type of sortie that Aqid Larka and Mr. Ignatov foresee, *without our inclusion* . . . to prevent a war erupting if someone among the Arabs is attacked, or perceives himself to be attacked, or his territorial sovereignty violated."

Jenny Land was fascinated by Seti's eyes; they were coal black with red-brown rims, like the eyes of a snapping turtle or a bird of prey.

Jay Adamson put his drink on the mantelpiece and walked over to stand between Jenny and Ford, facing Seti. Jenny was all too conscious that Ford had worn a gun to this meeting. If that were discovered, the results might be unfortunate.

Adamson said, "No special intel until I've cleared it. Which means that I have to know what 'it' is, Sarwat."

"Ah, so that's it." Seti's eyes didn't blink. His face didn't change. "You Americans do not trust me. This I knew." He put his hands in his pockets and everybody moved: Ford put his arm around Jenny's waist and pulled her three steps to the right. Adamson moved in to face Seti head-on. Farther back, Larka and Ignatov closed the distance between them, conferring in whispers.

"Aqid Larka, come and testify in my behalf to the Americans, who have been treating me like the bad guy ever since I introduced my houseguest of an evening, our friend Dalton here, to Meri Soukry."

Larka, from behind Jenny, said, "Seti's an okay guy, we are all sure of it. Only others in his department disturb us."

Ignatov rushed to cover Larka's bluntness, saying, "There is, of course, some leakage in any intelligence organization, as the American, Quantrell, found out."

Jenny, unable to help herself, blazed, "I don't understand what's going on here. What do you want, Mr. Seti? There's too much suspicion all around, and if you ask me, it's either your fault or that Soukry woman's fault!"

Now everyone was looking at her. She disengaged Dalton's hand from her waist, walked primly to the couch, and sat down before her trembling knees toppled her. Not the right situation to have walked into in high heels.

"Yes, Mrs. Land, you are astute, as usual," Seti said. "There is too much suspicion, and it has, we think, been sown by the Soukry woman. Although—" His raised hand couldn't forestall Ford's interruption.

"If Colonel Quantrell were here, we could talk about suspicion, starting with the name of a fat interrogator whom nobody remembers seeing at your HQ, despite the fact that everybody was dancing to this nonexistent person's tune."

"I am cleaning my house, Mr. Ford. Show me that you are cleaning yours."

"That's a deal," Ford snapped. "You first, buddy." He sat on the arm of Jenny's couch. His hands were balled into fists.

Adamson said, "I'm glad everyone's calm. Now, Sarwat, or Yousef, if you prefer, is there any other reason for this meeting besides setting up the Arab moderates to vet any—hypothetical—projected action?"

"To make sure," Seti said, "that any projected action meets with our approval. And to secure what intelligence sharing we can for such an action—which we *know* is in preparation. And we do not blame you Americans, or you Russians. But we must have a hand in it. This is our stomping grounds."

"But it is not your problem," said Larka in something that sounded more like an animal snarl than a human voice.

"You are wrong, Aqid Larka. When someone from this region is thought to be attacking spacecraft, it is a problem for all of us."

"We don't agree—" Adamson began.

"Do not treat me as a fool, please." Seti, with a smirk, moved to the bar and began pouring drinks. "You, Ford? You, Mrs. Land? You, Larka—a beer, yes?"

When he'd finished pouring and everyone had moved to the bar, Seti said, "Now, this is better. A friendly discussion. If I am a man who uses a work name—an assumed name—to protect his family, and you have found this out, then it should prove to you only that I am cautious enough to be fully trusted, not that I am untrustworthy. I am offering cooperation on a massive scale—you may interpret cooperation as a lack of interference, if we come to terms tonight."

Seti looked up from the glasses and handed Jay Adamson a cognac. "So, what do you say, Jay?"

"I'll ask," Adamson said grudgingly.

"And you, Mr. Ford?"

"I'm really fond of Glenfiddich," Ford said as he took the scotch appreciatively, "but I'm just here doing comms for Space Command."

"Yes, with the Russians; we know. Well, now you can do them with our help. It must make you feel better."

"Lots," Ford said, and toasted Jenny, who'd just taken a white wine from Seti. "To fun and games. And good relations, now and in the future."

Somehow, Jenny realized as she sipped her wine, she'd ended up where she'd always wanted to be: in the middle of something so real, so important, so imminent, that no one was treating her as a mere woman any longer.

If the stakes weren't so high, she might have been jubilant. As it was, she found herself wishing that Chan could have been here. But Chan couldn't be here. She had to handle their part of this on her own.

41

Day 18: The Egyptian-Israeli Border

"Just like that, an apology from Seti, an admission that there's trouble in his shop, and you're letting him audit this mission, Ford? Jesus, have you got sunstroke, or what?"

"Nope, Jesse. Just doin' my best to get this show on the road," Ford said, his face merely a flash of eyes and teeth in the dim, ruddy standby lights of the chopper behind him.

There was no sun up yet today, at the border pickup point Ford had designated. Dalton was leaning on the Quickfix IIB as if he owned the Blackhawk helicopter fitted for SIGINT/ECM (signals intelligence and electronic countermeasures), which Mackenzie had borrowed from the Army.

He had his black box under his arm, and a second hard case in his other hand. Because they were using "low-observables technology" whenever possible, there were no lights out here beyond the Blackhawk's minimal illumination. But if you'd survived to Quantrell's age in this business, you had learned to see in the dark.

And Jesse wasn't liking much of what he'd been seeing lately, and less of what he'd been hearing. But you couldn't get Ford to talk to you until he was ready.

He stubbed out his Salem and turned away. These kids needed full supervision if Quantrell was going to get them through this alive. None of them, except Mackenzie and possibly Kellogg, were what Quantrell liked to think of as seasoned combat veterans.

After this mission, the live ones would be.

"Jesse," Ford said softly.

"Now you want to talk?" Quantrell flipped the cover off his wristwatch and checked the time: "Your pickup's late."

"Jesse, let's get something straight: if you and Meri have something going, I'm not going to stand in your way. She'll be here any time now, so we need to clear the air."

"Ford, go fuck yourself. I just don't like secret mission parameters when I'm not privy to the secrets."

"Neither am I, Jesse—not yet. Meri's people are doing all the prepositioning. Mackenzie's good. You're fucking great. I'm not worried about your adaptability to Israeli battle strategies. You work it out. You go in. You take a look. You've got Israeli F-14 cover, with rockets underwing that you can call down for close air support, and helicopter extraction if anybody needs it or wants it in case of resistance. That's all I know."

"Resistance to what?"

"Resistance to Mackenzie and Marconi eyeballing what they've got in that station, if that's what it is, and maybe bringing home a souvenir or two."

Quantrell blew out a deep breath and lit another cigarette. "I could swear I just heard us hit the wall, Ford. How come you're saying 'you,' not 'we'? And what's this souvenir shit?"

"Look, Jesse, you can change anything you don't like about this battle plan once you get on the ground."

"You're still saying 'you,' not 'we,' Dalton."

"Yeah, well . . . I'm going in separately. Give you some real-time recon and on-site intelligence. I'll be in place and transmitting to Marconi by the time you guys—"

"How you gonna do that, Dalton? If what we've got for intelligence is any good, you'll blow the whole mission trying to—"

"Not with a high-altitude, low-opening jump I won't. I'm just going to float on down and sit there, set up toys, and pick my teeth until your team comes along with some firepower."

"Ford, you asshole. You're too old for—"

"This is my mess, Jesse."

"At least now we both know it's your mission. I don't like it."

"I'm not highly enthusiastic about it myself, but I've talked myself blue and that's the best deal I could cut. If we do it this way, we get full cooperation from the Israelis; the Egyptians give us some interoperating slack with border crossings and ancient rivalries, and—"

"*Egypt*ians? Oh, no, Dalton. Don't *do* this to me. You know how I hate operating with Egyptians. Soviet maps and—"

"Which reminds me, Larka and Iggy may show up."

Quantrell squatted down, stubbed out his cigarette, and looked in the general direction of Ford's silhouette, nearly indistinguishable from the Quickfix. "No way. No dice. I'm not runnin' a friggin' UN mixer; I'm doing a night mission. Recon and maybe some payback. Do my SAG boys look like expendable spare parts to you? Because we're not thinking of ourselves that way."

Ford came down to Quantrell's level. "Jesse, do you always have to second-guess me? Don't act like a prima donna. You know that if I could have done better, I would have. This isn't like dropping an integrated SF A-team into Beirut, for God's sake. We're trying to limit the possible repercussions."

"There's no possible way, with as many privy parties as you're contemplating, that this go has a chance of staying secret long enough to keep us from having to engage the enemy. You know that, Dalton. You're no kid pushing pieces around a topo table in a Washington war room."

"Screw you, Quantrell. I'm goddamn goin' in there by my lonesome, aren't I? To sit up there and talk you guys in?"

"Yeah, and you're giving me the go-ahead to take over your girlfriend. That's what worries me. Ford, you want to sit this one out, I'd feel better."

"My ass." Ford got up. "I gotta go show this last toy to Marconi and Mackenzie. If you want to at least pretend you're following the armed services into the electronic age, Quantrell, you can come along and watch."

Quantrell got up and followed Ford, saying, "You know, I'm going to take you up on that part about Meri Soukry. She's too good for the likes of you, anyhow."

"Fine. Great. Give you a reason to stop acting like a coach

and start acting like a player. You want to do the interfacing with the Israelis, I'm not going to be anywhere around to get in your way."

"Suits me. I hope you don't find out you're too old for HALO jumps the hard way. Christ, I wouldn't let my worst enemy try—"

Quantrell shut up. They were too close to the team to show open discord. Ford walked over to the shapes sitting on the ground and hunkered down: "Marconi, Mackenzie, I want to give you guys this little present before the Israelis arrive."

He bent the red-tipped penlight in his breast pocket to shine down, lit it, and opened his case.

Quantrell had to get in close if he wanted to see what Ford had.

"I'd like you boys to meet STICS: Scalable Transportable Intelligence Communications System. STICS is UHF/Sat-Com, so Marconi—" Ford handed Marconi something about the size of a portable radio "—you can use this to keep in touch with me via my black box, no matter where we are." He pulled out something that looked like a sleeping bat and handed that to Mackenzie, who said, "No shit?" and opened it.

In the red penlight, the thing in Mackenzie's hand looked like a tiny umbrella; an oversized, black drink parasol; or what it was: a tiny, collapsible dish antenna.

"Thanks, Mr. Ford," said Mackenzie as if Ford had made Mackenzie his heir.

Marconi said, "I saw one of these before. Used it, or one generation back from this one. I won't have any trouble, but if you want to test it with yours now . . ."

Ford looked up, as if he'd heard something. Quantrell looked up too.

"No time," Ford said judiciously. "I trust you, Marconi. Just remember, don't leave the dust-off area without me, even if I lose contact. Because I'll be there."

"We'll find you, Mr. Ford," said Mackenzie. "Don't you worry. You tuned this thing already, to the right freq for your transmissions?"

"That's right." Ford stood up.

By then Quantrell could hear rotor blades, merely a distant

thunking against the air, more of a pulse on his eardrums than a sound.

Then he readied his people for imminent deployment to the pickup aircraft, while Ford went to give the Army pilot in the Quickfix some final instructions.

Instructions like ignoring everything he saw from that moment on, Quantrell was willing to bet.

When Ford came back, the Quickfix IIB was whining to life, sitting in the dark with no running lights, the way she'd flown them in.

The Israeli chopper was, it turned out, a captured Soviet Hind with desert camouflage. It came in nap-of-the-earth, maybe forty feet above the ground.

As it started to set down, Ford took Quantrell aside and yelled in his ear: "I forgot to tell you. I got X-NASP and Israeli targeting data for the site above Homs Gap that's going to blow your socks off when Meri gives it to you. So don't worry about viability, so far as the target's concerned. You'll have plenty of intel. Your boys can access any overhead they need with that STICS terminal, if I'm not up and running. And don't worry about the body count. I talked to my people. Nobody cares if any of those bastards survive, as long as we've got a piece of evidence to justify the damage we're hoping to do. If we can, we enter the facility, take an inventory, and then destroy it unattributably. If we have to, we destroy it without eyeballing the inside. If we can't do that, the Israeli air cover will destroy it for us, with rockets. But we really don't want this done with Israeli hardware, Quantrell."

"Yeah, Ford, I see your point." Nice of Ford to tell him, before he got on the Israelis' Hind.

He could piss his pants now, if he wanted to, and nobody'd be the wiser.

But he wasn't really surprised: Dalton always estimated your need-to-know right enough. It was just the lead time you needed that he underestimated.

Quantrell patted Ford on the back, hard, and went off to watch over Mackenzie while he formed up the men. You couldn't talk with two sets of rotor blades whipping dust and chop at you; you could barely see who was who.

But Quantrell didn't have any trouble recognizing Meri Soukry when she hopped down out of the Hind's slider and came running his way. Mackenzie was doing a good job getting men and equipment loaded, so Quantrell took time to hug the woman and give her a kiss before he swatted her rump and hurried her toward the Hind again.

Ford was right there, watching, from over by the Quickfix waiting to take him wherever Ford was planning to go.

Quantrell waved once and jumped for the slider door, dust in his eyes and sand peppering his face.

When he'd scrambled to his feet and had grabbed hold of a strap so that he could look outside, Kellogg was slamming the door shut.

Quantrell caught just a glimpse of the Quickfix IIB lifting into the last bit of the night, headed back toward Cairo and running without lights, before the Hind roared off the other way, toward the Israeli border.

Meri tugged on his sleeve. He bent down. She said into his ear, "Come forward. Sorry we're late. We'll still make it into Israel before first light."

Funny, Quantrell hadn't been worried about that until she'd mentioned it. Following the woman up to the flight deck of the Hind, he wasn't sure he was worried about it now. They had close to thirty minutes flying time before dawn.

Israelis worried about everything, he reminded himself. It was what kept them alive.

42

"You're sure you want to put yourself on the line like this, Don?" Beckwith was feeling positively paternal toward Colonel Pollock, ever since the AFSPACECOM deputy chief for special operations had brought X-NASP home, bacon included, her windows methodically crosshatched with adhesive tape from the space plane's medical kit to keep shards from flying around the cockpit if the panes blew inward.

"If I said 'no, I can't say that for sure,' then what? Would you ask Conard to verify the space-radar sighting?" Pollock squinted at Beckwith as the two men headed for Beckwith's car, parked outside Pollock's office in the bright morning light. The sandy-haired colonel was clearly still defensive about cutting short X-NASP's flight.

Beckwith had to fix that, somehow. "I'd probably take a deposition from Major Conard, yes. Not that his opinion's going to carry as much weight as yours—and not that I'd bring him to a meeting where the subscription list of cognizant players is so short. But I won't think any less of you if you pass on this one, Colonel."

"What're you saying? That you think we're so far out on a limb that you want to protect me, in case we're wrong, because if this blows up in our faces, heads are going to roll? I know that. And I know it's the lowest-ranking head that rolls first. So what?" He thumped Beckwith's Cherokee and looked up. "I brought X-NASP home with no significant damage. It's arguable that, despite the foreshortened time frame, we accomplished our objective. I know a lot of men who'd have passed me over for somebody younger. You didn't. I passed my postflight physical. My debriefing's done. There's no favor you can't ask from me right now, Leo. I'm so damned grateful, I'd fly that lateral insertion over Syria for you, if you wanted."

"Lateral insertion." Beckwith, unlocking the Cherokee's doors, made a disapproving noise. "I don't know who thinks up these terms. Somebody who jumps out of a plane at high altitude knows damned well that he's doing something a bit more risky than 'lateral insertion' makes it sound."

"I know. And Ford knows what he's doing. If I was young enough to fly X-NASP because skill's what counts, he's young enough to HALO into that target area. Don't worry, Leo. I'll back you all the way." Pollock got in the car, fanning the hot air away from him as he did.

Beckwith started the engine and the blower for the air conditioner before he closed his door. "All right. You're my AFSPACECOM special ops maven, and I'm taking your word that Ford can do this with a very low signature and without jeopardizing mission security. We'll hold to that no matter how the regional theater commander bitches." USSOCOM—United States Special Operations Command—at MacDill owed Beckwith a favor. "You've got a pilot and an aircraft already designated, I assume?"

"Ford rolled his own. And I like the whole package real well, from a SPACECOM standpoint."

Both doors slammed. "That's not going to be the major issue, initially: CINCSPACE doesn't need to know every detail. I need you to stand there while Fred Whelan and I convince Washington and Langley that your flight—foreshortened or not—and the covert satellite data Ford collected, clearly indicate that what we've got above Homs is a tracking and telemetry station."

"That's what I saw, Leo."

Beckwith backed the car out of its parking space. "Washington wants to hear 'sure, for sure,' out of us. CIA's offering to let us nudge one of its photo-return satellites a little off its current course to give us some extra photo-reconnaissance. Plus there's that covert bird you can use when its overhead, and the cheap sat."

"I give you my word, Leo, we'll cover every minute we possibly can. This special op's going to have more coverage than a presidential campaign. Just the intelligence we'll collect on the other interoperating parties will make it worth our while. And if we have to show what we did to some committee somewhere, and you want to do that, we'll have documentation up the arse."

"You've made me feel a whole lot better, Colonel Pollock." Beckwith, turning toward Fred Whelan's office, accelerated. "Let's go do it for the record. God, I hate teleconferencing."

"I know what you mean," said Pollock. "But if something goes wrong, it'll be nice to have made it clear we were monitoring our people every step of the way, on top of the whole program."

This was nice. Beckwith was actually feeling feisty again as he walked into the office of USSPACECOM's commander in chief with Pollock, the hero of the hour, at his side.

It never hurt, when you were facing Washington and Langley brass, to have something sexy to show, like a deputy chief for special operations who'd personally piloted X-NASP over the kill zone in question because he was so committed to your mission.

Especially when you'd already committed more than a dozen field people—from USSOCOM, not your own shop—to that mission's next phase, and it was virtually too late to issue a pullback order, even if Beckwith wanted to. Which he didn't.

Whoever was out there killing sats had to be stopped. Whatever else was out there had to be identified: The analysis of X-NASP's reconnaissance and Ford's Israeli data wasn't yet complete. If it was as serious a threat as Beckwith suspected, that threat had to be countered.

Now. Before it was too late and they'd lost the advantage of surprise.

43

Day 18: Homs Gap, Syria

Free-falling from the Learjet with Saudi markings, through the still night, Ford had plenty of time to think.

He didn't like thinking in free-fall. He liked floating, stretching out, kiting with his body and listening to the wind. But that was what you did when you were skydiving for fun, not when you were HALOing into hostile territory from 22,000 feet, wearing a black motorcycle helmet to which the mask feeding from your oxygen bottle was attached.

Ford couldn't hear the flap of his clothes against him; he couldn't really feel the peace that he knew was up here.

Down below, there wasn't much in the way of peace to be had, either. And above him . . .

The Learjet they'd borrowed from the Saudi moderates was gone now, shadowing its way along in the radar image of a charter, bound for Turkey out of Cairo West, on a regular route. Seti hadn't missed a trick, making himself useful.

If there'd been any way that Ford could have gotten in here without Seti knowing about it, he'd have felt better. But Seti had been bound to find out anyway, no matter how Ford played it, when he didn't show up with Quantrell's team for the nap-of-the-earth insertion.

He shouldn't keep worrying about it. He should watch his step out here—keep an eye on his altimeter and his descent curve. *Jabal* meant mountain, and Ford's drop between the

Jabal an-Nusayriyah range and the Anti-Lebanon mountains wasn't the easiest he'd ever tried.

Strange things happened with air currents when you had the ocean so close, two mountain ranges that almost met, and a river flowing through the gap between them.

The Israelis had known the area like the backs of their hands—what radars to watch for, where the airstreams tended to get tricky. Meri Soukry had gotten him everything he needed.

Ford was falling into the moisture-laden sea winds of the Jabal an-Nusayriyah's fertile, western slopes in the scruffy battle dress of one of the private militias of the Lebanese Maronites. He had a Soviet AKM-15 paratroop sniper rifle, instead of the AK-47s being carried by Quantrell's forces, but the rest of what he carried was calculated to identify his body, if captured, as belonging to a mercenary out of Lebanon.

Since you could see into the Bekáa Valley from his projected landing zone, and the Lebanese border was on the "Go to Shit" plan (if everything went to shit, you walked down into Tripoli and met at a bar there), Ford was comfortable enough with the legend. He had a British-made Racal PRM4735 Covert Personal Radio system, complete with earpiece and lapel mike, for communicating with Quantrell's troops on the ground; a couple hand-emplaceable jammers on his web belt, along with three Soviet butterfly mines, C-4, three concussion grenades and three thermite grenades of East European manufacture.

The only telltales that marked him as what he was—an American purple suit bulling his way into a Special Forces mission because, years ago, he'd led A-teams out here—were his custom electronics, and that couldn't be helped.

Ford wasn't going to miss this chance to field-test his black box. Hell, that was what he'd been doing here in the first place. He'd stripped the box out of its hard case and stuffed it into his pack, along with his other necessaries.

Like the Jack Crain survival knife he carried, it didn't fit well with his image as a low-tech mercenary. But then, neither did his high-tech dental work or his cyanide pills. If he decided to get dead, he'd blow the equipment first; if he had time before getting dead accidentally, he'd set the booby trap on the black box, although if you did that and forgot . . .

Everything seemed hypothetical, free-falling in a helmet while you breathed bottled oxygen. He checked his wrist-strapped altimeter again; mustn't forget to bury it with the helmet, oxygen bottle, and mask.

He wanted as low a chute opening as he dared attempt. The landing zone he'd chosen on the mountain's slope was one where he could hunker down and keep watch on the facility with his naked eye, just upslope of the radar signature.

He wanted to see the damned dish, if he could, from where he was going to dig in and wait for Quantrell's people.

You didn't want to wait long. Not if the other signatures they'd picked up were accurate. Not if Meri was right about troops and artillery massing just southwest of the Gap, for a push down through Lebanon.

But before Ford could worry about anything as peripheral to his current situation as being discovered on the ground, he had to land—on his feet, not his head, and preferably without breaking anything.

He wanted to think about it in terms of controlled descent. And he wanted his timing to be just right. But he couldn't help trying to see into the murk down there, as it came closer. And he couldn't help counting to himself as he got ready to pull his cord.

He pulled it.

He could feel the chute billow out. It was a kind of sixth sense you acquired, as if you could see through the top of your head; the same kind of sixth sense that would prompt you to step just to the left of a mine or to bend down to light a cigarette just when the bullet was coming your way out of the trees.

If you lost that edge, you were dead. Until he pulled his cord and knew his chute hadn't streamed, Ford wasn't sure he still had it. But he did, and when the comforting jerk of the chute pulled him up short, he was humming to himself, already disengaging one of the Velcro tabs on his mask so that he could breathe the salty air.

From here to the ground, Ford would get to find out if he was still the lucky bastard he'd always been. All the while he kept glancing at the global positioning handheld, while controlling his descent, part of him was remembering

Vladimir Matiosov's *Soviet Military Review* article on tracking techniques for shooting paratroopers from the ground: "*When firing at paratroopers, the lead is taken in paratrooper length reckoned from his waistband . . .*"

Ford put the GPS handheld back in his jacket pocket. If he'd calculated his drift right, he'd be well within the grid square marking his optimum position.

"*. . . the lead must be one less than the slant range expressed in hundreds of meters, and two less for weapons using rifle and 5.45-mm cartridges. . . .*"

A downdraft caught him, and tried to suck him south. He wasn't about to end up in that valley, sitting on a railroad car, trying to explain what the hell he was doing there. . . .

"*. . . the aiming point must be displaced . . . in the direction of the parachuter's movement, which depends on the direction and speed of the wind. . . .*"

There. Better. You could see the rough edge of the range now, dark against the sky to his left. Its average height was 1,211 meters. "Average" didn't mean much if you were walking terrain because you'd screwed up. What had made him say he could do this without night-vision goggles?

"*. . . After the first long burst, the sight setting or aiming point can be changed, after which the weapon should be set to the previous position and firing continuously until the target is destroyed.*"

Whap! Up out of the night came the trees as if they were reaching for him. Ford cursed as he yanked on his chute. He didn't want to be hung in the trees. A leafy branch caught in his half-disengaged oxygen mask and broke off, snapping him across the face, under the eye, as it did so.

Then the ground slapped him, hard, under the feet and his knees weren't good enough to keep his ass from hitting a bunch of sharp rocks. *Don't want to be dragged . . .*

Pulling in the chute, trying to get his balance and run with it while he squeezed out the air, he kept feeling a jagged pain in his leg. When he had his arms around the parachute silk and it wasn't fighting him, he still couldn't stop to worry about what might hurt.

The leg held him. Out of his harness, he gathered the chute

into a ball, stripped off his helmet, altimeter, and oxygen bottle, rolled them in the chute, and then began digging a hole to bury them, using his Crain knife.

The soil was rocky, but if you don't care how hard it is to do something, your adrenaline will do it for you.

Sometime after he'd gotten the hole dug, stuffed the damned parachute in the hole and shoveled dirt and small rocks over it with his hand, he remembered that his leg still hurt.

By then he was rechecking his position with his GPS handheld. *Walk half a mile uphill? Why not?*

Because it hurt, now that he thought about it. He stopped to check out the leg, and when he put his head down it hurt to breathe. He could feel his pulse pounding behind his eyes like something in there that wanted to bust out.

He couldn't find anything broken, although he thought he probably had one hell of a hematoma. *Walk uphill, you bet.*

Nobody'd shot at him, he thought, about the time he noticed that the quarter moon was rising over the mountains.

Half a mile straight up, it felt like.

He hiked, turning on his Racal PRM4735, in case it could pick up anything from Quantrell's party this early.

He didn't hear a thing, once he got the inductive loop played out and the button earpiece in his ear. He took the little palm-sized Racal remote unit out of his belt and hit the control which generated a short tone burst that would signal, if Marconi was listening, that Ford was on-site and in position.

Well, close enough, anyway. He put the palm-sized RCU in his breast pocket; the batteries would give him four active-duty hours before he had to change them.

He hoped to hell that was going to be enough. Maybe he wandered a little off course because his leg hurt, and he was instinctively taking whatever looked like the easiest route. Or maybe he was still as lucky as he needed to be, because while he was climbing toward the grid coordinates he wanted, a little upslope of the area where the space-tracking radar signal had been, he hit something with his sore leg.

And then he looked again. And blinked in the moonlight.

If he hadn't been climbing around in the dark, he probably never would have banged right into one of the dish supports—

or, more exactly, the concrete piling into which the support was set.

Even right on top of it, he couldn't see it for the overgrowth, and the dish itself was camouflage-painted to match the environment, set into a handy hollow.

He stepped back three paces, very carefully. If there were any seismics here, he'd just tripped one.

Then, trusting his instinct, he kept backing up, ten paces, in what he hoped and firmly believed were his own footsteps.

He was right on top of the goddamned thing.

Hunkering down there, he considered his options. And then he reached for the C-4 he was carrying.

It was going take him a few minutes to pack the supports of the dish and set timers, but it was an opportunity he couldn't let pass.

For all he knew, he could end up the only guy who made it to the site. Anything could—and did—happen on lateral insertions. Something invariably went wrong.

The timers he had with him were radio-controllable, if he wanted to delay them later, so he set them to maximum and then started backing up again, still using his own tracks as best he could.

His leg was burning like thermite from all that kneeling and scrambling, and he was very conscious that, if there had been seismics or motion detectors emplaced around the dish, he'd be getting a bullet in the brain any minute now.

But he managed to retreat from the dish far enough to detour to his left before he heard voices.

He flattened in the underbrush, while his mind was still telling him that you wouldn't want seismics or motion detectors out here, because of plant, animal, and other nonhostile intrusions: you'd be running back and forth on false alarms all the time.

But his ears were listening. The voices were upslope, a little to his right. He kept trying to see their source, or make out the words. But he couldn't.

There was a dark regularity up there that might be a building, or an entrance to an underground building, because the edge, from his vantage point, was so regular.

Two men were talking, and it was an Arab dialect, he was nearly sure. That wasn't surprising.

What was surprising was that the voices started receding, and then there was a sudden square of light, which narrowed before it disappeared.

Okay, his intelligence had been better than he'd given it credit for; or he'd misread his GPS. One way or the other, he was right on top of the ground station that, an hour ago, he wasn't sure was out here.

Damn his leg. He grabbed his thigh as he got up and headed off to the left of the station. Still had to make the rendezvous. Still had to make contact with Quantrell's team. At least, now, even if he bought it, the dish might still blow on schedule, if the plastique wasn't discovered.

It was Bulgarian C-4, he reminded himself. He'd have to remember to thank Ignatov for that. Without it, all Ford's suspicions that Seti/Hatim was setting them up to take a fall might really have been bothering him as he limped his way toward the SAG drop point.

It wasn't until he was almost there that he began thinking about setting up his black box. He had lots of intel to gather, yet. And if he could do it, without being discovered, before Quantrell's team dropped, so much the better.

Since he'd almost screwed everything up back there—blown the whole mission by getting discovered prematurely, just the way Quantrell would be worried he might, he ought to have a little something more than a few preset detonations to tell Quantrell about when next they met.

44

Day 18: Jabal an-Nusayriyah

"Okay, listen up," Quantrell said needlessly to the team, sitting with black-smeared hands and faces in the modified Apache. He'd scrounged the electronics-laden helicopter from the *Kitty Hawk* offshore, once he'd won the argument about what kind of helicopter to use for this nap-of-the-earth leg of the night mission.

Shit, whatever helicopter the Israelis would have given him was going to be an American airframe, anyway. So you took your best shot. His *Kitty Hawk* pilot and copilot were from Seal Team 2, out here for Bright Star and therefore commandeerable by Quantrell. They had all the radar cross sections for the venue down, so they knew where not to fly.

Before they'd left Israel, Quantrell had felt like his veins were icing, sitting in a Mossad bunker with Iggy, Larka, Seti, some AMAN major, and Soukry, while everybody was trying to play intelligence-swap with the lives of his people.

Now he was even more jumpy as he looked at the men watching him, waiting for their final tune-up. Mackenzie had that sleepy-eyed look you never knew whether to like; Marconi was strung tighter than piano wire; Kellogg was cleaning his overpowered handgun with manic intensity, all his five CIA fraternity brothers huddled behind him in a knot.

You wanted to protect your team's integrity, which wasn't so easy when it was mixed, and each man had the individualistic tendencies that came with the ability to do this job and do it well. Team integrity was another reason Quantrell had flat refused to let Iggy, Larka, the AMAN major or—for chrissakes!—Meri, come along.

Israeli women fought in combat, he understood that. He understood lots of things he didn't like, and wouldn't sanction.

So it was just his people in the custom-bellied Apache, augmented to hold his entire team, the way he'd wanted it. If he'd stepped on enough toes, maybe he'd end up transferred to a different venue, or even a different region. But he could live with that, if all his men lived through this.

"One more time, people," he said as gently as he could over the Apache's running noise; and in the back, down near the Apache's tail, Kellogg stopped cleaning his .451 magnum.

"Once we're at the drop zone, we salt the route with anti-personnel mines. We're going out some other way." He held up his hand and brought up one finger: "Extraction by Israeli helicopters, at the kill zone, if we're perfect." He held up a second finger: "Contingency plan, extraction by U.S. forces, probably under fire, at your alternate site, if we have to call in an Israeli air strike on the primary target."

Mackenzie palmed a yawn. Nobody else moved a muscle.

"E and E," Quantrell continued, holding up a third finger as he reminded them of the escape and evasion scenario: "Down into Homs Gap, or hit the Orontes riverside. Lebanese/Israeli boats will be along the river. Tickets are waiting at the railroad station. Soviet contacts too. Everybody's got phone numbers to call. On your way out, blow everything you can—fertilizer plants or grain storage bins if you see them, any kind of hardware or gas station. It'll help us find you."

He waited a minute. Nobody said anything. He waited another minute. Marconi shifted in place. "Yeah, Marconi?"

"Uh—I want to know, that is—if I have to ask for Soviet exfiltration in case of E and E, what do I do about my classified gear?"

"Your choice. Destroy it or hold onto it—tight." That seemed to satisfy Marconi. "Anybody else?"

Nobody said anything; nobody moved.

"Last, but not least, the Go to Shit's still the Majnoun Bar in Tripoli: we'll have somebody there until every one of you is accounted for, if it takes six months, but we'd really like all of you who can to be there by day after tomorrow, sunset."

If they couldn't make it down there by then, either they were on foot, wounded, or had exercised their cyanide option.

Kellogg put away his .451 and got out a Sykes-Fairbairn, which he began whetting. "Kellogg, you trackin' this program?"

"Uh, yes, sir. I was wondering . . ."

"Wonder away."

There was always one guy with a better idea at the last minute, because at the last minute his adrenaline jacked him up so high that any idea seemed good.

"I was just wondering why we can't meet at the CIA station in Tripoli?"

"If you want to do that, all of you who have that information, go right ahead. Send your resident to the bar with a head count."

Quantrell wished he had a straight Special Forces team for this. The CIA Special Activities Group people were very good, but they thought they were better than very good—they thought they were better than the rest of Quantrell's people because, to a man, all of them had been through college and every one of them had a valuable language specialty.

"Kellogg, you're the best Arabic speaker, so you'll be right with Marconi all the time. I don't want you Company people off talking Syriac, French, and whatever together, cutting your own deal with locals, unless we're in damage control."

Kellogg's startling blue eyes began to show pupils in his cammo-smeared face. "Yes, sir. I didn't mean that. I'm just worried about the multinational aspects."

"You know, Kellogg, that bothers me too. If I could, I'd have shot all those Israelis and the Egyptian as well. Then we'd have had only the Soviets to worry about."

"Yes, sir," Kellogg said. "I know we couldn't do it any other way."

"Till we get on site, Kellogg, that's the truth. Now, when we're down there, we're going to talk this whole thing through one more time, unless there's an immediate skirmish. So, everybody who has a good idea, hold it until then."

Each of these men had been through a rigorous selection process that weeded out the ones that couldn't think on their feet. Not a one of them had brought a similar side arm, commando knife, or even pocketknife: they lived by their preferences. Except for the AK-47s and RPG-7s, the team could well have been the mercenary outfit it was meant to resemble.

The pilot up front called back to Quantrell that he had ten minutes.

Quantrell got up, hunched over in the Apache, and stuck his head up front: "How's the signature?"

Behind him, Mackenzie gave the order to lock and load.

"Better than good, sir." The night-vision goggles on the pilot made him look like a robot as he turned his head slightly. "You can rappel down if you want, but unless something changes, we can get down off these treetops and let you hop out. That is, if you don't mind hopping four or five feet unassisted."

"You're the pilot," said Quantrell, and went back to his men.

This was too easy. He didn't like missions that started out easy. They always went bad. At least, sliding down rappelling lines from forty feet or so, you had a chance to get your first casualty the easy way.

Mackenzie and Marconi were checking everybody's personal radios against "fratricide": making sure the scramblers were set so that, if it became necessary to deploy hexjams to screw up local transmissions, they wouldn't screw up their own. Everybody had hexjams, the size of small cigar boxes, preset to jam from twenty to eighty megahertz, but fine-tunable to local bandwidths. You just wired one under the back of the enemy commander's jeep, if you encountered an enemy with a commander who had a jeep, and you were all set.

Quantrell talked into his radio when Marconi asked him to, and then turned away, looking out the window at the trees passing by under the Apache's belly.

Something wasn't right here. He could feel it. He tapped his breast pocket, checking for the cyanide pills you always brought along. He hadn't wanted to issue them, but you always issued them.

All of a sudden, he was glad he had them. Syrians weren't famous for their hospitality in situations like this. And some of his high-tech specialists ought not to be any Third World power's guest for long.

Quantrell shook his head; he was getting too old for this, if he was thinking about cyanide. You never won unless you couldn't imagine not winning.

That's why he wasn't amenable to bringing a hodgepodge of foreign nationals along: he wanted to be able to narrow his concerns as much as he could. Winning meant getting out alive, with as many of his people as possible. But it didn't have to mean getting out with all of his people. You always expected to lose one or two.

That's why he hadn't gotten too close to them. Let Mackenzie worry about who was his best man at what, and how it was going to hurt to be without whomsoever.

Quantrell would probably never see any of these kids again, once this was over, unless they opted to come back here for a tour.

So he could go into this clear-headed, not the way he would if he'd had Meri and her whole circus to worry about.

Everybody was up and checking gear, webbing, rifles, rocket launchers, jamming black wool hats down on their heads and getting into position.

All of a sudden, the Apache banked sharply and started to climb.

Marconi nearly bumped Quantrell as he grabbed for a strap.

Up front, the copilot was swearing a blue streak and the pilot was calling Quantrell's name.

"Yeah?" He stuck his head between theirs.

"Uh—there's somebody down there. And they want to talk to you. And I don't like it." The last was through the pilot's gritted teeth.

The copilot handed Quantrell a headset with a dependent comm mike.

He listened for a minute, eyes widening, and said, "Okay."

Then he said to the pilots: "They're friendly," although he wasn't so sure about that.

"You want us to put you down there, then?"

"Right there," Quantrell confirmed and turned away, to hang his weight on a strap and look out at the dark, not talking to anybody because if he did, he was going to explode with rage he didn't want to explain.

The Apache was so low-signature that it had been right on top of the party waiting to greet them before it was noticed.

That was nice.

Quantrell watched the trees whip as the chopper came down, and then he watched his hands. Let Mackenzie unload the team first.

Otherwise, he might take one look at that sideshow and hustle everybody back into the chopper, leaving Dalton Ford and his foreign nationals to do this damned mission on their own.

Next thing, there'd be local press coverage.

Once everybody was out of the Apache but Quantrell and Kellogg, he moved to the open slider. Looked out. Shook his head. Touched the Desert Eagle on his hip.

Then he looked Kellogg straight in the eye: "Son, you know anything about those assholes being down there? Because this is the wrongest damned thing I've ever seen." You didn't put a trained team, whose lives depended on split-second timing, into the field with strangers along to trip over. You just didn't.

Kellogg cleared his throat and said, "Sorry about the ratfuck, sir. Adamson thinks interoperability's getting everybody involved out here where they can't do any talking. And the other governments were pressuring CIA to have their own observers on-site. I bet Larka feels just as bad about this as we do."

"That makes me feel lots better, Kellogg." The kid was obviously afraid that Quantrell might pull a total snit, call his people back, and just walk away from this mess here and now. But he wouldn't do that. He wouldn't give Adamson the satisfaction. If he couldn't stand it, he'd shoot the gatecrashers, every one: Meri Soukry, Seti, Larka and Ignatov. Then, when he got back, he'd shoot Adamson.

Goddamn circus.

Then he had to jump down out of the Apache. There was no excuse for endangering the heliborne ECM platform in a hostile venue just because he was pissed.

Once the Apache *whuk-whuked* its way up into the night,

Quantrell looked around the clearing which had been the designated drop zone.

He was going to go over to Dalton and punch him right in the mouth.

But Ford was the one person who *wasn't* on site.

Mackenzie, hands in his hip pockets, was standing in the middle of his widely grouped team, waiting for Quantrell to indicate how he was supposed to react.

"Go," Quantrell told the team. They knew what to do, and how to do it.

Mackenzie said quietly, "You heard the man."

The team moved off, hardly more than dark shapes in the night, as Meri came up to him. "Jesse, don't be angry."

"I'm not angry. You people want to have a picnic, that's fine with me. Just don't you don't be angry because I can't join you." And he started to back away from her, in the direction the team had gone.

She grabbed his wrist. Larka was waving, trotting toward them. Right behind him was Ignatov. Quantrell could hear the fat man's heavy breathing, even from this distance.

Seti was bringing up the rear.

"Jesse," Meri said in a tight, intense voice: "We cannot have you Americans taking the blame for this all alone."

"Even a woman," Larka said as he joined them, "tells the truth on occasion. Are you not glad to see us, my friend?"

"Larka, you know better than—"

Ignatov huffed up: "Please, we must not fall too far behind your commandos. I am not in the best of shape."

Last came Seti, whose teeth shone too brightly in the moonlight: "Quantrell, you must trust my judgment. Otherwise, if you are captured, there will be too much trouble having your stories believed."

Quantrell fought an impulse to sit down right here, to sacrifice himself for the mission, to delay and divert these fools so his men could get the job done.

Seti was wearing a Sig pistol on his hip. Somehow that struck Quantrell as funny, though everyone else was armed as well.

Meri still had him by the arm: "Jesse?"

"Okay, we walk to the rendezvous. I'll give you that much. If you people can convince me—quietly—that you can handle yourselves, you're on. Otherwise, I'm going to shoot two of you in the foot and leave you all. The others can carry the shot ones down to Homs. It ought to take all night."

45

Day 18: Cairo West Air Base

From her terminal in the Space Command tent, Jenny Land was in constant communication with Chan, aboard the *New Jersey*. The Army Space Command comms operator who'd usually worked with her when she'd been spending most of her time in Hangar 3 had been replaced by a "Space Command operations officer from J-3, Ma'am, fully deployable." The short, bespectacled fellow with a bull's neck had thrown her a sunny grin. "In case you need anything."

"That's nice. Thank you, Major Gold," she'd said, content that this fellow in the tent with her was cleared for whatever he might see, and familiar with the equipment so that she didn't have to worry about tutoring him.

At this point, she was so focused and so accustomed to Gold's presence that she hardly noticed that he was there.

Over the hands-free phone headset she wore, she and Chan were talking as they worked. In front of her, on her screen, was the Agency photo-return satellite whose orbital redeployment they were monitoring.

Some of the data she had were redundant, fed from CSOC in Colorado and its far-flung ground tracking stations. Some were coming right from FleetSatCom.

So when, in her monitor, she saw a blip she wasn't supposed to see, near the photo-return satellite, she said to Chan, "Do you see that?"

Even on scrambled communications gear, she'd learned to be careful. Chan, at his Fleet Intel terminal, could look at the blip in a number of signature modes. CSOC could have ALTAIR and ALCOR track it, if it was significant. The photo-return satellite itself could be directed to image the blip.

"You see it, too, Jen? I'm talking to CSOC right now," said her husband.

The photo-return satellite finished making its course correction. According to her equipment, the burn of its attitude thrusters shut down exactly on time.

She'd nearly forgotten about the blip. She looked back to it. Now it was gone. No matter. She was here to track the photo-return satellite's procession to a new orbit, not worry about what else was in the area. Anyway, she told herself as she watched her screen, the photo-return satellite was already out of the orbit that would have put it on a collision course with the blip at the time she'd seen it.

"I lost that secondary track," her husband's voice came out of her earphone. "Do you still have it?"

"No, it's gone." .

"Weird," said Chan. "Everything else okay from there?"

"Perfect," she said, sitting back from her terminal and stretching, her fingers laced above her head. "I'm going to take a break, honey. . . . I miss you."

Silence.

"Chan?" For no reason, a hand squeezed her heart. "Chan?"

"Yes, I'm here. CSOC took that secondary track as a group of expanding flecks. Conard said it looked sort of like a fire-cracker going off. You didn't see anything like that?"

"With this equipment? I'm lucky I could track the primary target. And what difference does it make? Even if it was something that exploded, it wasn't within collision range of the photo-return's new orbit—*oh!*"

"Yes indeed," came Chan's voice, deep with satisfaction. "'Oh' is right. We may just have solved our mystery, or at least part of it. Make sure you redundantly save that data, honey."

"Of course I will. I'm not an—Chan, when are you coming back?" He liked it over there. She knew he did. Lots of toys and lots of macho bull sessions.

"Um, I'm more use here. Look, I've got to go talk to people about this . . . 'exploding blip' phenomenon. Maybe the Porter Fleck was related."

"Maybe," she said slowly. "Maybe that's it. Dear, if you need me, I'll be here all night. I can't go back to my room until I know . . . until Dalton's safe. So if you want to talk about this anomaly, you'll know where to find me. Bye."

When her husband had signed off, she removed her headset carefully, trying to pull out as few hairs as possible. Then she slid her chair back.

"Oh, sorry, Major Gold."

The Space Command major had been right behind her chair. For all she knew, he could have been there the whole time.

She looked up at him and his face was grim. "Don't look so unhappy, Major. If that was something we happened to see because you can only see it under special conditions, or as it self-destructs, then we're ahead of the game. We saw it. We've got it logged. And the Agency satellite was out of harm's way, in its new orbit, before the event occurred."

"Yes, ma'am, but if that thing was meant to explode then and there, it was meant to explode and take the CIA—the photo-return satellite with it. And it would have, if we hadn't happened to move it just before the detonation."

"Detonation? Aren't you jumping to conclusions, Major Gold?" She had visions of spending the next eight hours in marathon conferences with worried government officials, when she wanted to be free to help with the imaging of Dalton's mission if it became necessary.

"Conclusions? No, ma'am. Can I get you anything? A cup of coffee?" The major's whole face had become one giant worry line.

Honestly, these men, so big and brave, became flustered by the littlest thing. The satellite she'd been here tracking was fine—safe and sound, and deployed to give supplementary intelligence to and about the team Ford had taken into the Syrian mountains.

"A cup of coffee would be lovely, Major. It's going to be a tense few hours."

46

Day 18: Cheyenne Mountain Complex

"The deputy director of CIA is on your STU, sir," said Beckwith's aide through the intercom.

"Good to hear from you—" Beckwith began.

The deputy's voice was thin and clipped: "Beckwith, we think it's now sufficiently clear how the satellites are being destroyed. I want an airstrike on that position. Maybe we can get the Israelis to—"

Beckwith imagined he could see the deputy smoothing back the white wings of hair over his ears: "Sir, I shouldn't have to remind you that we have people on-site there, verifying that the position is indeed a space-tracking and telemetry installation—"

"You have what? Nobody told me about that. Look, Beckwith, what if there's more of those things up there? Nearly undetectable? Hard to track until it's too late? It was only serendipity that the—sensoring platform—we were moving got out of orbit in time to avoid being destroyed. We want that ground station out of commission, and we want it done now. The President's willing to authorize an airstrike from our carriers offshore—"

"I said I have people in the immediate vicinity of that ground station," Beckwith snapped. Adamson had either never cleared the search-and-destroy mission with Langley, or else the Agency was exploring new heights of deniability. Then Beckwith remembered something: "Half of the operatives engaged in infiltrating that position are your people. They have orders to enter the area, do a thorough reconnaissance, even to securing a piece of physical evidence, and then disable or destroy the facility. Surely you don't want to endanger your own operatives in place."

"As far as we're concerned, Beckwith," said the deputy, "this is some unsanctioned cowboying we didn't know anything about. At least, I didn't. The President didn't. If you're not up to your hips in this, Admiral, I suggest you back out of the pond. If you are, be advised that in the case of even one more orbital attack on an American space-based asset, we're going to forget all about the rumor that there's some sort of mixed team in that area and destroy it immediately—with or without your help."

"I think the Israelis might have something to say about that. And the Syrians, as well. We've secured some pretty significant international cooperation on this." Beckwith was fighting desperately to keep his temper. He was actually seeing red. His heart was thumping madly. "I think you might want to talk to your own people in charge of Special Activities, to Jay Adamson in Cairo, to whomever you like in Mossad and Egyptian intelligence—before you go in swinging a stick as big as American air assault. Sir."

Beckwith, breathing hard, heard a faint voice say, "I'll do that, Admiral," before the phone clicked as the deputy broke the connection.

Beckwith put down the phone carefully and put his head in his hands. He was perspiring so that he could barely see. He had to get out of his underground office for a bit, even if only to walk around outside.

He'd go over to Peterson, he decided. If Dalton Ford and his people had just been cut loose to swing in the breeze, this was no time to be out of touch, no matter how claustrophobic, how sick, or how angry Leo Beckwith felt.

47

Day 18: Jabal an-Nusayriyah

Inside the secret ground station, total silence reigned. People looked at their feet, their hands, their knees, or shaded their eyes and stared in disbelief at their screens.

For Fouad Aflaq, frozen on the gallery, leaning on the railing and staring at the great overhead tracking screen, it was almost as if time itself had stopped.

He had failed!

He still could not truly grasp the enormity of it. He could hardly believe it, even now.

He tried to make himself move, but his limbs felt as if they belonged to another. Panic made him unsure of how to proceed. In his mind's eye, he kept seeing, over and over, the awful moment when it became clear that the target satellite—his last target satellite—was moving to a new orbit only minutes before Aflaq's last space mine was set to explode.

And explode it had. But it had not destroyed the CIA's despicable photo-return satellite. It had destroyed nothing, except perhaps the career—and even the life—of Fouad Aflaq.

The CIA photo-return satellite, as if it *knew* it was being hunted, had picked itself up and moved to a higher orbit, an orbit where none of Aflaq's forty thousand corundum pellets could harm it. And this new orbit was an orbit calculated to bring it directly overhead.

The CIA satellite, always a threat, was now the hunter,

rather than the hunted. On its present course, it would pass right over Aflaq's ground station.

And he didn't know what to do. It was going to come right over him! It was going to take pictures of his beloved ground-based space radar! It was going to find them!

This was a punishment from God, obviously. Aflaq must have erred grievously in the sight of Allah, sinned beyond measure. Perhaps it was the drinking of the champagne on Cyprus. He knew he shouldn't have indulged himself. Or perhaps it was allowing unveiled women into this station. Aflaq had always considered the station to be a holy place, consecrated to Allah, a temple from which His Will would remake the Earth.

Oh, what to do? He must stop standing here.

Below him, men were beginning to shift, to mutter to them-selves. One even leaned over and said something to his compa-triot. The other technician just bowed his head despondently.

Aflaq must take control. There were always ways to limit damage. He must—he would—*think!*

First, he unwound his hands from the rail. Next, he took a step toward his office. He wanted to get away from his work-ers. He didn't want them to look at him. He wanted to hide his face, his failure. He couldn't endure their accusatory stares.

But no one was staring at him, not yet.

Then there was still time. And there were, he realized at last, measures to be taken.

"Listen," he croaked. Then he tried again: "Listen very care-fully. The target satellite is going to come right over our heads. We must shut everything down. Everything. Everybody must stay inside. No one can leave. No one should move. We must all be very quiet, inside and out. Someone go tell the guards: Do not move an inch. Whisper when you talk, if you must talk. There is no telling what may be trained on us, soon, in the way of surveillance electronics. Understand: one man goes to notify the guards, comes back. Lock the doors. Even the guards, bring them inside." He wasn't sounding very organized. Could they tell he was rattled?

His mouth ran dry. He looked out on his workers. Now men were looking at him. Were their eyes glazed with shock and disappointment, or with hate? Would they rise up and tear him limb from limb as punishment for his failure?

But no, it was their failure too.

One man raised a hand, as if in school.

Aflaq calmed a little. "Yes?"

"I'll go alert the guards to come inside and be quiet, if it pleases you, *Mudir*."

The man at least still was willing to call him "director." In front of the others, this was a gift from Allah.

"*Na'am, imshi!*" *Yes, go,* he told the radar technician, and the man tiptoed off, taking exaggerated care to be quiet.

Others were whispering. He caught sidelong looks.

He must get away from them. He must think things through.

He moved unsteadily back from the railing. They had their orders. He could not stand there to make sure they followed them. Oh, would that he had not failed before Allah. If only he had not been so arrogant, perhaps he would not have been struck down and humiliated.

He needed to sit down. The best place for that was his office, his sanctum, his redundant miniature tracking station. When he got there, he saw on the screen of his micromini computer the same scene displayed on the great tracking screen in the main bay.

He saved the file, out of habit, before he shut off the system and sat down in his wonderful chair, his ergonomically correct chair from Germany that Gerhardt had given him as a present.

What should he do now? He dared not move from here. He dared not do anything.

It would be all right, he told himself, finally slumping forward, his head cradled in his arms. It would be all right. The Americans' CIA satellite would pass overhead, and then he could run away from the station. All his men could leave as well. They would turn off everything. The Americans would never find them.

And then, somehow, he would begin again.

Suddenly he sat bolt upright in horror. *The deployments!* Panic upon panic rolled over him in nauseating waves.

He picked up the phone. Then he put it down. He was being

silly. Not once had a deployment commenced without his personal okay, without someone checking with him first.

No deployments could go forward tonight. The chemical weapons, the last weapons, and the balance of the troops could not be moved in this uncertain—this dangerous, perhaps disastrous—climate.

If Allah had willed their success, this terrible fate would not have befallen him.

Again, he picked up the phone. He must tell someone, in case, overconfident, his compatriots assumed that no news from him was good news.

And he must do it as soon as he could decide whom to call, so that the chemical weapons could be returned to their warehouses in Libya, and not be caught in transit.

Finally, decided, he picked up the phone and made a long-distance call. The Egyptian, Sebek, would be the man to tell.

48

"What the hell are you running out here, Quantrell, a Swat Team Invitational?" Ford asked in a low voice from the bushes as Quantrell, bringing up the rear of his party, passed by.

Quantrell bent down in the moonlight, as if to tie his bootlace. "It's fucking oh-dark-thirty, Ford. Where you been?"

Ahead on the trail, Ford saw Larka stop, touch Ignatov, and fall back. Meri, noticing, stopped too. And Seti, beside her, followed suit.

"Monitoring message traffic. Quantrell, there's a whole damn battalion about ten miles downslope—PFLP General Command or something. Real mixed, lots of artillery, what looks like some pretty significant firepower—"

"Ten miles away is far enough. Whoever they are, they're not going to come up here looking for trouble." Quantrell stood up. "Gotta go. You coming, hotshot?"

Ford nearly said he wasn't. Then he half-stumbled out of the bushes. His leg was worse, not better. But then, he hadn't exactly been favoring it. He rubbed the place under his eye where the branch had swatted him. He couldn't look down with any accuracy, the skin there was so swollen. "How about you lead your multinational guests off in another direction, Jesse? Maybe you think that the noise we're about to make won't bring down any fire on us, but I'm not so—"

"Ford, you're only a purple-suited observer here, if you're anything at all. You think I invited those assholes? They know where we're going as well as we do. Say they'll attend the party on their own if we don't let them come on in with—"

Larka reached them, arms spread wide. Only a Spetznaz colonel could shout in a whisper: "*Glava* Ford! Dalton, my friend, you are come at last! Good. Now, tell the woman and the Egyptian that we cannot have two enemies who hate each other as much as they in our midst while we—"

And Ignatov thundered up, panting: "Ford! For the sake of my babushka, tell our friend Quantrell that you agree with me: after all, we've broken bread together. Drunk together. We, who are of the Soviet Union, should each have one of the RPG-7s. After all, without us, how would you have procured—"

"Iggy, go fuck yourself," Quantrell told the Bulgarian. "You wanted a rocket launcher, you should have brought one. I've only got six, and I'm not taking two of them from my men to give them to you—"

Up the trail, Meri was silhouetted in moonlight that came and went as the clouds covered and uncovered the moon. She had one hand on a hip and the other on Seti's chest.

Ford said, "How come something always goes wrong on one of these night assaults, Quantrell?"

"I dunno. But it always does. Let's go. We can talk on the way." Quantrell, too, had seen what looked like serious discord between the Israeli and the Egyptian.

Larka followed their stares. "Ah, an Israeli woman with a gun is a formidable thing. Seti should watch himself." Larka chuckled dourly and, shoving Ignatov before him, set off down the trail, loudly chambering a round in his Maadi AK as he went. The assault weapon looked like a toy in his hand.

Ignatov, nearly walking backward, said, "Dalton, tell me what you think. Shall we engage our enemies, tonight, or only our friends? In the Mossad station, you should know, Seti told the woman he had always known she was a spy and she told him that Israeli doctrine took into account that Egyptians were like camels: that they spit, they bite, but they kneel to the rider. This, I think, is not a good sign."

Ford was beginning to think seriously about slipping back

into the bush. "Jesse, leave them with me. Go run your assault. It's the only way."

"Then what happens when we need your goddamn intel?"

"Bullshit. Don't tell me you're worried I can't handle myself."

"You're limping, Ford."

"Yeah, that's so. And you're three years older than I am. My leg'll heal."

"What you got for me?"

Ford said, "Besides all those troops down there, and more, it looks like, just over the border in the Bekáa? Not much. The station came on, full power, for a while, according to the satellite data I took while I was waiting. Now it's all shut down." He slowed down, as if his leg were really bothering him.

Quantrell slowed too, saying, "Damn it, Ford. I'm going to order you to sit this out. I can do that, you know. Even if I have to knock you silly to—"

Ford went to one knee. Quantrell grunted, kneeling beside him.

"Jesse, I came in a little off target—right on top of the ground station. I saw—heard—two guys talking. It's underground, I think, with some kind of surface entrance." He pulled out his GPS, which he'd set to give him an area map. "Here." He pointed.

"Nice work. Thanks. About your leg . . ."

"Let me finish. Since I was there, and I had the plastic, I set charges, maximum delay, around the dish supports . . . gives us about another forty-five minutes if we want to surprise whoever's in the station, which is about twenty yards northeast of the dish itself. If you want to radio-reset the timers, you better tell me now."

"Up to you. You set 'em." Quantrell got up.

"God*damn* it, Quantrell, that's no answer."

"Look, Ford, can we just go kick some ass, please? If you're still alive and you think you want to stop the timers, later, you do that. Far as I'm concerned, you've facilitated destroying the objective. I don't give a good goddamn about anything as much as that, right now."

Ford got stiffly to his feet and Quantrell, despite his angry words, clapped him on the back as they went.

Ford knew he was lagging behind as much because of Meri as because of his leg, but he kept telling himself it was because he had too much to do, rather than because he didn't want to think about her being there.

They were less than five hundred yards from the dish when he finished updating Mackenzie, over their Racal radios, about what he'd been telling the Lands, intermittently, using his black box as a satellite uplink.

Mackenzie said, "I still think I better check in with Land one more time."

Ford couldn't even see the team captain. They were all spread out, readying for an assault on the rectangle of light Ford had seen.

It was almost as good as being here by his lonesome, except that Jesse kept bitching in his earpiece. Marconi came on line and said, "I'd like to initiate a STICS link, sir, and have you send your latest positioning data."

"You bet."

Ford sat down in the brush and put his prototype box on his lap. When he had it talking to Marconi's STICS, he sent the updated positioning information, made up of what he'd gotten from his on-site recon, the covert satellite's last overhead radar-seeking pass, and the up-to-the-minute photo-reconnaissance that Jenny Land had transmitted to him from the photo-return satellite.

Marconi's voice came back: "Got it. Thanks. But do you think there's still anybody in there? Sounds dead as a doornail in every bandwidth I'm set up to monitor, although I'm getting some heat signatures that might be human bodies."

"Yeah, I think they're in there. I would have seen somebody leave."

"Break it up, you two," Quantrell's voice broke in. "We're on the clock."

Quantrell gave the go order and Ford's pulse quickened.

He got his legs under him, repacked his black box, and started forward, his AKM-15 in his right hand, a hexjam in his left.

Everybody knew what to do. Whether Meri, Iggy, Larka

and Seti would do as they were told was another issue.

In the back of his head, a mental clock counted down the time remaining until the dish supports were going to blow.

If he'd been running this, he'd have stopped the timers, given himself that much leeway. But he wasn't running this; Quantrell was.

"Okay, I'm on target; hexjam in place." It was Kellogg whom Ford heard in his earpiece. Quantrell wasn't using military radio procedure in case, somehow, their scrambled transmissions were broken. Kellogg's voice startled Ford, after a long interval of hearing nothing but grunting and breathing as men took positions around the site coordinates Ford had gathered.

Then: "Ready, Can Opener." That was Mackenzie, who had his people deployed where Ford had seen the square of light, ready to blast open the door.

And then, in Ford's ear, came Meri's musical voice. He closed his eyes. This was a nightmare. You didn't want to hear a woman's voice when you were doing this—especially not the voice of a woman you'd had in your arms . . .

"Peanut Gallery in place," she said.

Quantrell's sense of humor was falling flat for Ford tonight.

Then Quantrell said, "All right, let's tear those tickets, kiddies. Remember, once you leave the theater, you don't get back in." Quantrell was reminding everybody of the antipersonnel mines they'd scattered as they'd come.

You were supposed to know where every one of those butterflies were. They looked like rocks or clots of dirt, in the daylight. In theory, you were supposed to know where you'd emplaced them. But in practice, you went out some other way—any other way.

Ford heard the first RPG round fired, closed his eyes, turned his head away, and heard two more leave their tubes before the first one hit the place they thought the door might be.

The shock wave kissed him, even as far back as he was. The noise followed: three ear-ringing concussions; then the flashes of the blasts.

In their wake, for an instant, he heard his own ear's reaction, a high, ringing tone. Then he realized he'd better move.

At least his leg didn't hurt. The chatter in his earpiece was confused, but understandable. He charged up the hill with the AKM like some kind of kid, free of pain, nearly free of thought.

He was listening so hard, he heard a thwack he didn't like, and a grunt he liked less, as Mackenzie's team thundered down steps (it sounded like) and met resistance.

Then the radio chatter was purely incomprehensible, and he knew there was fighting inside.

He dropped his hexjam when he found the steps. There was a body sprawled there, but it wasn't dressed like the SAG team.

He leaped over, forgetting to question the wisdom of leaping down stairs.

His right ankle nearly gave under him. Even in the smoke and confusion, he could still hear the snap of complaining ligament over bone.

But it held him, and he could hear a woman's voice, so Meri was alive, somewhere.

There was intermittent firing in the installation, which was dark whenever it wasn't lit by muzzle flash.

Then, somewhere, somebody flipped a light switch.

For a moment, Ford's eyes, trying to adjust, gave him a frozen-image photo of Kellogg, on top of a workstation, firing methodically in a circle around himself, while technicians defending the station cowered back.

Then his field of view widened, and he saw Jesse, in a corner with Meri Soukry pushed in back of him, returning fire from somebody crouched behind the rail of an elevated gallery; Mackenzie, trying to wrench his AK-47 out of the hands of three civilians piling on top of him; Marconi, bending over a terminal, oblivious to everything around him, a shot technician sitting slumped, arms dangling, in the chair he straddled.

Then somebody shot directly at Ford. He could feel the *whup* of air and hear the snap as the round passed by his ear.

He shot back, unthinking, in that direction.

And damned if he didn't see Seti over there, crouched behind an overturned printer station, shooting at whoever'd been shooting at him.

He saw the thermite grenade cook off as Marconi stepped

back from the computer where he'd put it. The molten steel would burn through and destroy the computer absolutely and completely.

Then Marconi either hit the deck or fell like a stone.

A hand came down on Ford's shoulder, while in his ear he heard Jesse: "Marconi? Marconi, you okay?"

Ford turned to face the guard or whoever had a grip on him, his finger already tightening on the trigger.

There, in the jagged opening that once had been a doorway, stood Larka, a big grin on his blackened face: "So, some fun, eh? Come this way, Dalton. A little surprise I have to show you."

Larka pushed the muzzle of Ford's AKM aside as if it were a water pistol. "Come, come on. Quickly."

Larka and Ignatov had been doing their own reconnaissance, Ford realized as he followed the Spetznaz colonel up debris-littered stairs and onto the raised gallery.

They detoured around three bodies, two of them methodically shot in the back of the skull, KGB fashion. "Where we going, Larka?"

"You will see, I promise." Larka coughed.

Until then, Ford hadn't noticed how much smoke there was in here. Acrid smoke. Nasty fumes from the thermite grenades burning into the computers.

Ignatov was leaning against a doorjamb. The door was closed. At first, Ford thought that Ignatov was just out of breath. The Bulgarian was far too overweight to be running around the way he'd been.

But then he saw a wound in the big man's paunch, over on the side where his love-handles were.

Ford's eyes shut of their own accord. He forced them open. Maybe it wouldn't be too bad, considering how fat Iggy was.

"So, Dalton, my beloved. Here we have for you the best present of your whole life, which we are giving you with the best wishes—" Ignatov coughed "—of my babushka. Call it our wedding gift." He coughed again.

Ford looked at Larka quickly. Larka, with a quirk of his lips, shrugged. "Open the door, Ford. We have saved this for you."

Open the door meant *shoot the lock,* Ford realized.

So he shot the lock, while Larka caught Ignatov as the big man stumbled when he moved away from the doorjamb's support.

Ford tried not to notice. You had to do the job. You had to expect things to go wrong. You had to want to keep going. . . .

Inside the door was a whole room full of electronics, and a man in a chair behind a desk. The man looked like he was asleep, until you noticed the reasonably neat hole that a small-caliber pistol had made in his forehead. Ford checked to the right, then the left: nobody else inside, alive or dead. As he stepped toward the desk to get a closer look, he saw a small-caliber pistol in the dead man's lap.

The electronics were so hot, so leading-edge, so complete that Ford just stared around him for a time while Larka, holding Ignatov up, grinned at him like a death's-head from the doorway.

Ford thumbed his remote; and then, for the first time, interrupted Quantrell: "Jesse," he said into his comm mike, "send Marconi in here, and whoever's got the Aerostat. This is what we want."

"Can't," said Quantrell back. "Marconi's KIA. Mackenzie, get somebody up there—Ford's with Larka and Ignatov, up off the gallery." In the background, Ford thought he heard another shot.

Damn, he'd thought the shooting would be over by now. It ought to have been. But then, there's always some guy in the bathroom or under his desk . . .

He suppressed the impulse to go back out there and see if Quantrell needed him. Quantrell had never needed Dalton Ford in his life for more than high-tech quick fixes or favors from the brass. "We're in a room back here, opposite the big screen," Ford said. "Hey, Quantrell, Iggy's hurt."

"Lots of people hurt, Ford."

Marconi's KIA—killed in action. Dead. Ford finally cycled the data. Then he looked at Ignatov. Lots of blood there. He'd better hurry, or Ignatov was going to be dead too.

"How about you patch that up, Larka, while we wait—"

Larka shook his head and at first Ford didn't understand why Larka wouldn't bandage his friend. Then he looked again at the amount of blood.

And he did understand. "Hey, Iggy, do you realize what this means, you finding this?" Ford said, unable to look at the big Bulgarian. His voice shook. "I bet that we'd have missed this." He walked over to the micromini and patted it as if it were a woman. "This is the proof we needed, I'd bet my life on it."

Wrong thing to say, for Ford's own composure.

He looked up again. Larka was still holding Ignatov, but the man was slumping badly.

And then Ford realized that Ignatov hadn't answered him, and wasn't even smiling.

Iggy was just staring at Ford out of those sad, bright eyes.

Shit, how long had Larka been holding his dead friend? How long was he going to hold him?

Ford mumbled, "Well, this is just terrific, anyway," and sat on the desk. He almost powered up the microcomputer to see what it had in it, but he looked for disks instead. He found a bunch of laserdisks and stuffed them in his pocket and still Mackenzie hadn't come in.

The noise of combat in his ear was nearly totally replaced by Americans swearing and grunting and the sound of equipment being destroyed.

With a start, still not wanting to look up at Larka, holding Ignatov in the doorway, Ford looked at his watch. "Jesse," he said in the direction of his collar, "we've got sixteen minutes left."

"That's about right," came Quantrell's voice in his ear.

And then Mackenzie was there, all sharp attentiveness and torqued-down can-do. He had one of his men with him, and the man had the Aerostat—a collapsed balloon with a skyhook receiver and cable attached—in his hand.

"This it, Mr. Ford?" Mackenzie walked right by Ignatov and Larka without noticing.

His companion noticed the two Soviets right away, and bumped into the desk as he stared: "Hey, that guy's—"

"Died valorously in the performance of his duties to the

State and our new policy of *glasnost*," boomed Larka so that
Mackenzie reached for the Hi-Power on his hip.

"Easy, Mackenzie. You know Colonel Larka. And you know
he's going to want to take home his dead."

Because that was what was going on here: Larka, the professional's professional, was unstrung enough to be totally
and completely unwilling to leave Ignatov's body behind. His
whole attitude screamed it so loudly that Ford was already
wondering how the hell they were going to deal with that kind
of problem.

"Uh-oh," said Mackenzie softly.

"I was thinking," Ford said, "about what a nice, fiery cre-
mation Iggy and Marconi were going to have together, here
where they triumphed over the enemy. I hate like hell to think
of Marconi going out all alone, and of Iggy missing the fun.
I heard Ignatov really liked fireworks."

Larka finally moved. He turned his head to his friend's head,
and said, "So, Iggy. Would you like to go with the American,
the brilliant, valiant Marconi, and have a wonderful crema-
tion, at great expense to the American government? With full
honors, and all of us standing by? You would? Good." Larka
kissed Ignatov on the lips and slowly, still holding Ignatov
by the arm Larka had over his shoulders, lowered him to the
floor.

Behind him, as he watched, Ford heard: "Okay, she's ready
to go, Mr. Ford. If you just want to check it?"

Ford checked Mackenzie's work. Then Mackenzie and his
man lifted the micromini between them. "You'll call in the
pickup?"

"You bet. Right away." Ford, still watching Larka, arrang-
ing his friend carefully, gently, fondly on the floor, made a
satellited call with his black box for a skyhook-equipped C-130
to snag the balloon once it was pressurized and airborne.

By rights, he should have used the STICS terminal, but the
STICS terminal had been with Marconi, and Ford wasn't about
to go pat down a corpse right then.

When he had confirmation that a C-130 with a skyhook
would fly over to collect the balloon with the dependent piece
of evidence, Ford went over to Larka and said, "Come on,

Colonel. Let's go see if there's anything we can do out there
to help. Then we can bring Marconi in here."

When they got out onto the gallery, Ford blinked at the mess.
Quantrell was standing in the middle of it. Kellogg was lying
on the ground, with Meri bending over him, doing a quick
patch.

Seti was wounded in the arm, walking around the room,
talking to himself.

"Ford," Quantrell bellowed when he looked up: "Let's get
our asses out of here. Now!"

Half the Special Forces people were already outside, Ford
realized. The rest were picking up hardware, and reloading
their rifles, forming up by the door.

Quantrell went over to Kellogg and said something. Meri
shook her head. Quantrell jerked her up by the arm and bent
down before Kellogg, lifting the CIA commando up in a fire-
man's carry. "I said, move, Ford," Quantrell snarled.

Ford didn't have time to explain to Jesse about Ignatov before
Larka was on his way down to get Marconi's body.

Then he started to, using his radio, as he headed for the
gallery stairs by the blown door, coughing because the smoke
was so thick here.

"I know. Let him do it. Marconi won't mind. You just get
out of here."

Ford looked at his watch again. And then he ran.

Where had the time gone?

"Jesse, want me to abort the—?"

"No!" His ear rang from the volume of Quantrell's shout
through the earpiece. "What do you think this is, a goddamned
Bright Star exercise?"

Outside, Ford could at least breathe. He realized his eyes
were stinging as he joined Mackenzie, who was watching the
inflated balloon go up.

You could barely see it, except when it crossed the moon.

Mackenzie noticed him and said, "That's what we needed,
right?"

"Might as well be," Ford said.

Then Quantrell was yelling for everybody to report, so he
knew he had all the live SAG people out. They weren't taking

prisoners; officially, they weren't here at all, so they couldn't leave any witnesses.

"Where's fucking Larka?"

"I'll get him," Ford said.

"No," said Meri's voice in his ear, "I will get him. You start. We'll catch up."

He and Quantrell started arguing at the same time, which meant that nobody won.

Meri didn't answer.

Ford decided he was never, ever, going out in the field again if he could just get home this time without losing anybody else. Iggy.

Poor Larka . . .

When Larka and Meri came out, arm in arm, Larka was shouting, "I have set such a beauteous pyre of plastic for them, no man has ever seen finer. Not a bit will be left, nothing!"

And he raised a fist at the sky once before Quantrell said, "Great, Larka, now can we goddamn run away before we get our own asses blown up too?"

Mackenzie already had his people started down the primary route.

Ford fell in somewhere behind Mackenzie and in front of Larka and Meri, and was surprised to find Seti beside him.

"Seti, how's your wound?" he said as soon as they'd made it far enough from the facility that Ford felt like talking.

"Oh, fine. Never—"

The dish blew, sending green and white and orange streamers into the sky.

Somewhere in back of him, another rocket went off: Quantrell, making sure, for sure.

But you didn't stop, once the fireworks started, to look back. The whole station was going to go next. Ford kept running down the slope, keeping an eye on the back of the person ahead of him.

The station went, in a blast that shook the ground and triggered everyone's reflexes so that the entire team hit the dirt, heads covered.

Ford looked up in time to see a few burning pieces arc down out of the sky into the trees behind them.

Marconi and Ignatov would have wanted it clean, but Ford had to settle for good enough: he couldn't check to see that the whole station was obliterated.

He couldn't.

When they hit the dust-off point and regrouped, Quantrell and Larka came over to him together.

Quantrell handed him a badly mangled dish antenna, and what was, inarguably, the STICS: "Larka fell with it in his pocket."

"Larka fell with it?"

"Yeah, well, before that, Meri and I used it to call down an Israeli strike on the facility—just some redundant cleanup."

"Cleanup. Right."

A low-profile Israeli strike wasn't the worst case they'd prepared for. But it was strange that Quantrell had ordered it himself, with Meri, using the STICS and bypassing Ford.

"Where is Meri?" A sudden suspicion made him ice cold, though a moment ago he'd been fine.

"Right here." She came over to him with Mackenzie. "There was a lot of pressure for some sort of airstrike, Dalton. We didn't have time to tell you."

"Tell me what?"

"Ah, now you'll see, Dalton Ford, what it is to put your trust in the Israelis," Seti said and sat down heavily, holding his shot arm.

Meri ignored him. "The Americans finally agreed that we should do something about the troops down below, before it was too late. So when we heard this, we thought, why not?"

"Meri—" Her face was unreadable, black and filthy.

"Ah, sir," Mackenzie said, coming over to him. "Mr. Ford, we had a bunch of last-minute orders, and they got kind of confusing. The way I make it, we wait for our Israeli helicopter extraction. There's going to be enough suppression fire laid down, because of the Israelis hitting those artillery positions and all those troops down in the valley, that we shouldn't have to use our E and E. Of course, if it doesn't come—"

"It will come," Meri said with complete certainty. Then, in front of everyone, she took out her pistol, trained it on Ford, and came toward him.

The pistol looked like an old Astra, he remarked to himself in the dissociated moment before certain death. He didn't understand why she'd carry something like that when she could have had her pick of anything Israeli Military Industries produced, and more.

"Was it something I said?" Ford, uncertainly, started to put up his hands. He had to make this into a joke, defuse the situation.

Meri squeezed the trigger and shot Seti in the head.

Everybody's weapons were aimed on her so fast that Ford screamed, "Stop!" and grabbed her.

Her gun's muzzle pushed against his belly as he did. He was shaking. She was shaking too.

"Okay," he whispered in her ear, "so you didn't like the man. You'd better tell them something."

"Quantrell knows," she whispered. "Jesse will not let his men shoot me. Now let me go."

Sure enough, Quantrell was telling everybody to put down their weapons.

"Seti shot Marconi, for sure," Quantrell said to the men around them.

"He fucking shot me, I think," croaked Kellogg, from somewhere in the dark.

"Kellogg," Mackenzie said, "I saw you get shot and I don't think—"

"Shut up," said Quantrell. "We thought Seti might have been part of the problem, but we didn't have anything but suspicions until we got in there. Meri, show them what you've got."

She held up something. It was a square of paper in the dark, or a single three-and-a-half-inch disk. It could have been anything. "Whatever this was, it's what Seti came to get. Marconi found it, and then Seti shot him."

Ford couldn't make out expressions on the camouflaged faces around him in the night. Maybe it was just as well. Execution wasn't Ford's style. He didn't think it was Quantrell's, either.

Quantrell said, "All I care about, at this point, is getting my people out of here alive."

Nobody could argue with that, but the team moved away

from Quantrell, Ford, Meri and the corpse on Mackenzie's quiet, insistent reminder that it was time for everybody to change their Racal batteries, or the radios were going to stop working soon.

Ford wanted to vomit. Quantrell sat down heavily and looked at his watch.

Ford said, "Meri, where're your choppers—"

"Shut up, Ford, okay?" Quantrell said. His voice was muffled, as if he had his head down. "Just shut up."

Meri didn't answer.

Then there was a crashing sound of someone moving around and everyone clutched their weapons, looking around.

"It's only me, Larka—who else but a friend would make so much noise coming upon crazy armed Americans in the dark?"

"Uh, Larka, maybe you'd better not come—"

"So you found out about Seti, eh?" Larka walked right over to Seti and toed the corpse. "We were going to tell you, when Moscow gave us permission. But we had to wait, you see, for that permission."

"Oh, Larka, thank you," Meri said in a voice that sounded tearful, and rushed over to hug the big Spetznaz colonel.

He stroked her hair. "Thank Ignatov, not me. It is his parting gift to you, little fox. We will get for you the documentation, and the name of the fat Egyptian cohort of his, a person in the finance ministry, who was so unkind to our friend Quantrell. Iggy would want you to have it, Meri Soukry. He always liked you, you know. Always."

Ford closed his eyes then, waiting for the heliborne extraction to arrive. But he couldn't banish the image of the big Spetznaz colonel, who'd lost his best friend, comforting the weeping Israeli woman who'd shot her worst enemy.

Hell of a way to run an operation, Ford thought, just before he heard helicopters and distant jets.

Somewhere behind them, shelling and rocket fire began, lighting up the night.

49

Day 19: Cairo

You come back with your data, your wounded. You leave your dead because there's no choice. Then some fool in a tropical shirt wants to know if you know what you've done.

Jesse Quantrell couldn't believe his ears as he stared at Jay Adamson. "Yeah—hell yeah, I know. But my part of this is over now. Identification of the corpses and assessment of the site damage isn't my purview, Mr. Adamson. The Syrians, along with the Egyptians and the Russians, are handling that."

Quantrell was always uncomfortable in Jay Adamson's clean room, more so than anywhere else in the Cairo CIA station.

"You know that isn't what I'm asking, Colonel."

He did know that. Quantrell shifted uncomfortably in his chair. What if it was Meri having shot Seti like that? He'd told everybody on that mission that he'd personally cut out the heart of anyone who said a word. But you never could tell what guys will say on stand-down, in a bar, or in bed. "What is it you are asking, Mr. Adamson?"

He really didn't like this Adamson. Some CIA people, like Kellogg, were all right. Kellogg's part of the team had performed so well that Quantrell had nearly forgotten, in the field, that they weren't from his alma mater. All the technical stuff, the comms, the identification of the various black boxes and computers at the site, and the after-action reports, were as professional and as smooth as they could be. He remembered thinking it would be nice if his boys could write reports like that. But prose wasn't a high priority in Quantrell's line of work. Survival was. Quantrell was really missing Marconi. He'd even gone to see Kellogg in the Cairo West infirmary, he missed Marconi so much. And Mackenzie . . .

"What was that, Mr. Adamson?"

"I haven't said anything, yet. You really don't know, do you? The computer your people put on that balloon—"

"Aerostat."

"Aerostat, yes. That computer contained the entire order of battle for a PLO/General Command–spearheaded assault on Jerusalem, plus a list of major backers, government officials from a number of hard-line Arab states who, without their superiors' direct knowledge, had supported the ground-station program or were in some way involved."

"So it's okay about the Israeli—" Quantrell snapped his mouth shut, hoping that in his relief he hadn't said the wrong thing.

Adamson was positively magnanimous. "It's fine, Mr. Quantrell. We're going to recommend than all our participants in your mission be awarded Intelligence Stars for courageous action, and that Mr. Kellogg be awarded the Exceptional Service Medallion as well, for injury in the performance of hazardous duties." Adamson beamed at him, managing to resemble a happy weasel.

"I get the picture. I'll put my people in for some . . . Marconi, anyway." If they hadn't been operating in a non-attributable environment, Quantrell would have done so before now. Medals didn't make up for dead soldiers, but they helped the living. "What about Ignatov?"

"We're handling that."

"If that's all—" Quantrell started to get out of his chair.

"I wish it were."

Oh, shit. Meri . . .

"The Israeli airstrike on that target of yours shouldn't cause any problems, since the pretext was a preemptive strike into Lebanon, which is hardly something new for the Israelis, and the ground station was so near Syria's Lebanese border. But—"

Here it comes.

"—the U.S. government did, however covertly, ask for that airstrike. We did have personnel inside Syria, guiding in that airstrike. So we are involved. And because we're involved, and the information may leak, despite best efforts, we're putting the entire Bright Star contingent on alert."

Quantrell slumped back in his chair. "What were we doing before, playing pick-up sticks? The goddamn DefCon—"

"—remains the same out here for the next few days, Quantrell. That's all. Let's hope we don't find ourselves in need of your services again in the next few days, because if we do, it will mean that this thing has escalated beyond all control."

"I'll be around, if you need me, sir. But if you're done, I've got a meeting with some Egyptians. They're doing some housecleaning over there and they want me to identify somebody."

"Well go ahead, Colonel. Have a nice time. Tell your Israeli and Russian friends we appreciate their help more than we'll ever be able to say publicly, but that we're sure a time will come when we'll be in a position to return the favor."

"Yeah, I'll do that," said Quantrell, and this time made it all the way out of his chair and to Adamson's door before the CIA station chief stopped him.

"One more thing, Colonel."

"Yeah, Adamson. I'm late for—"

"Please keep your interoperating foreign nationals on tap. Don't do anything to ruffle their feathers. If this story blows . . . turning from an Israeli airstrike that's survivable politically for all concerned into an overt case of Americans using force out here, we're going to really need your friends."

"I promise," Quantrell said heartily, "that all my friends are still friends. Now, can I get going?"

"Certainly, Colonel. And thanks again."

When Quantrell got back from identifying his personal fat Egyptian, whom Larka had told him would be referred to, in the ground-station intelligence, as 'Sebek,' he was going to call Meri and see if she'd have dinner with him. Then they could take a doggie bag back to Kellogg.

Maybe, if Quantrell's luck was holding, he could find Larka and make it a threesome. If he knew colonels, Larka was going to need some company tonight.

50

Day 20: Moscow

Take that! Shitov thought as he settled back into his Zil, telling
his driver to take him through Red Square before the customary
detour by the bakery. In his hand, Shitov still held the briefcase
in which was a commendation from the Executive President
himself.

Levonov had known this was coming, obviously. That was
why neither he nor his pig of a wife had been at the ballet last
night. Well, good. Hide, Levonov. Hide your face in shame.

Aleksandr Shitov had not felt the need to sacrifice a long-
time friend to save his career—only to tell the truth.

A part of the truth, at least. A vision of the truth. And
now he was vindicated. The Executive President's wish for
good relations with the Americans was fulfilled: there was no
longer any need to brandish submarines and move troops and
lase American pilots in their jets.

For the moment, anyway. And, for the moment, Shitov was
a hero.

The Executive President had called Shitov, personally, on
the telephone to tell him what a good job he had done. And
given him a week off, and invited him to the seashore.

"Driver," he said, sitting forward suddenly. "Stop at the
department store. I must get a present for my wife."

More important than bread, right now, was a new bathing
suit for Shitova to wear at the dacha. After all, many party

officials had also been invited to the Black Sea dacha.

There, Shitov would consolidate his gains. There he would be (as the Executive President had all but told him outright) the savior of *glasnost;* man of the hour. And Shitov deserved this honor.

He had worked hard. All night, some nights. He had used his influence with the Syrian government, who had used theirs with the Iraqi government, to make sure that there were no repercussions or reprisals (other than the customary minor sortie against the Israelis) because of what had happened.

Moscow drifted past outside the Zil's window, full of workers in summer clothes. What had happened, officially, was only that the Israelis had wiped out some more of their hereditary enemies. No one among the governments concerned was anxious to have it known that the Americans, the Russians, the Egyptians, and the Israelis had gone together up into Syria, where they had wiped out a technical facility and killed one hundred percent of that facility's personnel.

Of course, if the operatives had not killed one hundred percent of the enemy, it would have been impossible to maintain security.

Shitov had used his apparatchiki's influence on the Americans and, through them, on the Israelis, to make sure that the kill would be clean.

And he had lost a valued agent in doing so. Not the brightest of men, as the new generation of Soviet leadership measured such things, but a canny and dedicated man: Klement Ignatov.

Shitov's driver bulled his way through traffic. When one said "the department store" in Moscow, everyone knew where you meant.

This Ignatov, the single Soviet casualty, a man of Bulgarian extraction, who had worked under Bulgarian cover, was a hero in the true Russian mold. He had left behind an aged mother, and an ex-wife. Thinking about poor, dead Ignatov, of whom Shitov had hardly ever had anything good to say, he felt a sweet sadness.

Perhaps he would get something—a present—for the bereaved mother of this hero of the State who must remain unsung.

Yes, he would do it. He would bring baked goods to the home of Ignatova, and kiss her wrinkled cheek.

After all, if not for Ignatov, Shitov would never have been able to take all the credit for the destruction of the ground station which had shot down the Cosmos 2100, as well as the credit for finding a way to stop the escalating crisis in the Middle East before someone besides Israelis had to attack troops in that region, and a major conflict began.

To show his gratitude to the Americans, Shitov had gone through his files and found the name of the Egyptian collaborator known as Sebek, as well as the German, Iraqi, Syrian and Libyan involved, and given those names to one of his remaining Cairo agents, Colonel Larka, to give to the Americans.

It is no small thing, to stop a war. Shitov was feeling justly proud of himself, proud of his heroically slain Ignatov, and his as-yet-living Spetznaz colonel, Larka.

But mostly, Shitov was feeling relieved. He had beaten Levonov at Levonov's own game. He had driven Levonov from the ballet, as his proxies had driven the hard-line Arabs from their burrows in the Syrian mountains and the Bekáa.

He had won his war. The ballet was his. The bakery was his. And now, because he had won, his wife would get a new swimsuit, and Ignatov's mother would get a whole loaf of raisin pumpernickel.

He hoped the old babushka appreciated the sacrifice that Shitov was about to make, as soon as he had found his wife a swimsuit in which she would look her best when they visited the Executive President at his summer house by the sea.

51

Day 21: Falcon AFB, Colorado

Three weeks from the day that *HE-12* went down, the morning dawned hot and clear. Conard couldn't help thinking about *HE-12* as he drove over to the Officer's Mess at Peterson, where he was supposed to meet Pollock and Admiral Beckwith.

Conard's yellow 'Vette was running like a dream; the Def-Con was down to a comfortable level; and Conard was about to get a promotion.

Things could be worse.

When he found the Admiral's table, Beckwith shook his hand, and so did Pollock.

Once they'd sat down, Admiral Beckwith said, "Son, without that EVA of yours and the pellet you found, we'd have been up shit creek on this one. It was that pellet that got the CIA's attention. If we hadn't had it, we'd have made the wrong guess and flown off the handle—gone after the Russians, when it wasn't them at fault. Cooperation. Yes, indeed. That's the name of the game."

Admiral Beckwith looked odd this morning. His eyes seemed too bright and his face too pale. But it was still good to hear a compliment.

Pollock, who hadn't uttered a word so far, leaned forward, put both elbows on the table, and said, "The admiral's putting in for a medical leave, Conard."

"What's wrong, sir?"

301

"Just the ticker. Don't worry. I got your papers put through first. And I'll be back, even if it's with a lighter workload."

Then Conard looked more closely at Pollock. Was Pollock politicking for Beckwith's job? Was that what this was?

Pollock didn't exactly like Conard. . . .

The sandy-moustached colonel said, "Conard, I've been meaning to tell you how well you did up in X-NASP when the pucker factor went up." Pollock raised his coffee cup and sipped from it.

Maybe this was just a celebration breakfast, after all. But still, years of being the guy nobody liked kept Conard on his toes. He'd done great. He *was* the one who'd found the pellet, wasn't he? Neither of these men would be looking as good as they were to Washington if it weren't for him.

"What the admiral's saying," Pollock continued, "is that I'm going to have the honor of being his deputy while he's gone. So if you need anything, Conard, just give me a call."

Of course, Pollock would want him to hear it from the horse's mouth. Conard felt genuinely glad for the colonel, and genuinely proud. "We did really nail it, didn't we?"

"We did," said Beckwith, licking his lips. "When Ford gets back here, I want all you boys to get along."

"Ford?" said Pollock.

"Ford?" echoed Conard. *Oh, no. Not Ford.* But you couldn't say that aloud.

"I want everybody to get along, out here. I like a happy shop. And DIA's very sensitive about its perquisites these days."

"No problem," Pollock said as if he meant it. "They—Ford did one hell of a job out there."

"It'll be . . . nice to hear the rest of the story," Conard said faintly. Ford wasn't going to be Pollock's problem, so much as Conard's. Conard's intelligence function would put him right in Ford's face much of the time.

"Yeah, I can't wait," said Pollock wryly, and Conard didn't understand precisely why Pollock had said that the way he had. But he knew he'd find out, soon enough. Ford. Well, you couldn't win them all.

52

Day 21: Cairo

"Come on, Jenny, come out to Cairo West with me and see a real Bright Star exercise," Quantrell boomed over the music to which belly dancers gyrated in the exotic *Auberge aux Pyramides*.

Meri Soukry watched the American woman covertly, wondering what was amiss. Everyone was relaxed. Both the real combat upcountry and the combat alert in Egypt were over. She had taken home the computer disk that Seti feared would be so incriminating, and Mossad had shared its information with the Americans.

Then Jenny Land replied, "No, Jesse. I can't. My mother just died and . . . ." She couldn't finish the sentence.

"I'm so sorry," Meri said quickly.

She noted the blank look on Jesse's face. He was still mourning Ignatov and his young Marconi. And this was perfectly healthy, and natural. She, too, was still feeling the effects of the mission.

"It's really . . . a blessing," the American woman confided. "I'm free, now. Finally. I've decided not to rush home for the funeral; it's not that I'm callous or . . . You'd have to know what it's like to realize that there are some deaths that are a relief. It would be lying to pretend I'm not glad."

Meri knew just what the woman meant. Seti was at last where Seti had long deserved to be. The only trouble was, she didn't feel good about it. And she knew that Quantrell was still looking at her askance.

She hardly heard Dalton come back from wherever he'd gone. But she felt his hand trail across her back as he took his chair.

So it was the four of them. Odd, that they looked so much like a group of happy, married tourists when . . .

"What's with Chan, Jen?" Ford said brusquely. The scratch on his cheek was already a faded line; his limp was nearly imperceptible.

The Land woman flushed. Behind her head, Meri could see the belly of the closest dancing girl, who was in enviable physical condition, describing multiple figure eights.

"Chan . . . I told you, Dalton," Jenny Land replied, "I'm taking care of it."

Her husband had done a good job of alienating the major players, because of his pathological need to report everything up through channels. Meri knew it had caused trouble, but not how much, until Ford said, "*How* are you taking care of it?"

Then Jenny Land said, "I'm staying on a week or so. He went last night. He has his Virginia debriefing, after all." Bitterness was there.

Meri knew that the things which really destroyed relationships were not big things, not overt fights or terrible public misjudgments. Those were simple: the loud, brash argument was soon forgotten in a sea of kisses and a flood of apologies. The difficult things to overcome were quietly done and hardly noted—a moral incompatibility, a simple act which bespoke an unforgivable intent which welled from the soul.

She had been there. "A trial separation?" she guessed, although it was none of her business.

Yet the American woman wanted to talk. Everyone had lost something during Bright Star, evidently. "He's got to decide if it's me, or his job, that matters the most. Personal betrayal is simply . . ."

"We know," said Meri, who disliked most women but suddenly felt kinship enough to reach out and pat the other's hand. "Believe me, we know."

"If you're staying here, Jen," Dalton said slyly, "that means I've still got a chance."

Meri watched Ford flirt with the woman, thinking it was kind of him to offer such healing attention.

She had her own wounds, and they were not receiving any such balm.

She caught Quantrell's eye. He was still too quiet. When men like Jesse were quiet, it meant that they were thinking things through. "Jesse, it's early, but I really think I should—"

"Me, too."

The big man got up and came around to pull back her chair in a show of attentiveness.

Ford and the Land woman looked up. Dalton and Jenny seemed more like siblings than lovers. Meri said, "Thank you, Dalton, for dinner and—everything. If I don't see you—"

"I'll be around at least another week before I have to start revamping my *Hawkeye* project. You'll see me."

Quantrell had her by the arm.

When they reached his minivan, he helped her inside without a word and they drove for a time, unspeaking.

Cairo was hot and hazy tonight as it rolled by the window. Meri didn't object when she realized that Quantrell wasn't driving her home, but out to the Pyramids. Only an American would think that was a place for the kind of talk they had to have.

So Ford was going home to launch another satellite like *HE-12*: his reputation and his beloved project were safe and sound. And the American woman, whose mother had died, sounded genuinely relieved. She and her husband would do what Americans always did: negotiate a settlement and never really lose touch with one another, whether it was a settlement of reconciliation or a settlement of divorce.

And Jesse Quantrell had his Delta commandos, his regular post here as a regional Special Forces officer of some rank.

"It's nice that Ford's got proof there was nothing wrong with his prototype—it was really his baby," Quantrell opened.

"Which? The box or the satellite?" She was still a Mossad officer; he was still with the American government contingent here.

"The satellite." Quantrell glanced at her, away from the road. "You know, what happened out here's proved better than we could have hoped—better than any war game—just how much constant, real-time surveillance and quick reaction to a threat can mean in the context of global security."

"Jesse," she giggled, "are you writing your report? Is that what has you so distracted?"

"Yeah," Quantrell admitted sheepishly. "I'm tryin'. I hate paperwork."

"I am very good at paperwork," she said softly.

"I bet you are. Well, you're good at lots of things. With your help, we just pulled off the most amazing example of interoperability in recent history."

"No one will ever know it," she reminded him. "Unless we are very unlucky."

"We're not that unlucky," said the big man. "And I'll know it." He glanced at her again. "Meri . . . "

Here, now, would come the lecture about killing in cold blood, and morality. Americans never understood what it was like to be so small and weak that every strike against the enemy was crucial. . . .

"Meri," Quantrell said again, "I'm not good at this stuff . . ."

"What? The report? If you wish a report about, as you Americans call it, 'mutually enforceable peacekeeping,' from a ground commander's perspective, I can help you with that. It's easy."

"No. Ford's . . . I mean . . . Dalton's going back to the States."

"I know this," she said patiently. Soon they would be turning off toward the Pyramids. In the parking lot, all the magic of the ancient silhouettes drained away before the crass commercialism of stalls and lights and . . .

"Meri, I want to spend more time with you. I know I'm not Jewish and I'm probably going to be viewed as a security risk by Gazit and your Mossad—"

She burst out laughing. So that was it. Delight and relief flooded her, giving her laugh a hysterical edge. She'd been so sure that her action against Seti would be repugnant to him.

"Colonel Quantrell, my superiors would heartily approve any attempt on my part to cultivate you."

He pulled out of traffic, over into a parking slot. The Pyramids were still far enough away to be beautiful.

"I just want to know if I have a fighting chance—I mean, with Dalton still in the picture."

And then she knew how to respond. "Colonel, I assure you, you'll always have a fighting chance, no matter who else may be in the picture."

She could never promise more; she was too fond of Quantrell to promise what she could not deliver.

But there was something real between them—although what it was, she thought, had more to do with risking their lives together than with spending their lives together.

"Great," Quantrell said, and reached out to take her hand in his.

Just then, someone knocked on the window.

"What the hell?"

It was Larka.

Quantrell lowered his window.

"Larka, what's the . . . ?"

"I have been blinking and honking and nearly killing everyone else in this traffic to get your attention. Good evening—" Larka ducked down to grin at her through the window "—Meri Soukry. I have for you everything concerning all the perpetrators of the ground station and a certain telecommunications company. I will give a copy of this to Quantrell, too, if he is very, very nice to me."

"How nice, Larka?"

"I have, in my car, your Captain Mackenzie, and our friend Kellogg, and three other commandos I think you will remember. We six are off to, as Captain Mackenzie proposed, 'tear a new hole in Cairo.' Of course, I am cleaning up his language, in deference to the lady. But you two, we hope, will join us."

"Meri?" Quantrell wanted to know what she thought, his big face unreadable.

"Surely I can't turn down such an invitation."

"You're on, Larka," Quantrell said. "Where do you want to start?"

"The Camel's Eye. And there I will give you the intelligence from—"

She knew what Larka was going to say so she said it with him. So did Quantrell: "—from Ignatov's babushka."

Somehow, even though the joke was not that funny anymore, Meri laughed until she cried as Quantrell jacked the minivan around in the murderous traffic, following Larka's lead, and they all headed back into the Cairo nightlife.

53

Day 68: Peterson AFB

In his office, Dalton Ford read the letter again:

Central Intelligence Agency
Washington DC 20505

Commander, US SPACE COMMAND
Attn: SCIN-DDN (Mr. Ford)
Peterson AFB, CO.

Reference: MIPS 01-750

Dear Sir:

A recent review of agency financial records reflects an outstanding balance of $128,597.32 due in response to the CIA SF9379 597-47 (copy enclosed) and reference document accepted by this office on that date.

Your prompt action in clearing this outstanding balance would be appreciated. If you require any additional information please contact Morton English of this office on (703) 555-3089 for assistance.

Sincerely,
Jos. J. Averton
Assistant Director of Finance
for Liaison

Ford put the letter down. McMurtry. Ford hadn't thought about McMurtry for weeks. He picked up the phone to call the Space Command CIA liaison about the letter and then put it back down.

McMurtry had died testing the mirroring box, and Ford was now being billed for the box. It wasn't anything to worry about, just something he had to run through channels.

But he didn't do anything about it right away. He stared at the numbers. The kid who'd died was someone Ford had never met. Not like Iggy and Marconi. But what McMurtry had done was worth more than the price of the box to Dalton Ford.

He rubbed his eyes. He'd been at this desk too long. He nearly had the specs of his new *Hawkeye* prototype ready for the contractors. If it performed to expectation, then maybe Ford could concentrate on to the next milestone of the project.

He had a deadline to meet, and then he could get some rest. He ought to get back to work.

But the bill from the Agency wouldn't leave him alone. Finally, he sat back to make a phone call, but not to anyone in Space Command or CIA.

He called Egypt, and he got lucky:

"Hey, Quantrell, how's it going?"

He wanted to talk to someone who'd lived through Bright Star and the night assault on the Jabal an-Nusayriyah station.

"About like a rabbit down a pilot snake's gullet, Ford. How're you?"

"Just . . . working hard."

"Well," said Quantrell, "you ought to stop that. Get your butt out here, where something's happening. Shit, come for my birthday, next weekend."

It was crazy. It was nearly irresponsible. But Ford looked at his calendar. "Yeah, I can make that."

"Great. See you then."

When he hung up, McMurtry's bill was still on his desk. Well, he'd deal with it in a minute.

The numbers weren't what mattered. He tried to imagine what Dennis McMurtry might have looked like, out there in the rain at the Soviet space facility. . . .

. . . A big kid, soaked and muddy in peasant clothes, holding the black box that would get him killed . . .

The kid looked up at him. Ford said to the image in his mind's eye, "It's okay. We're holding our own. We'll get there yet. You did great, McMurtry. Great. We couldn't have done it without you."

Then he got up, took the bill, stuffed it in his back pocket, and left his office. He'd walk over to Al Nesbitt's and get this thing straightened out.

You didn't want loose ends flying around. Not in Ford's line of work.

It's one man against the clock, as missiles, warplanes, radar systems, and satellites converge in a terrorist battle for control of the Middle East.

MISSILE ZONE

HERBERT CROWDER
author of WEATHERHAWK

David Llewellyn, hero of the best-selling *Ambush at Osirak*, returns—in an explosive novel of suspense and intrigue pitting him against a group of Palestinian terrorists who have hijacked the most powerful ballistic missile in the Middle East and aimed it at a major Israeli city.

Coming soon in hardcover to bookstores everywhere.

G. P. PUTNAM'S SONS
a member of The Putnam Berkley Group, Inc.

HIGH-TECH ADVENTURES BY BESTSELLING AUTHORS

____**DAY OF THE CHEETAH**
Dale Brown 0-425-12043-0/$5.50

In Dale Brown's newest *New York Times* bestseller, Lieutenant Colonel Patrick McClanahan's plane, the Cheetah, must begin the greatest high-tech chase of all time.

____**AMBUSH AT OSIRAK**
Herbert Crowder 0-515-09932-5/$4.50

Israel is poised to attack the Iraqi nuclear production plant at Osirak. But the Soviets have supplied Iraq with the ultimate super-weapon . . . and the means to wage nuclear war.

____**ROLLING THUNDER**
Mark Berent 0-515-10190-7/$4.95

The best of the Air Force face the challenge of Vietnam in "a taut, exciting tale . . . Berent is the real thing!"—Tom Clancy

____**FLIGHT OF THE OLD DOG**
Dale Brown 0-425-10893-7/$5.50

The unthinkable has happened: The Soviets have mastered Star Wars technology. And when its killer laser is directed across the globe, America's only hope is a battle-scarred bomber—the Old Dog Zero One.

For Visa, MasterCard and American Express orders call: 1-800-631-8571

FOR MAIL ORDERS: CHECK BOOK(S). FILL OUT COUPON. SEND TO:

BERKLEY PUBLISHING GROUP
390 Murray Hill Pkwy., Dept. B
East Rutherford, NJ 07073

NAME _____

ADDRESS _____

CITY _____

STATE _____ ZIP _____

PLEASE ALLOW 6 WEEKS FOR DELIVERY.
PRICES ARE SUBJECT TO CHANGE

POSTAGE AND HANDLING:
$1.00 for one book, 25¢ for each additional. Do not exceed $3.50.

BOOK TOTAL $ ____

POSTAGE & HANDLING $ ____

APPLICABLE SALES TAX $ ____
(CA, NJ, NY, PA)

TOTAL AMOUNT DUE $ ____

PAYABLE IN US FUNDS.
(No cash orders accepted.)

231a